THE PECULIAR INCIDENT AT THISTLEWICK HOUSE

JENNI KEER

B

Boldwood

First published in Great Britain in 2025 by Boldwood Books Ltd.

Copyright © Jenni Keer, 2025

Cover Design by Alexandra Allden

Cover Images: Shutterstock

A CIP catalogue record for this book is available from the British Library.

Paperback ISBN 978-1-83656-087-6

Large Print ISBN 978-1-83656-086-9

Hardback ISBN 978-1-83656-085-2

Trade Paperback ISBN 978-1-80656-022-6

Ebook ISBN 978-1-83656-088-3

Kindle ISBN 978-1-83656-089-0

Audio CD ISBN 978-1-83656-080-7

MP3 CD ISBN 978-1-83656-081-4

Digital audio download ISBN 978-1-83656-084-5

This book is printed on certified sustainable paper. Boldwood Books is dedicated to putting sustainability at the heart of our business. For more information please visit https://www.boldwoodbooks.com/about-us/sustainability/

Boldwood Books Ltd, 23 Bowerdean Street, London, SW6 3TN

www.boldwoodbooks.com

For my Occold Book Club ladies
Thanks for making me read outside my comfort zone –
it has taught me so much
May your knickers always be exactly where you
thought you'd left them

AUTHOR'S NOTE

Please be aware that this novel contains terminology reflective of the historical period in which it is set. Some of the words used to describe characters, particularly in the earlier timeline, we wouldn't use today, but this language is included for the sake of authenticity and is not intended to cause offence.

1

THISTLEWICK TYE, NORFOLK, 1895

'Did she survive the night?' Barnabas asked, his face etched with concern and his lack of sleep apparent from the smudges of grey beneath his red-rimmed eyes.

He'd anxiously grabbed at his housekeeper's sleeve and was bracing himself for her reply, having stumbled from his bed when he'd heard footsteps on the landing. The thought that his beloved Emma might have left him alone in this world and passed over to the next was unbearable. She was his everything.

His wife's fever had been raging out of control the previous day – her breathing laboured, her speech incoherent, and her skin positively afire. Dr Appleby had expressed grave concern at her racing pulse and then shaken his head, almost imperceptibly, and let her limp wrist drop back down onto the silk quilt. He'd asked Mrs Drayton to make up some further mustard plasters and apply regular cold compresses to bring down her temperature, but everyone suspected these ministrations were futile because, when the doctor finally took Barnabas to one side, he informed him the outcome was now in God's hands...

Barnabas studied his housekeeper's face, frantically looking for an answer to the question before she could articulate her response.

'She's still with us, sir. Praise God. The fever's abated and she's out of immediate danger but—'

'Then I must go to her at once.' Relief flooded through every molecule of his being, and he sidestepped the older lady and hastened down the hall.

'But I must warn you, sir, that she's not quite herself...' Her voice followed him into the bedroom, where he found Emma on top of the covers, wrestling with their housemaid.

'I want my mummy,' his wife wailed, clawing at the young girl, who was valiantly trying to tuck her back into bed.

'Emma, sweetheart.' He rushed to her side. 'You're confused. Your mother passed five years ago.' The housemaid took a step back and he perched gingerly on the edge of the bed, reaching for his beloved's hand. She immediately snatched it from him and shuffled her body backwards, a look of pure terror in her eyes.

'Go away, strange man. *Everybody go away.*'

Didn't she recognise him? An uncomfortable feeling swirled in his stomach. And then she began to cry like he'd never seen her cry before, launching herself face down and drumming her fists into the bed – a sudden outburst that resembled the despair of a child.

'She's been asking for a Zella.' Mrs Drayton was behind him now. 'And talking of sleeping in a waggon. It simply doesn't make sense, sir.'

There was a knock at the open door as Dr Appleby alerted them to his arrival and stepped into the room. Barnabas stood up, walked over to greet him and they shook hands.

'Your man, Wright, let me in. He tells me the patient has improved considerably overnight.'

'The fever's gone, Doctor,' the housekeeper confirmed. 'In fact, rather miraculously, most of her symptoms have disappeared, but her mind's awfully muddled.'

Emma was still wailing into the bedcovers, managing to get a few words out between sobs.

'Dying hurt. I didn't like being dead.'

'My darling, you're going to make a full recovery. It will just take time.' Barnabas tried to soothe her. Perhaps it *had* felt like dying to her, as she'd been awfully close to death.

'Mrs Shaw...' The doctor approached her and placed his medicine bag on the floor. He took his pocket watch from his waistcoat and reached for her wrist, but she jerked herself upright and slapped his hand away.

'Call me properly!' she screamed, tears still cascading down her pink cheeks. 'Call me Esfir. And make my legs go short again.'

Emma paused for a moment, then narrowed her eyes. She grabbed the doctor's outstretched arm and sank her teeth into the crisp white shirt, and consequently the flesh beneath. He cursed and jerked his arm from her grasp. It was a totally unprovoked assault.

Barnabas started to panic and looked to the good doctor for reassurance.

'What's going on? I've never seen my wife so much as swat a fly. Where's this anger come from? Is it a result of the delirium?'

Before the doctor had a chance to answer, Emma turned to her husband and shouted at the top of her lungs – which seemed much stronger than when she'd been wheezing helplessly the day before.

'My daddy'll get his big gun and make them dead, like I'll make you dead.'

She jumped from the bed, skirted past the doctor and ran at

her husband, her arms flying as she repeatedly pounded him with her balled fists, time and time again. He managed to pull her close, trying to calm her, but she changed tactic and began to kick out. He'd never known anything like it in their ten years of marriage. This was not how his gentle, unassuming wife behaved. Had the fever left her confused? Had she suffered some kind of damage to the brain?

'It's all right. I've got you,' he reassured her, as Dr Appleby rummaged in his medicine bag and pulled out a small red leather-bound box containing his morphine paraphernalia.

The gentlemen exchanged a glance to confirm they both understood what was needed. Barnabas held her tight as the doctor deftly slipped the needle into her arm, and the effects were almost immediate. Emma stopped fighting her husband and he felt her body go limp. After a minute or two, she slumped down and, between them, they manhandled her back into bed.

'Let her rest a while and I'll drop by again this afternoon.' The doctor hastily checked her pulse as he spoke and then packed up his bag. 'I'm running late today. Unfortunately, influenza is now rife in the village. I've just been to Low Farm, as their children are showing signs. Both are listless, with dry coughs, and we know Mrs Shaw was with them last week, helping at the Sunday school.'

'I think the kitchen maid has it, too,' the housekeeper volunteered. 'I've confined her to bed for the moment.'

Dr Appleby sighed. 'I'm to have a busy few weeks ahead of me then.'

He nodded his leave as a slurred mumble came from the bed.

'Want my sister. Want Zella.'

But Emma had no sister, and the name Zella meant nothing to Barnabas. As a man who'd always been open to things outside the realms of rational understanding, he contemplated an alternative explanation. Because the life she was talking of was not hers – sleeping in waggons, and strange names that didn't sound English.

Could it be his wife had been possessed of some troubled spirit when she'd been at her most vulnerable? He'd long since believed in the supernatural and attended many a séance before moving to Thistlewick Tye, repeatedly witnessing the dead successfully communicate through those with a spiritual gift. But was it possible for one such to enter the body of a living person? Emma had spoken of dying; of her legs being too long as though she didn't recognise her own body; of family members that didn't exist...

He desperately hoped her behaviour was a temporary aberration, but he also knew if this state of affairs continued, and if his suspicions were correct, there was only one course of action open to him. He headed for the staircase with a heavy heart, because that would mean contacting someone from his past. Someone who hadn't spoken to him for ten years. Someone who had every reason to hate him.

* * *

'We'll have to start without the doctor,' Lord Felthorpe said, half a mile away in Felthorpe Hall. 'There's much to discuss today and I want it all tied up before I leave for my appointment in Norwich this afternoon. Ideally, I'd like to give the builder the go-ahead this morning for the repairs to that little row of workers' cottages near the forge. The bad weather will soon be upon us and the elderly couple in the end terrace need to be dry and warm or I fear they'll not live to see the new year. Did you have any business, Reverend?'

Only two of the three members of the Thistlewick Tye Benevolent Committee were present for the weekly meeting – Dr Appleby had failed to appear. Reverend Fallow shuffled the pile of papers before him and peered at his notes.

'Old Frank has begged that he be allowed another week to find his rent, and the schoolteacher is hoping we can secure the funds to send the Hockley lad to the local grammar school. He shows such promise but his parents don't have two beans to rub together.'

Lord Felthorpe nodded. 'Of course, and they're such a lovely family. Always at church on a Sunday and often give of their time to help out their neighbours.'

At that moment, the door to Lord Felthorpe's study opened and Dr Appleby belatedly entered. His forehead was furrowed in confusion, and his cheeks pale, as he hurried to take his seat next to the vicar at the large pedestal desk.

'A thousand apologies for my tardiness, but I've just come from tending to Mrs Shaw at Thistlewick House, where I've witnessed the most peculiar incident...'

2

LONDON, 1895

Dark green, velvet curtains were drawn across the high sash windows of Edward Blackmore's modest West London dining room, and a fat beeswax candle flickered on the mantelpiece, giving off a slightly sweet aroma. An oil lamp, with a decorative claret-coloured glass shade, stood in the centre of the circular table, and was turned down low. In the middle of the sideboard there was a human skull carved from plaster, smooth and symmetrical, with two further candles either side. The room was silent save a wooden mantel clock, which gave a disconcerting heartbeat to the gathering.

The seated, and carefully vetted, guests, alternating male and female, were a collection of particularly wealthy and highly respected individuals. They'd all been greeted with a large, sweet sherry half an hour previously, and given the opportunity to mingle, before being instructed to take a seat and create an unbroken circle. Ten pairs of hands were linked together across the deep red, chenille tablecloth, and the air was heavy with expectation.

Edward instructed them to take slow, steady breaths and

think of the person that they wished to communicate with. To picture their face and try to recall the sound of their voice, their touch, their scent...

He smiled to himself as he studied the shadowed faces before him. This was his favourite part of the evening. The anxious, grief-stricken people from earlier were now more at ease, helped by the alcohol, as they recalled their fondest memories of the departed. They were already connecting with the person they so dearly missed, if they did but know it, and he often wished it were enough – that people understood the ones we love never truly leave us whilst we still hold them in our hearts.

But those left behind invariably wanted more, and this refusal to let the dead go had practically evolved into a religion of its own, with spiritualists now offering their services all over the country. Edward Blackmore was somewhat of a novelty, because the majority of these mediums were women. It was widely accepted that their sex was of a more caring and sensitive nature, enabling them to better channel messages between this world and the next, but he'd always been a gentle soul, right from childhood. Even now, his jet-black, shoulder-length hair, extraordinary ice-blue eyes and bone-white skin made him look fragile – even if some of his clients whispered behind his back that he looked more like a spirit than any picture book illustration they'd ever seen.

His perceived fragility, however, was offset by his flamboyant clothes. He often sported a coloured silk top hat, wore long, flowing overcoats, and loved a gaudy patterned waistcoat. He always carried with him an elegant walking cane with the most extraordinary carved ivory skull handle. It had two red crystals staring from the eye sockets, and he occasionally waved it at irritating children when they came too near. Had he been born a hundred years previously he would have been labelled a dandy.

But it was all about the misdirection. He got to decide what aspect of his person onlookers focused on, and his elaborate attire was part of the act.

He cleared his throat, tilted his head back and closed his eyes.

'Beloved spirits, we welcome you with open hearts and minds. Move freely amongst us and speak to me so that I may pass on your messages to those gathered here tonight...'

There was a prolonged silence and, as the clock counted out the seconds, nine hopeful faces searched the shapes in the shadows. Someone let out a stifled gasp as the candles either side of the skull extinguished themselves.

'No rappings, eh?' said one gentleman, who was somewhat of a sceptic but was there to support his distraught wife. 'I thought your lot got the spirits to play tambourines and ring bells.'

Edward opened his eyes and smiled, his blue eyes bright even though the room was gloomy, and answered in a low and steady voice.

'I see you've been influenced by the amateur dramatics of the charlatans. How can a spirit that has no form, no substance, knock against something, move a physical object or play an accordion? It is, of course, nonsense. They are an ethereal mist, a mass of emotional energy, the very essence of a person. That is what calls upon us this evening and sweeps about the living, hoping to connect with those they have left behind.'

'Spirits with unfinished business,' volunteered Mrs Wellington-Smith – a particularly fervent believer.

'Exactly that, dear lady, and we have two such restless souls here with us tonight. Can you not sense them?'

There had been a gradual drop in temperature since the séance began, but it was now quite noticeable. The older woman to his left shivered slightly as the curtain fabric gave the smallest ripple, even though both windows in the room were firmly closed. She raised her eyes to meet Edward's and he could see her expression was full of hope. He wanted nothing more than to ease the burden of her suffering and drew in a slow breath, focusing so hard that he could feel the stirrings of a headache.

'Our first visitor is the one spirit that I was hoping would not appear – and he wishes to talk with Lady Temple.'

'It's Alfred, isn't it?' Her voice was shaky and low. 'I know he's here. I can smell his cologne.' And it was true; the sweet but spicy scent of Bay Rum aftershave lotion filled the air. No one questioned how a mass of thought and emotional energy that couldn't rap on a table might be able to generate such a fragrance, or even snuff out a candle.

Edward didn't answer her question. He didn't need to. Everyone knew that her husband, Sir Alfred Temple, an explorer of some note, hadn't been heard of for seven months now. He'd gone missing somewhere in the Himalayan mountains of Tibet, where he'd been surveying previously uncharted areas. Accompanied by three other men, he'd fallen desperately ill and become separated from his party after crossing the Karakoram Pass. Everyone but his wife had accepted the sad truth.

'I was so sure he was still alive, convincing myself that I'd have felt something had he passed away.' Her voice cracked but she didn't allow herself to cry. 'As much as it pains me to admit it, I was obviously wrong.'

'He says he misses you, Nellie, and always will.'

Lady Temple turned to look at Edward. 'Then my husband really *is* here because he was the only person allowed to call me that. Everyone else addresses me as Petronella.' It was further proof, not that she needed it, that Alfred was there in the room with them. 'Ask him what happened. Will I ever be able to bring his body home?'

There was silence around the table, save the occasional sniff from Lady Temple, who was struggling to keep her grief in check, unable to wipe her eyes or blow her nose without breaking the circle.

Edward let out a long breath, knowing he was about to deliver some very unpalatable news.

'Sir Alfred informs me that he was not of his right mind, delirious and confused, when he left the camp. He was walking for some hours, but missed his footing and tumbled down a ravine. It was a quick and painless death. He didn't suffer but doubts anyone will find him in those treacherous mountains and could not accurately direct anyone to his body if he tried. But he begs you not to grieve. He died doing the thing he loved. Besides, he insists that he's watching over you now, and bringing home his bones will do nothing to make him closer to you than he already is.'

Lady Temple nodded her understanding – her own eyes brimming with unshed tears. 'Tell him that I love him.'

'Tell him yourself,' Edward said gently. 'He's behind you and says that he has a hand on your shoulder as we speak.'

There was a sense of reverence around the table as everyone respected the moment.

'There's one more spirit desperate to make contact,' he eventually continued, closing his eyes once more. 'A man who tells me that he was driven to the edge through desperate circumstances. He's here tonight to beg forgiveness. A Frederick – does that name mean anything to anybody?'

'My father?' Mr Cardew, who'd arrived with the unconvinced but curious medic-turned-novelist Dr Doyle, was astonished by the possibility. 'But he died thirty years ago. I came here tonight merely as an observer, and a sceptical one at that. Surely it can't be him?'

'I do not choose who seeks me out. I merely pass on their messages and try to ease the suffering of all concerned.' Edward opened his eyes and looked directly at the man, his face full of pity. 'Oh, my dear fellow, it was you who found him in the barn when you were a child?'

Even in the gloom, he could see the colour drain from Mr Cardew's face.

'That's not common knowledge.' He looked at his fellow sitters. 'There's no way he could know that.'

'Of course not,' Mrs Wellington-Smith chided. 'Your father is here tonight, speaking directly to Mr Blackmore. Did you ever doubt that he was genuine?'

'Well, I...'

'He's being pulled from me now, but asks your forgiveness, both for the act itself and because it was you who stumbled across his body.'

'Of course I forgive him. Let his soul pass over and finally rest in peace.'

Edward nodded and closed his eyes for the final time.

'We thank you, dear spirits, for coming to speak to us tonight. You may now leave us...'

The flames on the pair of sideboard candles suddenly reignited, even though no one was nearby, and the room grew a tiny bit brighter. The icy chill also dissipated as the temperature began to rise.

After a minute or two, Edward instructed his guests to break the circle and return to the drawing room where Delphine would serve nightcaps before the carriages arrived.

One by one, they walked out into the hallway, as Edward extinguished the candles with a small brass snuffer and turned up the oil lamp to better illuminate the space. The lingering smell of Bay Rum floated in the air and he noticed Lady Temple lurking by the door. As he approached, she thrust a small bundle of notes towards him, but he shook his head and waved them away.

'I don't do it for the money, madam. I do it because I must. From the moment I was aware that I could communicate with spirits, I knew I had to use my gift for good, even though it is both a blessing and a curse. It's my duty to be a mouthpiece for these troubled souls and I will not exploit the misery of my fellow man.'

The very fact that his visitors were amongst the wealthiest people in London and he made no attempt to overtly part them from their money only proved to everyone how genuine he was.

'I don't think you realise, Mr Blackmore, what it means to hear from my darling Alfred. The not knowing has been eating me up all these months but I can finally move on. Such peace is worth more to me than a few pounds and I won't take no for an answer.'

Her stubborn determination was apparent from the set of her jaw.

'And I refuse to take payment. There are far too many charlatans out there, making money from their parlour tricks and falsehoods. You can see I'm a man blessed with an adequate income. I drink fine wines, visit the best tailors and regularly take in theatre shows. I've no wife, no dependents and my inherited wealth is more than adequate for my needs. But, if you insist, then the sum in its entirety will be forwarded to my pet charity – the Cattisham Orphanage Fund. It feels right to provide some comfort to those who have no one.'

She nodded, holding the money out to him again. He reluctantly pocketed the notes, before they joined the others in the drawing room for a parting drink.

Edward stood in the corner with the two guests he'd not met

before. Dr Doyle was bemoaning his fictional detective creation, Sherlock Holmes, and relaying how his mother had begged him not to kill the character off. Mr Cardew, an ardent fan, was just raising a glass to the woman's successful petition, when Delphine – Edward's maid – entered the room holding a silver tray, upon which sat a solitary letter.

'This has come in the last post, sir.' She bobbed an awkward curtsey. 'If you'll notice, it has URGENT written across the top left-hand corner, underlined twice, or I'd not have interrupted.'

Edward nodded, glanced at the mantel clock, and took the envelope, sliding his bone-handled letter opener under the flap. Who could it be from? Demand for his services was hardly pressing – the dead were in no hurry, after all.

The looping and irregular writing in black ink was a hand he recognised but one he didn't relish corresponding with. That funny way of finishing off the descenders with a curly flourish, and the ridiculously oversized capital letters. He took a pair of thin wire spectacles from his waistcoat pocket and moved to the large brass oil lamp on the corner desk. His eyesight had always been poor. It had hampered his learning as a child, and his slow progress had been one of the many reasons his father had cause to be disappointed in him. Edward could only be thankful that his tutor had finally realised it was defective vision holding him back, and not stupidity.

Curious as to what his cousin Barnabas could possibly want from him, he began to scan the words. The man had taken everything from Edward years ago and the pair had cut all ties, with limited communication between them over the intervening quarter of a century, and certainly never anything of an urgent nature.

Thistlewick House,

Norfolk
October 16th, 1895

Edward,

I know that you'll find it strange to hear from me again but I need your help. How it must amuse you to find the boot so firmly on the other foot, but it's Emma – and whatever your feelings remain towards me, I know that you cared for her once.

She has recently been dangerously ill and I genuinely thought I was going to lose her, but to everyone's amazement, even the physician's, she survived the worst of the fever, and for that I am truly thankful. However, since her recovery, her behaviour has caused much alarm. The doctor believes the fever has affected her brain in some way, but I know something darker is going on. She claims her name is Esfir, and talks of things I know nothing about, yet her manner of speaking is childlike and rambling.

Having listened to her wild assertions and deranged proclamations for the last two days, I have come to the conclusion that she's been possessed of some spirit. There is simply no other explanation and, whatever our past differences, I do know you to be the very best in this field.

Whilst I appreciate that you have no reason to help me after what happened, please know that I can pay you handsomely The things she is saying are truly alarming and I'm fearful she will harm either herself or someone else. Please consider coming to Norfolk at your earliest possible convenience.

Yours,
Barnabas Shaw

'Bad news?' Mr Cardew asked, noting the frown on Edward's face.

'Just a letter from someone I knew a long time ago.' He shrugged. 'Nothing of importance.'

He placed the single sheet of cream paper back in the envelope and walked over to the hearth, where he let it slip from his fingers and into the crackling flames. He'd loved Emma once, even though their acquaintance had been brief, and had even been fond of Barnabas when they'd been younger. But there were some things a man could not forgive. His life no longer included either of them, and whatever trouble the man was in, he'd have to face it alone. How dare he try to manipulate his emotions. The tiny roar of flames devoured the letter in seconds.

There. It was dealt with.

The first of the carriages arrived and Delphine began to ready the coats and gloves. Two further gentlemen insisted on making discreet and extremely generous donations to the Cattisham Orphanage before their departure, and Mr Cardew took Edward's business card to pass on to a friend, so impressed was he by the events of that evening.

'We wondered if you might like to visit our country residence this Christmas,' Mrs Wellington-Smith enquired, as Delphine helped drape her fox fur stole about her shoulders. The dead, glassy eyes of the creature stared at Edward and made him feel uncomfortable. 'I understand you have no family and we have quite the gathering every December. Our Boxing Day hunt is one of the best in the county. And, of course, my daughter would so love it if you were to stay...'

'I'm not at ease in social situations, nor am I much of the outdoor sort. The invitation is kind but I cannot accept.'

'Nonsense,' Mrs Wellington-Smith replied. 'I'll not take no for an answer.'

But Edward knew it would be wrong to let the woman believe he had any interest in her daughter – which they both knew was the real reason for the invitation. She was an attractive young girl with adequate flesh on her bones and a ready smile, and her promised dowry was even more appealing. But he couldn't marry her, any more than he'd been able to marry Emma. It was a burden he would carry with him always.

Edward Blackmore would remain a bachelor until the end of his days, because to take a wife would mean revealing his secret, and he simply wasn't prepared to do that.

3

Edward couldn't get the letter out of his mind, even though all that remained of it was ash. How dare Barnabas contact him now, after all these years, purely because he wanted something. And yet his guilt at abandoning Emma in her hour of need weighed heavily on his shoulders.

To the casual observer, Edward was doing well. He had sufficient wealth and was well respected in his field, even if it was a profession viewed as humbug by many, and even dangerous by some. But he was lacking the one thing that really mattered, and that was love. His mother had never been around to show it, his father had blatantly withheld it, and the one person who might have truly loved him, he'd rejected. It was what he desired above all else and yet every time it was offered, he pushed it away, leaving many would-be brides and eager mothers unable to understand why, at thirty-six, he refused to settle down.

The disquiet he felt over ignoring his cousin's plea was added to when a second letter arrived later that week. The envelope had the same looping hand and curly flourishes, and he had the same sinking feeling in the pit of his stomach as he read the words.

Thistlewick House,
Norfolk
October 18th, 1895

Edward,

Two days have passed since I wrote to you and I've heard nothing back. I don't blame you for your reticence to answer my plea but am now all but on my knees, begging you to come to us as soon as humanly possible. The situation with Emma is becoming increasingly serious. She still maintains her name is Esfir, and repeatedly claims that she wants to kill us all. Yesterday morning she even ran at our housekeeper with a table knife. This is a serious situation and one I fervently believe only you can help me with. You always had a gift for communicating with the dead, Edward, and your reputation as one of the few genuine spiritualists out there has grown.

I understand you have no reason to look upon me kindly, but if you won't do it for me, do it for her. I know you cared for her once. Is there not a part of you that would help alleviate her suffering? I beseech you. Name your price and I will meet it, for I have no need of fortune without my dearest Emma to share it with.

You are our only hope.
Barnabas

Edward adjusted his spectacles and walked over to the drawing room window to read the letter a second time, rubbing at his clean-shaven chin in contemplation. There was a part of him that was almost gleeful to find his cousin in such a desperate situation. He could request a sizeable sum be donated to the orphanage fund, enough to make the man truly suffer for stealing his birthright – because seventeen years ago, his cousin had done exactly that.

When Jonah Shaw had died in the summer of 1878, and everyone had gathered to hear the reading of the will, Edward had every reason to expect that, as his only surviving child, he would inherit everything. He may not have been close to his father, but it hadn't been through the want of trying. An affectionate soul by nature, he'd spent his childhood surrounded by few people he could lavish his affections on. He'd adored his nanny – an elderly woman who had become a mother figure in the absence of his own – but she was no longer required when he turned twelve and so was dismissed. He'd had few playmates and was educated at home by a stern tutor – his father refusing to send him away to boarding school. His cousin, Barnabas, five years older than him, had been his only real friend – a boy who'd welcomed the opportunity to stay with his wealthy uncle and young cousin during the holidays.

Jonah encouraged the friendship, even though he had little time for his own child, and could barely even bring himself to look at him. Edward had long suspected his father thought of Barnabas as his own but, even so, at nineteen years old, when he sat in the offices of Haycock and Smith, along with his extended family and a few valued members of the household staff, he was totally floored to hear that it was his cousin who would inherit the maltings business and their moderate country home – and not Jonah Shaw's disappointment of a son.

Edward pulled out a map of England from a low shelf on the bookcase to his left, slid into a leather armchair and studied the pages covering East Anglia. He knew his cousin had returned to the place of his wife's birth shortly after their marriage, because the Shaw family home had been sold by a desperate Barnabas – a further betrayal that Edward could not forgive. Emma had been an only child, set to inherit everything, including a large country house by the sea, and was able to bail her then fiancé out of his desperate financial troubles. Edward had never been to Thistlewick Tye but, sure enough, there it was – a small village on the Norfolk coast, nestled between Cromer and Sheringham.

He thought back fondly to the young woman who'd captured his heart all those years ago. She should have been his, but then so should his father's maltings business *and* the Shaw family home. But he'd never wished Emma ill and so her condition worried him. Was there something he could do to help?

The truth was, however, Edward no more had the power to expel a malevolent spirit than he could turn himself invisible. He was as much of a fraud as the next man, but played a better game. Because if there was one thing he understood, it was people. The mind was a powerful thing and, unchecked, it could conjure up disturbing visions and destructive half-truths. Equally, with the right guidance, it could positively impact the health and well-being of an individual. Emma was clearly suffering from some kind of delirium as a result of her fever, but he could perhaps assist with her recovery.

And if he could truly name his price, the Cattisham Orphanage Fund might also benefit. Perhaps it wouldn't take him an anticipated further two years to accrue sufficient funds for his plans. Now wouldn't that be something?

Delphine entered the drawing room carrying a small copper watering can and headed over to the window. Edward relied on this young woman and her brother, Carl, for everything. They kept the house running and assisted with his spiritualist endeavours, as well as keeping his secrets. But their loyalty would only remain as long as he had sufficient funds to pay them. He was under no illusion that they cared for him; it was his purse they cared for.

'If I were to stay in Norfolk for a few days, would you be able to manage here?' he asked, as she poked the thin spout into the dense foliage of an unwieldy fern.

'But you never go away, sir.'

'It wouldn't be for long.'

'But how would you—'

'I'd be staying with someone I knew from before. I could manage. He knows. He's always known.'

She nodded.

'You have a séance next week for that government minister and his wife.'

'I'll be back by then. If I go. I've not yet decided.'

But the pull of seeing Emma again, and equally Barnabas's offer of payment, was getting stronger. The orphanage fund was not growing as quickly as he'd have liked, and it was a cause *exceedingly* close to his heart. For Edward Blackmore's mother had died in childbirth, and his father – who had always seen his son as somewhat of a disappointment – had died nearly two decades later. Although technically no longer a child at that point, he'd very much felt like an orphan at the tender age of nineteen...

Because what Edward Blackmore failed to tell the benevolent donors to the Cattisham Orphanage Fund was that he was the founder, administrator and *sole* beneficiary.

4

In the end, the decision was an easy one. Edward caught the morning train from Liverpool Street to Norwich Thorpe and changed lines to Cromer. He then procured a lift on a brewery waggon that was delivering kegs of beer to the Sailmaker's Arms in Thistlewick Tye, to complete the last leg of his journey. It was an uncomfortable ride, sitting up the front next to the driver, but he was finally deposited in the village centre, with the old man advising him to take plenty of walks along the cliffs to get the full benefits of the fresh, salty, ozone-rich air, and to indulge in some winter sea bathing. Like most people, he'd taken one look at Edward and worried for his health.

But it was not the season for brave dashes into the North Sea. There was a biting autumnal wind and Edward turned up the collar on his emerald green frock coat as he stepped down from the waggon, collected his baggage and donned his matching top hat. The cliff walks he might partake of, if time allowed, but the sea bathing, he most definitely would not.

Edward took stock of his surroundings. He plunged the end of his walking cane into the soft turf of the large grassy area that stretched before him, but decided to stick to the meandering path, not wanting to soil his fine leather shoes. The orphanage fund looked after him well.

The view was so delightfully green, but stippled this time of year with the emerging colours of earth and fire, as the trees began to shed their leaves. He'd been led to believe that Norfolk was a flat county but a high ridge of land was visible in the distance to the east. There was so much sky in this part of the world, whereas in London he had to force his head up to find it as he wove between the tall buildings and lofty plane trees. Here, Edward felt, the world went on forever, especially when he spun further to the left and got his first glimpse of the sea. A thick dark line on the horizon divided the calm blue heavens above from the ever-moving grey waters below. His vision may not be sharp with regards to details, but the sense of space before him took his breath away.

He approached the cliff edge, wary that there was a drop of perhaps three hundred feet to the beach, and no effective barrier to prevent a fall. At one point, a post-and-rail fence had evidently run along the top, but it dipped and sagged where the land had dropped away, and sections of it were missing altogether. To his right, he could see a swathe of dead thistle heads, the spiky silhouettes of the stems visible against the sky. It would surely have been a blanket of purple splendour in the late summer and clearly where the village had got its unusual name.

He was about to pull back and head for his cousin's house, when he saw the small blur of a figure scuttling across the wide expanse of flat sand beneath the cliffs. Likely a woman from the way she moved, she was wearing a heavy woollen hooded cloak, which obscured her face. Perhaps she sensed him because she paused and tipped her head up to the clifftops, before quickly dropping it back down and continuing along the shoreline.

He turned away from the sea and towards the village. The driver had told him that Thistlewick House was at the end of Copperpenny Lane, and he soon found a weathered wooden sign for the correct road. He followed the sandy track for a quarter of a mile until he saw a large mid-century brick-and-flint house set in a sizeable parcel of land. Emma's father had been a gentleman of independent means and had built the house upon his marriage. A square box of a building with, Edward guessed, perhaps six bedrooms. It was large enough for a well-to-do family and a handful of staff, but not as large as the Shaw family home that his cousin had inherited and subsequently lost to creditors.

Edward pulled at the rope to sound the doorbell, which was promptly answered by the housekeeper, and gave his name. As he stepped into the hallway, Barnabas appeared from a doorway to the left. The man had gained weight, he noticed. Marital bliss had certainly led to him piling on the pounds, whereas Edward's loneliness had always kept him slim.

The two men studied each other and it took him a moment to notice the defeated posture and dark circles under his cousin's eyes.

Barnabas dropped his gaze to the floor and turned to step back into the room he'd appeared from.

'You're too damn late, Blackmore,' he said, over his shoulder. 'She's dead.'

* * *

Relieved of his coat and travelling bag, Edward followed Barnabas into the drawing room and attempted to warm his hands in front of the open fire. His mind was racing – how could Emma be dead? She was such a force of nature and far too young to have passed away – somewhere in her thirties, like himself. He felt his stomach churn at this unexpected and devastating news.

His cousin gestured for him to take a seat, lingering by the mantelpiece and sizing up Edward with accusatory eyes. His grief was visibly weighing his shoulders down, like an overcoat of iron.

For the first few minutes, both men remained silent. All Edward could think about was her sweet face – how she'd looked at him back then, and how she'd made him feel. The knowledge that light had been extinguished was devastating.

Finally, his cousin spoke.

'I appreciate that you owe me nothing, and I had absolutely no right to ask anything of you, but I'd hoped the money might have been an enticement. We were both always driven by the pursuit of wealth as young men and, what with your father's unexpected legacy...' He couldn't finish the sentence, or perhaps decided it would be unwise to do so.

Edward scowled. 'I came for Emma, even though I admit the temptation to reclaim some of the money you stole from me was a factor. However, you must see from my clothes, and know from what you read about me in the newspapers, that I have sufficient means. What you so cruelly took from me, I have accrued for myself.'

Barnabas shook his head. 'Well, you didn't come soon enough. She's lying in a casket in the drawing room, stone cold and stiff. The clocks have been stopped, the mirrors covered – more important than ever if there are indeed rogue spirits floating about – and my life is over. But then maybe, that was always your plan. Leave it long enough for her to pass away and then arrive in time to gloat.'

'You know I was fond of Emma. I'd not have wished her dead.' Edward tried to hide his building emotions; horror at the revelation she was gone, anger at the subsequent accusation. Hadn't his father always said he was too sensitive? One of the many reasons he'd been such a disappointment to the man. 'Tell me what happened.'

'Were my letters not clear enough? She was possessed by an evil spirit.'

'Details, man,' Edward demanded, as his cousin tipped back his head and drew in a long and pained breath.

'She visited a distant relative in Norwich two weeks ago but quickly came down with influenza, which we have since discovered is rife in the city. The doctor prepared me for the unthinkable when the delirium was at its worst, not expecting her to last until morning. However, to everyone's surprise, she survived the night. Her health, if not her mind, was almost immediately improved, but she was a different person – childlike and confused.'

'Childlike?'

'She kept asking for her mother, even though the woman has been dead for five years. Her manner was aggressive and she had fits of temper like an infant, biting people and kicking out.'

'Then the fever must have affected her memory and she'd simply regressed to her girlhood.'

'It wasn't as simple as that. It wasn't *her* girlhood she was reliving. As I explained in my letter, she said her name was Esfir – the name isn't even English, for goodness' sake. And then, she began to carry around the doll that had sat idly on a chair in the bedroom for years. She actually screamed when she caught her reflection in the mirror at her dressing table, not even recognising her own face.'

Edward frowned. Emma had always been practical and not one to display a fanciful imagination or behave in a dramatic manner. Look how calmly she had taken his refusal of her all those years ago.

'Goddam it, man, she didn't know me or anything about our life together. She didn't recognise any of the staff and wouldn't let me touch her. Have you any idea what it feels like when your own wife pulls away from your embrace?'

There was an awkward pause. Barnabas must have suspected that Emma had been fond of Edward once, and he also knew the reasons that his cousin pursued a bachelor life. His comment had been thoughtless.

'The longer this strange behaviour went on, the more I knew it wasn't Emma,' he continued, 'but instead a girl from another time. Someone who stood in front of my wife's sewing machine and had absolutely no idea what it was for; who talked of cooking over open fires and living amongst waggons. There was an uncontrollable anger within her that I've never witnessed in my wife, and she repeatedly cried that they must all die – although I never found out to whom she was referring. Simply put, it wasn't that Emma had lost her memories, *it was that she had someone else's.*'

Edward felt uncomfortable. She'd often teased him for his supposed gifts, unlike Barnabas, who'd always been so gullible – firmly believing his younger cousin could converse with the dead. It would have been no act on her part, but unlike his cousin, he didn't believe she'd been possessed. It was a ridiculous notion and, even though he couldn't be absolutely certain spirits didn't exist, he'd certainly never encountered one. To his mind, people simply found it too unpalatable to accept that everything ceased with your death, and the spiritualist movement had grown from this fear. But the existence of a soul separate to the physical body was scientifically doubtful. Most mediums he'd encountered were blatant frauds, like himself, although he had attended a couple of unnerving séances that he'd never satisfactorily explained.

'But if she'd recovered from the fever, even if she was confused and suffering from delusions, what caused her to pass away?' Edward suddenly realised no explanation had been offered for her death. Hadn't his cousin indicated that she'd survived the worst of the fever? A relapse, perhaps?

Barnabas slumped into the chair opposite his cousin and it was obvious that talking about her final moments was difficult, as his voice began to crack.

'She was found yesterday morning with a syringe of morphia beside her on the bedcovers. Dr Appleby raised the alarm. I rushed in as soon as I heard the commotion and truly think it was the worst few moments of my entire existence, grabbing her limp hand and trying to rouse her. She looked so perfect, her pale pink cheeks and closed eyelids making it seem as though she were merely asleep.'

It was hard for Edward to watch as the tears streamed down his cousin's face. He couldn't summon up the satisfaction that he wanted to feel at seeing the man suffer. His grief was real and raw and, had they not shared an uncomfortable past, he might even have reached across to put a comforting hand on his shoulder.

'Dr Appleby could only conclude that her mind had been so deranged that she didn't know what she was doing. She must have accessed his medicine bag and stolen the box of morphia. We'd all witnessed him frantically searching for it the previous evening, only to assume that he'd left it at the surgery.'

So, Emma had decided to end it all. Perhaps she'd had enough about her to realise she was spiralling into madness and had taken the opportunity to avoid further suffering. How unbelievably tragic.

A manservant entered with a tray of tea but Barnabas looked

across and waved him away. 'Fetch us both a proper drink, Wright. My cousin is partial to absinthe. And ask the house-keeper to make up one of the guest rooms. If you could also tell Cook there's a gentleman staying for dinner and to order more food in for next week, I'd appreciate it.'

But Edward had arrived too late to save Emma, and his scheme to extract money from his cousin had been scuppered by her tragic death, so there was no reason for him to remain in Thistlewick Tye.

'There's no need. I won't be staying more than one night. You're my cousin by an accident of birth but we're not friends, Barnabas. You know that. Besides, as you so correctly pointed out, I'm too late.'

There was no love lost between them, and it was only the severity of the situation that had forced Barnabas to call on him. So why would his cousin want to prolong the visit now that she'd passed away? He had no desire to remain at Thistlewick House longer than absolutely necessary, preferring to return to London to deal with his grief privately.

His cousin's hands were clenched into tight fists and there was a grim determination in the set of his jaw.

'But I need answers, Edward. The spirits of both my wife and whoever possessed her surely remain in this house and, with your gift, you can contact them.' He thumped at the arms of his high-backed chair with his palms. 'Damn it, man, I'm begging you to get those answers for me. I need to talk to her again... I need to understand... I need to say goodbye.'

Wright approached with the drinks on a tray. Barnabas swept up the brandy and took several large gulps, as Edward took a small sip of his favoured green spirit. It burned his throat but helped to sharpen his thinking. Could he still extract some money from his cousin and make him pay for the past? Or would he get greater pleasure – a joy that you couldn't put a price on – by refusing? It would be payback for everything that had happened all those years ago.

'I appreciate the offer of a bed for the night but there is no sum of money that can undo your betrayal. I came to be of help to Emma and I'm as broken as you are that she has gone, but I leave tomorrow.'

Barnabas lurched forward.

'This is exactly why I need you – *why Emma needs you*. There are things going on here that you don't understand. We must get to the truth, Edward. I have long suspected that there is an evil presence in Thistlewick Tye, spiritual or otherwise, and I don't have the strength or the skills to seek it out by myself.'

Edward sighed. 'She was lost to her own mind, Barnabas, and made the tragic decision to end her life. There is nothing I can do for her now that she has gone.' He felt sorry for the man, having to bear the shame that his wife had taken her own life, but Emma's delirium would make people more sympathetic.

'I don't think you understand.' Barnabas leaned forward, staring at Edward with an intensity that made him uncomfortable. 'The hastily arranged inquest this morning may have returned a verdict of suicide whilst of unsound mind, but I am absolutely convinced that Emma was murdered.'

5

Edward knocked back the remainder of his drink in one gulp. Things had taken a darker turn than he'd expected.

'What makes you think that?' he asked.

'Because, whatever the doctor believes, I fail to understand how or why a woman who favoured her left hand, even though she'd been forced as a child to hold a pen with the right, would inject herself in the left arm. She reverted to her dominant hand unconsciously for most tasks. I haven't been thinking clearly since her illness but, sitting with her body this afternoon, I suddenly realised the error. I even pulled up her sleeve to check for myself, and the mark was quite visible.'

Poor, sweet Emma. She may have married his cousin after Edward's rejection, but she'd never been anything but kind to him. He was angry to think someone else might have administered the fatal dose and, if what Barnabas was saying was true, then he also wanted justice for the woman he'd once been in love with.

'Then demand that they hold a second inquest.'

Barnabas shook his head. 'And say what? An evil spirit

possessed Emma and made her kill herself? Because this Esfir is surely the one who was responsible. Besides, everyone in the household will swear that she was right-handed. Only her parents would have backed me up and they are both long dead. Our housekeeper spent the night outside her room and swears that no one entered or left from the time I bid my wife goodnight until the doctor arrived first thing, and I will not countenance that Mrs Drayton was in any way involved.'

'But would the spirit of a little girl know how to administer morphia, Barnabas? And even if the spirit did make Emma inject herself, then me contacting them will serve no purpose. Technically, your wife still died by her own hand and you cannot deliver justice to someone who is no longer alive.'

'Maybe not,' Barnabas agreed, 'but I must know *why* the little girl acted so. You're my only channel to them, cousin.' His voice was sounding increasingly desperate. 'Help me and I'll write a cheque for five hundred pounds to you this very afternoon, in lieu of your stolen inheritance.'

The shock of this offer put Edward in somewhat of a quandary. It fleetingly occurred to him that he could take this money *and* make Barnabas pay for the past. He could perform a séance and summon the imaginary spirit of a child called Esfir, claiming she'd stolen the syringe to end her own suffering, and Emma dying had been an unavoidable consequence. Ha – as if a spirit possession was possible. It was far more likely that a living, breathing person had administered that fatal dose. Mrs Drayton could have fallen asleep, the perpetrator may have accessed the room through a window or, despite his cousin's declaration, the housekeeper herself may even have been responsible.

If he had more time to poke about the house and talk to staff, he could make it quite convincing. Get further details regarding Emma's behaviour in the last few days and, depending how vindictive he was feeling, pass on some condemnatory messages to her husband. Barnabas would certainly believe him because Edward had spent half his lifetime perpetuating the myth that he could bridge this world and the next.

Ever since he was a small child, lonely and isolated, he'd craved attention, and he'd conceived of a way to receive it. Starting with simple card tricks and then progressing to more complicated magic, Edward discovered that you could dupe people into believing almost anything – from your ability to turn a woman invisible, to sawing off a man's head.

And then a stupid comment from a stupid woman about his almost transcendental blue eyes and the seed had grown. Because he'd wanted to get back at Barnabas for being his father's favourite, he'd convinced his cousin that he could communicate with the dead. It gave him power over the older lad – a boy forced to play with his cousin because Jonah Shaw didn't want his son mixing with other children.

But everything Edward did in his capacity as a medium was illusion, sleight of hand and careful research into the back-ground of his clients – much like his recent summoning of Alfred Temple, the man missing in the treacherous mountains of Tibet. He needed no proof of his death in order to invoke his spirit and give his wife the closure she so badly needed. Alfred's favourite aftershave mixed into the wax of the pillar candle, and Carl extinguishing the flames from behind the scenes, were mere chicanery.

It then occurred to Edward that he might be allowing a real person to get away with murder if he blamed this fictional Esfir, but it wasn't his responsibility to seek out justice. Perhaps it would be better to walk away? He'd travelled to Norfolk to save Emma but, heartbreakingly, had arrived too late, so why was he allowing himself to get sucked into all this nonsense?

'My answer is still no.' Edward rose to his feet, making him appear as powerful as he felt in that moment. 'You chose not to help me when I was at my lowest ebb and yet expect me to help you now.'

All the colour drained from Barnabas's face as he leapt to his feet in his despair and rushed at Edward, gripping his lapels and shunting him backwards.

'You utter bastard. You're loving this, aren't you? Seeing my pain, my heartache. I've a mind to kill you myself so that you can join her. You always coveted Emma, but I didn't think you could be this cruel.'

But, like many, he underestimated his cousin's strength and, within a heartbeat, he'd been gripped firmly by the wrists and pinned against the wall.

'I've had a gutful of your whining,' Edward growled. 'My father chose you over me. Left you the house, the business and much of his wealth. The paltry sum that came my way was small compensation. And you did nothing to redress that, even though the man was dead. You could have involved me in the business I loved, but instead ran it into the ground and gave me not one penny of my birthright. That was the real cruelty.'

Barnabas was squirming under Edward's painfully tight hold and he saw a further swell of tears in the older man's eyes.

'You're right; I thought the money would make me happy, but it didn't. Take the cheque *and* the damn house. It's worth another two thousand. Sell it for all I care. These last few days have made me realise that my life is nothing without Emma here to share it with. Contact her spirit and find out who did this and I'll pass Thistlewick House over to you. I swear it.'

Edward released his grip as a tear rolled down his cousin's plump cheek. He could hardly believe the stupid man was prepared to give up so much in a foolish attempt to understand his wife's death. But the stakes had suddenly grown. This could be the answer to Edward's financial predicament; he could sell the house and raise substantial funds within weeks. He'd expected another few years plying his dubious trade until he'd amassed enough to disappear and fund a quiet and comfortable life, but what Barnabas was offering would free him from all the lies by the end of the year.

The problem was, every time the Cattisham Orphanage Fund grew, he couldn't help but dip into it. Renting in a nice area of London was important for appearances, as were his extravagant clothes and fine foods – even though Delphine managed a modest household budget for the occasions when he was not entertaining. But if Barnabas honoured this rash offer, he could soon be dining on venison and lobster, pineapples and peaches, somewhere less bleak but far from the prying eyes and web of deceit he'd spun around himself in London. He'd always sought the shadows, happiest with his own company, but would rather wander those shadows in fine clothes, eating good food, and with biddable servants at his beck and call.

Perhaps he could buy himself time and properly investigate the situation. Back in London, Delphine and her brother were skilled at getting information out of people and picking up local gossip – even though Carl's methods were sometimes on the violent side of pleasant. He could send for his manservant and have an ally in his endeavours.

Barnabas sensed his hesitation and took it as a good sign, wiping the back of his hand across his face, sniffing to clear his nose, and standing a little straighter.

'Look, Edward, I may have committed a transgression of the highest magnitude against you, and perhaps God is making me pay for this now – a punishment I accept – but I have, at least, kept your secret all these years. I was greedy and selfish, but not malicious. If I can undo the wrong that your father did you, then we're even. And we can set about contacting Emma this very night, for surely she's still nearby, having passed so recently.'

'I accept your offer, but you must know that I cannot simply summon her on demand. I'm still in shock at the news of her death and it will affect my ability to focus, so may I respectfully suggest we bury your wife first and then turn our attentions to contacting her? Besides, it would unsettle me to speak with her spiritual self whilst her physical self remains in the house.'

Edward took a step back and Barnabas nodded. The man was broken. He'd agree to anything.

'Perhaps you're correct. I'll confirm the arrangements for her funeral and after we've buried her body, we can tend to her soul.'

Edward flexed his fingers and walked over to the sideboard to collect the brandy decanter. The balance of power in the room had shifted and he relished in performing this simple action that demonstrated so clearly who was now in control. All this would be his soon, if his cousin was to be believed. He topped up Barnabas's tumbler and replaced the stopper, before reaching for the absinthe bottle and doing the same with his own glass. He felt a foot taller.

'You understand that I require my privacy and must send for my man if I'm to stay for more than one night.'

'Of course. The bedrooms all have keys and can be locked from the inside, and there's a spare room next to my manservant, Wright's.' Barnabas placed his untouched brandy on the table between them and walked to a small bureau by the window. He opened the fall and began to rummage amongst the papers. 'Let me write the cheque and pen you a letter outlining my intentions regarding the house. Wright can witness it. I'll not renege.'

Edward narrowed his eyes, hardly believing his imminent good fortune.

'Then I shall begin my preparation for the séance in the morning.'

But what concerned Edward more was that someone in the household or the village may have murdered poor, innocent Emma, and with the doctor carelessly leaving his medicine bag about, he wanted to question the man about who had access to the morphia and, whether it was, indeed, an overdose of that narcotic which had led to her death.

Because Edward knew that the real evil here was undoubtedly the work of a living, breathing mortal, and he was determined to find out who that was. And the first suspect on his list was the doctor.

6

Tired from the travel, trying to come to terms with his grief and overwhelmed by his cousin's startling revelations about the nature of Emma's death, Edward slept late the following day. Barnabas had swung from being angry about his cousin's failure to come to Thistlewick Tye in time to save her, to anxiously tiptoeing about him, in the hope that he might connect with his beloved once more.

Edward's own anger had dissipated with a good night's sleep and he felt more kindly towards his host. Losing Emma was punishment enough for the man. He could help bring Barnabas some closure and relay kind words from beyond the grave. It would cost him nothing and, rather unexpectedly, result in financial rewards of a magnitude he'd not anticipated.

In order to make the promised séance convincing, he spent the morning talking to staff and reading some of the local history books and pamphlets he found in Barnabas's book-lined study. Mrs Drayton was in the drawing room, sitting with the body of her mistress. He stepped briefly over the threshold, hoping, or perhaps fearing, he would feel something to indicate that there was a trace of Emma left behind. He closed his eyes and willed her to come to him but felt nothing. Surely, if there was an after-life and she was going to make contact with anyone, it would have been him. Disbelieving she might have been, but she had always been gracious in defeat.

He quizzed the housekeeper for further details of Emma's passing and found her to be of the same mind as him; the fever had caused the delusions.

'The doctor had been over the previous evening, happy that she was over the worst of the influenza,' she said, 'but trying to calm her odd behaviour and wild claims. When he came down-stairs, he mentioned something about missing his morphia but decided he'd left the small red leather box at home. The mistress must have taken it when he was washing his hands, but we didn't know it at the time.'

'Could someone else have accessed the doctor's bag during his visit?' Edward asked.

'It's possible.' She shrugged. 'It was left in the hallway for a short while when he was updating the master about her condi-tion. But no one in the household wished the mistress ill. She was a kind lady. I took her up some supper, which she ate, and the master looked in on her before retiring to another room to sleep. He didn't feel right sharing with her whilst she was so confused.'

Edward could see how emotional the housekeeper was, as she spoke about the woman she'd worked for over the last two decades.

'Then poor Dr Appleby arrived early the following morning, saying he'd not found his morphia set and was anxious as to its whereabouts. He dashed upstairs to find she'd been dead for some time. Apparently, she did away with herself in the middle of the night.' Mrs Drayton's voice finally broke.

Either the woman was a consummate actress or her distress was real, so Edward decided to change the subject. He announced his intention to explore the village and perhaps go down to the beach. Living so far from the coast, he wanted to take advantage of the salty, fresh air whilst he could.

'Be careful down there, Mr Blackmore,' she warned. 'Our cliffs are falling into the sea at an alarming rate. Don't you be getting too close to them. A hundred years ago, there was a whole other village northwards and there's nothing left of it now. Some say you can still hear the long-submerged church bell occasionally on clear days – a ghostly reminder of its existence. Thistlewick Tye will eventually meet the same fate, but not in my lifetime.'

Barnabas was wandering about the house in a grief-induced trance, greeting the inevitable flood of sympathetic callers. A woman from the village arrived to wash and dress Emma in preparation for the burial, and Mrs Drayton took in a delivery of black-edged mourning stationery, which had been ordered the previous day. His cousin eventually retreated to the study to send out the necessary notifications and make the funeral arrangements, so Edward took the opportunity to escape before the evening meal was served.

As he was leaving, Wright offered him the loan of a small marine telescope to make the most of the views and perhaps spot some of the coastal wildlife. Edward graciously took the instrument and slid the small leather case into one of his deep pockets, before sweeping up his coat and cane. Armed with a letter summoning his own manservant, he retraced his steps back to the village centre and found the small postbox set into a long flint wall that ran along one edge of the common – so much easier to locate now that the country had abandoned green in favour of red. With luck, it would find its way to Carl by morning.

It was greyer than the previous day, having rained solidly until mid-afternoon, and the nights were drawing in with alacrity. But he'd always preferred the cosiness of autumn and winter, to the brighter, sunnier seasons. The smell of wood fires, the crisp air and warming, roasted food were comforts he relished, and he welcomed the soft light of early evening. Summer, certainly in the city, brought plagues of flies and the unbearable stench of effluent and decay.

Wright had told him that a sloping track to the left of the village water pump led down to the shore, through a gap known locally as the Thistlewick Rift. It was obvious from the geology that a river had carved out the space many thousands of years ago, but all that remained was a small stream feeding into the ocean. He followed the burbling water down to the sand, passing a couple of small abandoned wooden fishing boats that had been pulled up from the water.

The tide was high and the great expanse of flat beach he'd seen upon his arrival the day before was now a narrow band of wet, pale brown sand, peppered with lumpy grey and white pebbles – some as large as loaves of bread. These must be the flints that he'd seen so many of the local houses constructed from. A bitter wind swept in from the sea, so he turned up his collar to shield himself from the worst of it.

He'd wrongly thought, back in London, that a trip to the Norfolk coast would mean a thriving fishing industry, as the area was famous for its herring and crabs, but it was a stretch of coast strangely barren of fishing vessels. There was the odd one or two, but then maybe the flatness of the beach made the shore unsuitable for launching boats, as he suspected you could walk out for half a mile and the water would still barely come up to your shoulders. Had Thistlewick Tye been on a branch line, it would have been perfect for holidaymakers, who could safely paddle in shallow waters and build sandcastles in the long, hot summers, but he got the sense that it was in many ways an isolated village.

He took out the pocket telescope and surveyed the vast charcoal ocean, spotting a tiny vessel on the horizon. Spinning slowly around, he followed the clifftop from west to east but, with the tide in, he was too close to the land to see far. He'd have to return on a day when the tide was out to locate the impressive Cromer parish church tower. The almost ninety-degree angle of cliff face to beach served as a reminder that this dramatic landscape was precarious, as Mrs Drayton had warned, and he could see places further east where the sandy soil had slumped into the sea. It wouldn't take much, he realised, for a landslide to smother someone beneath. It would be foolish to stray too close.

He heard the crunch of footsteps from behind and turned to see a cloaked figure emerging from the rift, clutching the neck of a green, glass bottle. It was the woman he'd spied the previous day and, up close, she was not the old crone that he'd initially supposed, although likely older than him – perhaps in her early forties. She dropped her head when she noticed him, the deep sides of her hood obscuring her eyes, and stepped out of his path, closer to the land.

'I'm not sure it's wise to be so close to the cliffs at high tide,' he said, as she made to pass by. He reached for her cloak, not sure whether she'd heard him, but as he tugged at the material, she spun back, her arms like a windmill, slapping his hand away, as a torrent of abusive language came from her lips. Not wanting to enrage her any further, he backed away, almost getting his shoes wet as a rogue wave surged up the sand. Stupid woman, he was only trying to help.

She scurried into the distance and he watched her go. The sun was setting behind her and the edges of her black silhouette were bathed in a warm marigold-coloured light, at complete odds to the bitter temperature. When she was about a hundred yards away, she bent down to pick something up from the ground and tucked it into the folds of her heavy cloak, before continuing on her path. He watched her for a few minutes, becoming smaller and smaller, until she eventually disappeared to the left where, he assumed, there was another gap that allowed her access back inland.

He pulled his pocket watch from his waistcoat and checked the time. There was an hour until he needed to return to the house for dinner. Curious as to what the woman had collected from the sand, he followed the small imprints of her booted feet. The spiky outline of a small tree at a perilous angle on the clifftop caught his eye. Its exposed roots dangled in mid-air, like the tangly hair of some medieval princess leaning from her tower, and he could see that the edge of the small woodland on the land above was falling into the sea, one tree at a time. With winter on its way, Edward suspected that buffeting winds and lashing rain would soon accelerate the erosion, and it would only take one vicious storm for the tree to crash to the ground below.

He walked on a little further and, even in the rapidly diminishing light, he could see incongruous flashes of white in the soil above, a few feet from the surface. These were no chalky-coated flint pebbles, however, but longer streaks, jumbled and in a concentrated area. As he lifted the pocket telescope to his eye, he realised with a jolt that they were bones – partially exposed in the dark, umber soil. He saw the flat triangle of a shoulder blade, the narrow, curved crescents of several ribs and the wide, knobbly end of a femur jutting from the cliff face. Animal or man, he couldn't be sure. Perhaps this was evidence of a medieval butcher's pit, because there were too many to be from just the one creature. The cloaked woman had clearly picked up one of the bones, and he wondered what she might want with it.

And then he spotted a larger, pale sphere visible a bit further along. The light was poor but as he peered through the eyepiece, he saw two dark circles staring back at him. A shiver of something swept across his body and it wasn't the cruel north-easterly wind.

Because, without a doubt, he was looking at a human skull.

7

Edward let the telescope drop to his side. He had no idea if *all* the bones were human, but he knew that the skull most certainly was. What he didn't know was how long it had been there. A hundred years? A thousand? The local history volumes he'd looked at in Barnabas's study said Thistlewick Tye had been mentioned in the Domesday Book, so it had certainly been a settlement for a while.

He spun back to face the sea and another rogue wave rushed up to his feet. This time, it covered the toe of his boot. To the west, the cliffs ran into the distance, dark and dramatic, backlit by a sky that had turned blood-red in those last few minutes. It would be dark before long and he had no light with him, so he returned to the rift and trudged back up the track to the village centre.

In the inky canvas of night ahead, he saw several heartening squares of gold casting their cheery light out into the street. It was still early and a few figures darted about, most likely returning from a long day at work and making their way home to a roaring fire and hearty meal. A small group of men entered a low Tudor building, and a much larger rectangle of light briefly flashed onto the road as they filed through the door. These were thirsty men, sneaking in a quick drink before they returned to their wives and families, he realised, as the sign hanging above announced that the establishment was the Sailmaker's Arms. It was an opportunity too good to miss. He could purchase a pint of ale and make some discreet enquiries about Emma. Had she made any enemies in the village? In his experience, men merry from drink had loose tongues.

He walked across the long, damp grass of the common and pushed the heavy oak door open. The interior was gloomy, not helped by the low ceiling and smoky atmosphere. Decorated plates and stone jars were balanced across the top of the dark panelling that lined the room. A pair of rifles hung above the fireplace, barrels crossed, and the head of a stag was mounted above. The group of men who'd entered before him settled down at a table near the open fire, and a pink-cheeked man in a grubby apron stood behind the bar. As Edward approached, a scruffy mongrel got to its feet and barked at him. The man, who he assumed was the landlord, shouted at the animal to be quiet.

'Good evening, stranger. And why might you be finding yourself in Thistlewick this time of year?' he asked, wiping a pewter tankard on a cloth, as a scrawny young woman prepared a tray of drinks for the table of regulars. 'It's too cold for sea bathing, and only tinkers and traders visit when the weather turns.'

'I've just come from Thistlewick House,' Edward said, removing his gloves and carefully placing his top hat on the bar stool beside him.

Two men, both substantially older than him, were propping up the bar and they turned to see who'd disturbed their drinking. Were they father and son? Edward wondered. Brothers? Cousins? They were clearly related because they both had the same wiry eyebrows, square heads and wide noses, but one was older, taller, broader and had a more intimidating presence than his smaller, hunched-up, nervous-looking companion.

The oldest one was quite annoyed. 'We don't want no newspaper people sniffing about here after that woman's death. Leave poor Mr Shaw alone. He's suffered enough.'

'Now, now,' the landlord said, and held up the tankard to Edward with a questioning look, who nodded to confirm he would very much like a drink. 'Everyone is welcome in Thistlewick Tye.' The man had a disarming smile, with a distinctive gap between his two front teeth that made him look slightly comical.

'I'm not with the papers.' Edward settled on a high wooden stool. 'Barnabas Shaw is my cousin.'

The old boy narrowed his eyes and sniffed. 'You don't look much alike. He ain't got your boot-black hair or suspicious-looking blue eyes. And he certainly wouldn't wear such fancy clothes,' he added, as an afterthought.

'No,' Edward agreed. 'He takes after his mother's family, whereas my features came down the paternal line.'

'Mr Shaw mentioned contacting some relative who knew about spirits and the like when his missus went all strange in the head,' the landlord said over his shoulder, turning the tap on the barrel behind him and filling up the tankard.

'Is that right?' the old man asked, squinting at Edward. 'You some sort of medium?'

'Edward Blackmore, at your service.'

'Jacob Palmer.' The man behind the bar nodded in return. 'But I'm afraid we don't abide such nonsense here. We're good Christian folk who are minded to consider such practices akin to witchcraft.'

'Let me assure you, Mr Palmer, I have some of London's finest society amongst my client list: dukes, eminent professionals and even members of Her Majesty's government. Many of these men attend church and quite happily reconcile the two.'

'Bunch of frauds, the lot of yer,' the grumpy customer said, but he looked uneasy. 'Once you're dead, you're dead.'

'I can assure you that my gift is very real and I'm only disappointed not to have spoken to Mrs Shaw before she was so cruelly taken from us. My cousin hopes I'll be able to contact her in her spirit form, before she departs to the next life.' He smiled. 'But enough about me, let me buy you gentlemen an ale and we can talk of more cheerful things.'

The offer was accepted and Edward learned that he was sharing the bar with Silas Garrod and his much younger brother, Noah. It quickly became obvious that Noah was simple. There was something unfocused about his eyes and his head hung forward in a strange manner. The three of them chatted for a while about the village and its inhabitants. Edward learned that the men were unmarried, lived together in one of the terraced cottages near the school and both worked for Lord Felthorpe, who was the biggest landowner in the area. Silas claimed he was a fair and generous man, popular with his tenants and the villagers, even if he was occasionally quick-tempered and somewhat aloof. But he'd embraced the legacy of his father, the previous lord of the manor, and continued to administer the Benevolent Committee that oversaw almsgiving to those in need, as well as financially supporting the parish church.

Edward moved the conversation on to discuss the influenza that poor Mrs Shaw had inadvertently brought into Thistlewick Tye, hoping to find out if her peculiar behaviour had a medical explanation.

'Has anyone else hereabouts suffered the same troubled mind following such a raging fever?' he enquired.

In the same way that contracting rabies might drive a man to madness, could her illness have been responsible for Emma's delusions?

'Only that babe down at the forge last month,' Silas volunteered. 'Sickly thing all its short life and started acting right peculiar out of nowhere. Never known anything like it.'

'It was odd,' the landlord agreed. 'It wasn't influenza though. Measles, I believe. The mother thought she'd lost it in the night but it survived, only to display the most extraordinary strength the following morning – thrashing about and trying to crawl. Pulled itself right out of the cradle. She came in after hanging out the linen and found it dead on the floor. If we'd any witches living hereabouts, I'd have said a spell had been cast over the poor mite.'

The talk of witches made Edward think of the woman who'd just attacked him.

'I encountered a strange, cloaked woman on the beach. She certainly looked the part.'

'Maude Grimmer. Ha.' Silas banged his tankard onto the bar. 'Closest thing we've got to a witch but she ain't magic. She's just a dirty drunk who lives outside the Thistlewick boundary, beyond the woods, but you're best keeping out of her way. Got a pretty face – at least she used to have when she was a young 'un, before all the drinking. Nasty piece when she's had a few, though. Slapped her husband about until the poor bugger couldn't take it no more and left. That were about five years ago now.'

Edward had smelled the sour alcohol, despite the sea breeze blowing between them, and she'd been clutching a bottle of what he now suspected was gin. As for the slapping, he could equally vouch for that. He'd had first-hand experience of her lashing out with no provocation.

'No one thought he'd have the guts to leave her,' Jacob

Palmer chipped in. 'Real shock when he ran off, along with his wages, and she had to find a way to make a living. Started combing the beach and hawking the bits and pieces she found: bottles, scraps of metal, fossils and the like.'

So, she'd been collecting the bones to sell to the rag-and-bone man. It explained why he'd seen her down by the shoreline.

'Only comes to the village to buy essentials from Drayton's, the grocer. Gets the gin from Sheringham, mind, as she knows no one here will sell it to her.' The landlord rolled his eyes. 'Won't be making old bones, that one. Surprised she's lasted this long, to be fair. She's more pickled than these eggs.' He pointed to a large glass jar behind him. 'No family or visitors to speak of.'

The grocer's surname was that of his cousin's housekeeper, who must surely be related. As an unmarried woman, Mrs Drayton would have kept her maiden name but been given the title of Mrs as a mark of respect. Everyone had a connection to everyone in a village, he realised.

'Talking of family, how come we've not seen yer around these parts before?' Silas asked, sliding his empty glass to the landlord and wiping his mouth on his sleeve. 'Can't be very close to Mr Shaw if you've not visited him in the ten years of his marriage.'

'You're quite correct – I'm not. Barnabas and I are very different men but I was inordinately fond of his wife, and it was her I came to see. But then we don't get to choose our family,' he lamented. 'So, it's rather heartening to see how close you are to your brother.' He nodded at the younger man.

'Saved my life, didn't you, Bruh?' Noah said, who'd let Silas do most of the speaking thus far.

Silas's face briefly flashed genuine affection, as his cheeks flushed pink with embarrassment.

'I saved your life, Noah. That I did.'

'Poor Noah here was mucking about in the water when he was a lad and got swept out to sea,' Mr Palmer said, returning behind the bar. He'd slipped out to wipe down the table the group of working men had been sitting at. They'd been particularly restrained, Edward noticed, and only consumed one after-work drink before heading home. 'Silas swam out and saved him, but he contracted pneumonia shortly afterwards and nearly died a second time. Weakened his heart though, and he's lucky to still be here.'

'I'm a lucky man, aren't I, Bruh?'

Silas nodded. 'That you are, brother. That you are.'

The landlord's scruffy dog reappeared and put his two front paws on Noah's knees, revelling in the ensuing attention, as his tail frantically whipped from side to side. If dogs could smile, Edward would have sworn it had the biggest grin across his furry face.

'I love Banjo, don't I, Bruh? And Banjo loves me?'

'That he does, Noah. That he does.' The older brother smiled, before his suspicious eyes returned to the stranger.

Edward offered to buy the men another drink, hoping one more would loosen their tongues further, but Silas informed him that two drinks were sufficient for any man. The way he said it made Edward think it was an often-repeated phrase of his. The Garrods collected their coats from the hatstand and began to put them on.

'When I grew up here, it was a lovely little village,' Silas grunted, helping Noah feed his arms into the thick wool coat he held up. 'Everyone knew everyone, and no one was unkind or dishonest. I weren't ever keen on the railway coming to Cromer. It just brought more trouble and a load of strangers. Occasionally, some of them find their way here, poking about in our business, when all the good folk of Thistlewick want is to be left alone.'

'Oh, I don't know, Silas,' Mr Palmer said. 'It helps the fishermen further along the coast to get their catch to market quicker. We can't remain isolated forever. Times are changing.'

'Well, they rattle me – swanning about in their top hats, with their foreign ways.' Edward wasn't sure if the comment was aimed at him. 'But I've said it before, and I'll say it again: bad things always happen when strangers turn up.'

Silas threw Edward one final suspicious look, tipped his hat and ushered his brother out into the night.

8

_____

The following day and the weather was even more miserable than previously. The skies had taken on a gloomy hue that promised rain. Edward idly tapped at the glass of the barometer in the hall with his fingernails as he passed it on his way to the study. He was seeking out his cousin to ask that provision be made for the arrival of his manservant, who had replied by return of post and would be in Thistlewick Tye by nightfall. The bottom needle dropped quite dramatically, pointing to *stormy* with definite assertion.

Mrs Drayton walked past and shook her head.

'There's some really squally weather on its way, sir. Keep yourself indoors, today. Even the Cromer fishermen'll be staying home, if they have any sense. I was supposed to be dropping off some socks to the church that I've knitted for one of the poorer families, but I'll not head out in this. We'll be seeing horizontal rain, floods across Low Road and more of the cliffs falling away, to be sure.'

Talk of the rapidly eroding coastline reminded him of the skull.

'Was there a burial you know of, up the hill, where the common land meets the top of the cliffs?'

'All good Christian folk are buried in the churchyard,' she said. 'Everyone from the village is there, apart from a few heathens and a suicide, who are just outside the church boundary.' She coloured, realising the insensitivity of her words, and lowered her voice. 'But the Reverend Fallow has been most gracious in allowing Mrs Shaw to be laid to rest within the walls.'

'I only ask because I think a graveyard might be falling into the sea,' he explained.

'There's always bones and fossils found on the beach,' she said. 'Some of the things in those cliffs go back thousands of years – a woolly mammoth was found there sixty years ago. It's likely those pagan sorts who were here before the Romans. They worshipped many gods and buried people willy-nilly.'

'I doubt the bones are that old,' he said. 'They're very near the surface.'

Mrs Drayton shrugged. 'Animals, then,' she said, clearly not particularly interested in his discovery, and she carried on her way, so he didn't mention that there was at least one human buried up there.

He wasn't sure why the vacant eyes of the skull wedged in the soil were haunting him so, but if a bad storm was about to hit the village, then it was highly possible it would be dislodged and fall to the sand below. A more unscrupulous chap than he might consider acquiring it for himself to add authenticity to his séances, but he was strangely content with his plaster skull. Besides, the bones could be from someone who'd passed in living memory and still had relatives to grieve for them, or even someone who'd been murdered, and deserved justice. He felt uncomfortable messing with the dead and wanted any falling bodies treated respectfully. Perhaps he was more afraid of an afterlife than he cared to admit, because he felt it was important that he got to the skull before Maude Grimmer. He could then properly assess the right course of action – especially if she was just going to sell it on without any proper investigation.

Carl had indicated he'd arrive in Cromer by the late afternoon, and then planned to get a seat on the mail coach to Thistlewick Tye. Borrowing one of his cousin's mackintosh coats and a sou'wester from the boot room, Edward told Barnabas he was going to the hostelry for a drink, where he would await the arrival of his manservant.

'Damn foolish to venture out in this, Edward. I've another bottle of absinthe in the cellar, if you feel the need for a drink. It's a strange public house anyway. Mr Palmer is a landlord with a conscience and keeps a strict eye on his patrons, refusing to serve them after a couple of drinks. You'd think he'd wring them for every penny he could, but he won't even sell to the Grimmer woman. Besides, your man can make his own way up the lane. It's not for you to be of service to him.'

Edward shrugged and gave an excuse that sounded convincing. 'I don't mind. I feel the need for some fresh air and to distance myself from the confusing and powerful psychic energy in this house.'

'You can sense her?' Barnabas jumped to his feet, his face eager and his voice hopeful. 'Is she with us now? Let me call for the table to be set up and we can contact her this very afternoon.'

'I told you; I won't perform the séance until she's in the ground. You must stop pressuring me, cousin.'

'Of course, of course.' He returned to his seat, wringing his hands, and Edward took his leave.

* * *

Five minutes later, he set off down the lane, hypnotised by the swirls of dancing brown leaves before him, as a strong gust whipped them into a frenzy. The skies were oppressively dark, suggesting the storm was imminent and, indeed, the first heavy raindrops started to fall as he approached the village common.

There was a flash of jagged lightning above the swirling sea, as he began his descent down the rift, and he walked headlong into a buffeting wind that was determined to push him back from whence he came. A few seconds later and a loud crack of thunder echoed about his muffled ears. The rain was suddenly falling like stair rods. He knew it was madness to be heading to the beach but had decided, if he kept away from the bottom of the cliffs, he'd be safe enough. Should the skull be dislodged, perhaps it would roll towards the sea and he could safely retrieve it without courting danger. The pocket telescope would help him ascertain whether it was still in the cliff face. He didn't want Maude Grimmer picking it up and selling it to be ground down to powder – although he hoped that even a desperate drunk might stop short of turning dead men into fertiliser.

But to his horror, as he arrived on the sand, she was already scurrying about beneath the teetering tree, her cloak buffeted by the fierce winds rushing from sea to shore. It was obvious that some of the land had recently collapsed, as there was an enormous slump of soil cascading towards the crashing waves. He looked up and, in the half-light, he could see the earthy browns, streaked with burnt umbers and pale yellows, where fresh soil had been exposed on the cliff face.

There was a skittering of stones and tumble of earth as more of the land fell away and, alarmingly, he realised that the tree was now almost parallel to the beach. Did the stupid woman not realise how much danger she was in? As he made his way over to her, there was another flash of piercing white light, splitting the

black sky above, and a much shorter interval before the
following rumble. The centre of the storm was almost upon
them.

An angry sea hissed to his right, even though the tide was
half out and not near enough to be an immediate danger. The
waves, however, were high and the wind was howling about his
buffeted body, stinging his cheeks, as he stumbled a couple of
times in his haste to reach her. She had her back to him and was
clawing at the wet earth with her bare hands. There was a
hessian sack at her feet and she was frantically thrusting objects
inside. A ferocious rush of wind almost flattened him and he was
glad the sou'wester was tied tightly under his chin.

Finally, she turned to put what appeared to be a pelvis into
the sack, and her face registered her horror at being observed.
She stood upright and shouted something but it was carried
away by the escalating winds, up over the clifftop, and his gaze
was distracted by a movement in his peripheral vision. The tree
no longer had enough of a grip on the land to anchor it to the
soil and it cartwheeled, surprisingly slowly and elegantly, from
above. He grabbed Maude by her shoulders and pulled her
towards him, spinning her about, so that she could see why he'd
taken such sudden and intrusive action.

She wriggled free, turned and scowled at him, before shoving
him violently in the chest, with so much force it was a wonder he
wasn't pushed over.

'This is utter madness!' he shouted. 'Go home. If more land
should fall, you'll be killed.'

Whatever her reply, it was again swallowed by the roar of
waves and wind. She turned back to the cliffs, but at that
moment, the very thing Edward had feared happened right
before their eyes. A further section of cliff suddenly slumped and
fell towards them, like a dying man collapsing to his knees. Even

more of the pale bones were now visible in the rich red-browns of the earth – ribs, maybe a tibia or femur, the small spiky discs of a spine, and another pelvis, jumbled and separate, big and small, as they both froze to watch the horrifying spectacle unfold.

He instinctively reached for the brim of the borrowed sou'wester, ensuring it remained firmly on his head, as she took a couple of steps backwards, this time willingly embracing the shelter of his body. The air and the sea were both thrashing about wildly, as though engaged in mortal combat, but the sliding earth had come to an eerie halt. There was a beat and then a pale ball rolled down the slope and past their feet. It was a skull, but Edward had no idea if it was the one he'd seen the previous day, or another altogether.

She turned her head to his, and a thick lock of her damp, wavy hair, flecked with grey, slid from inside her cloak hood to fall across her face, obscuring one eye. There was a delicate fan of crow's feet at the corner of the other, highlighted by her weather-beaten skin. It made her difficult to age but she must have a good ten years on him. They stared at each other for a moment. She was assessing him, he realised, almost waiting for something... and then, as suddenly as it had materialised, the moment of connection was gone. She turned to the sea and refused to look at his face again.

'These bones are human,' he shouted, trying to be heard above the wind. 'And from the number that have fallen, and that remain visible in the cliffs, I'd say we're looking at several bodies. Shouldn't the constable be notified?'

She ignored him but, if she'd been collecting them over the past few weeks or months, she'd know this. Instead, she bent down and grabbed the skull, carrying it to the sodden sack, which was now partially covered in fallen soil. She tugged it free, and added the find, as something nearby caught Edward's eye. There was a glint of metal in the earth behind her and he bent down and pulled out a thick gold chain. Despite the driving rain, she saw it in his hands, lurched forwards and snatched at it. It slid easily from his wet gloves and before he realised what was happening, she'd gathered up her sack and was scrabbling across the scattered flints for home.

So, it was grave goods she was after, he realised. Sell the bones for pennies, but these people, whatever century they were from, had been buried with treasures, and the despicable Maude Grimmer was merely here to steal from the dead.

9

Edward made his way back to the Sailmaker's Arms, to wait for Carl out of the storm. He hadn't noticed before but the snug to the right was a coffee room. Jacob Palmer informed him that the current vicar, Reverend Fallow, was a temperance advocate who'd tried to enforce complete abstention on the village a few years back but there had been quite the revolt. Lord Felthorpe had suggested turning part of the Sailmaker's into a coffee house and supported the change financially when it turned out that limiting alcohol, rather than banning it, was far more effective. And running the two businesses made his hostelry sufficiently profitable. Edward ordered a strong coffee to warm himself and tried to thaw out by the fire, as Banjo came to sit by his feet.

'You're quiet tonight,' Edward observed, and the landlord stared at him in disbelief.

'That's because you're the only one mad enough to venture out in this obscene weather!'

'Myself and Maude Grimmer,' he said, settling on a wooden bench and patting the adoring dog. 'I've just seen her on the beach.'

Jacob shook his head. 'She's bad news, that one. No one likes her coming into the village but there's nothing we can do about it because she lives beyond our boundary. Even Lord Felthorpe has given her up as a lost cause. He's always looked kindly upon the unfortunate, like when he made sure Noah Garrod was given a house with his brother when others wanted him sent to an asylum.' He leaned forward on the bar to stress his next point. 'But he's also not afraid to root out trouble. When he's had lazy or dishonest tenants in the past, he's evicted them. In the case of one particularly undesirable family, God intervened and they all came down with some mystery illness that lasted weeks, becoming so sick, they eventually left of their own accord. Sometimes, there is no helping those who won't help themselves. Unfortunately, Maude's property is her own; we can't make her leave. Although, as she gets older, she keeps herself to herself more.'

'Did she have any quarrel with the Shaws?' Could she have been responsible for Emma's death? Edward fleetingly wondered.

'She's generally been unpleasant to everyone for her twoscore years. I even remember her being spiteful as a child, but I don't recall any specific quarrel with them. Why d'ya ask?'

Edward knew of old not to reveal his hand. He trusted no one. But would a drunk like her really have the cunning to creep about Thistlewick House? Even if she had, as someone prepared to snatch a gold chain from his hands, she'd surely have pocketed small items of value to fund her drinking. His cousin had reported nothing stolen.

'Because I came across her on the beach just now and she was rude to me again. I'm not sure she even knows who I am.'

Mr Palmer shrugged. 'She might have overheard talk in the grocer's. Mrs Drayton's brother owns it, so they'll have been told of your stay and, as Silas made clear, we're wary of strangers.'

'She was collecting some bones that have fallen to the shore from the cliffs this side of the woods, as there's been a landslide up towards Sheringham. I think it might be an unmarked grave of some description because she picked up a human skull. Who should I report it to? I feel the authorities should be notified, even if the burial is ancient.'

Palmer frowned. 'Can't think a pagan burial would be of any interest to the police, but that'd be Constable Lovett. Leave it with me and I'll tell him in the morning when I take Banjo out.'

The dog heard his name and opened his eyes, swivelling them hopefully towards his master without moving his head. Neither walk nor treat were forthcoming, so he closed them again.

When the mail coach finally arrived shortly afterwards, Edward braved the storm to meet Carl, pleased to find the driving rain had eased somewhat. His man had a small trunk with him, containing some more of his master's clothes and his spiritualist paraphernalia. Together, they lugged it into the post office and the postmaster arranged for someone to drop it down to Thistlewick House first thing in the morning. Carl's more modest belongings were in a large canvas haversack that he slung over his back, so the pair of them turned up their collars against the biting wind and headed for Copperpenny Lane.

'Lady Temple has organised a very public memorial service for her husband,' Carl said as they walked, updating him on events back in London. 'Looks like the old girl fell for it. I reckon you could squeeze more out of her. Get her along to another meeting when we've tied up this nonsense.'

'I don't think that will be necessary,' Edward replied, realising his man had not yet been apprised of his recent good fortune.

'Because if we play our cards right, there will soon be more money in the Cattisham Orphanage Fund than I could have ever hoped for...'

* * *

The funeral of Mrs Shaw was held two days later. Edward tentatively suggested to his cousin that a human hand was responsible for Emma's death, but he wouldn't have it. The perpetrator had been an evil child not of this world, he insisted, who had threatened to kill everyone. Had Edward come to Thistlewick when he'd first written, he would know this. As much as it pained Barnabas, however, he would not approach the coroner to reopen the inquest, because even he recognised that there was no ruling that would cover such a cause of death.

'It breaks my heart that she'll forever be thought of as taking her own life,' he said. 'But the Reverend Fallow has been very kind about it all. With the recent change in the law, she can be buried in daylight hours with the full Christian burial rites, as she was deemed not of sound mind. He's insisting the grave is tucked away in the far corner, however, but as I accept that technically it was her own hand that administered the dose, it's the best I can hope for. I anticipate that your spiritual enquiries will at least uncover *why* the child did such a heinous thing...'

Edward was part of the simple procession that followed the hearse, drawn by two black-plumed horses, up Copperpenny Lane, around the edge of the common and across to the small Norman parish church.

After the service, the Reverend Fallow left the handful of mourners to linger at the graveside – all sobered by the injustice of a death undoubtedly brought on by the insanity associated with her illness.

A very elderly lady, introduced as Mrs Cleyford, and assisted by her spinster daughter, tottered over to Barnabas to pay her respects. She expressed her sorrow at having outlived someone so young. Barnabas later confided, she was the oldest woman still living in the village, having recently celebrated her eightieth birthday. The Benevolent Committee had organised a small tea party in the church hall back in the summer to mark the occasion.

She eyed Edward suspiciously but did not address him.

'Everyone that passes away in Thistlewick is younger than me now. I've seen them all grow up and she was one of the best. Gave much of her time to planting flowers in the village and spent that whole summer looking after the butcher's children when they lost their mother. Such a shame she never had any of her own.'

Barnabas, who was on the brink of tears, found her kind words too much and merely nodded before steering Edward over to Dr Appleby and his father, making the introductions. The older man had been the village doctor for two generations before his wandering mind had required him to retire, and had brought Mrs Shaw into the world, so was naturally deeply upset to witness her leaving it. He might not know what he'd eaten for breakfast, the son confided, but historic events, like delivering Emma in the middle of a heatwave thirty-four years ago, were firmly etched into his withering brain.

'Should be me in that box. I've done bad things.' The old man raised a wrinkled hand and pointed to the hole before them.

His son put his arm out to calm his father and offered gentle words.

'Now, now, you're getting muddled again, Dad. Reading too many newspapers.' He turned to Edward and lowered his voice. 'It's his infirmity of the mind. He gets confused about what is real, what's a dream and what he's read somewhere. He told me not ten minutes ago that one of the tastiest things he'd ever eaten was a meal of zebra... Honestly, I don't know where his brain even goes these days.' He rolled his eyes.

'Damn fine it was, too,' the old man said and then raised a finger to his lips to signify the secretive nature of his words. 'But we mustn't tell anyone. Keep it just between us.'

Barnabas took his arm and led him to the lychgate, keen to hear his recollections of Emma as a child, whilst the doctor and Edward trailed behind.

'I hear you're one of those fellows who claims to contact the dead,' the son said, as the two men fell into step.

'Ah, as a man of science, you suspect me to be a charlatan.'

The doctor shrugged. 'As a man of science, I never rule anything out. Whilst it's not something I announce, I'm genuinely interested in spiritualism. I would, however, appreciate your discretion in this regard. In your professional opinion, Mr Blackmore, could the spirit of some long-dead person possibly have possessed Mrs Shaw?'

Edward felt flattered that the doctor saw his line of work as a profession. There was no recommended training or formal qualification you could take in order to set yourself up as a medium, which was part of the problem – anyone could claim they were a channel between this world and the next. He also wanted to laugh at the doctor's enquiry – the very idea that Emma had been possessed was preposterous. But as his whole reputation was built on similarly abstract ideas, he trod carefully, especially as Carl had arrived with news that the cynic Dr Doyle – who'd attended his recent séance – had been so intrigued by what he'd witnessed, that he, too, had made a sizeable donation to the Cattisham Orphanage Fund.

'I've never come across a person possessed before,' he

replied. 'The souls I communicate with have lost their physical bodies, and their spirit merely awaits entry to the next world. As you know, I arrived too late to properly investigate Mr Shaw's claims, but I suspect the fever had altered his wife's mind in some way. He has, however, insisted that I perform a séance to establish this. If her spirit is willing to speak to me then she may well have the answers he seeks.'

'Which aligns with my professional opinion – Emma Shaw had a raging fever, and such high temperatures inevitably harm the vital organs. She'd clearly suffered some damage to the brain, leading to her extreme psychosis, and the name she gave was undoubtedly one from fiction. Her tales of waggons, dancing horses and men on fire were equally likely from storybooks. I am, as you rightly suspected, not a man easily given to flights of fancy, and so spiritualism is an uncomfortable bedfellow alongside my strong faith but, in the interests of research, I'd be keen to attend should you conduct such a session.'

Edward considered the man's request. The doctor was being surprisingly frank with him, admitting that he was at least open to spiritualism, so he decided to trust him with his concerns surrounding Emma's passing.

'I understand you gave evidence at the inquest but perhaps I might ask why you believed Mrs Shaw's death to be self-inflicted?'

The doctor shrugged. 'She was highly agitated and was violent towards myself, and later Mrs Drayton, with no provocation – a woman who's served her family faithfully for years. We believe she stole the morphia box from my bag the previous evening but didn't know what she was doing. It may even be that she was trying to alleviate her own distress and simply overdosed. Whatever the truth, I'd isolated her, and the housekeeper was outside the bedroom for the duration of the night. When I checked on Mrs Shaw at six o'clock the following morning, it was immediately obvious that she had been dead for several hours, clearly choosing a time to leave this world when the household were asleep.'

'But my cousin informs me that his wife was left-handed, despite many years of forcing herself to adapt, and the syringe was injected into her left arm.'

Dr Appleby's head jerked in Edward's direction. 'Now that I do find interesting. I'd no idea she favoured the left hand and wish Mr Shaw had shared this information with the coroner.' He looked about to see if anyone was close enough to overhear their conversation and lowered his voice. 'It throws a very different light on events. If what you say is true, then I would agree with her husband – in a moment such as that she would have instinctively picked up the syringe with her left hand.' He frowned. 'Do you think someone else administered the fatal dose?'

Edward returned the shrug.

'My cousin cannot conceive of anyone who would wish her harm and it's why he remains adamant in his conviction she was possessed, and that it was the spirit of the child who executed the heinous deed.'

The doctor frowned. 'But why on earth would a long-dead little girl wish Mrs Shaw harm?'

It was a question Edward couldn't answer.

10

By the following day, Carl had garnered much of the information Edward needed about Emma's childhood, her marriage and the circumstances surrounding her illness. A bit of chit-chat over dinner in the kitchens, some harmless flirting with the aged housekeeper and a late-night tipple with Wright where Carl had slipped the fellow half a bottle of rum. Between them, Edward was happy they would be able to convince Barnabas that they'd summoned his wife.

The evening of the séance arrived and Edward was unusually anxious. He much preferred conducting such summonings in his own home. For a start, there was a sliding panel in the back wall that enabled Carl to slip in and out of the room when necessary, usually to snuff out or reignite candles, and there were long lengths of rubber tubing running under the floorboards where they manipulated the temperature. It was icy cold when the spirits appeared, and connected to the range when the meeting was coming to an end to warm the room once more.

But there were still things they could do to convince Barnabas that his wife was communicating from the Other Side.

Edward remembered that Emma wore lavender because he couldn't smell that particular flower without thoughts of her flitting through his head. As part of the letter he'd sent home requesting Carl to join him in Thistlewick, he'd instructed Delphine to make a candle with lavender oil in the wax. Once lit, and an inch down into burning, the aroma would fill the room. And their combined research had uncovered several little-known facts about her past that would reassure his cousin she really was present. The housemaid confided that she'd heard her mistress cry out for a 'Zella' during her illness and, after the shock of seeing herself in the dressing table mirror, Mrs Shaw had lain curled up on the bed, crying for her mummy.

Edward asked Mrs Drayton to sit in on the séance, as she'd witnessed the so-called manifestation by Esfir. Besides, women were prone to heightened emotions and generally happier to volunteer information when he communicated with the spirit world, or at least unintentionally indicate if he was on the right track, adding to his credibility. And Dr Appleby had announced his intention to bring Lord Felthorpe along. Barnabas was delighted, as he'd been nervous that he would be judged by his peers for his wild claims – Thistlewick Tye was simply not a place for this sort of nonsense. But even if they were there to mock, Edward knew he could put on a good show, and had converted many a sceptic in his time. He saw it as a challenge.

He'd met Lord Felthorpe briefly at the funeral and knew from his cousin that the Felthorpe family had lived in the huge house on the Cromer Road for generations. The current baron owned much of the land thereabouts, but had never married, so there was no heir. Now in his sixties, you could tell he'd been quite the presence in his younger days. Still retaining all the bearing and authority of wealth, he could pass for much younger, with his handsome, dark eyes, despite his thick silver hair.

'As close as the members of the committee are to the Reverend Fallow, no one has dared mention the séance to him,' Barnabas confided. 'He is a fervent Christian, and his sermons can be quite intimidating. Terribly old-fashioned ideas and won't move with the times. It's almost as if he was born a hundred years too late. But, generally, he supports what the doctor and Lord Felthorpe are trying to achieve, and I can honestly say that I've never known a community so prepared to help out its own. The farmers encourage gleaning to feed the hungry, and when a family is struggling, for whatever reason, we all pull together to see them through the storm. Everyone has been so kind to me after Emma's death and, even though I'll happily surrender my house to you, I'm not prepared to leave the village.'

Edward's dream had long been to lead an isolated life, away from prying eyes and unwanted interference, so he was immediately suspicious. People were generally judgemental and selfish creatures, so he found it difficult to believe the good people of Thistlewick were that altruistic. There must be something in it for them, he decided, forgetting that, for many, faith was its own reward.

Carl had helped to prepare the drawing room that evening but, with no sliding panels or pipes to manipulate, he would remain in the corner, on hand to dim the lamps and assist with the ghostly illusions. This was still Mr Shaw's house, so it was Wright who distributed the sherries to the four gentlemen, as Mrs Drayton stood quietly in the corner, clearly feeling out of place, and casting anxious glances at them all.

'The doctor informs me you're looking for a smaller property,' Lord Felthorpe said to Barnabas, as they gathered around the chenille-covered dining table and Wright pulled out a chair for the housekeeper. 'I'll happily sell you one of the cottages by the church, but am curious as to why you would give up Thistlewick House. I hope there is nothing nefarious afoot.' He gave Edward the side-eye.

'Not a bit of it,' Barnabas assured him. 'I'm ashamed to admit that I did my cousin here a great wrong in our youth and hope God will look kindly upon my gesture of atonement.'

Lord Felthorpe nodded. 'It is never too late to repent your sins, Shaw.' He patted Barnabas's shoulder. 'We all stray from the path sometimes. And talking of straying, let me be clear that my presence here tonight is in no way condoning a practice that I consider dangerously close to the dark arts.'

Edward wondered why the man was here if he was so adamant that communicating with the dead was unacceptable.

'There is nothing nefarious about my gift. Rest assured, I'm not about to summon the Devil. I largely speak with good Christian folk who simply have unfinished business in this world.'

'But there *is* evil at play,' Barnabas interjected, banging his fist on the table as he slid into his seat. 'Emma was possessed by the spirit of a little girl, and it was she who administered the overdose.'

'Are you here to perform some kind of exorcism, Mr Blackmore?' Lord Felthorpe asked. 'You say communicating with the dead is a gift of yours, so banish this wicked spirit. Send her to the afterlife and leave us in peace.'

'I'm not qualified to exorcise,' Edward said. 'Besides, do you not think we should discover who we're dealing with first?'

After issuing the usual instructions to link hands, and for the assembled guests to focus their thoughts on Mrs Shaw, Edward confirmed that Emma had, indeed, joined them. At that exact moment, the tall pillar candle on the sideboard extinguished itself – or rather, the fine black wire Carl had attached to the top of the wick was pulled sharply to dip it into the melted wax and put out the flame. Mrs Drayton gasped and his man was far enough away to be assumed innocent.

Edward closed his eyes and concentrated on the information they'd gathered and how best to present the necessary facts. He shook his head from side to side, as if to clear his head.

'She has joined us, Barnabas,' he said and allowed himself a dramatic pause. 'Yes, yes,' he repeated, as though he were having a conversation with her.

'What's she saying?' his cousin demanded.

The words that came from Edward's lips in these situations could make or break a man and he allowed himself to enjoy the moment. If Barnabas continued to push him, tonight he would break a man.

'Don't distress yourself, Emma. I forgive him,' he whispered into the air.

'What? *What?*' Barnabas's tone became increasingly impatient.

'Must we go over old ground, cousin? Emma should not be feeling guilty for the way *you* treated me.'

There was an uncomfortable silence as his cousin undoubtedly felt the scrutiny of those gathered around the table, followed by a moment of realisation as the smell of lavender hit his nostrils.

'My God, she really is here. I can smell her perfume. Emma?' His voice became a reverent whisper, before he turned back to Edward. 'Tell me what she said. Is this about the damn inheritance? For pity's sake, man, it was your father's decision, and you must tell her that I'm going to make amends. That I'm passing the house over to you.'

The doctor raised a surprised eyebrow but said nothing.

'Calm yourself, man. She knows about our arrangement and

says it's the right thing to do.' He paused, feeling some satisfaction at his cousin's embarrassment.

Edward then put his research to good use and had Emma talk to the room fondly of her childhood memories in Thistlewick, as well as recalling incidents from her marriage that Carl had garnered from staff and villagers. An hour spent with Dr Appleby's confused father, whom Carl had found wandering around the village, had proved particularly useful, especially as the senile old man had no qualms betraying the confidences of his former patients.

Edward employed a more serious but gentle tone. 'And she will always love you for your understanding about losing the baby, and the complications that followed.'

Mrs Drayton gasped and the doctor exchanged a horrified look with Lord Felthorpe. They may both have claimed to be non-believers but Edward knew they were impressed.

'I didn't know Emma had lost a child,' Lord Felthorpe interjected.

'Sweet Lord... she really is here with us.' Mrs Drayton sniffed. 'I may have doubted you before, Mr Blackmore, but that was not common knowledge.'

All eyes were on Barnabas, who again struggled to contain his emotions and merely shook his head to indicate that he couldn't bring himself to speak for a moment.

'Let her know that I never blamed her, that I miss her terribly and don't know how I will go on without her...'

'She says not to mourn her and instead look for reasons to be happy. Know that she will always be with you, whether you sense her presence or not.' Edward had decided to be kind and he noticed his cousin's tense shoulders relax.

Edward then asked Emma to tell them the truth of her

passing but, after a suitable pause, he expressed that she didn't know.

'How can she not know?' Confusion flashed across Barnabas's face.

'Because, as you so correctly surmised, her mind was invaded by another. The soul of a child – she has few recollections of anything after the height of her fever.'

'Then contact the dead girl.' Barnabas was angry now. 'Summon her and find out why she killed my wife.'

'That's not how it works, cousin, and you know that. Emma has come to us this night to confirm that her passing was not done by her own hand, and because she wished to give you comfort. She loves you and will rejoice the day you finally join her in the heavens, but the child is not in the room and I cannot make her appear if she doesn't want to make contact.'

'Damn this.'

'But there is another spirit... a woman of advanced years called Margaret.' Edward did not meet Dr Appleby's eye and instead chose to misdirect his attentions to Mrs Drayton. 'A relative of yours?' He feigned ignorance as the housekeeper shook her head.

'She is asking for forgiveness... something about a foolish indiscretion.'

Still the doctor said nothing but his body language was telling – he was biting at his lip and his frame was rigid. Both the housekeeper and Lord Felthorpe cast fleeting glances at him but neither said anything. Everyone around the table, including Barnabas, must know Margaret had been his mother and that she'd passed away eight years previously.

The doctor shrugged. 'Very common name.'

'She cannot move on until she has the forgiveness she seeks...'

With everyone linking hands, poor Dr Appleby could not move to mop his brow, but even in the dim light, Edward could see tiny beads of perspiration glinting on his forehead. Whether he truly believed in spirit communication or not, he was certainly uncomfortable that the brief affair his mother had conducted with her brother-in-law might come out. Carl had done his work well and it had certainly been fortuitous that his path had crossed with the old doctor's.

Edward let the pause become increasingly uncomfortable before delivering his final line.

'She is sad there is no one present prepared to talk to her but will come again. I'm losing her now.' He paused. 'I think... is she humming "By the Sad Sea Waves"?' Dr Appleby almost choked on his tongue but still volunteered nothing. 'And now she has gone.'

Edward concluded the séance in his usual manner and the guests retired to the drawing room of Thistlewick House, where he expected them all to emphatically reject his claim that Mrs Shaw had been possessed, but everyone was strangely contemplative.

He could also tell from the doctor's face that he'd hooked another fish.

11

TEN YEARS PREVIOUSLY, LONDON, 1885

Edward had left Cattisham, the village where he'd grown up, not long after his father's death and moved to London. Using the money from his mediocre bequest, he'd rented a small flat and tried his luck at earning a crust from the illusions he'd perfected as a boy. He'd changed his appearance and, to spite his father, his surname – even though the man was not alive to witness it.

When it became apparent that Barnabas would do nothing to address the injustice of the will, he'd severed all ties with his cousin, and would have been quite content never to set eyes on the man again. But, seven years later, he was annoyed to find their paths accidentally crossed in London. Although, as it was Edward who had introduced his cousin to the murky world of spiritualism, it was perhaps an inevitable encounter.

'By God! Is that you, Edward?'

They were both attending a lecture on psychic phenomenon by The Etheric Communion Circle, and Barnabas was seated in the row behind him. They recognised each other as everyone filed out of the lecture theatre at the end of the evening, and his cousin was clearly embarrassed to run into the man he'd betrayed but could not, in good conscience, ignore.

At first, Edward wanted to thump him, but they were in polite company and manners demanded he should save any such revenge until they were in a back alley and away from the judgemental eyes of gentlefolk.

'Barnabas.' He nodded but his hands were scrunched into tight fists and he could feel his jaw tensing. Barnabas was equally discomposed by the accidental meeting.

'The colourful, theatrical clothing and the hair—' They walked alongside each other and followed the crowd to the foyer.

'I appreciate that it's unfashionably long,' Edward hastily interrupted, 'but in my line of work, such eccentricity is almost imperative.' His jet-black, ramrod-straight hair rested on his shoulders, making him look like some bohemian poet or a young Franz Liszt. 'Please know that I go by the surname of Blackmore now and would appreciate your discretion regarding... matters relating to my childhood.'

'Of course. And I would be grateful if the courtesy extended both ways. I'm in London hoping to secure the hand in marriage of a young lady I met through friends in Norfolk, and would like her to think kindly of me.' The look that passed between them acknowledged the necessity to leave the past firmly behind.

'How is the exhilarating world of malting?' Edward had made no effort to investigate his father's company or the exploits of his cousin since leaving Suffolk. As a child, he'd been fascinated by the process of steeping, germinating and drying the barley to provide the essential sugars for the brewing process. But, back then, he'd wrongly believed it was to be his future occupation.

'As long as men drink, there will always be a need for malt,' Barnabas replied, avoiding a direct answer and then immediately changed the subject. 'From the manner of your dress, I assume you are doing quite nicely for yourself.' Was it Edward's imagination or did his cousin look jealous?

'I'm keeping my head above water, but I've had quite the struggle to establish myself, as I started out with practically nothing.' His cousin had the grace to bow his head and remain silent.

A fair-haired young woman across the room caught Edward's eye and his heart began an intense and uncontrollable thud. It wasn't that she was particularly beautiful, in fact, there was nothing exceptional about her at all. He couldn't explain or rationalise how meeting her eye suddenly made his whole world explode into beautiful colours, as though everything before that moment had been grey. She started to walk towards him, almost as if he were the fisherman, reeling in his line, and she were the fish, being pulled ever closer. Everyone around them blurred to an unfocused mist as their eyes locked.

He'd never before given credence to such fanciful notions as love at first sight. For someone whose growing reputation was based on amateur dramatics, he was, in reality, an exceedingly quiet and self-controlled man. He had no time to indulge in such emotions, largely because the affectionate side of his nature had been eroded by the treatment he'd received from his father. But this stranger had ignited a spark of unconfined joy, without so much as even having spoken to him. Perhaps there was more to the universe than he'd considered.

Barnabas noticed that he'd lost Edward's attention and turned to see what his cousin was looking at.

'Ah, Edward. This is Miss Emma Dunham. She is staying in London with her parents for a couple of weeks. Her father is here on business but the ladies have accompanied him to experience some of the things our wonderful capital city has to offer.' He swept up the woman's small hand as she approached and gently placed a kiss on her soft fingers. 'She is a... particular friend of mine.'

Edward forced himself to remain upright, feeling keenly the metaphorical kick in the guts as his cousin squashed him into the dirt for the second time in his life. This was the woman Barnabas was hoping to marry?

The introduction was brief and Barnabas was particularly keen to cut the conversation short, perhaps sensing Edward's interest. His cousin was staying at the same guest house as Miss Dunham and her family, and she'd insisted on collecting Mr Shaw from the lecture in her father's carriage, even though he'd said he was happy to catch a cab.

Once she realised that Edward was related to Mr Shaw, however, and clearly unaware of their uncomfortable history, she insisted that he was included in the concerts, gallery visits and park walks they'd planned for the remainder of her visit. Edward had no desire to spend any time with his cousin and could hardly look at the man without wanting to thump him, but his reasons for accepting were threefold. Barnabas was hiding something – he just knew it; his cousin absolutely did *not* want him anywhere near the young lady, so he would delight in doing exactly that; and Edward was so inexplicably enchanted by Miss Dunham that he would even suffer being in the same room as the man who'd betrayed him, just to spend more time with her.

Consequently, he spent the following three days in their company, knowing full well his presence at the National Gallery, an afternoon musical recital and a Shakespearean play at the Lyceum made his cousin uneasy – especially as Edward and Emma bonded so quickly.

His spiritualism, in particular, fascinated her, but she did not believe for one moment that any of it was real. She asked about his process, which made a refreshing change from his cousin's blind acceptance, and offered rational and intelligent explanations for the things he talked of – most of them uncomfortably close to the truth. But she did not judge. Instead, she found the whole thing rather amusing.

'If you are clever enough to dupe people, and they are foolish enough to believe you, then good luck to you all. They are paying for a show and I can imagine you are quite the showman, holding forth in your fancy waistcoats and colourful coats.' She paused. 'And yet I suspect you to be a private man, a gentle soul, hiding something. What's your secret, Edward? What is it that you keep hidden?'

He'd laughed it off without answering and Barnabas wandered over to ask what was so amusing, before deliberately placing himself between them, and the conversation dried up. But Emma's perception unnerved Edward. She knew he was holding something back, but he also knew that he couldn't divulge the truth to her, because she would end up distancing herself from him, as his own father had done. Even Barnabas had abandoned him once he no longer had to pacify his uncle.

Instead, Edward revelled in every shared joke and quiet moment over those few days with Miss Dunham. His confidence might have been an act but his feelings certainly weren't. He studied her face when he thought she wasn't looking, sometimes catching her studying him with equal fascination, and replayed these intimate moments over and over in his small, rented garret room at the end of each day, looking for reassurance that his feelings were reciprocated.

On the Dunhams' final day in the city, they met for a walk around the Serpentine in Hyde Park, even though the day was overcast. Barnabas had taken the opportunity to confront his cousin, away from the rest of the group, as they returned to the carriage to collect some blankets for the ladies to sit on.

'Now look here, Edward, I'll shortly be asking Emma to marry me, dammit, and I can see you sniffing around like a dog on heat. Back off, I say, or I'll tell her the truth about you. Do you not think she'll find out anyway? And then where will you be?' He puffed up his chest, feeling that he had the upper hand.

Edward had always known he was unlikely to marry, and had accepted that this brief flirtation was nothing but a pipe dream, but one he'd enjoyed, nonetheless.

'Then I demand you tell me what you're hiding, cousin,' he challenged. 'You've been evasive about the maltings and my father's house ever since we encountered one another. It's more than your embarrassment about the inheritance, and if you don't come clean then I'll lay bare the truth of your treatment of me before Miss Dunham. I don't think you a bad man, but you were certainly an opportunistic one.' Edward spoke slowly and calmly.

He watched his cousin's Adam's apple bob down to his sternum as he swallowed hard.

'I lost the company.' Barnabas's head was low and his voice almost inaudible.

'You did what?' Edward gripped his cousin's lapels and pulled Barnabas's face close to his. Two ladies scuttled past, arm in arm, looking most alarmed at what they could only assume was the start of a physical altercation, but Edward had never hit anyone in his life. He simply did not have the stomach for violence.

Barnabas began to wring his hands together as soon as he was released, and the coachman jumped from the driver's seat to hand them a pile of folded rugs.

'I was never interested in the maltings, like you. I did not care for the quality of the grain or the modernisation of the equipment. I took a lucrative deal with a local brewery and was made promises that never materialised.' He shrugged. 'I put all my eggs in one basket, and when the brewery went bankrupt, I lost everything. In the end, I sold out to Greene King...'

'And the house?'

Barnabas's inability to reply told him all he needed to know.

Edward couldn't believe what he was hearing. The business had been in the Shaw family for three generations and Barnabas had destroyed it within a few years. The gullibility that had enabled him to convince his cousin that he had a spiritual gift, had also led to the man being duped by a rival business. He couldn't stop a small laugh from erupting.

'My father must be spinning in his grave. He was so determined that I wasn't fit to take the helm and yet I'm certain I'd have done a far better job. There was nothing to stop you giving me a position in the company, nor asking for help when you realised things were turning sour – but you did neither of those things. You really are an unbelievably bull-headed man.'

His cousin glanced at the remainder of their party in the distance, and began to rub at the back of his neck with his free hand.

'But I've told you the truth and that's what you asked of me. The good Lord, in his wisdom, has taught me humility by bringing me low, and it is only meeting Emma that has enabled me to turn my life around. Don't take her from me, Edward. I beg you...'

Edward remained silent as they walked back to Miss Dunham and her parents. Although unspeakably angry about what his cousin had done with the family legacy, he wondered if the fact Barnabas had lost everything was punishment enough. He was half tempted to take Emma from him as further revenge, but he acknowledged that she would ultimately be the one to

suffer, and he couldn't bring himself to snatch away her chance
of happiness just to spite another. She deserved to marry a man
who didn't make his living preying on the bereaved, or have to
conceal parts of himself from those who would judge him, and
who could give her a houseful of healthy and perfect children.
She may profess to find his need of spectacles endearing but he
was constantly frustrated by them. He was frustrated by a lot of
things.

So, he decided that, much as he'd coped with the cruelty of
his father by distancing himself mentally from the man, he
would do the same with his cousin. They'd had no contact for
seven years and it was only by chance they'd reconnected, so
cutting ties once more would be easy enough. He was building a
solid reputation here in London. Emma had been a fun diversion
but he had always known that ultimately he'd have to give
her up.

The group spent a pleasant couple of hours watching families boat across the Serpentine and small children paddle at the
edge. All the while, Edward was conscious that the Dunhams
were leaving for home the following morning and he might
never see Emma again.

'Mr Blackmore, will you come with me to buy some ices from
the booth?' She pointed to the corner of the park where a small
wooden hut advertised raspberry and lemon ices. It was quite
proper, as they'd be in full view of her parents and Barnabas. He
agreed and she cast nervous repeated glances up to him as they
walked, finally finding her voice.

'Should you ever visit Norfolk, it would please me greatly if
you would call on my family in Thistlewick Tye,' she said. 'Perhaps you could even accompany your cousin when he comes up
next month?'

'I have many demands on my time in London, pursuing the

profession you think is poppycock,' he teased, trying to let her down gently. 'I cannot foresee any circumstances that would take me to your part of the world.'

They joined the queue for the ices and he halted his steps, as his face took on a more serious expression. 'Will you marry him if he asks you?' He tried to appear uninterested in her answer as though it made no difference to him either way, when the truth was it mattered more than anything. He brushed non-existent dust from his coat to avoid meeting her eyes and giving himself away.

'A few days ago, it was all I wanted, all I dreamed about, but things have changed... I have met another. Someone who excites and unnerves me all at once. A man who keeps parts of himself closed off, but who makes me laugh and has a lively mind. Someone who occupies my every waking thought...'

She turned her head away and he noticed the flash of pink that swept across her cheeks, saw how her hands began a restless twitching, heard the tremble in her voice.

'So, I don't know the answer to your question, Edward. What do you think I should do?'

He loved her, he wanted her and he could hardly believe that she felt the same, and for one magical moment, he considered proposing to her, himself. But there were so many reasons why this could not be – most of all because, whatever Barnabas had done to him, he could not bring himself to betray his cousin.

'I think, if he asks you, you should accept.'

She nodded at his words and he saw her bite at her bottom lip as she slowly digested his answer.

'Then that is what I shall do.'

Edward never saw her again after that afternoon, and by the autumn, Miss Dunham had become Mrs Shaw. He saw Barnabas only once, when he delivered the wedding invitation by hand,

and expressed his gratitude at Edward's gracious actions, hoping they might repair the damage of the past, but Edward gave him short shrift and decline to attend.

His cousin, however, for all his faults, never revealed Edward's secret to Emma, and so she never understood why the quiet young man with the long black hair, gentle nature and piercing blue eyes didn't fight for her.

12

THISTLEWICK TYE, NORFOLK, 1895

Barnabas, true to his word, immediately set about signing his house over to Edward, visiting a solicitor and requesting that the deeds of conveyance were drawn up – a process that would take weeks. He was pleased to have had the chance to say goodbye to his wife, but disappointed that he'd never know why the little girl had turned on her. Now that Emma was in the ground, however, he could hardly bring himself to rise in the morning. It was interesting that someone once so driven by wealth that he would not share it, had willingly parted with most of it now that he'd lost the one thing that genuinely mattered to him. Would Edward have given everything up for Emma? Possibly. Would he ever allow himself to fall for someone like that again and let his own desire for riches fall by the wayside? Never.

Edward had no intention of living in Thistlewick House. He planned to sell it and use the combined monies from Barnabas and the Cattisham Orphanage Fund to start again, somewhere new. With the sums involved, and by his reckoning, he could live a comfortable life, tucked away in a big house just outside a fashionable city, like Bath or Bristol, where no one knew who he was. If he was to spend his life alone, he would at least do so surrounded by opulent furnishings, and dining on pineapples and white truffles.

He wrote again to Delphine to apprise her of his plans, and also to his bank, instructing them to clear Barnabas's cheque for five hundred pounds. Wright offered to have both letters posted but Edward swept up his coat and his cane, despite the late hour, and set off down the lane. It would be good to get some fresh air and clear his muddled head.

As he was returning from the postbox, he saw two figures ahead of him on the edge of the common. It was the Garrod brothers. He recognised them from the evening he'd spent in the Sailmaker's Arms. Silas towered over Noah but the two were walking amiably along, with Noah muttering nonsense that Edward could hardly make out.

They hadn't seen him in the shadows but the full October moon illuminated them clearly. Noah was clutching a beer bottle by the neck, and occasionally taking a swig, as they made their way across the common. Edward realised the man was struggling, and at first thought he was drunk, even though they'd professed not to be big drinkers, but the youngest Garrod stopped in the middle of the dirt path, forcing his older brother to stop also.

'What the devil's wrong?' Silas sounded frustrated, doubtless keen to return to a warm house and get out of the biting wind.

Noah was staring ahead at nothing, and dropped the bottle to the ground where it smashed upon impact with the stony path. After a moment, his right arm went up to clutch the shoulder of his left, as he lurched forward.

'I don't half feel queer, Bruh,' Edward heard him say as he stumbled forward, his breath condensing in the cold night air before his face. 'Kinda dizzy.'

'I knew I shouldn't have got you that beer. It's been a long week and yer fair done in. C'mon, let's get home.'

But Noah's whole body froze for a moment, before his knees buckled and he collapsed to the ground clutching at his chest. A panicked Silas fell to his knees beside him.

'Noah! Is yer heart playin' up? What do I do? Noah!'

Edward, realising the seriousness of the situation rushed forward to assist, dropping to his haunches and feeling for the man's pulse. But it was a futile gesture. Noah's eyes were open but the man saw nothing. He was dead, likely from cardiac failure, and if that were the case, there was nothing further to be done. Hadn't Jacob Palmer hinted that the man had been on borrowed time for many years?

'I'm sorry,' Edward said, looking up at the bulky man. 'I think he's gone.'

'No. That ain't right. He can't go before me.' Silas's voice was shaky and the moonlight clearly illuminated the distress across his face. He placed his wide hand on Noah's forehead as he gently stroked a loose strand of hair from his brother's face.

'Don't leave me alone, Bruh,' he said, his voice cracking with the emotion, as he echoed Noah's favourite term of endearment. It was an intensely personal moment and reflected the love that this huge ox of a man had carried for such a vulnerable person, probably for most of his life. 'Appleby'll bring him back. He'll know what to do.' He pulled away from the body and started to wring his large hands together.

'I'll go,' Edward volunteered, knowing the outcome was out of even the most experienced doctor's hands. 'You stay with your brother and direct me to the surgery.'

Silas did exactly that and Edward whipped up his cane from where he'd laid it on the ground. He hastened across the common, coattails flapping as he waded through the overgrown, wet grass.

He'd barely gone twenty yards, when he heard a shout.

'Oi, mister, mister, he's back!'

Edward spun around and saw the silhouette of the younger brother now sitting upright – arms outstretched as he reached for Silas.

How could that be? There'd been no pulse. Edward was certain. If he'd been a betting man, he would have wagered everything he was shortly to own on the man being dead. He started to run back towards the pair.

'Oh, Noah. Thought I'd lost yer. Don't you be scaring me like that.'

Noah said nothing. Instead, his eyes expanded with horror. He stretched out his hands before his face, as though he'd never seen his own fingers before.

'I should still go for the doctor,' Edward said, now within a few feet of them. 'I think your brother has suffered some sort of apoplexy of the heart, although he has blessedly been saved, but you *must* seek medical advice. I'm certain he'll recommend bed rest and perhaps administer some opium.'

'I've absolutely no wish to see a doctor,' Noah said, surprising them both with his eloquence, now getting to his feet. 'I feel perfectly well.' But his face remained a crumpled frown and he was clearly still struggling to understand what had just happened to him. He spun about, as if to get his bearings and sort his head out. 'Thistlewick Tye?' he asked.

'Come on, Noah. We can stop by Appleby's on the way home. You scared me stiff. And Mister Blackmore, here, thought you was dead.'

'I can fetch the doctor out, if your brother is reluctant, Silas,' Edward offered.

'*Silas?*' Noah turned his head slowly to his brother and studied him with interest. Perhaps the cardiac incident had afforded him temporary memory loss or, at the least, caused the poor man a degree of confusion.

'I really think you should let the doctor see you, Mr Garrod,' Edward said. 'You don't seem quite yourself.'

Noah bent to the ground and picked up the smashed bottle that had fallen from his hand a few minutes earlier and, holding it by the neck, he brandished it like a weapon. The relief of moments before quickly unfolded into a violent nightmare, as he rushed at the much bigger man with all the determination of a stampeding bull. What started as a low growl grew into a primal yell – a cry of anger and unconcealed hatred.

His first swipe caught Silas across the cheek and, even in the poor light, the emerging dark line of blood was clearly visible. The big man's shock was clear from the expanded whites of his eyes. He'd not expected his brother to attack and hadn't even tried to defend himself but, as Noah launched himself at Silas again, he was better prepared for the second assault.

'*Svoloch! Svoloch!*' shouted Noah.

'What yer goin' on about?' Silas reached for his brother's wrist and held him firmly. It was not an even match as, although much older, he was infinitely stronger. 'Why yer speaking like that? You don't know no foreign language.'

'Calm yourself, man,' Edward said to Noah, who was positively seething, even more so now that he was restrained, his legs kicking out in an attempt to do some damage where the jagged bottle no longer could. Edward took a step back from the tussling men. He was anxious that Noah would bring on a second cardiac episode and this time might not survive, but his distaste for violence meant he was not prepared to get injured in the process.

'Stay out of this, stranger. It's not your concern,' Noah shouted over his shoulder.

He was right; this was a silly family quarrel between two men he barely knew. These were not his people; this was not his village; it was not his fight. Despite what they'd said at the pub the other day about his two-drink rule, perhaps they were both inebriated, although Noah seemed remarkably focused after his near-death experience. But these were grown men and he didn't want them to turn on him.

He tugged at the brim of his top hat and nodded his acquiescence before spinning on his heels and making for the beach. There he might find some solitude, whilst these silly men acted out their ridiculous feud.

The sound of the crashing waves and gushing wind rushed up through the rift, overseen by a lamplight moon. Some time near the sea would help him clear his head. He was carrying a degree of guilt for lying to Barnabas and now he was worrying about the Garrod brothers – both of which were needless distractions, when he generally tried to remain emotionally detached from others. He shouldn't have come to Thistlewick Tye, despite the money, because he could feel himself being dragged into the lives of these people, adding unnecessary clutter to his already jumbled thoughts.

As he stepped onto the flint-littered sand, he saw a blurry figure in the distance, illuminated by the full moon. Almost certain it was Maude, he could see her scurrying about on the beach in the shadows to his left. The tide was high, leaving only a thin strip of land running underneath the cliffs to Cromer in one direction and Sheringham in the other. She appeared to be collecting flotsam and jetsam from the tideline, but sensed she was not alone and looked across at where he was standing.

Maude, Edward realised, was part of his muddled thoughts.

His mind had repeatedly wandered back to her in his reflective moments, but he wasn't sure why that should be the case. She was simply a violent drunk, scraping a living by scavenging, who had no social skills and had never even had a civil conversation with him. But his subconscious had clearly picked up on something that his rational mind had yet to properly work out.

'I mean you no harm,' he called across to her. 'I merely wish to walk along the water's edge. Let me pass in peace.'

She stood to the side, her head bowed and the deep hood of her cloak covering most of her face, as usual. As he approached, he heard further shouts from the cliffs above. It was the Garrod brothers continuing their petty dispute. They must have made their way towards the edge and he was alarmed at how loud the voices were. He didn't like how near Maude was to the foot of the cliffs either. Any slip of land could prove dangerous, especially with the two men tussling so close to the verge.

He looked up as a blood-curdling yell of 'Bastard!' echoed around them and saw, to his horror, a dark shadow fall from above. In the fraction of a second that followed, he realised Maude was directly beneath the plummeting mass, and unaware of the rumpus above. Edward acted without thinking, grabbing her slender shoulders and pushing her out of the way and onto a clear patch of sand, as a sickening thud landed behind them both.

With his heart galloping faster than a herd of charging horses, he turned back to see the broken body of Silas Garrod behind them. His skull was crushed and one leg was bent back at an unnatural angle.

Much like his brother's only minutes before, his vacant eyes stared out at absolutely nothing.

13

Edward stared at the horrific sight that now lay not two yards from him and felt a sudden rush of nausea. He turned away from the rapidly spreading pool of blood coming from Silas Garrod's head which, in the poor light, looked like thick black ink. The man had hit a large lump of flint, which had caused the wound, but he'd have been dead regardless after a fall from that height.

'What the hell?' Maude whispered under her breath as she, too, stared at the broken corpse. She was on her back from where Edward had pushed her to safety, eyes wide and her long, dark hair blowing loose about her face where her hood had slid from her head. Edward reached out his hand.

'Are you hurt? I'm so sorry.'

'Don't apologise – you saved me.' She looked at him properly for the first time and accepted his offer of help. 'Thank you.'

He pulled her up and she examined her palms, grazed from where they'd broken her fall. The faint smell of juniper berries drifted between them as she started to brush the sand from her clothes.

'This is all damnably odd,' he said. 'Noah was with Silas

when I was up on the common just now.' He tipped his head to the clifftop. 'Suffered some kind of heart incident and I honestly thought he'd died, but then he sprang to his feet, acting most peculiarly. Started attacking his brother. It was all so out of character, and I left them to it. But now this...' Edward was so confused that he spoke aloud, in an attempt to sort the muddle of events out in his head, but stopped short of making any accusation. He hadn't seen Noah push Silas, after all. 'I must alert the people in the village to what's happened. The body needs to be moved. Come back with me. There's nothing you can do for him now.'

'I'll stay with him,' she said. 'I've seen death before. I'm not afraid.'

He nodded and ran back to the Thistlewick Rift and up the hill that led to the village. It was only as he dashed across the common that it occurred to him that Noah would still be wandering around. He might attack again, either himself or, he realised with horror, Maude – a lone woman on the beach. What a fool he'd been to leave her there. He could protect himself with his cane but, even though he knew her to be handy with her fists and aggressive by nature, she was of slight build and undeniably the weaker sex. He mustn't linger and should return to her as soon as possible.

He flung open the door to the pub.

'Silas Garrod has fallen from the clifftop. He's dead. Come quickly.'

He had no time to give any further details about the incident, nor did he say anything about suspecting Noah of the crime, but the gathered customers in the pub didn't need telling twice. Someone shouted that they would fetch Constable Lovett, and there was a scrape of chairs as people got to their feet.

A small group of men returned to the beach with him, as he

yet again told himself this whole affair was none of his business. But there was something strange going on, and he knew it. By concealing his suspicions, he was both protecting himself from unnecessary involvement and giving himself time to think through the implications of what he'd witnessed. The tiny seed of doubt, planted by Emma's bizarre behaviour before her death, had sprouted into something dark and twisting. Noah's resurrection had been no illusion – that man had been dead – but he'd heard of people dying on operating tables, only to spring back to life after their heart had stopped beating. Perhaps he was over-thinking what was a simple medical anomaly.

The scene at the bottom of the cliffs a few minutes later was chaotic. Jacob Palmer, one of the tallest men there, held an oil lamp aloft, as Dr Appleby examined the corpse.

'You don't need me to tell you that the poor man is dead, but if a couple of you younger lads can get him up to my consulting rooms, I can properly assess the body.'

'He must have stumbled in the dark,' Jacob said. 'Neither he nor Noah had drunk to excess. They only stopped by for one drink, and then Silas bought his brother a bottle of beer to cheer him up because he wasn't feeling himself – which he took with him. Why did he wander so close to the edge? He knows the dangers.' He shook his head in disbelief. 'We must find his poor brother. He'll be distraught; he doted on him.'

'What exactly happened here?' the constable asked, a late arrival, pushing through the circle of onlookers. He'd clearly been woken from his slumbers and was none too pleased to find himself on a wind-buffeted shoreline in the middle of the night. The doctor was covering Silas's body with a coat – the sight too much for most men, even in the half-light.

'Mr Blackmore raised the alarm,' Dr Appleby said. 'He'll know better than us.'

Edward met Maude's eyes across the gathered group. How much did she know? What had she overheard or seen? Her eyes dropped away almost the moment that they met his and she seemed to shrink into the background. An unpleasant thought crossed his mind. Had she asked to remain with the body so that she could rob it?

'I'd been in the village posting letters and came down here afterwards. I briefly encountered Mrs Grimmer on the beach but we'd hardly exchanged two words when there was a noise from above.' He told the constable how he had pushed Maude to safety as he saw the figure fall.

'An unfortunate accident,' Constable Lovett concluded. 'Stupid fool should have known to stay away from the cliffs, especially at night. We'll need to erect another fence to stop this happening again, but as soon as we put one up, a couple of years later we lose it to the sea. I'll speak to the Benevolent Committee about securing the funds.'

There was a burst of activity as Silas was lifted by some of the men and they carted his body back to the surgery. Everyone began to return to the village and Edward turned his collar up to shield his face from the bitter wind. He looked around for Maude to ask her what she'd seen, but she'd disappeared.

He stood by himself, facing the angry sea, his heart racing faster than it ever had, along with his mind. The more he thought about what he'd witnessed, the more an alternative scenario occurred to him – one that was much more other-worldly than a simple medical miracle.

Because if Noah Garrod really had died up on the common that evening, then his recovery had been most peculiar. For an inarticulate and slightly simple farm labourer, he'd suddenly spoken incredibly coherently. Initially appearing confused about who and where he was, his ensuing attack on his brother had been completely unprovoked. He doted on Silas and owed him his life. And yet, although Edward could not be certain, he suspected Noah was responsible for pushing a man to his death. None of it made sense, unless...

He thought back to Barnabas's wild claims about Emma being possessed, and they no longer seemed quite so ridiculous. He'd just witnessed an almost identical personality change in the youngest Garrod brother. Emma's behaviour had also altered dramatically, the very night after she was so very dangerously ill that her husband had not expected her to live until the morning. Perhaps, Edward considered, she *had* died that night – slipped away when no one was awake, as the fever took hold, allowing someone or something to slide into her body. And then there was the sickly baby mentioned by Silas Garrod. The mother thought she'd lost it and yet it had not only lived to fight another day, but had also pulled itself out of its cot...

Had this Esfir, whoever she was, possessed Mrs Shaw? Because the word shouted by Noah had sounded Eastern European and Esfir was definitely a foreign name... These incidents must surely be linked.

Despite the circles he moved in, he'd never seen any evidence of a dead person's soul communicating with the living. As someone who had learned all the tricks employed by the mediums, and developed a few of his own, almost every manifestation he'd come across could be easily explained away. If spirits were truly contactable, then every unavenged murder victim in history would be queuing up to reveal the perpetrator. And yet, he couldn't categorically state that they didn't exist...

It occurred to him, standing alone on that windswept and desolate beach, that the afterlife he'd been so confident was nonsense, fabricated merely to appease the bereaved and reassure the faithful, might actually exist.

14

The following morning, Edward was late to rise. He'd instructed his man to let him sleep after the drama of the night.

'Have you heard if Noah Garrod has been found?' he asked, as Carl sharpened the cut-throat razor on the strop, before embarking on the close shave that his master always demanded.

'Yes, he was wandering the streets, sir, disorientated and seemingly not knowing where his house was. Not good on such a bitter night. He took the news better than expected, however. Told the constable they'd had a quarrel on the common outside the pub, and Silas got all fired up over nothing, but he'd left him alive and well. Some stranger in a fancy top hat had interfered and Noah left the two men bickering. The implication was that this stranger might be responsible... He must be talking about you, sir.'

Edward nodded. The youngest Garrod brother was lying but he hoped Mrs Grimmer would vouch for his whereabouts when Silas had fallen. She might be a drunk but she'd have no reason to implicate him in the death, especially as he'd saved her from possible injury. But what struck him most about

Noah's words was that Edward was no stranger to the Garrods, as they'd spent that evening together in the pub. The man was a bit slow, but Silas had addressed him by name and Noah should have recognised him as Mr Blackmore, even in the dark.

'What exactly's going on, sir?' Carl took the blade to Edward's face and there was the satisfying scraping sound as he slid it through the white shaving cream.

Edward shared his suspicions that something other-worldly was at play and that malevolent spirits were possessing the good folk of Thistlewick Tye. He didn't care if Carl thought him silly; he was paid enough to agree with everything Edward said and to do his bidding, regardless.

His manservant wiped the blade on the cotton towel and snorted. 'You're telling me that the very nonsense we spend all our time trying to convince people is real, might actually be the truth, after all?'

Edward shrugged. 'It's a possibility.'

'Nah, I don't buy it.'

Carl tipped Edward's chin to the ceiling to see if he had missed any stray hairs and then wiped the remainder of the lather off with the towel.

'For a start, where are these spirits coming from? A soul is pretty much the essence of a person, right? So, someone has to die for that part of them to float out?'

Edward thought back to the night of the storm and the bones raining down onto the beach. It was the grave of at least one person, likely more, who'd not been buried in the churchyard for some reason. Mrs Drayton said that all good Christian folk had that privilege, so who did that leave? Criminals? Heathens? Those who'd died long before the church had been built? Or maybe even foreigners who worshipped other gods?

'The Thistlewick Tye cliffs are collapsing and a grave has been exposed. Maybe these are the spirits.'

Carl's face was reflected back in the mirror in front of Edward and the man's expression was of disbelief, as he raised one eyebrow. 'One hell of a jump there, sir, if you don't mind me saying.'

'Maybe, but there's definitely something off about those bones. You don't bury people willy-nilly in common land, and certainly not in well-established and civilised villages. A gold chain fell to the shore in the same place, and the grave isn't deep enough to be truly ancient. So, I want to find out who they were. Because if we're told that a group of people from a foreign shipwreck was buried near the cliffs two hundred years ago, for example, then at least we'd have a connection between a girl called Esfir and Noah talking another language.' Carl looked unconvinced. 'Maude Grimmer collects things from the foreshore to sell, so if anything else of interest has been exposed, then she's the person to ask.' He thought back to how she'd snatched the gold chain from him.

'Do you want me to pay her a visit, sir? I could make her talk.' He raised his eyebrow again but in a more disconcerting manner. Even though the woman had attacked him on a previous occasion, Edward didn't want her harmed or scared.

'I'll do it. But I'd still like you to ask around. Find out if there's a legend attached to the village – the arrival of foreigners, pirates or gypsies. I didn't come across anything when I went through my cousin's library, but not all history is documented.'

'Very well, sir.'

There was a knock at the bedroom door and Edward glanced in the mirror to check his appearance was satisfactory before he announced they could enter.

'This was found on the doorstep first thing, Mr Blackmore.

And the constable is here, wanting to have a few words about Mr Garrod's death.'

Mrs Drayton presented a small basket containing a pair of pale grey kid leather gloves, a green silk neck scarf, a luxury hair tonic and a small bottle of cologne. It had been left at the back door, which was most unusual, and she couldn't think why the person who'd delivered it hadn't rung the bell. She handed him the small card tucked into the front.

'*Your help contacting my beloved mother was appreciated and I feel I can finally move on. Please take this gift as a thank you.*' He turned the card over and frowned.

'Is there a name, sir?' Carl asked.

Edward shook his head. 'They must be especially grateful to have tracked me down to Norfolk. Perhaps your sister passed on this address. It's surely not from Dr Appleby. He wouldn't even admit Margaret was his mother. Be so kind as to put it on the bed for now, and help yourself to the hair tonic. I won't use it,' he added as an afterthought.

Carl didn't need telling twice and swiped the small glass bottle. 'Might give me an edge with the local ladies,' he joked. 'Got to be some benefits to being away from home.'

And he winked as he left the room.

15

Constable Lovett left Thistlewick House happy that Silas Garrod's death had been an accident. Noah, he said, had clammed up and not repeated the accusation against Edward. Besides, the man was overwhelmed with grief and too simple to be a reliable witness. Everyone knew how devoted the brothers were, so no foul play was suspected. Mrs Grimmer had confirmed Edward was on the beach when the incident happened, and Edward said nothing about the brothers' quarrel. He had no proof the man had been pushed and didn't think spirit possessions came under the remit of the police.

After a delayed breakfast, he set off for Maude's house, which was just outside the village boundary, over a mile away from the centre of Thistlewick Tye. Edward asked for directions from Mr Palmer, who was out looking for Banjo. The dog apparently had a habit of jumping the back fence and getting out onto the common.

He advised that the cottage could either be accessed from the beach, by heading towards Sheringham and walking through a smaller gap in the cliffs, or by skirting the common and going through the woods. Edward chose the first option, taking the opportunity to scour the sands for further bones, but the weather had improved, and the cliffs had been stable since the storm. There was nothing new on the shore and the lapping waves had taken much of the fallen soil away.

As he continued westwards, the height of the cliffs started to decrease and there was another gap, smaller than the Thistlewick Rift, just as Jacob described. He scrambled up the bank of soil and squinted, seeing an isolated flint building in the distance. Hopefully, the woman hadn't started on the gin yet, and would be in a reasonable frame of mind and less likely to attack him. It was, however, exactly what he intended to use to win her over. Carl had secured a bottle of mother's ruin from somewhere, and he had it with him, tucked into his long green overcoat.

He knocked on the low door and Mrs Grimmer opened it a crack, her surprise evident in her startled expression.

'What do you want?' It was aggressive and challenging. This wasn't going to be easy. Perhaps Carl would have been better placed to get information from her, but he was here now.

'I wanted to thank you for confirming that I was on the beach when Silas fell, and to check you didn't have any injuries from when I pushed you out the way. What we witnessed last night was extremely unpleasant and I was worried about you.'

She narrowed her eyes and snorted. 'I've seen worse; besides, I'm not the sort of person others usually care about. People will think it odd that you've come all this way to see me.'

'And I'm not the sort of person to care what other people think,' he countered. 'Look, I want to ask you some questions and I've brought you a gift in exchange for ten minutes of your time.' He lifted up the bottle.

She stared at it for a few moments and then nodded.

'May I come in?'

'No, you may not. This is my house and my refuge. Be quick about your questions and then pass it over.'

She was far from friendly but at least she was willing to talk. Perhaps remaining on the other side of the door might also prevent her from launching another attack.

'I've been told you make a living by collecting things from the shoreline to sell, and I've seen you picking up bones and the like.'

'What of it? There's no crime in that. I do what I must to survive,' she snapped.

'Absolutely, Mrs Grimmer, and I'm not accusing you of anything. I'm here to ask for your help. When we were both caught in that terrible storm last week, a large section of the cliff collapsed and exposed what I believe to be the burial of several people. I'd like to know more about them.'

'There's all sorts of bones in those cliffs. People often come to Thistlewick Tye looking for fossils and such. Animals and sea creatures that died thousands of years ago. They like to display the shells and bones in their fancy houses.'

'Agreed, but these bones are near the top of the cliff, so I don't believe them to be prehistoric, nor do I expect you to have the answers I seek, but if I could look at them more closely, or any objects you found with them, I might learn when they were buried and why. You must agree, it's odd for them not to be in the churchyard. And we both know you snatched a gold chain from me – a closer examination of it may yield answers.'

'Finders, keepers,' she barked, and tried to pull the door shut, but he'd wedged the toe of his boot in the gap.

'I'm not after taking it from you. I merely wanted to see it. You can hold it, if you don't trust me. I wondered if it might offer a clue to who they were: gypsies or foreigners, perhaps.'

'You're too late because I've sold it.'

Edward sighed. What had he expected? This woman would do anything to fund her drinking habit.

'Can you at least describe it to me? Was it part of a necklace? Was there any engraving?'

'It was just a chain,' she said, and her shoulders shrugged. 'And I've not found anything else near that part of the cliffs. Only bones from people no one remembers. Leave them be.'

He doubted she'd even looked at the chain in any detail. As soon as she'd realised it was gold, she'd have sold it to the first person she met.

'You've lived here all your life, could you at least tell me if this is the only instance of bodies being exposed, and how many skeletons have fallen to the beach?'

'I only knew it was people when I came across the skulls, and I've found four of them, if that's important to you, but others could easily have been washed out to sea. They've been falling from that part of the common for the last couple of months. We had some strong winds back in September.'

She shrugged, clearly not caring about the identity of these people, merely how she could benefit from what she found.

'Do you still have any of them? Or have you sold them to the rag-and-bone man?'

He knew animal bones were used to make knife handles and other decorative ornaments, for soap making or even ground up as bone meal. Would the desperate woman even care which creature they had come from?

'I know what people think of me, mister, but I wouldn't sell human bones. Most of what I find on the beach, I sell, but people? That's different. They were living, breathing men and women once and deserve to be treated with respect. I take them inland, as far from the destructive devil of the sea as I can, and I bury them...' She paused. 'But I'm not telling you where so you can dig the poor beggars up again. I've told you all I know. I want my gin now.'

Realising he'd get nothing else from her, he slid his foot from the threshold.

She stuck an arm through the gap and he placed the bottle in her hand. It was snatched back and the door slammed shut. He wondered if it would even last the day.

'And a very good day to you, too, madam,' he said to the closed door, and made his way back to Thistlewick House, thinking that the baby living near the forge had displayed its unusual behaviour back in the middle of September. If nothing else, the timing of these bones falling from the cliffs, and the curious behaviour of the baby, Emma Shaw and Noah Garrod, fitted perfectly.

16

Edward knew that death was a part of life. A quarter of children wouldn't live to see their tenth birthday and most people felt extraordinarily lucky if they reached the Bible's promised three score and ten. However, it struck him that there were a surprising number of such fortunate people in Thistlewick Tye. Mrs Drayton, who had grown up in the village because her father had owned the grocery store, claimed that the wholesome benefits of the sea air, a diet of fresh fish, rich in protein, along with the caring community that looked after its own and saw no man go without, gave the villagers a longer than average life expectancy. It made the loss of Emma and Silas, both seemingly at the hand of another, even more tragic.

It also made Edward wonder if he'd got his priorities wrong. Few of the wealthy folk that he knew in London walked around with the beaming smiles of the Thistlewick Tye families. Perhaps money wasn't the answer to his unsatisfactory life after all, but instead, it was living somewhere where you knew your neighbour would always lend a willing hand, your children would receive a good education and no one would see you go hungry.

There was even talk that the doctor was raising funds to build a small cottage hospital. What more could a person want?

The Benevolent Committee, Carl confirmed from his enquiries, was at the very heart of this largesse. It had been established over fifty years ago, by the previous Lord Felthorpe, along with the then vicar and old Dr Appleby. It was now run by their successors: three well-respected men who ensured that the church was central to everything in Thistlewick, and who had initiated a fascinating scheme to deal with sinners. If they repented, they'd be given the chance to make amends through the undertaking of good deeds. Apparently, the vicar had drawn up quite the list of jobs and services needed by the community, and trespassers were expected to give back, with joy in their hearts, when their sin was discovered. The baker's son had been caught scrumping fruit in the autumn and spent three days repainting the interior of the church hall, and the postmistress had been overheard saying unkind things about the state of her young neighbour's house and was instructed to mind her children for a couple of afternoons so the poor woman could get on top of her housework.

'Lord Felthorpe, in particular, takes his duty as *paternalistic custodian* of Thistlewick Tye very seriously – them's the vicar's words, not mine,' Carl added. 'As long as his tenants prove honest, hard-working men, he treats them well – keeps the properties in good order and the rents reasonable. And he ain't the only one, neither. Dr Appleby doesn't charge the poorest folk for his services, and in the September storm, the whole village turned out to help repair the roof of the school. Real community spirit here that I ain't seen nowhere else.'

Thistlewick Tye appeared to have a good system to Edward. If you helped someone in their hour of need, they would likely reciprocate when you hit hard times. And the whole idea that the punishments, where necessary, were designed to benefit those who'd been sinned against was clever. It was an incentive to lead wholesome lives and probably why Barnabas said he'd hardly ever seen any drunken or violent behaviour – Maude Grimmer's habits and Noah's unprovoked attack on Silas aside.

'The Grimmer woman gets away with it because she ain't technically part of the village. She refuses to attend church and is a slave to the demon drink. Most people I spoke to seem amazed she's lived this long and wouldn't give you ha'penny for her chances of lasting much longer. I mean, I enjoy a drink with the best of 'em, but apparently she walks to Sheringham and buys three bottles of gin a week. She's the only rotten apple in the barrel but we know she didn't push Silas from the cliff and has never stepped foot in this house, so's unlikely to have anything to do with the death of Mrs Shaw.'

But was the serpent in the Thistlewick Tye Garden of Eden of this world? Or had Emma and Silas, in death, become empty vessels, allowing the immaterial essence of another to occupy their earthly bodies? And did these spirits have murderous intent? Every bone in Edward's body told him that there must be a logical explanation for their astonishing personality changes, but their behaviour had been so peculiar that he truly couldn't think of what that might be.

And then he mentally stepped back, once again, from his role in all of this. Why should he care about this backwater? His cousin had promised him Thistlewick House and had already given him a sizeable financial payment – seventeen years too late, but still. He could use the money to finally put an end to his lies, even though he'd always tried to convince himself they were never unkindly meant. He merely offered a service to the bereaved, and those who visited him were invariably happier when they left. The spiritualism had been a means to an end.

Much like Lord Felthorpe's system for the village, it felt right to Edward that the trespasser – his cousin – should recompense the victim. He should take the money and run.

'Ah, cousin.' Barnabas lifted his eyes as Edward entered the dining room a little while later. They were red from crying and dark shadows hung across his face. The man was not sleeping or eating, broken by his grief, and the plate of congealed eggs before him had not been touched.

'I appreciate that you've upheld your end of the bargain, but I would consider it an enormous favour if you would undertake one last séance to try and reach the evil spirit who took my precious wife from me,' he said, raising his head and looking for all the world like an abandoned puppy.

Organising Emma's funeral had kept him busy and given him a purpose, but with her burial came the full stop to the chapter that had been their life together, and he was understandably struggling to begin the next.

'I'm not a spiritual telegraph service,' Edward pointed out. 'Séances are very draining. I told you, cousin, I cannot summon spirits at will.'

Edward pulled out the chair opposite Barnabas and helped himself to a slice of toast from the rack, not having much of an appetite himself.

'It's only those with unfinished business in this life who come to me. This Esfir, even if she remains suspended between our world and the next, has no reason to make contact. In fact, if she is guilty of this nefarious deed, then quite the opposite is true.'

'But you can try. I've already promised you the house. What more do you want from me? If it's to see me suffer, then I can assure you I will bear the weight of Emma's death until the end of time. You won, cousin; I'm a pathetic, empty shell of a man.'

Edward looked across at the person who'd been left a

thriving maltings upon the death of his uncle, but who'd destroyed the company within five years, and married the only woman to ever steal Edward's heart. And then he'd moved to his wife's birthplace after her parents had died and inherited *yet another* house. Barnabas may not have been responsible for the decisions made by Jonah Shaw, but he'd done nothing to address the injustice after his death. Edward had neither forgotten nor forgiven these actions.

It was as he helped himself to a plate of kippers that the housemaid burst into the room, screaming.

'Your man!' She addressed Edward. 'He was down in the kitchen having breakfast and started going all peculiar; shaking and jerking about. He's collapsed on the floor and his lips have gone all blue. Mr Wright has gone for the doctor but it is a terrible sight to see.'

'Good God,' Barnabas said, pushing back his chair. 'Surely not another possession? Have we unwittingly invited the very Devil into our house?'

The pair rushed to the kitchen and Carl was indeed thrashing about, as his back briefly arched and the most horrific grimace flashed across his face. Edward knelt beside him, suspecting a poison, and from what he could see of the symptoms, strychnine.

'He was complaining of an itchy scalp and feeling queer when he first came in,' the cook said. 'Kept touching his head.'

Dr Appleby arrived blessedly quickly and Edward apprised him of the situation. Carl was given opiates to ease the spasms and the doctor ordered a hot bath to help the muscle contractions. Accepting that the doctor was better placed to tend to his man, Edward took himself upstairs, now suspicious of the gift basket after the cook's words – in particular the hair tonic. He gathered everything up, even the gloves and scarf, not certain whether it was possible to apply poison to fabric but not prepared to take the risk, and then went downstairs to Carl's room. Sure enough the hair tonic bottle was open next to the wash stand, so he put the stopper in and collected that up, too. Mrs Drayton told him that Carl had now been transferred to her small sitting room, and he found the doctor still tending to him, so passed the bottle over.

'This may be the culprit.'

The doctor nodded and took out a large handkerchief to handle the item, and then placed it in his medicine bag.

'I'll test it and let you know.'

'Will he pull through?' Barnabas asked, wringing his hands. Thistlewick House had seen more than its fair share of drama in the last two weeks.

Dr Appleby shrugged. 'He's young and strong. It appears that he only used a small amount... Maybe,' he said. 'We'll just have to wait and see. But I'm mightily concerned if the tonic is to blame. An accident in the manufacturing process, do you think? Some of these preparations contain the most dubious of ingredients.'

'It was a gift, but the sender did not put a name on the card.'

'Ah, beware of anonymous Greeks bearing gifts.' He raised an eyebrow. 'This house is becoming quite a dangerous place. Take care, Mr Blackmore.'

Edward knew the poisoning was deliberate. The fact that the note had been so vague and, in his heart, he knew Delphine wouldn't have divulged his address to anyone. Which meant one unpalatable and disturbing thing: he'd been the intended target.

It was only his generous action of giving the hair tonic away that had saved his life, and possibly cost Carl his.

17

Carl survived the night but remained terribly unwell and the doctor advised that his recovery would take some time. The seizures had subsided but he was still in a lot of pain, and no one could guarantee he wouldn't suffer permanent nerve damage. Edward was now beginning to wonder if he'd been sent the poison because he'd given credibility to the spirit possessions. In his séance, he'd fraudulently claimed to have contacted Emma and confirmed that her body had been taken over by Esfir. Anyone present could have passed this information on to others in the village. The vicar would certainly be angry that Edward had given credence to such nonsense, but he liked to think a man of God wouldn't send him a poison gift basket in retaliation.

He decided to visit Emma's graveside, desperate to feel *something*, and still hoping that if anyone would reach out to him from the Other Side, it would be her. He remained unsettled after witnessing the peculiar incident with Noah. Perhaps a part of him also wanted to defy those who would see him scared after the threat to his life.

Barnabas had been drinking heavily when Edward had

retired the previous night. An empty brandy decanter stood on the sideboard and there was still no sign of him by mid-morning, so he asked the housekeeper to notify his cousin that he would return for a late luncheon and set off for the village.

The parish church was further inland, clustered together with the schoolrooms and village hall, and the walk was pleasant, the weather dry. There would be no headstone on Emma's grave for months, to allow the soil to settle, but he noticed that someone had arranged a pretty border of pebbles and shells to mark the burial. Nearby, he could see a hole had already been dug for Silas. The coroner had probably never been so busy, but had recorded a verdict of accidental death, and Edward understood the funeral was imminent. Perhaps he should have spoken up at the inquest but, yet again, doubted that an other-worldly possession by a murderous spirit could be cited on the certificate.

The Reverend Fallow spotted him as he knelt down to be closer to Emma's mortal remains, seriously wondering if her soul was now free and he could connect with it somehow. The reverend couldn't be much older than Edward but had gone prematurely bald, so that he had a half-circle of curly chestnut brown hair that ran from one ear to the other, around the back of his head. They'd met briefly at the funeral and he'd come across as somewhat of a zealot, but then Lord Felthorpe, and no doubt his father before him, would have taken the selection of the parish priest seriously.

'Good morning, Mr Blackmore. Might I enquire what you're doing in my churchyard, when you're a follower of a somewhat alarming movement that is at odds with everything I teach?' His tone was polite enough but Edward sensed his animosity and understood it perfectly. The church saw spiritualism as a harmful practice – which was how he viewed religion, so he didn't much care.

'I'm not here to corrupt your flock or perform any unsavoury rituals,' he reassured the vicar.

'I'm pleased to hear it, because one of the reasons I took the Thistlewick Tye living eleven years ago was the reputation of its sincere and devoted congregation.'

'Even if you do view me with suspicion, please understand I'm only trying to help my cousin understand more fully what happened to his wife.' He nodded to the mound by his feet. 'He believes she was possessed of some demon spirit,' he ventured.

'Indeed, for it's come to my attention that you performed a séance at Thistlewick House and I was most disappointed that the doctor and Lord Felthorpe saw fit to attend. Our misguided Catholic cousins give such things more credence. Mrs Shaw was likely suffering from some form of hysteria – something women are sadly prone to. I tried to deliver pastoral care but she was quite lost to her own mind. So, I don't believe you contacted her spirit for one moment and would ask you not to feed my parishioners such hogwash. They are godly people.' He paused. 'When *exactly* will you be returning to London, Mr Blackmore?'

Edward decided to give this stuffy man something to stick in his pipe.

'I may yet decide to remain permanently in the village, as my cousin is currently in the process of signing Thistlewick House over to me.'

The vicar pressed his lips tightly together and his nostrils flared.

'Yes, this was mentioned at our committee meeting yesterday. But I'm not convinced you'll fit in around here. We're a quiet village, not given to drama or theatrics.'

Edward had to laugh. 'There's been more drama in the few days that I've been here than in a month back home: a dangerously ill woman claiming to be a reincarnated little girl; the poisoning of my servant by persons unknown; and a man falling to his death from the cliff. I hate to think what you consider real mayhem.'

'Ah, poor Noah Garrod. I spoke to him only moments ago. The unexpected death of his brother has affected him badly and he's not himself...'

Again, Edward wanted to laugh. The vicar had no idea how accurate his words might be, but if the man was nearby, it would be a good opportunity to speak to him about the incident.

'Which direction was he heading?'

'Towards the woods, but I—'

Time was of the essence if he was to intercept him, so Edward made his excuses and headed that way. Once he reached the common, he saw Banjo racing away from the Sailmaker's, clearly having just escaped the yard again. His tail was wagging and he hared towards Noah – one of his favourite people – who was striding across the grass in the direction of the woods. But as he got near, the dog stopped short and began barking, sensing something was wrong. He arched his back and bared his teeth, forcing the youngest Garrod brother to stop, and enabling Edward to catch up with him.

'I'm truly sorry about Silas,' he called out.

Noah didn't acknowledge his comment and turned to walk back the way he'd come, not wanting to engage in conversation or confront the dog, but Edward hadn't finished.

'I wanted to ask, however, why you initially told Constable Lovett that you'd left me and Silas together on the common, when it was I who left the pair of you? Especially, as I didn't mention to anyone about our encounter just prior to your brother's fall – how you'd collapsed and your subsequent unprovoked attack...'

Noah, who still seemed much sharper than on their first meeting, swung his head back and narrowed his eyes.

'Because, the thing is,' Edward continued, 'I heard shouts from above when I was on the beach, only moments before the tragedy.'

'You think I pushed my brother?'

'Did you?'

'I left him on the common and went home. We were both three sheets to the wind. He wasn't in control of his actions and must have slipped.'

Edward knew he was lying. He'd seen the signs a hundred times before. Noah couldn't meet his eyes and his body stiffened.

'You didn't know who I was.'

'Like I said, I'd been drinking.' But the Garrod brothers never drank to excess. If his cousin was to be believed, no one in the village did.

'Who am I then, Noah? We spent a whole evening together at the Sailmaker's Arms when I first arrived in Thistlewick Tye. What did we talk about?'

'You're related to the man who lives in Copperpenny Lane. I didn't recognise you the other night because I was in my cups and it was dark. Look, I've just lost my brother and don't appreciate being accused of things by you.'

Edward decided to test the water and see how this man would react to his accusation. Could the dead rise again? The dog was certainly unhappy about something.

'Silas was not your brother because you're not Noah Garrod. You know it, Banjo knows it and I know it.' If you stated a thing as fact, it was surprising how people buckled. Look at the success of his séances.

'You know nothing.'

'It's you who knows nothing. Let me tell you exactly who I am, as you seem to have forgotten. I'm Edward Blackmore – eminent spiritualist at your service.' He briefly tipped his top hat and bowed his head. 'I've devoted my life to communicating with the dead – those tortured souls trapped in this world who need to unburden themselves before they move on. I was called to Thistlewick Tye a couple of weeks ago by my cousin, because he believed the psyche of a dead girl called Esfir had inhabited the body of his seriously ill wife.'

Noah's face jerked back in his direction and Edward thought he'd never seen a man look more shocked in his whole life. All the colour drained from his face and he started to shake. He closed the gap between them in a heartbeat and gripped at Edward's collar, pulling him closer and spraying spittle as he growled.

'A girl claiming to be Esfir? Where?'

Despite the pain of Noah's knuckles digging into his neck and the close proximity of this angry man, it was Edward's turn to say nothing. It was almost as though he knew the girl Emma had claimed to be. An uneasy feeling swirled in Edward's stomach. He suddenly knew, beyond all doubt, that spirits existed, because Noah was definitely possessed by someone no longer of this world. And he knew this, not because he was blessed with any supernatural gift, but instead because logic and reason told him there was no other explanation

'Do you believe in life after death, Mr Garrod? That it's possible to die in this world but for your soul to live on?'

Noah released his grip and Edward took a step back, preparing for his biggest lie of all. He swapped his cane from one hand to the other, sliding his right hand up to twist the brass collar under the knob in readiness. Noah Garrod had killed once and could easily do so again. He must be prepared.

'...Because I summoned Silas Garrod and he told me that you'd murdered him.'

The horror Noah felt at this announcement was apparent in the way his mouth gaped open, his whole body tensed and his eyes rapidly expanded.

Spirit possession was claimed in a variety of cultures across the world – from Christianity to Hinduism, from the Americas to deepest Africa. Edward perfectly understood that these roaming souls need not necessarily be demonic, and *could* be benign but, having witnessed the brutal attack on Silas, it was clearly not the case here. Whoever had taken possession of Noah Garrod was a bad man – killing poor Silas, who'd devoted his life to caring for his brother. By confronting him, he was putting himself in an extremely dangerous position.

Banjo began a low growl, and Edward felt reassured the dog was on his side. It was two against one. Besides, he didn't believe Noah to be armed on this occasion and was poised to whip out the long, thin blade hidden within his cane. But the man before him suddenly darted to the left and ran through the overgrown, wet grass of the common and towards the woods. He'd expected further anger and aggression, but instead sensed that Noah's overriding emotion had been fear.

Rather than attacking him, he had simply fled.

18

Edward let Noah scamper away, wondering if the spirit possessing the youngest Garrod brother was responsible for the hair tonic. He certainly had every reason to want the truth of Silas's death kept quiet and must be bewildered that Edward hadn't publicly pointed the finger at him.

Banjo, now that he had no one to growl at, brought a small stick over and dropped it optimistically at his feet. Edward threw it half-heartedly a couple of times before walking down the rift and onto the beach to clear his head.

The tide was out and he felt a mere dot on the wide expanse of flat sand. The sky was so big in this part of the world, he mused, and the view a far simpler affair. Three distinct strips of colour faced him: the brown of the shore stretching from his feet; the thin grey line of ocean; and the pale blue sky dotted with ragged white clouds. He'd always loved spending time in opulent surroundings – the rich reds, greens and golds of the theatres, wandering around galleries and museums full of valuable and intricate items, or visiting the homes of wealthy clients, where the rooms dripped with ornaments and artwork. So why did

being here take his breath away when there was little colour in
the landscape and not much to see?

He headed west and, as he approached the area where the
bones were falling, he noticed another slump of land. It wasn't as
dramatic as the collapse when the storm hit, but the sienna-
coloured soil had added a fresh coating to the landslip of before.
There were a couple of smaller bones exposed, from hands or
feet, he supposed, but what caught his eye was the glint of something metal poking from the earth.

He bent down and pulled out a small silver coin, before
donning his spectacles to see the profile of a young Queen
Victoria looking to the left – the date of 1843 beneath her head.

Edward surveyed the cliffs. If the coin had fallen with the
bones, then the bodies had been put in the ground sometime
after 1843, but not before. His first thought was this date was in
living memory for the older residents of Thistlewick, and yet,
despite the enquiries Carl had undertaken, no one admitted to
knowing anything about the grave. The current Lord Felthorpe,
old Dr Appleby, Mrs Drayton – in fact, anyone over sixty would
have been a small child or older, and the coin only suggested the
earliest possible date of burial – it could have been more recent.
His knowledge of decomposition was limited, but he estimated
that with bodies buried in damp, sandy soil, and not in coffins, it
would take a minimum of twenty years for the organic material
to disappear and leave only skeletons. These people had been
put in the earth somewhere between the eighteen forties and the
eighteen seventies. Surely such a dramatic event could not have
gone unnoticed by *everyone* in the village?

Edward pocketed the coin before returning his busy mind to
the encounter with Noah. He should have been more direct with
his questions. Not many minutes had gone by since the man had
run from him. Could he track him down? If he'd made for the

woods, he'd come out near Maude's cottage. Edward felt a rising panic. He was a desperate man who had very likely committed a murder and Mrs Grimmer was a woman alone. Was she to be the next victim of this vengeful spirit? Might Noah accidentally stumble across her cottage and try to rob her? Or had he bolted in that direction deliberately because he had a score to settle with her? Either way, Edward felt it his duty to check she was unharmed.

As he clambered up the smaller, more westerly, gap in the cliffs, he could see two figures in the distance. As he got closer, he recognised Maude from her long, woollen cloak. She was talking to someone – which was odd because she didn't like people and they didn't like her. Out of breath from the climb, he started to increase his pace when he realised that the other person *was* Noah, and she was leading him inside.

Fearing for her safety, he quickly arrived at her cottage and started banging loudly on the door.

'Open up. Maude, I know you're in there.' He used the end of his cane as the ivory skull was louder than his gloved fist. 'I'm not leaving until you answer. I can be out here all day if necessary.' His voice was hoarse from the running and his heart rate racing.

After a few moments the door was pulled slowly inwards.

'What do you want?' Maude's face peered through the slender crack.

'I know that you have Noah Garrod in there with you. I saw him enter as I came up from the beach.'

She said nothing, but her eyes narrowed. Edward leaned in closer and lowered his voice, not sure whether Noah was near enough to hear their conversation.

'You must realise it's likely that he pushed his brother from the cliff? Whatever the provocation for doing so, when I asked him about it just now, he ran, which only serves to confirm his guilt. What if he turns his violence on you?'

Edward wasn't prepared to tell this belligerent woman of his suspicions that Noah was someone else – a resurrected spirit who'd killed Silas without any obvious motive. She wouldn't understand and it might frighten her more.

'I've known Noah all my life. He hasn't got an angry bone in his body and adored his brother. You're a stranger to these parts and don't know their history. He's not as... sharp as most people. I can't have him taken off and questioned for something he didn't do, Mr Blackmore. He's vulnerable and might be made to say things he doesn't understand.'

'Let me take him to the local constable and explain himself. I'll make sure he isn't taken advantage of, but you and I both heard the shouts before Silas fell from the cliffs. We know he wasn't alone up there.'

'I heard nothing,' she said and tried to close the door but Edward had wedged his foot in the gap as soon as she'd opened it. 'Besides, he isn't here. Whatever you thought you saw, you're wrong.'

They stared at each other for quite some time, until Edward realised this was a stubborn woman who would probably stand on the other side of the door until nightfall, if necessary. He'd warned her of the danger and that was all he could do. It was entirely possible that she'd agree to anything for payment, even harbour a murderer. Besides, if Noah had wanted to kill her, would he not have done so by now? It even occurred to him that she might be in league with the man and he had this all wrong. Perhaps *she* was responsible for the pit of dead people? She was hardly blessed with a wholesome reputation and could have done away with them all twenty years ago. Maybe it was Noah who was in danger.

Not for the first time, Edward questioned why he was getting sucked into the lives of those at Thistlewick Tye. It was this meddling that had doubtless seen the attempt on his life. He must step away.

'Fine.' He removed his foot. 'Perhaps I shall take my suspicions to Lord Felthorpe and have the constable—'

But Maude had already slammed the door and disappeared.

19

Frustrated by Maude's stubborn behaviour, and wondering if he should have shared his suspicions with the constable from the start, Edward decided to pay a visit to Mrs Cleyford – the elderly woman he'd met at Emma's funeral – on his way back to Thistlewick House. Even if the bodies had gone into the ground in 1843, she'd have been in her late twenties and old enough to know if foreigners had visited or lived in the area at that time. The daughter, Miss Cleyford, let him in but warned Edward that her mother was tired and not in great spirits.

'Poor love, everything's wearing out,' she said. 'Her mind's as sharp as it ever was, but I worry she'll catch the influenza that's doing the rounds. You have no symptoms, I trust?'

'No, only the kitchen maid at Thistlewick House came down with it,' he reassured her, 'and she's since made a full recovery.'

'I'm making a pot of tea. Will you join us?'

Edward declined. His cousin would soon be wondering where he was, so he couldn't stop long. As they entered the tiny parlour, he saw the mother lying in a small bed that had been made up in the corner. Old Mrs Cleyford's twisted hands clutched the edge of the quilt as she eyed the visitor with suspicion.

'Well, you're a colourful one,' she exclaimed. 'I've heard you gad about the village in coats of emerald green and midnight blue. At least you had the decency to wear black for the funeral. Might be all the rage in London, but we're simple folk. Coming here with your spooky mumbo jumbo.' This lady was someone else who viewed him as corrupting the good people of Thistlewick Tye, he realised, but he didn't comment.

'What a pretty embroidery,' Edward said, noticing a framed sentiment about friendship hanging above the mantelpiece.

'Someone I was incredibly fond of gave it to me years ago,' Miss Cleyford said, a light briefly flashing across her eyes. 'It means a great deal to me.'

Her mother tutted. 'Always getting gifts. My daughter's got a secret admirer, it would seem. Little presents left on the doorstep for a couple of years now. Not that she should be thinking about romance at her time of life,' she scoffed.

Miss Cleyford coloured and bowed her head, obviously uncomfortable at her mother's observation. She must be in her fifties, and Edward thought it rather sad that there was a limit imposed on the age for finding love.

'Had her eye on the baker when she was young, but he up and married someone a bit more grounded than this one.' She tipped her head towards her daughter. 'Always had her head in a book, dreaming about romance and adventure, but look where it got her?' She sniffed.

'And Thistlewick men like their women to do their duty to family and church,' Miss Cleyford mumbled, a slight edge to her voice. 'Besides, it's been somewhat fortunate for you, as I've spent my life helping run your household.'

Her mother didn't respond but spun her head back to Edward.

'What do you want, then?' the shrewd old lady asked, giving no credence to her daughter's observation. 'No one visits me any more unless they want something.'

Edward smiled. 'I'm after some information. At some point in the last fifty years, I believe a group of people either from, or visiting, Thistlewick Tye were buried on the common, and now that the winter weather ravages your coastline, their resting place has been disturbed and they're tumbling into the sea.'

Mrs Cleyford looked slightly alarmed and shuffled further up the bed. 'No one was buried out there in my lifetime. They'll be older than that, I'm reckoning. A plague pit maybe.'

'A gold chain and a coin were both found with these bodies, and so I'm fairly certain that these people have not been in the ground more than half a century.'

Mrs Cleyford sniffed again. 'Lots of people travel through. Once had a whole lot of foreigners staying here for a week when their cargo ship sank in a storm.'

Edward frowned. Esfir was a foreign name and Noah had spoken that one exclamation in a language he'd not recognised. 'When was this?'

Mrs Cleyford shrugged.

'About twenty years ago,' the daughter volunteered. 'Think they were Spanish, if I remember rightly.'

'And what happened to these sailors?'

'They stayed until the weather improved and then got passages home. One of the men married a Cromer girl and took her with him.'

'And it was all men? No children? No little girls?'

The old woman sighed. 'Of course not. Why do you ask?'

'You've heard, I assume, of my gift? Of the reason that Mr Shaw called me to this part of the world?'

The daughter pulled up a chair for him and mumbled something about stirring the pot.

'Of course I have. Everyone's been talking about you. Strangers stand out in Thistlewick, and the word is that you're one of those spiritualist types.' Mrs Cleyford clearly did not approve. 'Calling up the dead and getting them to perform silly tricks, when they should be left well alone.'

'I am indeed. Were you aware that Mrs Shaw, suffering delirium after her recent illness, claimed to be a girl called Esfir?'

Behind him, there was a clatter as the daughter dropped something in the kitchen. Edward heard it but didn't turn to draw attention to her clumsiness.

'What sort of silly name is that?' Mrs Cleyford scoffed.

'It sounds Persian or Russian to me,' Edward said. 'Perhaps a form of Esther? And she was asking for someone called Zella – another curious name. You're a quiet village, and the arrival of any foreign peoples would have created gossip and intrigue. Gypsies, perhaps?'

'Gypsies have occasionally camped on the common over the years, and whilst it's my Christian duty to be kind to everyone, even travellers, they're nothing but trouble, in my experience. Coming here and causing mayhem. They steal and lie, and lead such wicked lives.'

'It's not fair to judge all travellers the same,' Miss Cleyford said, returning to the room with a small fruit cake, which she placed on the dining table. 'The earliest of peoples led nomadic lives, following herds and using up the natural resources of one area, before moving on to the next. We welcome the arrival of tinkers to mend our pots and pans, and farmers rely on seasonal labour to gather in harvests.' She sighed. 'I wonder if we'll always persecute those who are different to us, when we should be embracing them.'

'Always were soft in the head.' Her mother tutted. 'Reading about actresses, opera singers, royalty and the like. As if your world was ever going to include such people.'

'But it did, Mother. Do you not remember when I was younger and the circus came that winter? Camped up on the cliffs.'

'Circus?' Edward's ears pricked up.

'Silly notions about their glamorous life and sneaking off to look at the animals when you had chores to do. Ugly freaks – tiny men and deformed women – filling your head with nonsense and practically kidnapping you. You've no idea how close we came to losing you, because you were only a child.'

'They were fascinating people, Mr Blackmore. Everything was so colourful.' Miss Cleyford ignored her mother's words and looked misty-eyed for a moment. 'They performed wonders that you couldn't imagine: vaulting on the backs of beautiful white horses, breathing fire, shooting arrows at silk hearts, walking across tightropes in the sky...'

'You were so young,' her mother said. 'You didn't know about the filthy things they got up to. Drunkenness and debauchery. Light fingers – the lot of them. A pig went missing, they stole some of the church plate and set fire to Farmer Tutter's barn of grain. Nearly killed poor Lord Felthorpe's dog – Master Felthorpe, he was back then – smashed windows the night they left, and one of their dirty horse hands took advantage of poor Mary Tutter. Wicked, they were.'

'What year was this?'

'Oh, I don't know.' The old woman was getting irritated now. 'My daughter was about ten. Maybe forty years ago.'

'And what happened to them?' Edward was curious. The date would certainly fit with the coin.

The old woman shrugged. 'They weren't even putting on shows. It was the start of the winter months when they pitched up. Just resting, they said, but they came to cause mischief. Heathens, mostly. And those that did have a faith were worshipping other gods. The swarthy man with the snake – ringing bells and burning scented sticks. Weren't right. *Thou shalt have no other gods before me.* Says it right there in Exodus.'

'I wish you'd show some tolerance, Mother,' her daughter said, angrily snatching at the knitted blanket on her mother's bed and straightening it.

Could the bones belong to a circus troupe, Edward wondered? Perhaps some illness had struck them when they were visiting and, unable to bury their dead in the churchyard, they'd dug a grave on the common. Something like an outbreak of typhoid fever? But then, surely the villagers would remember such an occurrence, if only because they would have been anxious that any such disease didn't spread through Thistlewick.

'Did any of them pass away during that time?' he enquired. 'Illness or accident?'

'Not to my knowledge. Only here a couple of weeks and then they moved on. I'm sure the Reverend Marsham – he were the vicar back then – said they'd gone to King's Lynn, with plans to sail abroad.'

So, the circus had come to Thistlewick Tye and brought chaos in its wake. These had been bad people, stealing from the locals and attacking innocent young women – godless drunkards, disrupting village life. Edward had encountered travelling folk himself and come off badly, even though in many ways he identified strongly with people such as these. They were often outsiders, like himself, and they relied on illusion as much as he to earn their crust. Even P. T. Barnum, the circus showman, had embraced his moniker as the Prince of Humbug. He claimed his trickery was harmless and purely to amuse, as he exhibited Joice Heth – a woman reportedly one hundred and sixty-one years old – or the taxidermied body of the Feejee Mermaid. But Edward also knew that what old Mrs Cleyford had said was true; wherever outsiders went, trouble followed. Travellers of all descriptions generally, were people who lived by their own rules, and so would naturally clash with those who lived differently.

Miss Cleyford announced the tea had brewed and Edward took the opportunity to take his leave. As she opened the front door to show him out, she took a piece of paper from her apron, standing so that her back obscured her actions from her mother. It was a faded handbill, he realised, advertising *Samson's Circus of Astonishing Spectacles*, and Edward took out his glasses to focus on the line she was pointing to.

Watch aghast as the Daredevil Zella walks the tightrope...

She slid the leaflet back into her pocket and hastily ushered him out the door, but not before he'd noticed that, several lines below, the Russian Madame Katerina was also listed – a fortune teller.

'Everyone says the circus was run out of town, but I think otherwise,' she whispered. 'Jacob Palmer has a small dilapidated barn behind the Sailmaker's. Some of the boys at Sunday school confided in me recently that they'd been hiding in it and had made a curious discovery. Don't let anyone catch you, but take a look inside.'

And with that mysterious instruction, she returned to tend to her mother, who was grumbling about the tea being stewed.

* * *

With his heart beating wildly in his chest, Edward made for the Sailmaker's. He knew it would be infinitely more sensible to return to Thistlewick House and wait for Carl to do the snooping, but the poor man could be bed-bound for days, if not weeks, and he wanted to seize the moment.

What on earth could be in Jacob's barn? And could it be connected to the handbill Miss Cleyford had just shown him? Of all his wild guesses, the idea that the bones might belong to a circus troupe certainly hadn't occurred to him. But with the name Zella on the handbill and the dates fitting with what he'd discovered on the beach, it was now a strong possibility.

There weren't many people out and about in the village, maybe because it was lunchtime, but he still took care not to be seen. He crept up to the barn and found it padlocked, but took his pocketknife from his coat and quickly picked the lock – a skill the unscrupulous Carl had taught him. He slipped through the door, and gaps in the boarding allowed the filtered light to illuminate shapes in the dark. It was dim inside and it took his weak eyes a few moments to adjust, but before him were a couple of empty barrels, a rusted Sailmaker's Arms pub sign and some broken benches awaiting repair. He pushed his way to the back and found a rolled oilcloth propped up against a wall. It was six feet high, and he could smell the linseed oil and see the sturdy metal grommets at the corners. As he began to unroll it, he realised that it was a hand-painted advertising banner, and the large ornate letters across the top started to reveal '*Samson's Circus of...*'

The space inside the shed was small, but on the unwound section he could see colourful illustrations of various circus acts dotted across the cloth, with details of who they were beneath.

The Daredevil Zella under a slender girl walking the tightrope; *Samson the Strongman* with a muscular, bald-headed man balancing a woman on each arm; *The Giraffe Woman* showing an Oriental-looking lady with a long neck of gold rings...

There were half a dozen dusty tea chests in the corner and Edward peered inside. He pulled out some of the items: a crystal sphere wrapped in a square of velvet with a tarot deck, the tatty remnants of elaborate sequinned costumes, now chewed by rats and reduced to shredded rags, a set of wooden juggling clubs, a cracked leather saddle with curious handles on the side...

He tidied the items away and slid out of the shed, returning the padlock and ensuring he wasn't seen. And as he walked back down Copperpenny Lane to his cousin's house, one thought kept circling around his bewildered head: if the troupe had moved on, as Mrs Cleyford had claimed, why had they left a barn full of their equipment behind?

20

The calendar slipped into November and only the beech trees clung to their copper-coloured leaves. Somehow, Edward had been in Thistlewick Tye for nearly three weeks when he'd only ever intended to stay one night. So much had changed in that short time, however. He no longer felt quite so bitter towards Barnabas; he was soon to be a man of independent means; and the lie that he'd built his entire livelihood around had turned out to be true, after all. Spirits really did exist.

Dr Appleby dropped by to confirm the hair tonic contained strychnine, having injected some under the skin of a frog and witnessed the same spasms. It proved that someone wished Edward harm but, whereas previously in his life he'd shied away from danger, he felt strangely compelled to stay and fight.

Constable Lovett called round a couple of days later to question Edward over who could have sent the basket. He was tempted to reply that the spirit of a long-dead circus performer might have possessed one of the villagers and tampered with the contents. But perhaps someone else had been taken over by a malevolent ghost. Maude claimed at least four skulls had fallen, so it was possible four souls had been exposed. But in the end, Lovett couldn't trace the anonymous sender so didn't take the matter further. He did, however, suggest Mr Blackmore might be safer in London, giving the distinct impression that he, like the reverend, would be pleased to see Edward leave Thistlewick.

Carl's recovery was slow, but Edward was perfectly capable of shaving and dressing himself – it was more than a gentleman in his position was expected to have a man, and it made things easier for him. Wright offered to step in, but even Barnabas knew his cousin wouldn't accept.

Reassuring Delphine that her brother was on the mend, Edward wrote to instruct her to clear his diary for the foreseeable future. Knowing her detective skills to be nearly as good as her brother's, although her methods were decidedly less dubious, he also asked her to find out what she could about *Samson's Circus of Astonishing Spectacles*. Within three days she'd written back, enclosing a newspaper clipping from April 1856, when concerns were raised about their disappearance. Most of the troupe had cut ties with their families, they owned no property and paid no rents, but when the season started up again that spring, it was fellow showmen who'd noticed their absence.

MISSING CIRCUS!

Concerns are growing for Samson's Circus of Astonishing Spectacles, which has not been heard of since last winter. The small troupe were seen travelling through East Anglia in the autumn and there have been subsequent rumours that they secured passage on a ship bound for the Russian Empire. Fellow circus owner and competitor, Kingsley Heath, said it was unusual for Samson Ballard not to convene in London at the start of the season. Mr and Mrs Ferris, known for their stilt walking and contortionist acts, had expected Mr Ballard to be in contact with a view to renewing their contracts and are also anxious to hear from them. If anyone has information regarding their whereabouts, the editor of this paper would be most pleased to hear from you.

Edward was now convinced that the bodies were from this missing circus but still had no idea why they'd ended up in a pit on the Thistlewick Tye common. Perhaps there had been infighting amongst the performers and some had turned on the others; it was well known that there was no honour amongst thieves. Could those responsible then have sailed for foreign shores, in order to escape justice? That would back up Mrs Cleyford's story that they'd headed to King's Lynn. But if they'd been killed by their own, why were they coming back in spirit form to perpetrate such terrible acts against the villagers?

Edward's thoughts returned to Maude. Having not seen her for a few days, he wondered if the younger Garrod brother had done away with her and was living at her cottage – which was isolated enough for him to do so undetected. Mrs Drayton had heard rumours that Noah had not turned up to work for over a week, and she wondered if the trauma of his brother's death might have turned his mind. Efforts had been made to track him down but had been unsuccessful, so Edward decided to investigate, especially as he was pretty certain no one else cared enough to check if Mrs Grimmer was still alive.

He chose the coastal route again, curious to see if anything else had been exposed in the cliffs. But as he stepped onto the beach from the Thistlewick Rift he saw her familiar figure scuttling about on the shoreline. The tide was in again and the sand was a thin, flint-scattered ribbon running between the sea and the cliffs. Noah hadn't murdered her then.

'Mrs Grimmer!' he called out. She lifted her head, saw him and immediately began to hurry westwards. But he was determined to get answers from her this time. Had Noah said anything to her about a circus? 'I need to speak to you.'

He began to gain on her until they hit a patch of flints. She was far more used to scrabbling across these slippery rocks than him and her swift feet skittered over them. The uneven surface caused him to wobble a couple of times, as they were wet from earlier rain and slimy from the seaweed, making his journey hazardous. Such was his desperation to reach her before she could disappear up to the cottage and lock the door on him, that he wasn't concentrating properly and caught his foot, tumbling forward, unable to prevent the inevitable. There was a searing pain across his ribcage and the agonising crack of his right hip smacking into stone. His involuntary cry alerted her to his distress, and she spun around to gauge the situation, her hood falling to her shoulders.

His top hat had tumbled to the ground in the fall and he groaned again as it rolled towards the sea. Panicking, he sat up and smoothed his hair back into place, then looked down at his white shirt and noticed the thick red stain where he'd cut himself on a jagged piece of rusty metal wedged between two of the flints. The wound stung like hell and he was embarrassed to find himself in such a vulnerable position. Momentarily winded, he didn't have the energy to get to his feet as she approached. A strong breeze coming from the sea blew the loose tendrils of her silver-streaked hair across her face, and she angrily swept them away, but her concern for Edward was apparent.

'Are you hurt?' She crouched next to him and her hands went to his chest, hovering above the bloodstain, wary of touching him, and looking for permission to investigate his injury.

'I'm fine. Leave me be.' He couldn't have her manhandling

him but, equally, he couldn't hide the agony he was in, as his face scrunched up and a stab of pain forced deep grooves to appear across his forehead.

'That's a lot of blood and I need to see how deep the wound is.' She wasn't taking no for an answer. At the mercy of her investigations, because of the way he'd fallen, Edward could only stare, open-mouthed, as Maude reached over to his shirt. It was tucked into his trousers, but she slid it upwards to assess the extent of the damage. When she saw the trails of hairs leading down to his groin, and those scattered across his chest, however, she paused.

Their eyes met and he knew that his secret was out.

'It's a nasty gash and it's deep.' Lifting up her thick woollen skirt, she tore a strip of cotton from the hem of her underskirt and rolled it into a pad. 'Press this on the wound.' He did as she bid. 'We're only a little way from my cottage. I've ointments and bandages, and a basic understanding of healing. How's your ankle? Can you bear weight on it?'

She got to her feet and put out her hand, saying nothing of what she'd seen.

He stared at it and then shook his head to refuse her offer, feeling even more vulnerable than before.

'You wanted to speak to me so badly you've raced recklessly across these slippery rocks and injured yourself. I'm offering to take you to my home, a place I don't allow anyone to enter, where you can do just that. Your refusal makes no sense.'

Her hand remained outstretched.

'You have Noah there.'

'Not everything with that man is as it seems, but it would appear you have secrets, too, Mr Blackmore. I'm not sure why you are so determined to dig about in things that don't concern you, especially as I overheard there was an attempt on your life, but I think p'rhaps it's about time we had a civil conversation and I'll share with you some of what I know. Noah is long gone, so are you coming or not?'

The pain was getting worse and his choices were limited. Return to the village, where the doctor would inevitably be called, but he didn't want Dr Appleby seeing his chest any more than he'd been happy about Maude seeing him so exposed. Go with this difficult and insular woman, and assess whether she was likely to divulge his secret – or at least ascertain if she planned to blackmail him for keeping the information about his condition to herself. Or return to Thistlewick House, deal with the injury to the best of his ability, and ignore the pain – and, frankly, it was a pain he couldn't ignore.

Returning with her to the cottage would at least prove whether her words were true and Noah had left. And she was offering to share information with him. What was he so afraid of?

Refusing her help, he managed to push himself up. His ankle would bruise but it wasn't broken and he began to make his way to the large patch of flat sand beyond the rocks. But he'd got to his feet too quickly and felt himself sway. Maude noticed his moment of dizziness and slipped herself under his left arm, taking some of his weight and guiding him towards the gap in the cliffs.

Together, they made their way up the shallow bank and stumbled along the path to her home. His chest was throbbing like crazy, but he no longer cared about concealing his truth if she could only give him something to ease the pain.

21

Five minutes later and Edward was ducking under a low lintel into Maude's small parlour, surprised how cosy the interior was, despite the smoke and unpleasant smell of cheap rush lighting. He'd expected mess and chaos, to reflect the neglected nature of the exterior. The priority of a drunkard, after all, was the next drink, not the cleanliness of their home.

'I thought you didn't let strangers in.'

'You're no longer a stranger, Mr Blackmore. And despite everything, I feel I can trust you.'

'Because you can now blackmail me?'

'I've no interest in extracting money from you. I manage on what I earn from combing the beach, and can afford to purchase what I need to get by.'

Yes, mainly gin, he wanted to reply, but bit his tongue. The pine-like smell of juniper berries was apparent even now, as she lowered him onto the stark wooden bench near her open fire. She collected two small pieces of driftwood from a basket on the hearth and slid them into the flames. They crackled and spat, but he could feel the warmth begin to thaw his frozen extremities and it was a comfort.

'I have some strips of cotton I can boil as bandages, and gin in the pantry to clean the wound. A stronger spirit, like whisky, would be more effective but it'll have to do. And a nip of it might also take the edge off the pain. It won't take long to make a poultice from the root of the marshmallow. Watch the kettle whilst I dip outside and harvest some.'

She slipped through the low door and Edward was left alone. All he could think of in the ensuing silence was the promise of gin and how it might alleviate his suffering. After a few minutes he rose from the bench and walked over to what he assumed to be the pantry. He usually drank absinthe – the choice of artists and intellectuals – but anything that would numb the pain was welcome. Even the cheap gin of an alcoholic.

He pulled back the door and his face crumpled into a frown, because in the tiny room, neatly stacked on the shelves, were rows and rows of dark green, rectangular gin bottles, and they all appeared full...

'How dare you pry into my cupboards!'

Her angry rebuke startled him. He spun back to face her, as she stood in the doorway, the pale, thin roots of the marshmallow in her hands.

'I don't understand.' He gestured to the bottles.

Maude placed the roots on her small, scrubbed table, bolted the front door and stomped over to him. She dipped into the pantry and brought out one of the bottles, firmly closing the door behind her, her nostrils flaring in her indignation, as she thumped it down on the table. Her fingers anxiously clenched and unclenched, as she looked around for the things she needed to tend to his injury.

'I invited you into my home because I thought I could trust

you. I didn't invite you in so you could go snooping around the second my back was turned.'

'Sorry. The pain... I was trying to help.' He felt embarrassed and confused. A room full of untouched alcohol didn't make sense in the home of someone notorious for her drinking but he shouldn't have invaded her privacy.

Still silent, she poured him a measure of neat gin. Her eyes narrowed as she handed him the tumbler, and he didn't blame her for being cross. He downed it quickly, spluttering a cough at the bitterness of the liquor. It burned a fierce pathway down his gullet, the heat of it like fire, but it quickly started to numb the pain.

Feeling like a reprimanded schoolboy, he watched as she took a folded piece of cotton from a small drawer on the dresser. She proceeded to rip it into strips, which she placed in a chipped ceramic mixing bowl. Then she lifted the kettle from the pot hook and poured boiling water on the rags.

Edward returned to the bench as Maude began angrily scrubbing at the roots, before chopping them up and grinding them into the mortar with a wooden pestle. After a while, she returned to the fireplace, with everything she needed to tend to him gathered together on a tray. She brushed her skirts to one side and perched on a rough-hewn milking stool.

Their eyes met and held. She was waiting, he realised, and began to unbutton his shirt, shrugging it from his shoulders. As she washed the wound, he watched her focused expression, determined not to make a fuss.

Finally, she spoke. 'Not that it's any of your business, but I haven't touched a drop of liquor since my husband left me,' she said, in reference to the contents of the pantry.

Edward raised an eyebrow.

'But I've seen you, clutching half-drunk bottles by their

necks. And, no offence, but there's often the distinctive smell of stale alcohol about your person.' Even now, he thought to himself.

'I dribble it on my clothes and still buy it to maintain the pretence that I drink, but I don't.' Maude shrugged, and dabbed some of the neat gin on the deep gash.

He sucked in a sharp breath through his teeth. God, but it stung. Another whole minute passed in silence, with only the sounds of spitting wood from the fire.

'I woke up in a pool of my own vomit on an unbearably hot July morning four years ago, remembering nothing of how I got there. I'd also soiled myself and was running a terrible fever. The stench was unbearable and, had I anything left in my stomach, I'd have emptied it all over the floor again. Instead, I staggered to the door and threw it open to the most beautiful day – a day that made me thankful to be alive. A cloudless azure-blue sky and the fresh salty sea breeze. The birds were chattering away and dots of colour from the meadow flowers made the whole scene look like something out of a picture book.' She gave a sour laugh. 'But my overriding feeling was the disgust I felt at myself for the situation I was in.'

She laid a bandage across the wound, lifting up his arm to thread it behind and then bringing it back under the other arm. Her hands were cold but her touch was gentle. Edward didn't interrupt her tale.

'I took myself down to the shore, stripped off every stitch I had on and threw myself into the sea. As I'm sure you know, even on a warm summer's day, it's a shock to the system, but it was also a clarion call. I had to change my ways.'

Why the thought of a naked Maude in the sea should cause Edward to blush, he wasn't sure, but it was an image he held on to for longer than he should. She wasn't so old that she'd ceased to be attractive, especially now that she wasn't scowling at him.

'If you've not touched the gin in all these years, why would you want people to think you were still reliant on it?'

'The villagers have long since made their minds up about me and wouldn't understand that I'd had an epiphany, bobbing about in the North Sea. I suffered a few days of sweats and suchlike as my body adjusted to my sobriety but when I walked into the village to beg fresh milk, I was still whispered about. People turned to get out of my path, not wanting to meet my eyes, and called me everything from a sot to a whore – even though there's no basis in truth for the last accusation. Ha.' She laughed to herself, but it had a bitter edge. 'If only.'

He sucked in a sharp breath as she tucked in the loose end of the dressing and accidentally brushed against the wound.

'But Thistlewick Tye is full of such godly people. They pride themselves on their forgiveness and compassion. Wouldn't the congregation welcome a repentant sinner?'

She snorted at that. 'And yet, I rather think they like having a local pariah. Mothers pointing at me and warning their children about the consequences of their actions. *Look at what happens when the demon liquor gets a hold.* It's easier to let people believe what they want, not least because they generally stay out of my way. Let's not forget, I used to beat my husband and know that I don't deserve forgiveness or compassion. I once overheard a woman say that when I was at my most intoxicated, I hit him over the head with a chair and nearly killed him. Can't say I recall the incident, but I certainly don't blame him for running off.'

She shrugged, as though it was just one of those things, but her sobriety explained why the tiny cottage was so neat inside.

Driven to the edge by her addiction, she'd given up the drink and mended her ways.

'So let them point and call me names because sometimes it's better to draw people's attention to one thing, to distract them from another.'

She sighed, and he understood completely. Wasn't it exactly what he was doing with his colourful clothes and dramatic appearance?

'I'm not a believer in God, Mr Blackmore; he's done little for me in my lifetime. To be welcomed back into the fold holds no appeal. I'm answerable to no man and enjoy my simple life. I eat well enough – the sea offers up its bounty, if you know where to look – and I've a few vegetables growing out the back, not seen from the path. What I find washed up on the beach makes me enough to get by. Every morning I stand on the cliffs and am grateful for the stunning view and fresh air. And the best part of it is that the chirping birds flitting about in my hawthorn hedge and the rabbits grazing on the short grass across from my gate don't judge me.'

For a man who'd spent so much of his life in the pursuit of wealth, he was beginning to appreciate her point of view. Wasn't the natural beauty of the countryside as stunning as the fine architecture of the city? And that wholesome air – he was constantly pulled to the beach. The savage nature of the sea and the sweeping winds so refreshing after the city smog.

'Why did you attack me that first day? You went at me like a wildcat and I'd done nothing to you.'

She shrugged. 'You were a stranger and I didn't want you prying into my business.'

'So, if I keep your secret, will you keep mine?' he asked. She'd said nothing of what she'd seen beneath his shirt but he could see her eyes were drawn to his chest, even now that the wound was dressed, and knew she was wondering the truth of it all, so decided her honesty deserved his.

He put his hand to his jet-black hair. The dramatic contrast between that and his pale skin was an image he'd long manipulated to his advantage – because a man who looked as though he'd risen from the dead was surely best placed to contact the spirits of the departed.

With one sharp tug, he slipped off the wig and revealed the close crop of snow-white hair that covered his head and matched the hair across his body.

For Edward Shaw had been a bitter disappointment and brought everlasting shame to his father.

Edward Shaw had been born albino.

Edward Shaw was a freak.

22

Edward's wig was of the finest quality and had taken six heads of human hair to make. The strands were hand-tied onto a flesh-coloured lace cap, and it had been custom-made in Paris – all paid for from the Cattisham Orphanage Fund. He'd previously experimented with dyes of boiled walnut hulls or silver nitrate, but the latter gave off a purplish hue in certain lights, and the white growth of his roots showed within days, making the whole process time-consuming and far from satisfactory. The colour faded quickly and left stains on pillowcases and the collars of his shirts. In the end, a wig had proved the best option.

He shaved his face twice daily, to avoid the tell-tale white stubble from showing. His flamboyant and flowing clothes hid most of his body hair, apart from that on his face, but he dyed his eyebrows with the walnut hulls and used a stick of E. Rimmel's black cosmetique to darken them even more and colour his lashes. All very well until the heat of a blazing summer day or the driving rain of winter caused the dark stain to run.

As part of his condition, the lack of pigment in his body gave him the most piercing blue eyes, but had also affected his vision.

He struggled to see objects near to him so needed spectacles to read, and was sensitive to bright light. It was one of the reasons he kept out of the sun, preferring winter and night-time – the other, of course, being that his pale skin would burn easily. But he knew many people with his condition had it worse. He'd once seen a little girl with red eyes – much harder to conceal and pass yourself off as 'normal' – whatever that meant. But with the help of Delphine and Carl, he'd successfully pulled the wool over most people's far more clear-sighted eyes.

Maude didn't flinch as he placed the black wig on his lap, but then she'd seen the snow-white hairs covering his broad chest when she'd pulled back his shirt on the beach. She could now be in no doubt of the secret that he kept so closely guarded. The secret that had forced him to move away from the people he'd grown up with, to reinvent himself, disguise his appearance and even change his name. Blackmore – how could he resist?

He was the second child in his family to be born lacking in pigment, but the older sister he'd never met had only survived a few days. And then when Jonah Shaw's son was also born an albino, he'd sworn never to sire another child. Edward was a bitter disappointment and had spent a great deal of his youth trying to prove to his father that his fragile appearance didn't mean he was weak – physically or mentally. But there are none so blind as those who choose not to see, and nothing he could do made Jonah Shaw proud. Instead, over time, the man turned his hopes and attentions to his nephew, Barnabas, determined to have a Shaw run the maltings after his death, because he refused to countenance his freak of a son at the helm.

Edward reached for the gin bottle and poured himself another half tumblerful – it wasn't as if Maude was going to drink it.

'Your secret's safe with me,' she said, and they locked eyes.

Did she see his pain as he saw hers? Because there was something about her that told of a cavernous emptiness – a haunted look and her defeated body language – that he understood. She was not a good woman, but then he'd not always been a good man. He'd spent the majority of his life lying to people and extracting money for a gift he didn't possess. His clients believed they were donating to a worthy charity, when in truth the orphanage was fraudulent.

He noticed her gaze drop to his open shirt again and was suddenly embarrassed to be so exposed, pulling the two sides of the cotton together and refastening the buttons. A faint pink tinge bloomed across the apples of her cheeks. All the while he thought she was a hostile drunk, their sex had hardly come into their encounters, but now that he'd discovered she was a perfectly rational woman with a head clear of drink, albeit slightly older than him, he was acutely aware that such intimacy was inappropriate.

'Thank you for your kind ministrations,' he said, rising to his feet, picking up his wig and deftly placing it back on his head. He winced as he put weight on his ankle. 'But I must head back to Thistlewick House. Barnabas will be wondering where I am.'

In reality, Edward doubted his cousin would notice his absence. The man hadn't left the house since the funeral, and continued to look for reasons to live in the bottom of his whisky tumbler.

Maude stood with him and the pair walked over to the door. As she fumbled with the bolt, Edward looked down at her. She was quite tall for her sex but even so, at nearly six feet, he towered over most people.

What was it about this strange woman that made his heart suddenly accelerate? Her weathered skin told of a hard life, and the soft crêpe of her skin around her eyes and on her neck attested to her age. She was on the attractive side of plain, but not a particular beauty, and, for most of their short acquaintance, she'd been downright unpleasant to him. But he sensed there was something deeper to her – something he'd only begun to unearth that afternoon, in the confines of her small cottage. Alcohol was a ruthless master. It had turned her into something that she wasn't. The shock of her husband walking out, and her subsequent sobriety, had allowed this more reasoned woman to resurface. Look how she'd tended to his wound. But perhaps he'd always subconsciously been aware that she was not what she pretended to be. Her level-headedness on the night that Silas had fallen from the cliffs was a prime example. Everyone deserved a second chance.

'Do you not get lonely?' he asked, unable to stop himself from reaching for her hand to help her draw back the bolt. Her earlier confidence seemed to have deserted her as she stared at his fingers, wide over hers, and tipped her head up to meet his questioning gaze. Was it his imagination, or was she trembling?

'Sometimes.'

Her simple, honest reply, and vulnerable expression, had a bewildering effect on him. Edward's breathing felt momentarily constricted, as though someone was pushing a firm hand down on his breastbone. His heart flipped upwards, replicating the sensation he felt when the carriage went too fast over a humpback bridge – a feeling of seasickness and discombobulation.

He ran his tongue across his lips and, with the same inevitability as gravity, his head was pulled towards her slightly open mouth. He inched towards her, almost imperceptibly, and her head remained defiantly tilted upwards, before he chastised himself. What the hell was he doing? This was a married woman with a disturbing past. Added to which, he'd made the decision long ago not to complicate his own life by becoming involved with a woman.

His unfortunate condition meant he'd never entertained the idea of a wife. If his own father could hardly bear to look at him, why would a young woman feel any different? Especially in the bedroom, where he could no longer hide behind wigs and long, sweeping clothing. And who would risk bringing albino children into this world? To society at large, he was Edward Blackmore – the man with black hair and pale skin – but the intimacy of marriage would reveal the truth, so he'd refused to pursue any meaningful romance. He'd even stepped away from the one woman he'd loved, without ever revealing why.

But Maude knew about his albinism now. Did it matter to her? She was still frozen, but whether that was because the potential kiss was an unwelcome shock, or she was steadying herself in anticipation of it, he couldn't be sure.

His focus, which had been entirely on her lips, now darted back up to her eyes, and she snapped out of her hypnotised state and shook her head, pulling away.

'I can't do this,' she said. 'It makes me uncomfortable.'

He'd been fooling himself that she felt an attraction to him. Like everyone else in his life, he realised, she didn't want to be associated with a freak.

Edward slid back the heavy bolt and opened the door. Limp light from the miserable day flooded the cottage, but the chilly atmosphere that swirled about them wasn't just down to the breeze.

'I'm sorry. You're married. The gin… What was I thinking? You've been so kind and my behaviour was unforgivable.'

'Mr Blackmore—'

'Please, call me Edward.'

'Despite my determination to live an independent life, I *am* lonely. If you can bear the chatter of the gossips, then I could use a *friend*,' she admitted, emphasising the platonic nature of their possible relationship. 'There are strange things going on and I think you're the only person who can be trusted to do the right thing.'

Edward hesitated, half over the threshold, and then stepped back inside, drawing the door to a close again. He banished all thoughts of romance. They'd been fleeting and ridiculous. The alcohol had blurred his judgement, and the truth was that he often felt lonely, too. But he'd run after her on the beach because he believed she could help with his investigations, so he should return his focus to the matter in hand. She'd told him the truth of her past and assured him she wouldn't reveal his secret. He could trust her.

'I could also do with a friend,' he said. '*And* your thoughts on the accusations of spirit possessions, and how they might be connected to the falling bones.' She'd been collecting them for weeks, and had spoken to Noah – a man he knew was not who he claimed to be.

How to approach such a preposterous hypothesis.

'Where do you stand on the afterlife?'

Maude shrugged. 'I've never given it any thought.'

'But you must know that I was called to Thistlewick Tye by my cousin, after his wife claimed to be a small child called Esfir?'

She shook her head. 'I keep myself to myself and don't get involved in gossip.'

Edward went to his breast pocket and took out a small tortoiseshell cardholder, slipping one of his calling cards from within.

Edward Blackmore Esq.
Spiritualist & Medium

Conductor of séances. Guidance from the spirit realm.
Appointments by Invitation Only
17b Ambury Lane, London

'Guess it explains the fancy clothes.' She gestured for him to return to the bench. It was obvious to both of them he was going nowhere for the moment. There were things to discuss, and he was relieved that she was open to such a conversation. 'And you spoke to this supposed spirit?'

'To my everlasting shame, I arrived after Mrs Shaw had passed away. But I witnessed Noah Garrod's death up on the common, and saw him come to life moments later, talking in a manner that was most peculiar and attacking his brother. I believe he's also been possessed.'

'Because you can communicate with spirits and can sense when they are near?' She looked most unconvinced.

He swallowed hard.

'No. I can't. I'm a fraud. Until I came to Thistlewick Tye, I thought spiritualism was nonsense, and was merely peddling the lie that I could communicate with the dead to make a living.' He paused and shrugged. 'Like you, I did what I could to get by. But the things I've witnessed in this village lead me to believe I was wrong to dismiss the afterlife.' He leaned forward to stress the earnestness of what he was about to say. 'And I'm starting to suspect that those bodies falling into the sea are somehow linked to it all.'

'Is that why you've been asking about the bones?'

He nodded and noticed that she'd folded her arms – a clear sign that she felt defensive.

'I won't tell you where they're buried. It's not right to dig up the dead.'

'I appreciate that, besides, there's not much they can tell me, especially as I think I've worked out who they are.'

Maude looked mildly interested and let her arms drop back to her lap.

'In 1855, before you were born...' He paused. The woman was of indeterminate age. 'Or possibly when you were very little, a travelling circus visited Thistlewick Tye. They caused a great deal of trouble and there were issues with the locals. These travellers were wicked people, debaucherous and violent, but they also disappeared that winter – the whole troupe. Most villagers seem under the impression that they only stayed a short time and then moved on. But I recently made an intriguing discovery – Jacob Palmer's barn is full of circus equipment.'

Maude's eyes expanded in surprise. 'So, what happened to them?'

He shrugged. 'That's the thing. Mrs Cleyford insists they were run out of town, and left for foreign shores. But if that were true, why would they leave their belongings behind? And even more chilling is that one of the names Mrs Shaw talked of when she claimed to be Esfir was Zella, who I've subsequently discovered was the tightrope walker with the troupe. But if it *is* their transmigrated souls popping up in the bodies of villagers, then I can't explain how some or all of them have ended up in a big burial pit on the cliffs. I thought perhaps there had been some accident, or an outbreak of disease, but then why aren't the good people of Thistlewick being honest about it? Forty years is certainly long enough for bodies to become bones and for clothes to disintegrate, but other things, such as objects made of metal, would survive. It's why I wanted to look at the chain.'

'There really was nothing special about it,' she confirmed. 'And I needed the money.'

'Then may I request that if you find anything else as the cliffs fall, that you sell it to me? I have money and will give you a fair price. Or, at the very least, tell me about it?'

'Of course, but surely you can simply confront the villagers who are old enough to remember their visit and ask what really happened to the members of the circus?'

Edward sighed. 'I've only spoken directly to Mrs Cleyford so far, but I must tread carefully because I believe someone has made an attempt on my life.' And he told her about the hair tonic. 'I can only assume that another person has been possessed but is clever enough to conceal the truth. If only I could sense these spirits, as I've claimed all these years, and knew when I was in the presence of such an entity.'

'If only,' she agreed.

'Even when I talked with Noah, it was purely logic that told me his behaviour was not that of the man he claimed to be. There was no sense that I was standing before the ghost of a dead man. It would seem Mr Palmer's dog has more psychic ability than I do.' He snorted and rubbed at his chin with his hand. 'The spirits of these people are doing bad things. I want to find out why, but I also don't want to announce my suspicions and put myself in greater danger.'

Maude narrowed her eyes and leaned forward, confusion apparent across her brow. 'Do you genuinely believe that someone from a circus several decades ago has possessed Noah Garrod?'

He nodded, relieved she was taking him seriously.

'Because that would explain some of his curious behaviour when he came to the cottage. You're right – there was something off about him because he had no idea who I was or anything about my reputation. And when you arrived, banging on the door, you rattled him, and he left shortly afterwards. But at no point did he threaten me; nor did I think I was in danger. He told me he intended to walk to Great Yarmouth and catch a boat to Belgium or Germany because he believed *himself* in danger. Perhaps there's another side to what happened up on the cliffs,' she suggested. 'Perhaps you can uncover the truth of *his* story?'

'Did he give a name?' Edward asked.

'Yes,' Maude confirmed. 'It all seemed nonsense to me at the time, but he kept insisting he was Samson Ballard.'

And Edward's mind flashed back to the newspaper clipping Delphine had sent, the handbill that Miss Cleyford had given him and the banner in Jacob's barn. The name on all these was now more important than ever – *Samson's Circus of Astonishing Spectacles*.

23

Edward returned to Thistlewick House, a journey that took longer than anticipated because of his injured ankle, explaining to Barnabas that he'd fallen, down on the beach, but that someone from the village had tended to him, managing to avoid mentioning Maude by name. Mrs Drayton wanted to send for the doctor but his cousin, well aware he would not want to be examined, backed him up.

They sat together awaiting luncheon, when the Reverend Fallow called. He made it painfully clear that he was there to speak to Mr Shaw and Edward was not welcome. But loitering in the adjoining room, Edward heard most of their exchange, which included a particularly admonishing talk on temperance and the evils of drink. As the vicar was shown out, he informed Mr Wright how disappointed he was that the household had facilitated their master's descent into unacceptable behaviour. He strongly suggested that Mrs Drayton reduce the amount of spirits she purchased, requesting that she keep all household receipts for him to inspect upon his next visit.

Unable to hold back, Edward stepped out into the hallway and confronted him.

'Surely, Reverend, it's not for you to tell a man what he may or may not do in his own home?'

'I disagree completely, Mr Blackmore. That is exactly my duty. I serve to educate my flock as to the difference between right and wrong, and drinking to excess is wrong.' Wright helped him on with his coat and handed him his gloves. 'We care for our neighbours in Thistlewick Tye,' he stressed. 'The schoolmistress sends the children to me at the first sign of laziness or dishonesty, and we find the child concerned rarely transgresses again. The Bible can be a very powerful tool.'

'Depends what you do with it,' Edward said, flippantly. 'A whack across the backside with a book that heavy might make a small lad think twice.'

'I'm a firm believer in spare the rod and spoil the child, and it's yielded excellent results for me over the years. Nearly every adult in the village can read – Noah excepted.'

Whilst that was an impressive achievement, it concerned Edward that the church was overstepping its reach. Of course, he knew it wasn't acceptable to commit heinous crimes against one's fellow man, but the whole point of the Christian faith was that people had free will. Every decision in life came with consequences, good and bad, but surely it was not within Reverend Fallow's remit to enforce that. Certainly not to the extent of speaking to Barnabas's staff. The poor man's life had totally collapsed and if alcohol was helping to see him through that for the short term, whilst it was far from ideal, it was his choice.

After the reverend had left, he voiced his concerns to Mrs Drayton.

'But the vicar and the doctor have always worked together in this regard – overseeing the physical and spiritual health of the villagers,' she said. 'Besides, God works in mysterious ways. Not long after Charlie Tutter started a fight with some visitors last summer, he was dreadfully sick. Divine retribution.' She folded her arms as if that was the end of the matter.

He peered back into the drawing room, sad to see Barnabas, stooped and silent, standing at the windows and staring out over his gardens. Strangely, he felt no elation over this state of affairs. His nineteen-year-old self would have relished such a reversal of fortunes, but he no longer wanted to exercise such power over his cousin. He knew Maude's unexpected kindness had disarmed him and it was a reminder that *everyone* was redeemable and deserved a second chance. He stepped into the room.

'Emma loved you,' he said. The most peculiar sensation swept over him as he spoke the words. 'Right from the moment you first met. To my knowledge, she never wavered in her devotion, despite what you thought that summer in London. It was only ever you she wanted, Barnabas.'

His cousin turned his head, blinking furiously. 'And that's the truth?'

Edward nodded. 'Of course. You rightly surmised that I was as enchanted by her as you were, but my feelings weren't reciprocated. Besides, we both know she wouldn't have accepted me once she found out about my condition.'

'There, cousin, I think you're quite wrong. It wouldn't have mattered to Emma. When she loved, she loved fiercely. Your father was not a good man and he coloured your view of the world. Not everyone sees a person's differences as a reason to exclude them. It wasn't your albinism that made me cut you from the company; it was my pride and my greed. I knew you'd do a better job than me, and I didn't want my inadequacies highlighted by your competence.'

Edward felt a lump form in his throat. His cousin's honesty meant the world.

Wright entered the room to attend to the fire and then asked his master if he would like a nightcap.

'Splendid idea,' Barnabas replied, and Edward's mood dipped as he contemplated another evening of watching his cousin sink into drunken oblivion. 'Would you join me in a hot cocoa?' he asked, and a tiny part of Edward hoped that his kind words had helped to bring about such a small but significant change.

* * *

The following morning, after a bracing walk along the beach, Edward decided to check on Carl. He'd seemed more chipper the previous day, and he hoped his servant might soon return to his duties. But when he stopped by his room, he found it empty.

'Where is my man?' he asked Mrs Drayton.

'He left not long after you, sir.' She frowned. 'Did Mr Shaw not say? I got the impression you knew about it. Going back to recuperate, he said, and took your big trunk with him. Wright ran him to Cromer in the trap, so he could catch a train to London, but he left you this.'

She handed over a folded note.

Mr B

    Sorry but I aynt dying for no one. This spirit stuff has got wyrd and I don't want nun of it. Don't try to find me. I know people.

    Carl

And Edward returned upstairs to his room to find that, along with his manservant, most items of value that he had with him in Thistlewick Tye had disappeared.

24

As if things couldn't get much worse for Edward, he joined Barnabas in the dining room, hoping for some sympathy with his mutton chops. But after the touching honesty of the night before, he was surprised to be greeted by his cousin's thunderous face.

'What's the meaning of this?' Barnabas thrust the morning edition of the *Daily Telegraph* in front of Edward, who had to adjust his spectacles and hold the newspaper at a more convenient distance to read the headline.

Sir Alfred Temple Found Alive after Eight Months!

The intrepid explorer and former diplomat Sir Alfred Temple has made contact with British authorities in Leh, having been believed dead since he went missing in the Kashmir region earlier this year. Sir Alfred had been surveying uncharted areas of the Himalayan mountains when he became separated from his party, soon after suffering extreme delirium from an illness contracted a few days previously. Not of his right mind, he wandered from the camp in the night and, with no word from him in months, has long been assumed dead. Lady Temple recently sought to contact her husband with the help of the renowned spiritualist Edward Blackmore. He claimed to have summoned Sir Alfred during a séance, where he was said to have confirmed that he had fallen to his death...

Edward's heart sank to his fine leather boots as he read of the man's remarkable survival. According to the article, he'd wandered southward, through the desolate Karakoram Pass, and was found on the brink of death by a band of yak traders, of all things. He was nursed back to health, and for weeks he remained in a bewildered state, unable to recall his name or origins. With no proof of identity or means of support, he was eventually conveyed to Leh, the remote British outpost in Ladakh, where he finally recovered his memory and dispatched a desperate telegram to his wife.

Absolutely furious to have been deceived into believing Sir Alfred had died, Lady Temple had been only too happy to talk to the newspapers about Edward's deception. It wouldn't take long for talk of the scandal to seep through London society and reach his other clients.

He carefully folded the newspaper up and handed it back to his cousin.

'Well? What do you have to say? Dammit, man. You told the woman you'd made contact with her dead husband, and all the time he was alive. They're denouncing you as a fraud. Will there be further tales of such deceit seeping from the woodwork? Have you been lying to *me* all these years?'

Considering his world was about to come tumbling down in the most dramatic fashion, Edward was surprisingly calm. He could claim that he had spun Lady Temple the tale as a kindness, that it had been a one-off and all his other spirit communications had been genuine, but that would be more lies and he didn't want to be that man any more. Barnabas had a valid point, though – others would soon start to query his legitimacy. And he was pretty sure if there was a way to make money out of the scandal, Carl, still bitter about the poisoning, would sell his story to the newspapers and spill all his secrets. It was only a matter of time.

He said nothing.

'Did you really contact Emma when you performed the séance for me? Or was that a sham, too?' His cousin was shaking now, and he could see the desperation in the man's eyes. Edward knew there was a part of Barnabas that wanted him to refute the newspaper report, because he needed Emma's comforting words to be real – that final goodbye had cost him five hundred pounds and his house.

His cousin read the silence correctly and slumped into the chair opposite, shaking his head. 'Just tell me the truth, Edward.'

There was no point continuing the charade.

'I cannot, and never could, contact the spirits of the dead. Not once in my thirty-six years have I communicated with anyone during a séance. You're quite correct: it's all been illusion, careful planning and detailed research. But I'm not minded if you think badly of me, because I did what I could to earn a crust when my father all but cut me from his will.'

Barnabas had the grace to look uncomfortable.

'Well played, sir. You got your revenge and I hope you'll be happy at Thistlewick House. Even though you did not deliver the services I required, I shan't dispute the legality of our agreement. This whole situation is divine retribution and I graciously accept my punishment for doing nothing to address the unjust nature of your father's actions. More fool me for believing such poppycock. Which just proves how useless I am without my beloved wife.'

'You're missing the point, though.' Edward leaned forward to emphasise the earnestness of what he was about to say. 'Because I'm now utterly convinced that spirits *do* exist and that you were correct in your belief that Emma was possessed—'

'Enough. Don't try to play me for a fool twice. Take the damn house and either live in it or sell it and move back to London. I care not.' Barnabas slammed his fist down on the table and his cutlery jumped.

'With my reputation in tatters? Besides, I suspect Carl and his sister will have cleared out my house and be long gone.'

He'd written to Delphine but expected no answer. As soon as her brother had returned, with tales of possessed villagers and the true horror of his poisoning, which Edward did feel guilt over, the pair would be off. And now with the news of Sir Alfred, they might see another opportunity to make money, and he didn't blame them. Even before his lie had been exposed, Edward had felt uncomfortable about his old life. Yes, his hand had been forced with regard to timing, but he found he didn't mind as much as he should.

'What I said to you about Emma was true,' he continued. 'I know you were conscious of our special friendship, but it was always something that meant more to me than it did to her. The conversation we shared as we went for the ices that day in Hyde Park was her letting me down gently when I revealed the extent of my ardour. I always let you think her feelings were greater for me than they were as part of my bitterness for what you did to me in the past.'

Barnabas's jaw visibly clenched as he stared at his plate of food.

'But I *will* get to the bottom of what happened to her. There are strange things going on at Thistlewick Tye. Bones are falling onto the beach from the burial of circus folk who came to the village forty years ago and disappeared in mysterious circumstances. The names mentioned by Emma in her delirious state, and the recent unusual behaviour of Noah Garrod, are linked to these people.'

'More tales to suck in your gullible cousin?' Barnabas batted the comments away with an uninterested hand.

'This is the truth. I swear on Emma's grave. These people came to Thistlewick Tye and caused all sorts of trouble, and seem intent on causing even more harm as they rise back up.' He was agitated now, needing someone on his side. 'Don't you see? They must be stopped before they kill again. It's because I've been looking into it all that someone sent me the contaminated hair tonic.'

Barnabas narrowed his eyes. 'This is not a joke?'

'I swear it, cousin. I can only assume someone else in the village has been possessed and is after me. Until the newspaper story broke, they may even have believed me capable of detecting spirits – which would naturally have made me a target.'

'How do you know I'm not possessed of a dead man, if you say you don't have the power to sense them?'

'Because I know you, Barnabas – your mannerisms, the way you speak and the very fact that we've been sitting here discussing our shared history. You're exactly who you say you are.'

His cousin shook his head. 'I'm almost certainly being taken for a chump, again.'

'Do you want justice for Emma?'

His cousin nodded.

'Then trust me.'

* * *

As word of the newspaper report spread through the household, Edward detected a change in the staff's attitude towards him. Wright spoke to him with deference but his eyes told a different story. And he overheard Mrs Drayton talking to the cook, angry that he'd played on Lady Temple's grief and sore that he'd soon be her new master. Edward stopped short of stepping into the kitchen and announcing he no longer required her services.

Two days after that, he received correspondence from his landlord regarding the apartment in Ambury Lane. He requested that Mr Blackmore find other accommodation, although he noticed that many of his possessions had already been moved, and asked for the final rent payment.

As Edward suspected, Carl and Delphine had quickly sold him out, with exclusive interviews about their time working for the charlatan spiritualist, revealing all his tricks and illusions. Interestingly, they didn't mention his albinism. Perhaps Delphine had more compassion than she let on, or maybe Carl, after years of helping Edward conceal his condition, understood that Jonah Shaw's cruelty had nearly broken his master. They were after money, not revenge.

Lord Felthorpe saw fit to visit Thistlewick House when the news reached him. As a passing acquaintance of Sir Alfred, he was angry at Edward's deception, and possibly also furious that he'd been duped into attending the séance.

'I'm greatly concerned that the scandal will follow you to our lovely village. May I strongly suggest you return to London and deal with the mess. I realise the constable hit a dead end with the poisoning of your man, but if nothing else, it's proof that you're not welcome here. There may be a further attempt on your life and my first thought is naturally for your welfare.' The man was being disingenuous but Edward said nothing. 'We've had too many deaths in the village recently, and with the doctor's father and several children from the school now ill with influenza, we've enough to deal with. I think it would be best for everyone if you left Thistlewick Tye.'

'And yet the greater scandal brewing in the village, you cannot lay at my door. There are several bodies buried on the common land by the cliffs, the bones of which are now being exposed as the soil falls into the sea. Those responsible clearly didn't think the erosion of the land would expose the dead in their lifetime, but the evidence suggests they were put there forty years ago. That's the real crime, Your Lordship.'

Lord Felthorpe frowned. 'Why was I not told of this? We need to get Constable Lovett to investigate immediately and determine whether the coroner needs to be involved.'

It was Edward's turn to frown. 'I mentioned all this to Mr Palmer days ago and he said he'd do exactly that. I assumed the constable had been investigating. Or at least waiting for more bones to fall, as the land has been stable recently.'

'I don't believe Mr Palmer has done any such thing. Constable Lovett would have told me. Are you even sure they're human?'

Edward was confused why Jacob hadn't passed on the information. That man was hiding things – not least a barn full of circus paraphernalia – and he racked his brains to think if there'd been any indication that the landlord of the Sailmaker's was not who he said he was. Surely Banjo would be the first to react had his owner been possessed, having sensed all was not right with Noah Garrod.

'I've seen the skulls for myself – they're people, all right – but come high tide, the sea claims them.' He didn't want to involve Maude at this stage. The villagers didn't need any more reasons to vilify the poor woman. 'But, more alarmingly, as the dead fall, their spirits are rising. I believe my cousin was right to claim that his wife had been possessed.'

'And why should this interest you, Mr Blackmore? A man with no faith, who we now discover has built a career laughing behind the backs of those who believe in spirits?'

But Edward was definite in his assertion.

'Because whatever you think of me, I do not condone the murders of Mrs Shaw or Silas Garrod. And because I am the only person who believes spirits are responsible, I am the only person who is likely to get to the truth.'

25

The rain that night was torrential, keeping Edward awake for hours. When he finally stirred, he realised Mother Nature had also decided to throw freezing fog into the mix. The plummeting temperatures had condensed the saturated ground and moist air, so that the day started with a thick cloud of white draped over Thistlewick Tye. As he drew back the curtains, he could see the intricate fern-like patterns of frost inside the panes of his bedroom window, icing-sugar feathers adorning the edges of the beech tree not ten yards from where he stood, and puddles of glass reflecting light back at him from the ground outside. Everything beyond that had blurred into grey.

He sighed, and pulled his dressing gown tighter, before embarking on his close shave and touching up the dye on his eyebrows. He had no reason to remain now the scandal had broken. The transfer of the house could be sorted from London, and the five hundred pounds Barnabas had given him upon his arrival had cleared, so he could easily rent somewhere short-term to avoid his previous clients harassing him...

But, as he'd indicated to Lord Felthorpe, things had changed, and the most important of these changes was that there were now two people in Thistlewick Tye whom he cared about. He didn't like seeing his cousin so miserable and he was fighting building feelings for Maude. They made no sense but they were there, smouldering beneath his skin, nonetheless. Added to this, and despite spending his life playing others for fools, he knew someone in the village was jerking at his strings. There was a puppet master out there, manipulating him, and Edward was determined to flush them out.

'I don't think old Dr Appleby will last much longer,' his cousin said, as Edward sat down later to a luncheon of bread and soup. 'He's contracted this damn influenza that's doing the rounds and may even have passed in the night. Mrs Drayton said his son has engaged Miss Cleyford to nurse him so he can continue with his practice, but his father has been approaching the shadow of the grave for a good many months. One nasty illness was always going to see him off...'

At first, Edward let his cousin's meaningless chatter wash over him, pleased that they'd reached an understanding, but as Mrs Drayton placed a steaming bowl of beef broth in front of him, he suddenly realised the implications of Barnabas's words. If there was likely to be another death in Thistlewick Tye, then it was possible a further possession would follow. And then he considered the weather of the previous night – driving rain. He suspected no one had jumped into Silas's body because no new bones had fallen from the cliffs, but such horrendous weather could easily have dislodged more soil overnight. He wasn't even sure how it worked. Did the entire body have to be exposed for the soul to be free? Or just the skull? And how could he ever establish this, when everything fell in such a jumble that he couldn't possibly know which bone belonged to which body? Regardless, he needed to get over to the doctor's house and check that another spirit was not about to cause mayhem.

He pushed back his chair and swept out of the room without trying so much as one spoonful of soup.

'My hat, coat and cane, please,' he said to the housekeeper, as she followed him into the hallway.

'And your luncheon? You've not touched a drop. It wouldn't be wise to head out in this weather, sir,' she said. She may have cooled towards him but she still knew her duty. 'Whatever's got you all of a tither can surely wait?'

'It's imperative I call on old Dr Appleby before he passes away. I need his help.'

He very much doubted the muddled elderly man would remember anything of the circus, but it wasn't the doctor he wanted to see. He was anxious to confront whoever found themselves in the body of a recently deceased septuagenarian and prevent any violent reactions. Miss Cleyford had struck him as a nice woman, alerting him to the circus visit and the contents of Jacob's barn, and he didn't want her to be attacked by a vengeful spirit.

He wrapped a thick woollen muffler around his neck and started to stride down Copperpenny Lane, noticing that the fog was lying in patches. When he reached the common, where the ground was higher, it had cleared out slightly, although the view ahead was still beclouded.

There was a shout to his left and he heard Jacob call for Banjo, quickly spotting the mischievous hound running about madly in a circle, with a small stick in his mouth. As soon as he realised there was someone new to play with, he bounded over and dropped his prize at Edward's feet.

'Damn dog got out again,' Jacob said, wheezing as he approached. Banjo yapped at the pair of them. 'He wants you to play with him, and clearly doesn't mind that you're a wrong 'un, claiming to be a spiritualist when you're nothing of the sort...'

The dog looked up at Edward expectantly, mouth open and tail wagging, so he tossed the stick a few yards. Banjo promptly retrieved it but dropped it at the feet of his master this time, as Jacob bent to pat his head.

'Reckon this fog is only going to get worse. I'd head back to Thistlewick House, if I were you. And then consider packing a bag. This village doesn't condone liars.'

'I don't care what you think of me, but I do care that, whatever I might have believed about the existence of spirits when I first arrived in Thistlewick Tye, villagers are being possessed. I may have peddled a trade in contacting the dead when I have no such gift, but I can assure you these displaced souls are real and they're killing innocent people.'

'Rubbish.' He threw the stick for Banjo again.

'You may not be aware that when Mrs Shaw was ill, she asked for a woman called Zella. Or that Noah, before he ran off, claimed he was Samson Ballard, a circus owner from several decades ago. I now have every reason to believe these are names from a troupe that disappeared in the winter of 1855. And, as their bones fall from the cliffs – bones you failed to report to the constable, may I add – the dead are rising. You do realise that when the old doctor passes away there is every possibility that he'll be possessed too?'

'Poppycock and nonsense.' But Jacob's face had turned as pale as the fog surrounding him. 'I'd leave well alone, if I were you, Blackmore.' Edward couldn't be certain if his words were a warning or a threat.

'You were living in Thistlewick at the time the circus came to town, right?' he asked. The man must be about sixty.

Jacob blinked. 'I was just a lad. About seventeen. Working for the previous Lord Felthorpe back then.' He put his hands up in a defensive manner. 'I didn't see anything.'

'I didn't ask if you did.' Edward narrowed his eyes. 'But you'd certainly have been aware of Samson's circus if it pitched up in such a small village as this.'

'Maybe, but I had nothing to do with them. And then they left.'

The fog suddenly descended and swirled about them so that Edward had to step closer to the man to see him clearly. He felt in that moment as though they were two actors on a stage, blinded by the lighting and unable to see the audience below. It was an eerie sensation.

'But they didn't leave!' He was getting agitated now because Jacob was hiding things. 'At least, not all of them. Their bodies are buried up on the clifftop, near the woods. Years of vegetation have covered the grave and it looks no different to any other part of the common now, but there must have been a time when that land was freshly dug over. A pile of disturbed soil that I can't believe no one in the village noticed.'

'They were bad people...' Jacob finally managed to reply.

'I don't doubt it. And I completely understand that the villagers were frightened of them then, and have every reason to be frightened of them now, but someone needs to start talking because evil things are afoot and I want to prevent anyone else being murdered.'

Jacob didn't question why Edward had nominated himself as the person to investigate.

'But what I *really* don't understand, Mr Palmer,' he said, resorting to a more formal manner of address, 'is that even if this troupe came to Thistlewick and committed the most heinous deeds, why did so many of them end up dead? There are bones still suspended in that cliff that suggest there are several more bodies up there, and yet, if it had been something like an outbreak of illness or some of the troupe had turned on their own, then surely the good, *honest* people of Thistlewick would have been upfront about this from the start. Instead, I've been fed lies about them all leaving, when they clearly didn't.' It was time to play his trump card. 'Which then begs the question, why do you have a barn full of their circus equipment, including banners advertising *Samson's Circus of Astonishing Spectacles*?'

Jacob looked rattled and started to shake his head. 'You've no business nosing about in places that don't belong to you, but since you ask, they sold their stuff before they set sail.'

'Really? And a young lad of seventeen, with no money, bought himself some souvenirs?'

Jacob's brow wrinkled in confusion. He was becoming increasingly uncomfortable with Edward's enquiries.

'It was already in the barn when I was given the Sailmaker's.'

'*Given*?'

Banjo had now picked up on the animosity between the two men and began to bark.

'I don't have to explain myself to you. Believe what you want. They were a bad lot – a *very* bad lot, and then they went. I've got no more to say. You're in no place to be asking questions. The newspapers said you're a liar. I strongly suggest that you leave this village before someone makes you.'

And with that, he launched Banjo's stick as far as he could, roughly in the direction of the pub, and strode off into the dense fog.

There was a beat of a minute or two. Suddenly Edward wasn't sure which direction he was facing, plus he had the unnerving feeling he was being watched. He spun about but there was no one there. Perhaps he was being haunted by ghosts – which would be ironic. Just because he couldn't sense them didn't mean they weren't nearby. But then, with the rapidly deteriorating weather, he couldn't see what was a murky cloud of low-lying ice crystals and what might be a spectral visitant.

It was becoming increasingly difficult to get his bearings, but he set off in what he hoped was the direction of Dr Appleby's, seeing a few dim blobs of golden light ahead. The doctor's house was on one of the small streets that edged the woods, near the schoolrooms and the church, so the hazy row of thick trunks on his right-hand side was a good sign.

Out of nowhere, there was a frightening crack and, almost simultaneously, he felt a sharp pain on the side of his head. He put his hand up to his ear and then looked at his glove to see a smear of crimson.

Had he just been shot at?

'Hey!' he called out. 'Mind what you're doing! You nearly got me.' What the hell was someone thinking, hunting in conditions like this? There was barely a beat and then a second bullet whizzed past his head and he realised the gravity of his situation. The shots were no accident and he began to run towards the woods, and away from the direction of the gunfire, hoping the trees would offer some protection.

It was alarming how thick the fog had suddenly become. One minute, it was patchy, with clear areas, and the next, he could barely see five yards ahead. Suddenly, the woods were a blur of swirling pale grey, and all he could make out were the spiky black skeletons of the trees in his immediate proximity. It was as if someone had taken a giant paintbrush to the view ahead and coated the scene in whitewash. He squinted, his eyesight poor without the added complication of the blasted weather. His panicked breaths condensed before him and he felt as though he was in a dream, surrounded by misty nothingness. He stumbled on, losing his footing on a couple of occasions, and wondered if whoever had sent the contaminated gift basket was here to finish the job. Jacob, he realised, would've had enough time to return to the pub and fetch a gun. He knew damn well that the man had a pair of rifles mounted above the fireplace.

A third shot was fired, and there was an alarming crack as a small section of the oak tree ahead splintered. He spun madly about looking for the perpetrator and trying to work out the direction of the shots, but he was completely disorientated. He ducked down to make his body smaller, now certain he was the thing being hunted, as panic flooded through his veins. With a thumping heart and a throbbing ear, he half ran, half crawled in a straight line, to cover as much ground as possible, hoping against hope that he was heading away from the shooter, and not towards either him or the edge of those lethal cliffs.

His raspy, anguished breaths in the bitterly cold air stung his lungs but he raced on, over the rough ground, as frozen puddles shattered and cracked beneath his scurrying feet. Creeping brambles tore at his coat and the scarlet dots of bright red hips and haws, the only flash of colour in this milky landscape, whizzed past his eyes. Eventually, he emerged from the trees, not sure where he was, but noticed a silver ribbon of frozen water in the ditch running alongside him. He was on some sort of track, so followed it until he saw the outline of a low house emerging from the fog.

It was Maude's cottage.

Fumbling with the gate, he yelled her name and was relieved when the low door swung open.

'Mr Blackmore? What on earth...? Oh my stars, your head is bleeding!'

'Help me?' he begged, as she stepped back to allow him entry. 'I've been shot.'

26

Edward was quickly ushered inside, relieved to find that the interior was as cosy as before. Maude turned to bolt the door but asked no questions, and pulled out the solitary kitchen chair, indicating for him to sit.

'Remove your wig and your scarf,' she instructed, in a no-nonsense voice. 'Both are matted with blood and I need to assess your wound.'

He laid them on the table beside him, suddenly extremely self-conscious of how he looked, and patted at his velvet crop of white hair. Maude gave half a smile.

'That's better. Apart from anything, the black makes you look sinister.'

'It's a look I've deliberately cultivated,' he said, his heart rate slowing now that he was inside her cottage, although the truth was he felt exposed without the wig. Even though she knew his secret, years of his father's cruel comments made him feel weak when he was Edward the Albino, and it was more important than it should have been for him to feel potent and strong in front of her. He wanted to be seen as a man, not a freak.

She tipped her head to one side. 'I go about in a hooded cloak for much the same reason, but we're friends now, are we not? Please keep your head still as I clean the wound. Although, it is becoming quite the regular occurrence – me dressing your injuries. P'rhaps I should start charging for my nursing,' she said.

Edward felt a stab of guilt that she had indeed been of service to him before. And now, here he was, bursting into her house, seeking refuge and demanding help a second time. He did as he was told and she set about dabbing a wet piece of cloth on his ear.

'The bullet's only grazed you,' she said. 'You're lucky; couple of inches to the left and you'd be dead. It must have been Lord Felthorpe or one of his men – they often come for the deer in the woods. Maybe he mistook you for an animal.'

Edward shook his head. 'This was no mistake. I was followed long before that. And I shouted out after the first shot to alert them to my presence. Whoever was holding that gun was deliberately aiming for me a second and third time. As I told you on my last visit, I'm a target because I'm investigating the circus. Someone wants me silenced.'

Jacob Palmer had definitely been rattled back on the common, but was he rattled enough to shoot Edward in cold blood?

Maude hesitated for a moment. 'Are they going to turn up here and murder us both?' she asked, wrapping a thin strip of cotton around his head, finally tucking the loose end into the folds and pulling back to admire her handiwork.

'Unlikely. I lost them in the trees and they'll have been as disorientated as me. Besides, I'm convinced whoever's behind this wants to make it look like an accident. Like you say, if I was shot in the woods on a foggy day like this, it would be easy to assume I'd been mistaken for a deer.'

His injury now dealt with, she took the wig to the sink and carefully rinsed out the blood, setting it on an upturned milk jug to dry. She then lifted the net curtain and peered through the tiny window above it.

'I can barely see beyond the windowsill, so I don't think you're going anywhere for a while. Sit near the fire and warm yourself. I'll make us both some food.'

'I can't impose—'

'Nonsense. Like I said before, I get lonely. So long as you're happy with simple fare... I can't afford luxuries such as meat, but gathered some bladderwrack yesterday.'

He nodded. It would be sensible to wait out the dreadful weather in her cottage, if only to avoid being shot at again... and even if he had to eat seaweed.

'Aren't you worried that a gentleman spending the afternoon in your home will damage your reputation?'

She looked at him in disbelief and started to chuckle to herself.

'I assume you're making a joke at my expense, Mr Blackmore. *What* reputation? It's long been supposed that I fund my drinking with whoring, so it'd be your good name at stake, not mine.'

In turn, he snorted his response. 'And yet, I care less about people's opinion of me as the days pass. Did you not hear? I've been exposed as a fraud. Having built up a solid standing as a leading spiritualist over recent years, it's all come crumbling down because a man I claimed to have communicated with has turned up very much alive. My reputation is in tatters and the upstanding members of Thistlewick Tye have strongly suggested I leave.'

'Then you'll be returning to London?'

'Possibly, but there is little for me to return to. I'm not sure I can face a host of angry, bereaved relatives and I understand my former manservant has stolen from me. And yet, even though I'm shortly to take ownership of Thistlewick House, I'm not wanted here, either.' He shrugged. 'The vicar certainly won't welcome me in his pews. Though I'm of a mind to remain here after all, just to irk him.'

'Ah, but you'd miss the culture, fine dining and the eligible young ladies of London. We're too rural for the likes of you. I'm afraid there are no fancy gentleman's outfitters or theatres in the village.'

'Those things aren't as important as they once were,' he replied honestly, because he rather liked the bracing walks along the rugged coastline and the small community feel, away from the stench of the Thames and crowds of the city. 'It's my intention to sell Thistlewick House and use the money to buy another property somewhere I have no connections. But I'm not in the hurry I initially was and feel a duty to get to the bottom of these spirit possessions. The fact someone wants me dead just makes me more determined to do so. Only then will I sell up and be off to pastures new.'

'Don't you want to remain close to your cousin? Is there no one here you'd miss if you left?' She focused intently on clearing away the things she'd used to dress his wound, as though his answer was of no consequence.

He wanted to believe that she was fishing over their tentative friendship but that would be quite a leap. She was a married woman with a dark past, and the silly feelings he kept trying to squash were merely the result of his bachelor status, the drama of everything that had happened since his arrival and her recent kindness towards him. She was, however, despite everything, the only person in this village, aside from his cousin, that he trusted. She also made his stomach flip and his heart flutter and, did she but know it, both those things were happening to him in that instant.

He avoided her question because he suspected he *would* miss her if he left Thistlewick Tye, and that was rather a surprise for him to admit to himself after so short an acquaintance. But then, it had never taken him long to form romantic attachments, even those he'd no intention of acting upon.

'You're quite correct that I should wait out the weather, and I skipped luncheon so something to eat would be most welcome.'

'Good,' she said, spinning around to pull a small onion from the string hanging on the wall behind her. 'Then you can help me prepare it.' She smiled at his startled expression. 'Ah, you're used to calling on your manservant or summoning a maid?' she correctly guessed.

Preparing food was the preserve of women and he'd little experience of such an activity, but her look brooked no opposition and within minutes he found himself, shirtsleeves rolled to the elbows, scrubbing and then peeling a wrinkled potato and a large turnip. Maude collected grains and dried herbs from her pantry and set a kettle of water to boil from a chimney crane above the fire. She scraped some of the hot ash to one side of the hearth and fried some slivers of fat in a pan on a trivet, before adding the vegetables to brown, and transferring everything into a larger pot. She poured on some of the hot water, covered it all with a lid and then used the remaining kettle water to make a tea from some leaves he couldn't identify.

'It'll take a while to be ready, but that fog's not lifting today. Sit awhile and drink this.' She handed him a chipped mug and he brought it to his nose, smelling lemons. 'Dried sweet balm – I can rarely afford tea. Besides, the villagers are convinced I'm downing neat gin for most of the day. And yes, it's ridiculous to spend my precious pennies on liquor that I don't touch, but I've a disreputable image to uphold.'

Her eyes crinkled as she smiled and they settled together on the bench. Maude stretched out her legs to warm her toes. For someone used to a fine Darjeeling or an Earl Grey, Edward was surprised how pleasant the drink was. The faint citrus smell was refreshing. Their enforced domesticity had distracted him from the threat to his life, and the panic of earlier was slowly seeping from his body, despite the unsettling sensation every time she'd brushed past him in the confined space.

'Shall we play a hand of cards whilst we wait for our meal?' he suggested.

'Is that how you spend your time when you await the food your staff have prepared?' She was teasing again. 'I'm afraid I've chores to complete as soon as I've drunk this. I've socks badly in need of darning and a floor to sweep. And that doesn't include the jobs I can't contemplate in this weather, like chopping wood, drawing water from the well on the common or foraging for food.'

She really had turned her life around and was completely self-sufficient. If only the people in the village knew the truth. He looked about him at her homely and ordered interior, in complete contrast to the exterior. She'd cleverly not tended to any part of the house or gardens that would draw suspicion, wanting everyone to believe she remained the abusive threat she'd been four years ago so that they'd leave her alone. Her simple life was surprisingly appealing. Such isolation from society at large had always appealed to him, but he'd hitherto assumed he would need a degree of wealth to take the edge off his loneliness. Perhaps this level of self-sufficiency, however, would keep his mind and his body active, and bring its own rewards. It was certainly a new way of looking at things.

'If you've a mind to be useful, you can help me replace the rotten floorboards upstairs. I have some tools left by my husband, and managed to oil a rusty saw and cut some planks to size from wood washed up from a shipwreck last winter. But I don't have the strength to pry up the damaged boards.'

'I've never so much as held a hammer in my life.' She looked disappointed and he felt somehow inadequate. 'But, if you direct me, I can try.'

They mounted the steep, curved stairs in the back corner of the room and entered a dim attic space. Edward could see she'd set up two low stools as trestles and cut mismatched lengths of reclaimed wood to the correct lengths. There was a rusty chisel on the floor, which she picked up and handed to him, and he slid the blade into the gap at one end of the first rotten board and pulled. But he was strong and the board was weak, so the spongy pine crumbled almost immediately, sending him flying backwards into Maude. They both tumbled to the floor, Edward landing on his bottom between her legs, and his head falling against her soft stomach. He looked up as she looked down and, after a beat, they both burst into laughter.

Despite the poor light, they worked efficiently together. As each board was removed, she sawed it into short lengths and took the pieces downstairs to stack by the fire. He nailed the new planks into place, quickly learning from her how to hold the hammer and reduce the risk of injury because, she joked, she was running out of petticoats to turn into bandages.

They returned downstairs nearly two hours later to eat the food they'd prepared – the light from the day now all but gone, but the stubborn fog still smothering everything outside.

The stew was only of vegetables, grains, seaweed and a little bit of meat fat, and yet he honestly thought it was one of the best meals he'd ever tasted. She'd worked magic with the herbs, and the fact that he'd contributed to its creation, combined with his weariness from the hard, physical work, made him appreciate it all the more.

'I must pay you for the food,' he said, realising that he'd probably eaten her rations for the next three days without thinking. 'Despite the betrayal of my servants and collapse of my reputation, I'll shortly be far wealthier than when I arrived, and certainly far wealthier than you. I've abused your hospitality and must give you something for your trouble.' He had some shillings in his pocket and placed them on the table between them.

'I can't be bought with coins.' Maude's mood turned in a heartbeat. She looked most alarmed and he wondered if she suspected he was trying to secure other, as yet undisclosed, favours.

'No, you misunderstand. I'd pay for a meal in a coaching inn, and I'd like to pay for the meal you've so kindly provided today. Besides, I have money and you don't.'

'Thank you, but no. I don't need your charity and won't be beholden to any man.'

He was impressed with her desire for independence but she was cutting off her nose to spite her face. 'And yet, surely charity is what you have bestowed on me these past two occasions.'

'That's different,' she huffed. 'You know I expected nothing in return.'

'Apart from the removal of your floorboards,' he teased.

'Then we're even,' she said, and he nodded his agreement. 'Will Mr Shaw be worried about you in this weather?' she asked, as he scraped the tin spoon around the chipped earthenware bowl to collect up every last drop of the stew.

He shrugged. 'Both he and Mrs Drayton thought I was foolish to come out in such terrible fog, but I was anxious to speak to Dr Appleby's father. As soon as it's safe to do so, I must call on him.'

They both stood and she moved to the sink to wash the bowls. As she brushed past him again, he reached for her free wrist and pulled her close, not knowing quite why he'd been so impulsive or what he would do next, but knowing that he couldn't fight the urge to hold her a moment longer. He must look ridiculous with the cotton bandage wrapped around his head, but she was paying no attention to that. She had her eyes locked on his and he felt she was looking deeper into him.

Edward could hardly focus, as a cascade of thoughts coursed around his giddy mind. He wanted nothing more in that moment than to kiss her, but it was a completely illogical desire. She had a dark past, and as she was a married woman, they'd have no future.

And yet, she hadn't pulled away, even though there was an unmistakable hesitation on her part. Was his albinism the issue? The immorality of her situation?

'I like you, Edward—'

'But you're married. I understand. I'm sorry, I wasn't thinking.' He dropped her wrist and put his hands to his shorn head, running his fingers through the velvety crop. What the hell was going on? Because there was definitely something weird floating around the tiny space between them.

She looked at him for a long time and he couldn't quite understand her distracted expression. It was as though she was turning something over in her mind. She put the bowls on the tiny wooden draining board and turned back to face him.

'There's something I need you to see. I haven't been entirely honest with you. Please try to understand that I've been so very frightened... so very alone, and I didn't know who I could trust.'

She squeezed past him and walked over to an ancient blanket

box that stood by the far wall and lifted the heavy lid. When she turned back to face him, she was cradling a pale skull in her hands, her expression anxious. It took Edward a moment to realise that there was something strange about it, because the surface was covered with bony deposits, like tiny half-eggs, and there was something odd about the teeth.

'Is this one from the cliffs?'

She nodded and he noticed how she bit at her bottom lip, as though she was in trouble.

'Did it fall recently? Will you bury it with the others?'

'No, this was exposed four years ago when a violent storm swept across Norfolk. It fell to the sand, along with the rest of what remained of Mallory Hornchurch, a young woman of twenty-nine who was part of *Samson's Circus of Astonishing Spectacles*. She was also buried up on the clifftop forty years ago, but much closer to the edge. This skull, Edward, is mine...'

27

Edward stared, open-mouthed, as Maude waited for him to respond. He felt almost physically winded by her announcement, and couldn't pull his eyes away from the obvious deformities.

The skull was hers?

She was one of them?

'You were…' He couldn't find the right words. 'An oddity? A freak? Part of Samson's circus?'

He couldn't hide his surprise. It was the moment he realised she was as much of an outcast as him, and wondered if it explained the pull he'd long felt towards her. Even when he thought her a violent drunkard, he'd struggled to reconcile her reputation with her behaviour. But he'd not once guessed the truth – she was one of the circus troupe and her spirit was trapped in Maude's body. The shock was written across his face, even though he quickly adjusted his expression, but she'd seen it, and she stared at him with narrowed eyes, mistaking his reaction for disgust.

Her nostrils flared, and he heard the snort that followed, as she placed the skull gently on the small pine table.

'I prefer to think of myself as a *lusus naturae* – a whim of nature. A little game she played and I was the result. My whole body was covered in unsightly lumps and it made me a thing to be stared at and pitied. So, yes, I'm a freak, although Samson was kinder than you, billing those of us who were different as marvels, wonders... I'd hoped for your support and understanding, Edward, not your ridicule.'

His already pale face drained of the last vestiges of colour, but he hurriedly tried to explain himself.

'I'm not passing judgement. You've got this all wrong. Are you forgetting my affliction? I could easily have found myself as a sideshow, especially had I been born into poverty. Barnum always had albinos on his books – Unzie, the Aboriginal Albino, and the Martin Sisters – and I'm painfully aware that those with my condition are exploited, even now. But I chose another life for myself. I chose to conceal my albinism.'

'How delightful to have the choice,' she said, and he felt bad for his thoughtless comment. 'Proving our situations are very different. People turned away from me in disgust, but when I saw you for who you truly were, I thought you were one of the most beautiful creatures I'd ever seen. You look like an angel.'

His stomach constricted at the unexpected compliment but he was confused. Reading women could be tricky. What they said and what they meant were often at odds. He'd believed she'd pulled away from him because she found his albinism unattractive. That she could be friends with him but never anything more intimate. But perhaps it was *her* secrets that had kept her at bay. Did she feel something for him beyond friendship?

He also realised that he couldn't respond in kind and say he found her beautiful, too, because she'd just admitted the face he was becoming so fond of wasn't hers at all. And, even worse, that she'd suffered from a deformity that had made her a thing to be mocked. Was it a trap? One never knew with women.

'I'm no angel.' He didn't know what else to say.

Turning to the hearth, he tried to work out the consequences of her admission. Maude was not Maude at all, but someone who'd passed away forty years ago. All this time, whilst he'd been investigating the bodies and trying to work out if spirits really existed, she'd known the truth. Recalling how he'd postulated and speculated, he felt a building irritation. She could have saved him so much time by being honest but instead she'd lied to him. Or, at the very least, kept this vital truth to herself.

He spun back to face her.

'Here I am, desperately trying to understand what happened when the circus came to Thistlewick and prevent more murders, and now you tell me that *you were there*?' He was frustrated by her deception. 'I told you my secret and you still kept this from me?'

She slammed her fist down on the table, angry now.

'You didn't choose to tell me; I found out when you fell. Besides, how dare you judge my actions. You've no idea how alone and frightened I've been these past four years. I trusted no one until you entered my life but perhaps doing so was a mistake. Even now, I struggle with how you make your living – defrauding the bereaved. I heard the villagers talking about the scandal with Lady Temple as I queued for my flour.'

She walked over to the fireplace, scowling, but he wasn't having that. He'd carried enough guilt in his life and didn't need her adding to it. He'd long believed he'd let down the living, but if Maude was part of this missing troupe, was it also possible that he'd let down the dead?

'How dare *you* judge me,' he snapped. 'Don't you understand how lonely *I've* been for the past thirty-six years? My mother died in childbirth, my father couldn't bring himself to love a freak and my cousin betrayed me. I've never dared take a wife, for fear of her either rejecting me, or of passing on my condition to my children, and so made my living the only way I knew how.'

They stared at each other for several moments, both furious, but her anger subsided first.

'I'm sorry for that. I don't think either of us have had an easy life, but the circus was like family to me, which makes their horrific murder even harder to accept.'

'*You knew they'd been murdered?*' he shouted, his anger boiling up again. He'd started to suspect this was the case, but now she was standing here confirming it. 'For God's sake, woman, you've got some serious explaining to do.'

She sighed and her defiant posture slumped. 'I agree, and if you calm down, I'll tell you *exactly* what happened.'

She gestured to the bench and he nodded, but knew he still had the biggest frown across his face. He wasn't prepared to make this easy for her. She seemed to understand his annoyance and slid to the floor, her back resting against the seat, as though by being at his feet she was best placed to offer up her confession. He was the priest; she was the penitent sinner.

The fire cracked and spat, and the bitter smoke circled in the air around them. As he kneaded at his temples with frustrated fingers, she started to tell her story in a low, unhurried voice – not the one she'd peddled about being married, spiralling into alcoholism and abusing her husband – but the story of Mallory Hornchurch, the Toad Girl, and one of the sideshows in *Samson's Circus of Astonishing Spectacles*.

28

THISTLEWICK TYE, NOVEMBER 1855

Mallory wasn't normally allowed in the covered waggon. It was for the Ballard family only; Samson, his Russian wife Katerina and their two daughters. Well, Esfir was actually their grand-daughter but to the outside world the child was Katerina's. But, in many ways, the circus was Mallory's family now, because she'd learned that family could be chosen and need not be blood, and was especially thankful that this was the case because her real father had never wanted her.

Gathering up the laundry she'd come in search of, she ducked her head under the small baskets, blackened pots and bunches of dried herbs hanging from the bowed ceiling. It was a cramped and cluttered space, but homely, with brass lanterns on the wall and two beds, one above the other, at the far end. Far more comfortable than the bedrolls of wool and straw that most of them slept on in the large communal tent.

She suddenly knew she was being watched and thought at first that it might be Zella, returned from the village, because at three, Esfir was too little to see up into the waggon through the open door. But as she turned, drawing her cloak further over her face, she saw a young, fair-haired girl peering in, and the Ballard women were all dark, with hair like liquorice and eyes to match. The child darted away as soon as Mallory approached the steps and ran into the bushes, believing herself better concealed than she actually was – almost quivering behind the bare stems of the hawthorn. She wasn't part of the troupe so she must be a local girl. And locals creeping around the camp was never a good thing.

'What do you want?' Mallory shouted, keeping her face covered. 'Come to nose? Steal stuff? Or just have a jolly good laugh?'

Ashamed at having been caught spying, the small figure stood up and took a few steps towards her. The child was brave, she acknowledged, but then had it been Samson stepping down from the waggon and confronting her, the girl would have run for the hills. He was over six feet tall, with a shaved head but the bushiest mahogany-coloured beard, and muscles that made him nearly as broad as he was high. A giant of a man, he wore a permanently fierce expression, enough to scare anyone, although the truth was, he always looked intimidating, even when he was happy.

'Mother said there were travelling performers camped up near the cliffs.' The young girl, who Mallory guessed was about nine or ten, had her head bowed, as though she were standing before a schoolteacher or a priest. Her voice dropped to a reverent whisper. 'I heard her talking to our neighbour about how you were circus people: acrobats, jugglers and fortune tellers. I've read about such in the penny chapbooks she buys from the pedlars. I wanted to know if you were going to perform, and wondered if you had an elephant because I've never seen one. I was... I was curious.'

Mallory's tone softened. This girl wasn't here to tease or

gawp. She simply had an enquiring mind and a desire to experience things outside her undoubtedly narrow village life.

'No elephants, I'm afraid, and we don't put on shows in the wintertime. Our horses are exhausted and we're here to rest, practise our acts and get everything in order for next spring, when we'll be on the road again.'

They were a ragtag bunch – the assorted performers and hangers-on at *Samson's Circus of Astonishing Spectacles*. They numbered nearly thirty in the summer months but many of these were casual labour – men employed to help erect the tents, rustle up trade and look after the animals. They were only half that number now.

Possibly encouraged that the cloaked woman hadn't shouted at her, the girl took a few steps closer.

'We usually stop in November and start performing again at Easter, when the roads are easier to travel on,' Mallory continued. 'It's tough going for the poor horses this time of year. We'll only be here for a little while, but there's much to be done. Samson, the owner, has a head full of ideas for new acts he wants to try out, the women will be busy mending and sewing the costumes, and the hands must make repairs to our equipment and give the waggons a lick of paint.'

To be truthful, Mallory wasn't sure why they'd travelled up to the barren coastal village of Thistlewick Tye at all. It seemed an unnecessary detour to her. They could easily have remained in Oxfordshire, where they'd performed their final shows of the season. But she'd overheard Katerina and Samson arguing about money, and it was implied that Thistlewick Tye might offer a solution to their current financial predicament. So, the waggons had been loaded and the arduous journey undertaken. Perhaps, she speculated, they were chasing a new act, but had asked no questions, fearful that she was the act they were replacing.

They'd camped a fair distance back from the cliffs but the other side of the common to most of the village, overlooking the endless sands of the Norfolk beaches. Out the way of the locals but close enough to make use of their amenities and buy provisions. From what Zella had told her after scouting around that morning, it was somewhat of a backward place, and their arrival had led to the usual mix of curiosity and fear. Both, she understood completely.

'You won't be putting on any shows for us?' The young girl sounded bitterly disappointed. 'I shan't get to see galloping white horses and young men walking across tightropes?'

'In *Samson's Circus of Astonishing Spectacles* the tightrope walker is a young woman. Zella is our acrobat and only seventeen years of age. Here...' She pointed to the side of the waggon where a couple of their handbills had been pasted to the wooden boards. The information was out of date now as they'd lost their juggler – a double blow as he'd also played the fiddle and been the musical accompaniment to many of the acts. Next season, Samson hoped to acquire a clown, complaining the show needed more laughs.

The girl peered up to read the information. It was printed in a bold scarlet because Katerina insisted the extra cost of red ink would make it stand out – which it did. The large, fancy block lettering was surrounded by smaller engravings of some of the acts. The dramatic language was also Katerina; words such as 'astonishing', 'Herculean' and 'Daredevil'. Mallory had long been suspicious that the enigmatic fortune teller was not Russian at all but instead a well-educated English speaker. To be fair, she looked the part, with her dark colouring, kohl-lined eyes and flowing headscarves. She used words such as *da* and *nyet*, occasionally came out with the odd Russian expression and had a thick foreign accent, but

Mallory had never heard her speak fluently in her alleged native tongue.

The young girl began to read the words aloud, her eyes wide with unconcealed awe.

Samson's Circus of Astonishing Spectacles

Gasp as Samson the Herculean strongman lifts a woman with each hand and bends iron bars!

Watch aghast as the Daredevil Zella walks the tightrope!

Laugh at Rag Doll Sally – the elastic contortionist!

Witness the enigmatic Serpent Master, Hazibub, charm the deadly cobra and swallow fire!

Dare to have your destiny revealed by the mystical Russian Madame Katerina!

Be astounded by the knife juggler, stilt walker, dazzling equestrian displays!

And gaze upon our Living Wonders:

Giraffe Woman, Little Cupid and the Toad Girl!

Admission 6d

'And you?' she asked. 'What do you do in the circus? Do you swallow fire? Balance on the horses?'

Mallory tugged at her hood and let it fall to her shoulders, exposing the disfiguring lumps across her face.

'I'm the Toad Girl.' She shrugged.

Mallory had been quite like other children until her early adolescence when these unsightly bumps started to appear. Admittedly, her teeth had always been rather peculiar, with an extra row behind those that people could see. And, in recent years, she'd become painfully thin, finding blood when she used the pot. The tumours, which were only apparent on the outside, were, she'd long suspected, also growing on the inside.

She wouldn't make old bones. But, strangely, with the appearance of the lumps had come a life that she'd not trade for one three times as long without them.

Mallory Hornchurch was the only daughter of a Derbyshire coal miner who'd desperately wished for a son. She was already a disappointment when her sex was announced by the midwife, and even more so when her mother passed away two days later. It had all somehow justified her father's naming of the small, wailing infant twenty-nine years ago, for Mallory meant ill-omened and unfortunate, and to him she was both those things.

He'd never loved her but he'd never been cruel – possibly because he was rarely home to administer frustrated blows or lash out with hurtful words. They shared a small end-of-terrace stone cottage with her paternal grandmother, where the two women did piecework for the textile industry – embroidering small flowers on bonnets, dresses and linens – whilst her father worked long hours in the mines. One summer, the circus came to town and he'd had the idea that his unfortunate burden of a daughter might be at once both off his hands and fare better in a place where she wasn't the only oddity. Perhaps there was some kindness in his actions – Mallory chose to think so. They'd very little money and she was becoming increasingly lonely, with people giving her a wide berth as the growths started to proliferate.

Gazing into the speckled glass of her hand mirror at nineteen, she accepted that she'd never marry. What did life hold for her? And then a pinch-faced Katerina Ballard had been invited to their tiny cottage and given her father the princely sum of twenty pounds to take his daughter on the road with them. She promised the girl would be clothed, fed and experience the most incredible sights outside her small life in the outskirts of Chesterfield.

Given the choice between her continued isolation and the opportunity to be a cog, however inconsequential, in a machine that drew crowds, made people gasp and laugh, and received rapturous rounds of applause – the decision was not so difficult, after all.

Her father didn't kiss her the day she left and she made no promises to correspond – her literacy was basic and his was non-existent, so there was no point. And the last ten years had indeed been filled with wonder and adventure, even though her life was far from easy.

So, she absolutely understood the curiosity of the young girl sneaking about the waggon.

The child hadn't flinched when Mallory dropped her hood. Instead, with the innocent and wondrous way that children look at the world, she pulled up her skirts and rolled down her left stocking to show a frightfully scarred shin.

'I spilt scalding kettle water down me last year when I tripped on the kitchen tiles.' It was as though she was playing a game of snap – one disfigurement to match another. She shrugged and then her mind flitted back to her fascination with the circus, as though they'd merely announced a shared interest in stamp collecting. 'Tell me what it's like,' she begged, pointing back to the handbill, and Mallory found her enthusiasm infectious.

'The main tent is really something when it's all set up for a performance,' Mallory said, no longer conscious of her face, and allowing the weak November sun to fall across her imperfect skin. 'It's a gigantic waterproof canvas supported by huge pine poles, anchored down with thick ropes and long iron stakes. The men'll start to put it up this afternoon when the grass has dried out a little. Inside, when we're performing, we set out rows of wooden benches that can seat nearly two hundred people. In the centre is an oval ring, where the shows take place, but we also have smaller tents for the fortune telling and the Living Wonders, like me. I'm there to be looked at and have no special talents. Although, sometimes, I help with the magic tricks and do a comedy turn. My face rather lends itself to mockery...'

'Who's Rag Doll Sally? Is she really a doll?'

Mallory smiled. 'No, she's a woman who can twist herself into the most unnatural shapes. Her husband, the stilt walker, gets her out of a tiny box and throws her about, as if she's a rag doll. It's very clever.'

'And the tightrope walker?'

'Zella. She's a marvel.' Mallory's smile stretched from ear to ear. 'The tight wire is set twenty feet off the ground and she carries a long pole as she skips across it. Sometimes she's paired with Cupid – he's a dwarf and shoots targets with a bow and arrow, including firing at a red silk heart held aloft by her as she walks across the sky with a rose between her teeth. And when all the torches are lit, the flickering light makes the whole space feel magical.'

It was one of Mallory's jobs to make the tiny heart-shaped cushions and stuff them with horsehair or straw – a task that would fill the long winter evenings ahead. She also made the artificial roses from starched fabric and wire, and knew she was valued as much for her sewing skills as her bizarre looks.

'And if she should fall?'

Mallory shrugged. It wasn't something she wanted to contemplate. 'I guess the danger adds to the thrill of it all. Everyone is fully aware it's a possibility. The Caley sisters do breathtaking somersaults and flips on the backs of our trick horses, Star and Beauty, as they trot around the ring, and any slip on their part would be just as catastrophic. Katerina wants Zella to be part of their act next season, because she is uncommonly pretty and our leading light.'

Samson often watched his daughter from the sidelines – his eyes shining with pride. She was his princess, so the unexpected pregnancy had been particularly hard for him. But that was thankfully behind them now.

'I wish I could see such sights.' The girl sighed and picked at her nails. 'My life's so small. I've never travelled further than Cromer. The most exciting thing that ever happens about these parts is things washing up on the shore from a shipwreck – some barrels of honey turned up once – but no one does tricks or magic, and everywhere smells of fish.' She wrinkled up her nose and they both laughed.

'Ah, but I'd never seen the sea until I was nearly twenty. Imagine that. And you've had that pleasure all your life.' Mallory looked at the child's sulky face. 'Look, how about I sneak you in the back of the big tent when they're all rehearsing one afternoon? It's not quite the same, but you'd get an idea of our performances.'

The returned smile was almost as wide as her freckled face.

'Truly?'

'Truly. But you must be silent and keep out of sight or I'll get into a great deal of trouble.'

They shook hands and arranged to meet the following day, when Mallory would show the curious little girl with the small life all the wonders of the circus in the big tent.

29

After the girl, who had belatedly introduced herself as Sarah, had scampered back home, Mallory took the gathered washing down to the stream and set about the backbreaking task of doing the laundry. Soon it would be almost impossible to dry the clothes, but the day was mild and it was gusty on top of the cliffs. She would throw the garments over some bare bushes and hope for the best. Back in September, they'd been camped near the most glorious lavender bushes and the washing had never smelled so good.

Po Po, a tiny Burmese woman with the most extraordinary, elongated neck supported on brass coils, appeared with another basket of dirty clothes on her hip. Sarah would have been astonished to come across this shy member of the troupe. Samson billed her as the Giraffe Woman and she was another of the Living Wonders. The poor soul had been stolen from her people and everything she knew many years ago, but the details of this were never discussed. Samson had acquired her from another circus but Mallory felt there was something dreadfully wrong about taking Po Po from her country and culture for the entertainment of others. And yet it was only the animals – the horses, zebras, snakes and monkeys – that were tethered and caged. Yes, they'd all signed contracts binding them to Samson, but had Po Po chosen to run, there was little anyone could realistically do about it. The truth was, as a foreigner, and a woman in a strange land, she'd be foolish to try and find her way home. The troupe knew that they were at least fed and protected by Samson. Better the devil you know.

The pair walked to the nearby stream that ran down to the sea, and worked silently but diligently, scrubbing the soiled clothes with lye soap and rubbing them against the washboard. The water was icy cold, and their hands were raw and red, but the flowing water carried away both the dirt and the soap. They then stood opposite each other and twisted the washing between them, to remove as much water as possible, before bundling it all back into the baskets and returning to the camp.

They'd only been at Thistlewick Tye for a day and it took time to make a new pitch feel homely, so everyone had been allocated tasks to help them settle in. Katerina had gone to see about buying hay and maybe some turnips for the horses, and Samson was seeking out the blacksmith to discuss a lost horseshoe. Zella and Esfir had been sent by their mother to the grocer's to buy vegetables and the Caley sisters had been given directions to the dairy to collect fresh milk and butter. A small group of their men were trying their luck at the village public house – the Sailmaker's Arms. The final leg of their journey from Bury St Edmunds had been arduous, and even Katerina acknowledged the stable hands needed to let off steam. Getting drunk and fighting with the locals was the usual way they went about it.

Only Mallory, Little Cupid and Po Po remained at the camp. They were the Living Wonders, the freaks, the oddities. And, as Katerina constantly reminded them, if people were prepared to pay for the privilege of seeing them up close, they shouldn't be minded to provide a free show beforehand.

Cupid's real name, if it had ever been known, was long forgotten. He'd been with Samson for well over a decade, a year or two longer than Mallory, and was selling cheap trinkets on the streets of London when the Ballards found him. He had wide blue eyes and a cherubic look about him, but in reality was miserable and foul-tempered unless he had an audience to impress. He was also a rotten drunk.

Po Po was equally melancholy, often sitting cross-legged in dark corners, consulting chicken bones that she threw before her onto the ground. Mallory hoped it gave her the answers to the questions she was asking, but she spoke little and never smiled. Harry, the coarse-spoken ruffian in charge of the animals, had laid unofficial claim to the woman, and she didn't seem to mind, possibly because she didn't understand all the unpleasant things he was saying as he did the deed. The canvas wasn't soundproof, and there were often occasions when everyone was too intoxicated to care, including Po Po herself. Sometimes he didn't even give her the dignity of taking her out of view of the others. Everyone knew what they were doing, but then the sexual freedoms of the troupe were part of their lifestyle. Zella and Mallory were the two exceptions, both of whom Katerina guarded fiercely. The Ballards' precious daughter attracted men wherever she went but her pregnancy had cost the company dear. The men generally avoided Mallory, however, possibly because they couldn't be sure that her lesions weren't contagious.

But then, they all had their vices and did what they needed to do in order to greet the sun every morning and plaster smiles across their faces for the paying audiences. It was a different life to that which most people lived, Mallory acknowledged. One seen as debaucherous and wicked by others. But everyone who belonged to *Samson's Circus of Astonishing Spectacles* felt like an outcast for one reason or another, and were treated as such everywhere they went, so why should they follow the rules and religions of the people who chose to mock them and treat them as though they were nothing?

Mallory began to throw the laundry over the bushes as Po Po scurried off with the empty baskets. There was the rumble of hooves from behind and she turned to see a young man on a noble-looking bay hunter approaching, with a liver-and-white pointer trailing along behind. The rider was in a smart red coat and his horse was outfitted in the finest tack. Instinctively, she pulled her hood back over her head.

'You part of this damn circus?' he asked, pulling on the reins as he came to a halt. His thick black hair was parted at one side and he sported neatly trimmed side whiskers.

Mallory dipped her head, to shield her shame even more, but said nothing as the dog caught the scent of something and ran off.

'Captain!' the man called but the dog didn't react. Getting no response and clearly not really caring what his hound was up to, he returned his focus to Mallory.

'How long are you intending to camp here? Not for the whole damn winter, I trust? I don't want your sort causing trouble. My father owns most of the land hereabouts and we respect the countryside. I can already see your rubbish piling up.'

She finally found her voice. 'Just a couple of weeks, I believe.'

The quarrel that she'd inadvertently overheard between Samson and Katerina confirmed this wasn't to be long term, and they'd be gone before Christmas. He was keen to return to London, but his wife insisted she could pick up a sizeable sum of money here. In response, Mallory had heard him shout, '*Radi*

Boga!' – one of Katerina's familiar curses, as his use of her language was only ever in exasperation.

'We need to rest the horses and repair some of our equipment, but we'll be on our way shortly.'

The gentleman nodded just as his dog wandered back with a long-handled wooden spoon in its mouth.

'That belongs to us.' She pointed at the spoon.

'Then you shouldn't leave it lying about on common ground where Captain can find it.'

He tugged at the reins again to turn the horse about, but as he did so, they both spotted Zella returning with a basket of vegetables. Esfir was clinging to her skirts and chattering away – at that age when she demanded answers to everything. Why didn't the sun fall out the sky? What happens when you die? Why aren't people very nice to us?

Mallory knew it had been hard for her friend to relinquish the role of mother, but had instead focused on being the best big sister she could be. It was the bargain she'd struck with her mother after having Esfir at just fourteen. The lad concerned had been her age and she'd believed herself in love, but the circus had moved on, and her parents had assumed parental responsibility – partly to avoid a scandal, but partly because Katerina was better placed to bring up the child.

The man paused, as men often did when they saw Zella. If he was enchanted by her appearance in her long cotton dress, hair loose and pale cheeks flushed by the strong sea breeze whipping across the common, then he'd be utterly bewitched by the sight of her in her fleshings, fitted close to her slender body, under a highly decorated bodice embellished with sequins, glass beads and silver threads, as she gracefully swept across the rope, twenty feet in the air.

'More of your kind,' he said, with feigned distaste, but there was not one person on the planet who wouldn't be captivated by the sight of such a beauty, skipping through the damp grass, head to the heavens as she laughed at something the small child beside her had said.

'They're sisters,' Mallory said. 'Zella is our high-wire performer. You should see her when—'

But the man had encouraged his horse to trot towards the two girls, leaving Mallory talking to herself.

With her hood still screening most of her face, and returning to the task of hanging laundry, she observed them talking. She envied Zella's confidence, as she stood defiantly with one hip jutting forward, twirling her hair around her fingers and jutting her chin up towards the stranger. Her friend knew the power she had over men and used it to full advantage. He slid from the horse, towering over the two girls, and his body language changed subtly the longer Mallory watched. Initially, aggressive and confrontational, he was soon nodding and smiling – his whole body more relaxed.

Because that was Zella's vice – the attention of young men was like a drug to her and, despite the result of her previous folly tugging at her skirts demanding attention, the young woman revelled in it. It had been her undoing once before, and with a strange lurching in her stomach, Mallory wondered if it would prove to be the case a second time.

That evening, with the big tent now up and everyone exhausted, the troupe sat together around a small fire, where a piglet was roasting on a hastily made spit. The animal had been acquired somewhat dubiously during the afternoon but Katerina, who laid down the moral law the troupe abided by, had been told Harry had purchased it from a local farmer.

Mallory welcomed the fire; she felt chilled to the bone and would happily sit in front of it for the several hours it would take the pig to cook. The delicious, slightly sweet smell of the sizzling pork fat, however, was torture when you knew you wouldn't get to bite into the crispy crackling or taste much of the moist meat.

She was pleased to currently be in relatively good health, as there were often times when the pain in her abdomen was unbearable. Samson always recommended strong liquor, whereas his wife insisted working through the discomfort would yield the best results – but then Katerina was conscious they had bills to pay and thirteen people to support through the bleak winter ahead.

The Ballards had paid for her to see a doctor when the

bleeding had been particularly bad, but the man was clearly baffled by Mallory's symptoms. He pronounced she was suffering from 'multiple anomalies' and that her growths were tumours, but could be no more specific than that, and had absolutely no idea how to treat them. And then, with no thought to Mallory's feelings, he'd gone on to express an interest in leading her autopsy to Katerina, without even considering she was in the room to hear the unpalatable discussion of what might happen to her body after her death.

He gave them poultices for what he believed were haemorrhoids, and laxatives for her constipation, but she suspected what the doctor did not – all her ailments were linked to the lumps. He recommended a bland diet of soft foods and an expensive course of bloodletting, which had resulted in no discernible improvement, especially as Mallory feared she didn't have a lot of blood to spare.

Not wanting to make a fuss, she declined Samson's offer to consult another physician and undergo further unpleasant examinations. Hazibub, their snake charmer, had a soft spot for Mallory, and occasionally and discreetly passed over preparations of opium when she was at her worst. During a particularly bad spell, late that summer, he'd taken her to one side and given her a small blue corked bottle from his locked miniature cabinet of medicines – a beautifully inlaid decorative wooden box that resembled a tiny wardrobe. If it ever got too much, he told her, the liquid within would give her a final escape from all the pain of this earth in the most pleasant way. It would be their secret and her decision. She pocketed it and thanked him by adding tiny, embroidered snakes to the edges of his cotton handkerchiefs – which he found highly amusing.

'Tomorrow we need to start repainting the waggons before the wet weather comes. Hazibub tells me we have a week before

the storms arrive.' Samson addressed his troupe as he passed a
bottle of spirits around.

'I was not meaning a storm of weather but a storm of anger,'
Hazibub piped up. 'I am telling you, many times, we must be
leaving this place. It will not end well.'

Mallory cast nervous eyes at Zella. If their mystical foreign
friend was predicting bad things, then bad things were sure to
happen. But Katerina was having none of it and she inhaled
deeply on her thin Russian cigar before commenting.

'*Nyet*. Ve leave when I say. Troubles is part of our living, but it
comes from a place of jealousy. They do not like that you and I
are free, that ve do not rise in the morning to the same view for
years and years. I am not tied to Samson vith some legal docu-
ment. I do not follow the ridiculous rules of a church that has
enough money for silver plate but not to feed its poor and dying.
I am not ashamed of my body and choose who I share it vith.
These people are trapped by their stupid rules and hate to see
those who are not.'

'But if Hazibub believes there's danger ahead—' Little Cupid
was half a bottle of cheap gin down and wriggling uncomfortably on the wooden bench, his legs sticking out in front of him.
The mystical snake charmer had something of the soothsayer
about him and had been proven right before.

'I told you all,' Katerina interrupted, 'I see good fortune in my
crystal sphere. Ve leave here vith enough money to see us
through the vinter and buy new acts for the coming year.'

The last time the troupe had encountered good fortune,
Katerina had employed blackmail – Mallory was scant on detail
but Harry said it involved threats to reveal a compromising situation that a wealthy gentleman had found himself in with one of
the Caley sisters. Everyone knew Katerina's crystal ball could no
more predict the future than Po Po's bones. She was skilled in her

craft though, able to make astute observations about the person sitting across the table from her, and offer dramatic but vague pronouncements. Overeager customers supplied the information she needed, delighted to think good things were on the horizon, and adapted her words to suit their circumstances. Her reputation spread because 'You vill be blessed before Michaelmas' could mean the arrival of a baby, a new job or recovery from an ailment. But if she was predicting good things, and Hazibub bad, then Mallory knew whom she was inclined to believe.

The Ballards had met in Liverpool, but Mallory only knew this because Samson occasionally talked about it when he'd been drinking. Apparently, Katerina had run off with a free-thinking Russian artist in her youth and lived with him for a couple of years, but it had ended badly. This was where Mallory suspected she'd picked up the odd Russian word and possibly why she pretended to be from a country she clearly didn't hail from – her dark colouring suiting her tale. But many of the troupe had secrets. You only ran away to join the circus if you had something to run from, and there was an unspoken agreement not to pry into the past of another.

Katerina was the level head behind the troupe. She harnessed Samson's wild ideas, knowing which of his grand plans were viable and which were pure folly. For a mighty man, Mallory observed that he often behaved like a child: overexcitable one minute, and with a raging temper the next. But he loved the woman he called his wife, and he loved his circus, in equal measure.

'We're going to teach Beauty to remove my hat, scarf and mittens,' the oldest Caley girl announced, changing the subject and feeding scraps to the small capuchin monkey sitting on her shoulder. The sisters, close enough in age to be passed off as twins in their act, had grown up around horses and had an affinity with them, speaking their language almost as well as their own.

'In this weather, you'd be better off teaching him to put them on,' Little Cupid joked. 'In fact, try training the stupid beast to steal some for us.'

'This is not a place I vant headaches with the locals,' Katerina said. 'Just two weeks I ask you to stay out of troubles and then ve can be on our vay. Scraps outside the taverns are harmless but you *must not* get involved with the peoples,' she warned.

Mallory knew that even Katerina would find ways around the law when the needs of the troupe depended on it, but she didn't countenance outright theft. Harry, however, had no such scruples. All eyes met across the piglet but no one spoke.

'There was a smart gentleman on a horse at the camp this morning,' Mallory said. 'He asked me how long we were staying but talked much longer to Zella.'

Katerina choked on her cigar and turned to her daughter. 'I have told you about this, Zella,' she snapped. 'The men are only after one thing. Do not let them have it.'

The young tightrope artist glared at Mallory, who immediately dipped her eyes. She hadn't intended to cause trouble for her friend.

There was a sudden thundering of feet and Samson jumped up from the bench, grabbing one end of the strong greenwood hazel branch they were using for the spit. Hazibub immediately grabbed the other, and they whisked the pig out of sight. Within seconds, the three hands, led by Harry, came running to the fire, chased by a couple of locals. They'd clearly been fighting, as the start of a shiner was visible on Harry's left cheek, and one of the village lads had bleeding knuckles and a fired-up look about him.

'Where's the piglet, you thieving bastards?' The accuser was perhaps twenty, with a square head and wide nose.

'What pig?' Zella said, her wide eyes full of innocence.

'I won't have no one taking stuff from Lord Felthorpe,' the man shouted, shoving Harry to the side and approaching the fire. 'I can damn well smell it. Late litter. Nine there this morning and only eight in the pen now. We know it was you. There's always upsets when your sort pass through. Like the fucking gypsies. Nothing but thieves, cheats and whores.'

Mallory felt uncomfortable because she knew the piglet had been stolen and, although she didn't like the words used or the tone, all of those descriptions could apply to her friends. She tried to skirt behind the bench and make her way to the big tent.

'What the fuck is *that*?' A gap-toothed adolescent pointed directly at her.

'Not the missing pig but she's certainly pig-ugly.' The older lad roared at his rather pathetic joke. Mallory felt the twist of humiliation, even though she'd endured a lifetime of name-calling. But he was in his element and looking closely at the faces of the circus troupe in the flickering firelight for someone else to ridicule.

'And here, some foreign woman with her head balanced on a pile of gold rings. Look, a flea-infested monkey. And bugger me if it ain't General Tom Thumb,' he said. 'Jesus, I ain't never seen so many freaks.'

It was the wrong thing to say to Little Cupid. Jealousy was a difficult shadow to step from because he'd constantly bemoaned the unparalleled success of Charles Stratton, a person of similar stature, who was known to the world as General Tom Thumb. He was Phineas Barnum's star act and had even toured Europe, earning more money than Cupid could dream of, performing for the likes of Napoleon III and German nobility. It had played no small part in Cupid's downward spiral from enjoying a drink with the rest of them, to pitiful alcoholic over the intervening years, and it broke Mallory's heart to see.

Cupid threw his empty gin bottle to the floor, where it smashed upon impact, and wriggled from the bench. The young lad smiled, amused by the thought of the tiny man taking him on in some foolhardy show of might, when Samson strode out of the big tent with a loaded shotgun in his hands. That was the thing about this troupe; if you picked on one, then you'd better be prepared to take on them all. Yes, they bickered amongst themselves, but when an outsider attacked, they banded together like family.

'I don't want trouble but I'm telling you we don't have your pig and you can bloody show my people a bit more respect.'

He walked over to the most vocal of the men and squared up to him, as the younger lad spoke up.

'Leave it, Silas,' he said. 'He'll shoot you as soon as look at you. One little pig isn't worth getting yourself killed over.' He tugged at his friend's arm and Mallory could see the other one grinding his teeth, as he contemplated the reality of the situation. Even without the gun, Samson was an intimidating presence. Six feet three of brawn and solid muscle, and a face that she'd once heard someone say needed to be beaten handsome again.

As the local lads slunk back to the village, Katerina stood up and walked over to the hired hands, all five feet of her looking up to the three burly lads who'd thundered back to the camp from the village.

'You stole from Lord Felthorpe.' It wasn't a question. 'There will be no pork for you.' And she reached up and slapped each one of them hard across the cheek, proving, yet again, who really ran this circus.

31

The following day was colder than previously, because Jack Frost had sauntered nonchalantly through Thistlewick Tye overnight, leaving a dusting of white sugar over everything, from the spiky tree branches, to the drooping, overgrown grass beneath Mallory's feet. The circus women had been out early scouting for kindling, whilst the men slept off their sore heads and nursed the bruises and scrapes from the altercations of the night before. By midday, Katerina had roused them all and Samson had set the hands to waggon repainting and was leading a full afternoon of rehearsals, as Mallory cleared up the pots and dishes from the greasy pork and watery vegetable stew.

Mealtimes were her favourite part of the day. Her previous life had been one of piecemeal embroidery work and domestic duties and, in that regard, not much had changed. As part of the circus, she was a one-trick pony – there simply to be gawped at by those who praised the heavens that they weren't so afflicted – so she was lumbered with many of the more unpleasant jobs to keep the troupe on the road. She emptied chamber pots, washed clothes and dealt with the ailments and injuries of her fellow workers. But this was different to before. Here, people said thank you. Here, people hugged her with soft, warm arms and genuine smiles. Here, she was as odd as everyone around her and, in a strange way, her abnormalities made her fit in. And that was never more apparent than when they all sat together on the long wooden benches at trestle tables, or around a smoky campfire, to share food. The flagons of ale were passed to everyone, including the ugly girl with the face covered in strange lumps, as they celebrated their successes and rued their failures. The jokes flew thick and fast, and they were all teased; from Samson for his broken nose and impetuous decisions, to Cupid for his size and, even occasionally, if someone was feeling brave, Katerina.

That afternoon Mallory met Sarah in the copse. The young girl had slipped away from home as soon as her chores were completed and she shyly handed over a large whelk shell, announcing the Toad Girl would always be able to hear the sea now, wherever in the country she was. Mallory put it to her ear, and the whispers of the waves made her smile. What a thoughtful gift.

They chatted as they walked back to the camp and Sarah told her that, now she was ten, she no longer attended the village school but instead stayed at home providing nursing care for her elderly grandparents, so that her mother and father could work.

'Although the school was closed for a week recently after the schoolteacher became violently ill,' she said, skipping along beside her new friend. 'Mother says it was probably something he ate. Grandmother said it was divine retribution because he'd been caught gambling.'

They stepped from the trees and came up behind the tethered horses, close to the waggons that held the monkey cages. The six carthorses, even-tempered beasts and good workers, pulled the waggons, and the two beautiful grey Arabs were the equestrian act. The Caley sisters performed with, and trained, the animals but Harry and the other two lads did all the heavy work: mucking out, grooming and breaking in. Harry had worked in stables all his life but had fallen foul of the law and spent time inside, consequently losing both his job and any possibility of decent references. People he invariably antagonised, but animals seemed to like him.

'Treat 'em with kindness and they'll learn faster,' he'd always say. Cupid, on the other hand, had no patience with them. Another reason he would never rival General Tom Thumb.

Sarah petted Beauty, the gentle grey gelding who was grazing nearest to the woods.

'We're a small troupe but the horses are by far the largest portion of the show,' Mallory explained. 'Circuses started out as equestrian displays, and it's only in recent years other acts, like tumblers and clowns, have been included.'

'What sort of tricks can the horses do?' the young girl asked.

'Beauty and Star can stand on their hind feet, kneel down, roll over and even shake hands. There are two specially adapted saddles with handles and straps for the Caley girls to hold so they can do handstands and vault over them. But,' she confided, 'they're quite plain and people pay to see the extraordinary, so Zella's high wire steals the show every time.'

Sarah was only half listening, distracted by the sight of two smaller, more eye-catching beasts, huddled together further back.

'Zebras!' The young girl could hardly contain her excitement.

Samson's most recent idea had been to purchase and train up four zebras. The deal was struck without Katerina's knowledge, over a few drinks in a backstreet London tavern. It was a huge mistake. He might be the creative genius but she was the voice of reason – the sensible head. She'd been furious when he returned, because she knew more about these creatures than her husband. He hastily tried to persuade her that the stunning beasts would be an unparalleled draw.

'Imagine,' he'd said, 'the spectacle of such eye-catching animals prancing around the ring! It's never been done before.'

But zebras were almost impossible to train. They had a reputation for aggression and a strong flight instinct, and weren't even capable of carrying a rider, like a horse. Their backs weren't as sturdy and their gait was different. *There was a reason no one had done it before.* So, they'd been lumbered with the stupid things and mounting debts. Samson, the big man with the small brain, had been duped.

He'd managed to sell a pair of them to a small zoological gardens, but they still had two remaining, added to which, the miserable climate did not suit these African creatures. One, in particular, Harry didn't think would last the winter. As striking as they were, they did very little. They could be paraded through the towns as an advertisement for the circus but, despite Samson's best efforts, they were untrainable and merely visual novelties – much like Mallory herself – except a zebra was exotic and coveted, and she was not.

'Don't get too close,' she warned the young girl. 'They can be unpredictable.' As if to prove her point, the one nearest to them flattened its ears to its head and bared its teeth. 'Come see the monkeys instead. They're much friendlier.'

Checking there was no one about, she heaved Sarah on to one of the covered waggons and they crept over to the three capuchins. About two feet tall, with tails as long as their bodies, they were brown, almost black, with cream-coloured heads and shoulders. The circus had travelled up to Liverpool six summers ago to buy them, as anything and everything went through this centre of global trade. It had been a fraught trip, as, although they technically weren't married, the Ballards had all but divorced over Samson's threat to purchase an elephant.

'That little one does flips and rides the horses.' Mallory pointed at one of the monkeys. 'And this one here dances jigs and steals hats. I make tiny waistcoats for them and they look so smart.'

'Oh, look at their darling little pink faces!' Sarah was fascinated by the inquisitive creatures, with their wide eyes and nervous expressions. Samson was not always the most patient with those in his care, and Mallory often felt uncomfortable about the way he trained them – their short leashes yanked violently when they failed to perform. Harry was much kinder to the horses.

'How thrilling to live with such amazing animals,' Sarah said. 'If I was part of the circus, I'd spend all day admiring the zebras and talking to these darlings. I'm not sure I'd ever get any work done.'

'When you live with the exotic and unusual, it becomes ordinary,' Mallory pointed out. 'Not that I don't love my life but it's not all sparkles and glorious rounds of applause.'

It was degrading to have people mock her unsightly skin, especially when it was covered in umber and sienna-based greasepaints – yellow ochre around her eyes to make her look as toad-like as possible. To be pointed at in disgust and hear cruel things. As part of her act, Katerina ordered her to eat mealworms and crickets and, at first, the insects turned her stomach, but no one refused Katerina. The Ballards had spun increasingly fantastic tales about who she was and where she'd come from, and she endured the curious faces that peered at the girl who was purported to be the result of a scandalous union between a gigantic warty amphibian and a plucky female explorer who'd become separated from her party and violated by this beast. A monstrous half-breed who had been found in the jungles of the Amazon as a baby, and whose mother had died shortly after their rescue. It seemed to Mallory that the more preposterous the tale, the more the public lapped it up.

'I don't like being laughed at,' she admitted, 'and have the same feelings and emotions as everyone else. But I try to remember I'm probably more content than most of the over-worked, underpaid and unhappily married souls who pay to gawp at me. Everyone at the circus is someone I consider a friend. We're all very different but I've found that people who have something to teach you, whose experiences are different to your own, make excellent company.'

'We're different, too, aren't we?' Sarah's wide freckled face looked up at hers and Mallory had to smile, guessing where this was leading.

'We are indeed and so would make excellent friends.' She heard the chatter of the Caley girls approaching. 'Come, let's see what acts are rehearsing and give you a taste of the circus.'

32

They climbed down from the waggon and Mallory ushered Sarah under one of the heavy canvas flaps at the back of the large tent. It was used all year round, even when they weren't perform-ing, because most of the troupe slept in it, and it was where they refined their acts and sat together to eat, especially in bad weather. Currently they were using a couple of the audience benches for meals, but most of the seating stayed strapped up on the waggons over winter.

The girls crouched down behind two enormous folding screens where, during the shows, the performers prepared them-selves for their grand entrances. Mallory explained to an awestruck Sarah that Samson's earliest shows had been outside, in a ring of rope, as the trick horses performed their intricate movements and riders balanced and somersaulted on their backs. Gradually, he'd introduced other novelty acts and the show had expanded, but he'd always been at the mercy of the unpredictable British climate, and was sometimes forced to cancel shows in high winds and rainstorms. He tried hiring venues for a while, but then read about the travelling tent shows touring America and realised that canvas could be easily packed away and transported in waggons, enabling him to take the show to more rural communities who wouldn't otherwise experience such things.

Beauty was led into the tent by the oldest Caley, who began to walk him around the ring.

'The daring feats of horse and rider require skill and absolute trust,' Mallory whispered. 'Most of the training involves developing the bond between them.' They could both see the Caley girl whispering into the horse's ear and stroking him gently, before she even attempted any tricks.

In the far corner, Zella was warming up with stretches, watched by her adoring father.

'Everything's an illusion,' Mallory said, knowing that the biggest illusion of all was that the great strongman and leader of the circus was Samson, when in reality it was his tiny wife – a woman of uncertain origins but who Mallory was convinced was no more Russian than Robert the Bruce.

'Samson's real name is Simon but *Simon's Circus* doesn't quite have the same ring to it.' Both girls giggled.

'That man's so small,' Sarah said in hushed tones, pointing to where Cupid stood on an upturned wooden crate, firing arrows at a target. He was approaching thirty but no bigger than a three-year-old. Esfir, to her great delight, had overtaken him in the summer.

'If only you could see him in his costume,' Mallory whispered back. 'He has the most breathtakingly beautiful set of wings made from the foot-long flight feathers of turkeys, and wears nothing but those and a blue silk loincloth, embellished with pink and red silk flowers. He is the Roman god of love, after all.' She was too modest to admit that the embroidery was her handiwork and it was fine stitching indeed.

Sarah gasped, as Po Po appeared and began scurrying back and forth, retrieving the arrows.

'That woman has a neck of gold!'

Mallory tried not to smile at the astonishment on her face. This was exactly what they strived to do with their shows – amaze and entertain. What a shame there wasn't an opportunity for the young girl to see them perform properly. Perhaps Katerina could be persuaded to bring the circus back up to Norfolk next year. It was bleak and cold at the moment, but Mallory was desperate to walk along the glorious, wide sandy beach that she'd seen from the top of the cliffs, and could only imagine what a wonderful place that stretch of coast would be in the summer.

'It's one long brass coil which, over time, has pushed her shoulders down to give the appearance of a long neck. In her culture, it's seen as desirable.'

'She is *very* elegant,' the young girl agreed.

But like Mallory, Po Po suffered for her appearance. The rings made it hard for her to bend for long periods, or turn her head, and she had aches in her limbs and back. Hazibub had created a salve that eased the muscles, and he'd taught Mallory how to apply it, gently massaging the poor woman's shoulders. It was yet another example of how they all looked after each other.

'Sally Ferris, the contortionist, has work in the music halls with her husband over the winter, but I wish you could see her. It really is the funniest thing when she's thrown about like a rag doll. But they'll find us again in the spring and, with a couple of new acts and some more hired hands, we'll double in number.'

The girls sat together for some time, as Katerina arrived and watched her daughter being taught how to vault onto and dismount the horse. She was keen for her to be as accomplished as the Caleys, but there was no trace of a smile on her face, her tiny eyes narrowed as she barked her observations.

Out of nowhere, a large pointer ran into the tent. Mallory immediately recognised it as Captain, the gentleman's dog from the previous day. It started to bark at the strange smells and angry faces, spooking the horse by its sudden arrival. Just as Zella dismounted, Beauty reared up onto his hind legs in fright and, on his way down, caught her leg with his hoof. She cried out in pain as the Caley girl tightened the rein and calmed the horse.

'Not Zella!' Mallory exclaimed under her breath. 'Stay here,' she instructed Sarah, and scampered out from behind the screen to help her friend. Any injury in their line of work was a worry. The girl who walked the tightrope when Mallory had first joined the troupe fell and fractured her leg so badly that she could never bear weight on it again. Katerina had no room for charity and had to let her go. God only knew where the poor woman ended up.

Several people gathered around, concerned for Zella, especially as a thick patch of blood was now seeping into the fleshings where the sharp edge of its shoe had cut her calf, but Katerina reassured everyone no bones were broken.

'Captain?' The owner strode into the tent, as though the place was his, and looked about for his dog, just as Zella was helped to her feet by Hazibub and Samson. He froze as he noticed the young woman in her costume, hopping towards a bench. Mallory could see what he saw: her curves and elegance, her mystery and hypnotic allure, as the tiny glass beads and silver threads caught the daylight and made her a thing of wonder.

'Is this your goddam dog?' Samson shouted, squaring up to the interloper.

'Yes. And this is also my family's goddam land. I'm Christian

Felthorpe and my father is lord of the manor. You may have rights of common, but my dog can run whheresoever he pleases.'

'Even if he startles my beasts when they're working and causes injury to my daughter?' Samson's hands were balled into fists and his tone aggressive.

Katerina, who'd usually take control of a situation such as this, had disappeared. Mallory scanned the tent for her but there was no trace. This was odd because the calm but feisty woman was much better at defusing such situations than her husband, who everyone knew solved things with his fists rather than diplomacy.

'Yes. Even then.'

The two men stared at each other until Hazibub walked over and placed himself between them.

'I am thinking Zella will be mending. It will bruise and perhaps be scarring, but will heal.' He placed his hands together, as if in prayer, and bowed at Master Felthorpe, calming the tension.

Satisfied Zella would be all right, Mallory retreated behind the screen and ushered Sarah from the tent, worried that they'd be discovered. The pair scampered behind the waggons and ran silently into the woods. When they were out of sight of the camp, they sat together on the trunk of a fallen oak.

'I'm glad your high-wire lady is not badly injured. I wonder if I can string a line between some trees and learn how to walk a tightrope. If I could, would you let me join Samson's circus?' she asked. 'Maybe when I'm a bit older and Grandma is dead,' she added as an afterthought.

Mallory smiled. 'P'rhaps it's a good thing that you saw the accident and realise that our life is not all glamour. Horses can be dangerous, even when well trained. That's half a ton of animal that can come crashing down on you, if you're not careful. And no, I wouldn't want you to live this life. My options were limited but the whole world is open to you.'

'You're wrong,' Sarah said. 'My world is small. I've been nowhere and seen nothing, and it worries me that I'll end up like my mother, stuck here forever.'

'But Thistlewick Tye is such a lovely place. Zella said the streets are incredibly clean, the houses so neat, and I honestly don't blame those local lads for fighting with Harry and the others. We've disrupted your peace.'

'I suppose we are lucky, but the vicar is stern and I never did enjoy school much. One of the boys in my class was whipped for taking the Lord's name in vain, and although he's never dared to utter such blasphemy again, he'll have those welts on his legs always. I do understand that if you go on big adventures, bad things might happen, but I'll never travel outside Norfolk or walk across the sky in a beaded tulle skirt, and my duty to my family will keep me in this village forever.'

'It is strange how back to front our lives are,' Mallory observed. 'You're so pretty but lead such a dull life. I'm ugly and lead a life so full of colour.'

Sarah leaned forward and put her small arms about Mallory, squeezing her tight.

'I think you're beautiful,' she said. 'Especially on the inside.'

Now anxious that she'd been away from home for too long, and not wanting her mother to notice she'd disappeared, the young girl skipped back to the village, with promises to meet up again in a few days.

Mallory headed back to camp, but as she got closer, she heard voices. Slowing her steps and tucking herself behind the wide trunks of the ash and elms, she crept forward. Zella was leaning back against one of the trees, a thick woollen shawl wrapped about her body. Her injured leg was tentatively resting on the ground, as she played with the ends of her loose hair. With his back to Mallory, stood the Felthorpe heir – his dog circling his feet, and sniffing at the dusty fallen leaves and strange scents left by the woodland creatures.

'I'll make amends. My attitude towards your father was unforgivable.'

'He's just protective of me.'

'Understandably so. You're a treasure worth protecting...'

Mallory had seen this play out before. Zella was the star act, not only because of her talent, but also because she was beautiful. Even as a young girl, this meant she attracted the wrong sort of attention and Samson had occasionally been involved in fights to protect his daughter's virtue. Part of the problem was, growing up in this world, she'd never had a childhood, and both behaved and was treated as much older than her years. She'd worked long hours since she was tiny and was surrounded entirely by adults leading unconventional lives and embracing sexual freedoms she might not otherwise have been exposed to. Yet, conversely, she was kept on such a tight rein that Mallory understood her desire to rebel.

And then, at the disturbingly young age of fourteen, she'd fallen pregnant – apparent by the first weeks of sickness that Mallory had initially helped her to conceal. But it wasn't long before the swell of her stomach was visible in the skin-tight costumes she wore, and the truth came to light.

Katerina had been furious. The legal age of consent may be twelve for girls but, in reality, her daughter's age, and the fact she was unmarried, was utterly scandalous. Mallory heard the shouts and screams, and saw the scarlet cheek where Zella later confided her mother had struck her, in her fury. The beautiful high-wire girl was one of their biggest draws and so attempts were made to hide her condition with a longer skirt of stiff tulle about her gradually expanding waist. Eventually, she was dropped from the bill and kept out of sight until she'd given birth to the child. One of the benefits of their itinerant nature was that, forever on the move, the troupe simply arrived at the next town and announced that Samson and Katerina had been blessed with another daughter.

Mallory knew little about the father, or how Zella felt about the arrangement within her family, but the truth was never spoken of. The young girl had no say in Esfir's care, or Katerina's decision that the child would become an acrobat, like her biological mother. The poor thing was stretched and twisted from a young age, with the idea that she could start performing properly by the time she was five. Mallory knew Katerina had even chosen her name – as Esfir was a Russian name meaning star.

But Zella continued to revel in the attention of men, perhaps because her mother was so hard to please. There was no 'well done' or 'you look beautiful' for her daughter, or indeed anyone in the troupe. For Katerina everyone had to try harder, be better, shine brighter. Only in recent months had she eased off her criticisms towards Mallory, perhaps because it was obvious to all that she was dying.

Despite Zella's previous misjudgement, Mallory could see she was enjoying the attentions of this wealthy young man. It felt wrong to be spying on them, but she couldn't pull herself away. What was it between these two young people that had her so mesmerised?

Master Felthorpe slowly leaned towards Zella, who still had her back to the tree. Mallory could see how their eyes were locked and their bodies were mirroring. But as he got closer, she ducked under his arm and avoided the kiss, panicking at the last moment. She must know this encounter was wrong and couldn't possibly have a happy ending.

He gave an amused snort and then smiled, not put off in the slightest. The pair separated, and Zella limped back to camp, turning at the last minute to lock eyes with the young man. They both smiled, and then he whistled for his dog, who totally ignored him, and he set off in the opposite direction.

Mallory lingered a while, anxious that her friend was playing a dangerous game. It occurred to her then, as someone who had spent a lifetime longing to be beautiful and command admiration, that being cherished was not always a positive thing.

33

In return for Mallory showing Sarah something of her life, the young girl promised to share her favourite place in Thistlewick Tye with her new friend – the beach. Growing up in the land-locked county of Derbyshire, Mallory had enjoyed a lush green landscape of rolling hills and limestone peaks, dotted with pretty stone cottages. She'd seen the fast-flowing streams power the cotton mills, and occasionally travelled to the canals that trans-ported coal, pottery and textiles to and fro, but she'd not seen the sea until she was nearly twenty, when the circus her father had sold her to pitched up in Scarborough, and her love for the coast began. They'd been camped up at Thistlewick Tye for five days now and she'd ventured no further than the woods, and certainly not into the village to be mocked and ridiculed, so she was excited for this rendezvous.

'Vere are you off to?' Katerina barked, spotting her wrap a thick shawl about her thin body, as she tried to hide the worst of her face before setting off.

'To explore the shore,' she said. 'My pains are bad and I

thought walking might help. It's such an overcast day, I don't expect to meet many people.'

'Have you done your chores?'

'Yes, and Samson doesn't need me. He's rehearsing with Hazibub.'

Katerina nodded her assent and Mallory gratefully headed down to the Thistlewick Rift, as Sarah had instructed, passing only a grumbling man working on the hull of his small, careened boat, and paying her no attention.

Sarah was hidden around the bend of the cliffs, skipping about on a large cluster of flints. Mallory had only seen the beach from above, peering over the cliff edge, getting as close as she dared, but down here, the height of the land made her feel small and exposed.

'We mustn't get too near the bottom. Great chunks of land fall into the sea from time to time,' the young girl explained, after throwing her arms around Mallory's thin waist in greeting. 'Twenty years ago, the bones of a big hairy elephant were discovered and lots of serious men in smart clothes turned up to take them away and study them. Mother told me all about it.'

It was low tide and the sands seemed to go on forever – a flat landscape disappearing into the distance, as though the world had no end. She was here for the glorious smell and sense of space, but coming from her colourful world, it felt somewhat dull.

'The view of the sea is humbling, but there's little to see.'

Sarah looked at her like an admonishing parent. 'That's because you're used to big things,' she said. 'Lights and flames and jumping and sparkles. You should see the common in the summer, when the purple heads of the thistles cover the ground.'

Perhaps she was correct. As a child, Mallory had revelled in the beauty of a frost-covered spider web or watched a green tiger beetle, no bigger than her thumbnail, walk along the top of a stone wall. Had the excitement and glamour of circus life made the simple joys of nature seem mundane?

Sarah began to show her the different seaweeds floating in the shallows, and explained which ones were edible and how to use them in cooking. Mallory determined to return with a basket and collect up the bladderwrack to make their camp meals go further. Together, the girls hunted for periwinkles and each gathered a pocketful as her friend explained that winkles and mussels were less common in Thistlewick; the former more likely to be found in the salt marshes, and mussels more abundant further west, in Wells-next-the-Sea.

They walked along the tideline looking for things of interest that had washed up: bits of net, rope, driftwood and dead crabs. Sarah had amassed quite the collection of seashells, she confided, which was where the large whelk shell had come from.

'Sometimes pieces of sponge wash up, and Mother is glad of them. We use them for washing. And look.' She bent down to pick up a piece of blue glass, holding it up to the autumn sun. 'Treasure!'

She chatted merrily away about how to catch a crab, with a string and fish heads for bait, and then how to pick it up without getting nipped. As they walked back towards the cliffs, she pointed to some abandoned gull nests. 'In the spring, there are those who'd have the eggs from the nests. Fine for baking but a bit funny-tasting for me.'

The day was biting but Mallory felt a warmth within. This simple walk along the shore with someone who paid no attention to her disfiguring lumps was one of the nicest afternoons she'd ever had. It was almost enough to make her forget the pain in her body.

'What can you tell me about Christian Felthorpe?' she asked, wondering if her friend could shed any light on the man she'd seen with Zella.

'Handsome, isn't he?' Sarah giggled. 'He's all right for a rich person. They act differently to us. I suppose there's an order to things, and Grandma says those with money and a good education know what's best for the rest of us, even when we don't want to hear it.' She shrugged. 'But, like everyone, all he wants is people to be kind to each other and for Thistlewick Tye to be a nice place to live. His father is away at the moment so he's strutting about like a feathered peacock, but I feel sorry for him, not having a mother. There's a little boy called Noah in the village who also lost his mother, but his big brother looks after him. I guess I'm lucky to have mine, even though it doesn't feel like it when she's telling me off for daydreaming...'

Mallory's brain was quite exhausted listening to her circuitous chatter but then she said something of interest.

'...He's not married yet and my grandmother says he simply isn't the sort for dallying. She says boys who dally with girls are wicked because it's always the girls who have to pay, and that his father has brought him up proper.'

Did this mean Christian Felthorpe's intentions with Zella were honourable? The beautiful Ballard girl really had cast a spell over the poor fellow then, because anyone could see that a romance between a circus girl and the heir to the Felthorpe estate had no future. Perhaps it was just an innocent flirtation that would be over before it had even begun. She hoped so.

After a while, and aware that she'd been absent from the camp for a couple of hours, Mallory thanked her young friend for showing her the bounty and beauty of the coastline and they both headed back, following the stream and coming out on the common.

'Sarah?' a furious voice shouted. 'Where have you been? I've been worried sick. Our Jack said he thought you'd come down here but there are jobs to be done and your grandmother needs help washing. You can't just skip off when you feel like it, young lady. And who's this?'

She turned to Mallory, who pulled her shawl back slightly, feeling it only polite to show some of her face as she was being addressed. The horror on the woman's face was immediate.

'A circus freak? What are you doing with this *thing*?' The way she spat the word out, unable to even acknowledge that Mallory was a human being, stung more than her fingers when she'd plunged them into the tiny rockpools to investigate the creatures within.

'Mallory's my friend,' Sarah insisted, as her mother grabbed a handful of collar and jerked her young daughter away from the stranger.

'You don't want to be making friends with the likes of them.' The woman looked disgusted. 'Good for nothing except gawping at – the lot of them. I've just come from the grocer's where the big fella was shouting at young Freda Drayton about a sack of potatoes he'd been sold, complaining they was rotten, when we all know he's just after doing the shopkeeper out of more money.'

But the sack *had* been rotten. Mallory had made the discovery when she'd been preparing vegetables that morning. A few decent tubers on the top and then her hand had sunk into the wet flesh of those beneath, as a noxious smell drifted out. It often happened. They were sold the low-grade produce or spoilt goods, with locals knowing they had the travellers over a barrel.

'You're being unkind,' Sarah protested, standing up for her friend. 'They're clever people who know magic and perform the most incredible and dangerous feats. I envy them. Perhaps I shall walk tightropes when I grow up.'

Sarah's mother looked horrified at the thought, and turned her temper on Mallory.

'Have you been putting wild ideas in my daughter's head? I've heard of your lot kidnapping innocent children to work for no pay... or worse. Keep away from her or there'll be trouble. Do you understand?' Her nostrils flared, as she growled her threat and stormed across the common with her protesting daughter.

Mallory watched them disappear into the distance, with Sarah turning back, only to be jerked onwards. Pulling her cloak further across her face, she eventually wandered back to the camp, her apron pockets full of treasures and her head full of the injustice.

34

Later that day, Mallory was walking past the Ballards' covered waggon when she heard Samson and Katerina arguing inside.

'For God's sake, woman, we need to leave before there really is trouble. We've come all the way up here for reasons I don't truly understand, and there's still no sign of the money you promised. I don't like it here. There's something about this place that sends a chill through my bones.'

'I told you, next veek. Be patient. I am not liking this place either. And then ve return to London and you sell the ridiculous zebras to the Kingsley man for his silly circus.'

Not wanting to be caught eavesdropping, Mallory returned to the big tent. Hazibub was outside on the grass, in the dim light of early evening, practising his fire-eating act. He took a flaming torch, tipped his head backwards and popped it into his mouth, whereupon the fire was immediately extinguished. It looked impressive and thrilled the crowds, but Mallory knew that heat travelled upwards, so by being beneath the flames, they were directed away from him. The trick was to quickly exhale as it approached and then to close your mouth around the fire, starving it of oxygen. That wasn't to say it was risk-free, and he still occasionally suffered burns, using preparations of honey and chamomile to soothe the blisters.

He smiled when he saw her, but his eyes were sad. This was most unlike him, so she was immediately worried. She had a soft spot for Hazibub and knew it was reciprocated, but the man himself remained a mystery. No one knew where he was from, only that it was somewhere far away and eastern; Persia perhaps, India or maybe Egypt. Even his name was no clue, as it was another fabrication of Katerina's. Unlike most of Samson's troupe, who professed to have no religion, he quietly worshipped his gods, but no one was quite sure *which* gods because his prayers and ceremonies were intensely private. But there was also something other-worldly about him. Of all the acts she'd ever seen who claimed to have psychic abilities or that they could perform sorcery, he was the only one who seemed to possess real magic – not the illusions and sleight of hand that others employed to dupe a gullible punter out of a shilling, or to make a body levitate or disappear. There was an energy about him that she couldn't explain.

Most snake charmers, for example, had tricks to make the cobra compliant. They removed the fangs, drugged the animal or, rather alarmingly, sewed the mouth shut. But Hazibub did none of those things. He played a haunting melody on a long wooden instrument, as the speckled, tan-coloured creature rose up from its basket. Its tiny black eyes, like elderberries and so much smaller than those adorning its distinctive wide hood, were completely mesmerised by the man who'd disturbed it. As Hazibub swayed with the music, the snake swayed too, and then he chanted some incomprehensible words, as the six-foot-long body writhed and thrashed on the ground, tying itself into a perfect knot. Every time. There was no trickery involved, just a bewildering understanding between man and snake – a creature impossible to train.

He stuck the torch in a pail of water to ensure it was properly extinguished. It sizzled and steamed, as he met her eyes.

'What's wrong?' she asked. Had it been anyone else he'd have brushed the question off but there'd always been an honesty between them.

'I am knowing that I will be dead before the month is out.' He shook his head from side to side. His eyes were wild and white against his dark skin, making them seem even bigger.

'Are you ill?'

He shook his head. 'No, this will be the doing of others. But I'm not knowing when this will be happening or how.'

Hazibub's unnerving second sight, which he largely kept to himself, not wanting to overshadow Katerina and her theatrics, was occasionally shared with Mallory.

There was an uneasy swirling in her stomach. He'd already predicted bad things were on the horizon, but this pronouncement was chilling in the extreme.

'I know my time is coming, too,' she confided. 'I constantly feel sick and have terrible pains in my stomach.' She held out her arms. 'Everyone can see I'm losing weight. Something is slowly killing me from within.'

He reached his bony brown fingers out and rested them across her chest. 'And yet—' the old man frowned '—I have always been knowing that you will live the longest of us all. Whatever will be happening to me, there is a much-deserved happiness in your future. I am seeing a few years of the waiting but be patient because I am also seeing happy times ahead. A man who is loving you very much.'

Mallory wanted to laugh out loud. That she should have finally found a place where she belonged and was accepted for what she was, was a wonder in itself, but to think she'd one day find love was utterly ludicrous. Besides, she wouldn't live many more months, never mind years. However, she said nothing because Hazibub's words unsettled her. Katerina's fortunes were as fake as her accent, as she gazed into the glass ball that stood on its ebonised plinth, or traced a delicate finger over the lines of a woman's upturned palm. But the enigmatic snake charmer used no tricks or props to predict the future. He simply reached out to touch you and closed his eyes, before quietly delivering his alarmingly accurate predictions.

'You must be getting out of this cold,' he said, lifting a flap of the tent for her to duck under. The light was fading fast now and her stomach grizzled. Given the time, she and Po Po should probably start to prepare the food.

They had a small kitchen area set up inside the tent this time of year, although it was far safer to cook in a pit outside. She set about washing the periwinkles she'd collected earlier, and then skinning and gutting some rabbits Harry had caught in the woods.

There was a scrabbling sound behind her and the black nose of Master Felthorpe's pointer appeared under the canvas. Within seconds, Captain had pushed his way in and was sniffing around the table, obviously drawn to the smell of the meat and looking for scraps of food. Po Po shooed him away and he lifted his leg and urinated over one of the benches in defiance.

'Someone get the dog out,' Mallory shouted, from behind the trestle table, but everyone was busy doing their own thing and no one could be bothered. She was up to her elbows in rabbit guts and watched as he wandered aimlessly about the space. Alerted to the presence of another creature by his strong sense of smell, the dog nudged at the snake basket, and she was horrified, as it chewed at the string and shook its head back and forth to free the lid.

'*Someone get the damn dog out!*' yelled Mallory a second time. 'It's at the snake.'

It all happened in a flash.

The lid tumbled to the ground and there was a loud hiss before the wide head of the cobra shot out at the dog, who yelped and threw itself backwards. Finally, her friends paid attention.

'Fetch Hazibub.' A frantic scrabble of feet. The sound of a whimpering animal and agitated mutterings.

Mallory wiped her bloodstained hands on a cloth and dashed over. The dog started to tremble, wobbling on its legs, until it collapsed completely. It was obviously having difficulty breathing and she noticed the puddle around its rear as it wet itself.

'Will it die?' she asked.

'It's damn well not our fault if it does,' Samson replied. 'That Felthorpe lad was warned. Needs to keep the bloody dog under control.'

Hazibub appeared with his small cabinet and fell to his feet beside Captain, soothing noises coming from his mouth as his hands worked quickly to gather what he needed from the bottles and pots within.

'Can you save it?' Katerina asked. 'I do not need this troubles.'

Hazibub shrugged. 'The venom is in his system. It is depending on the strength of the dog.'

After a few minutes, he announced that he'd done all he could. It was now in the lap of the gods, and Captain was carried out of the tent by Samson, who was presumably taking him back to Master Felthorpe.

An hour later, he returned from the hall to say that the

gentleman had been out – no one knew where – but that the dog was calmer and still breathing when he'd left it with staff.

It was early evening by the time Mallory realised that she hadn't seen Zella all afternoon.

But when the oldest Ballard girl finally reappeared, and they all sat around the fire to eat their food, Mallory noticed a thin silver chain around her neck. It was new and obviously a gift.

And it didn't take a genius to work out where it had come from.

35

Three days later, the troupe sat down to eat their evening meal inside the tent, as it was wet and windy outside. Mallory was feeding Esfir, who was happily perched on Hazibub's lap. Both Ballard girls looked upon him as a grandfather figure, partly due to his age, but partly because he'd brought Esfir into this world. Zella had gone into labour when they were travelling between Nottingham and Derby and, as unusual as it was for a man to deliver a baby, the drama of a breech birth had left them little choice.

The troupe were seated in two rows, either side of a trestle table and were midway through their food when they heard voices outside. Harry opened up the tent and a strident voice demanded to speak to Samson Ballard.

A small group of villagers were invited to step inside and an angry-looking man, who announced he was the Reverend Marsham, appeared to be their self-appointed spokesman.

'We want you gone,' the vicar said, without preamble, as soon as he'd been introduced to the owner. 'Now. Tonight. The villagers have come to me extremely concerned by your continued presence in our quiet, respectable community.'

Samson stood up and approached the group. Mallory noticed the reverend's Adam's apple bob up and down as he took in the size of the man he was now confronting.

'We're on common land. Our animals have the right to graze and we're not obstructing any byways. Our stay is temporary, and my wife reckons we'll be good to move on in a few days. We're not causing you any harm so just let us be.'

'No harm? *No harm*?' the vicar repeated, incredulously. 'You've been stealing and fighting. The boys in our village don't normally get involved in physical altercations – they wouldn't dare. Yet you arrive and I find young members of my congregation turning up to church with bruises and scrapes.'

'Your lads started it,' Harry said, sullenly, from down the far end of the trestle table.

'Bollocks did we.'

'Jacob!' the vicar admonished. 'Language.'

The young lad bowed his head and mumbled an apology. 'But they were flirting with some of the girls from the village. It just ain't right. Their snake attacked Master Felthorpe's dog and we know they stole that pig...'

'I have, indeed, had several concerns raised, including that yourself and Mrs Ballard are not, in fact, legally man and wife, and you've also been overheard in the high street proclaiming all religion is fantasy. Blasphemy of the highest order—'

'There is no needing for this,' Katerina interrupted. 'A piece of paper to satisfy a God I do not care for. I have seen what your God does. Men who beat their wives in His name. Persecute those who do not believe, or are different. And the judgement... always with the judgement.'

'You may not care for him but he's watching and you *will* be found wanting.'

So much for Christian forgiveness, thought Mallory.

'They were planning to take my Sarah!' A woman stepped forward. 'Your Toad Girl freak has been filling her head with tales of adventure and life on the road. My poor mite's only a child and has been bewitched. I found she'd packed a bag and written me a letter explaining she wanted to walk across the sky and eat fire.'

'You simply cannot steal other people's children,' the vicar stressed. 'We're already fully aware of your lack of religion and sexual debauchery, but to lure a child away from her loving home is wickedness beyond measure.'

'No one's lured anyone,' Samson said, his face getting redder by the minute. Mallory was worried he'd snap and thump the man before him, but Katerina had her hand on his arm and was whispering calming words. 'Who even is this Sarah?' he asked. 'I've not seen anyone at the camp. Mallory?'

'She wanted to see the horses performing. I let her watch our rehearsals.'

Katerina clenched her teeth and Mallory knew she was in trouble.

'Ve are not in the businesses of kidnapping. Those who join us do so from choice, but even if your daughter begged us to take her, ve vouldn't. The only children in this circus are mine.'

Harry threw his legs over the bench and stood up, walking over to the group and squinting at the vicar, as though something had just occurred to him.

'Hey! You're the bloke who was peering through the tent the other night when I popped out to water the daisies.' He studied the reverend for a moment, as a silence descended and everyone looked at the vicar. Even Katerina focused her kohl-lined eyes on him.

Mallory remembered Harry mentioning a figure in the shadows but no one paid him much mind as the things he'd been smoking made him hallucinate. She'd been trying to sleep but Cupid was blind drunk and had taken on the Caley sisters in his wild carnal pursuits – both of them.

'I'd heard rumours of the debaucherous behaviour,' the vicar spluttered. 'It was my duty to investigate, for the sake of my parishioners. And I was disgusted to witness the most heinous and despicable acts.'

'Not sure you needed to witness them for half an hour,' Harry said. 'Quiet as a dormouse, at the back of the tent, and still lurking when I went out later to check on the horses. I saw where you put your hand, and it wasn't lifted up to the other one in prayer.'

There was general tittering amongst the troupe but the vicar looked positively apoplectic and Mallory half imagined she could see steam pouring from his ears.

'You dirty bugger,' Cupid slurred from his seat, slamming his tumbler down on the table. 'Copping an eyeful of something that you don't get at home?' He jumped down from the chair and shuffled over to the table that held the drinks. 'Getting hard watching a little fella like me riding one of the girls? That's closer to the truth, ain't it, your reverendness?' His face twisted into a wry smile as he tipped his head back to look up at the vicar. 'Got caught with your hand in the biscuit tin and now you gonna stand there and tell us all you don't like biscuits?' He snorted, retrieved the gin bottle and hopped back up onto the chair.

The reverend was now practically spitting teeth. Mallory noticed Sarah's mother throw the man a perplexed look, clearly unaware that the vicar had gathered his information first hand.

'I condemn you all, every last one of you.' He lifted his shaking hand and waved it across the tent. 'Paul tells us in Corinthians that we must flee fornication. "Every sin that a man doeth is without the body; but he that committeth fornication sinneth against his own body." May you rot in hell for your wickedness and lies.'

'Hey, I thought you were supposed to forgive the sinners,' Harry said, echoing Mallory's earlier thoughts.

The tension was now palpable and Mallory slipped from her seat to stand behind little Esfir, who was happily dipping crusts into her bowl of soup, not really paying any attention to the atmosphere in the tent. Should any fighting break out, it was important that the child was removed from the situation as quickly as possible.

Preparing to lift her from Hazibub's lap and sneak her out the back, everyone was distracted when the young Master Felthorpe strode into the tent.

'I say, what's all this fuss about? Dr Appleby said there was some sort of contingent down here, trying to move the circus people on.' Mallory saw how he sought out Zella with his eyes, and the pair of them exchanged the briefest glance, before his attention returned to the villagers. No one else noticed but she was looking for it, knowing of their budding romance.

The young man she now recognised as Silas spoke up. 'We want this lot gone, sir. They broke into the outbuildings at the hall and stole a young pig.'

Christian Felthorpe batted away the accusation with a flick of his hand. 'I was compensated for the theft and had an apology from that young man.' He pointed at Harry, who looked as surprised as everyone felt. 'Isn't that right?'

Harry nodded slowly, his eyes narrowed in suspicion.

'Besides, we've not been very welcoming to these good people.' Cupid nearly choked on his mouthful of gin, finding himself being referred to in such glowing terms. 'The Bible reminds us that welcoming strangers is akin to welcoming Him. If Jesus can forgive the prostitute, surely we can try to be more understanding of these people and their ways?'

'But their snake nearly killed your dog. You said yourself that there'd be trouble when they first arrived.' The vicar was clearly confused by Master Felthorpe's change of heart.

'It was irresponsible of me to allow Captain to wander into the camp, and I understand this dark-skinned fellow rushed to save him as soon as the accident happened. I plan to speak to Father upon his return and allow the circus to remain over the winter.' He spun to face the village folk. 'Where's your Christian charity? Your compassion?'

But the only reason the young man was prepared to tolerate them was to keep Zella nearby. Mallory noticed how her eyes shone as she looked across at Christian. How could no one else see it?

He turned to address Samson. 'I don't agree with your lifestyle or your morals, but I'll pray for you all and hope you come to see the light. Keep to the common and stay out of the Sailmaker's and perhaps we can live alongside each other. And now—' he turned to the vicar '—we should leave these people to finish their meal in peace.'

He ushered the villagers from the tent, but as the last of them slipped through the canvas, Silas turned back and muttered a threat. 'Watch your backs. I'm warning you,' he snarled, and strode out into the night.

'What the fuck was that all about?' Samson said, turning to speak to Katerina, who had been sitting behind him, but she was no longer at the bench, at some point since the arrival of the villagers having taken herself to the back of the tent.

'It means ve must be leaving soon,' she said. 'And it means ve truly must be vatching our backs.'

36

The following morning, as Mallory returned to the big tent after relieving herself in the bushes, she saw Hazibub standing in the low rising sun, as it cast long shadows across the damp grass.

'What are you doing?' she asked. He held a small sack of salt with a tiny hole cut in the bottom and allowed a trail of the white crystals to trickle out behind him. Curious, she followed as he walked around the perimeter.

'Protecting us. Please be waking everyone inside the tent, gather the stable lads and be rousing the Ballards. I must be doing this important thing.'

'Surely, they were just making idle threats to scare us. And,' she pointed out, 'some of the accusations were true.'

Hazibub looked at her and shook his head. 'I am knowing bad things are coming but cannot clearly see what. Trust me, being cautious is always the most wisest of options.'

Harry and the other two lads were already awake, tending to the horses. They were murmuring softly to the animals as they worked, brushing them down and checking their feet for stones, and she asked them to return to the tent. She knocked on the door of the covered waggon and explained to Katerina that Hazibub wanted everyone together, and eventually found Po Po standing near the cliffs, looking mournfully out across the sea, probably longing for her homeland.

They all made their way inside to see an iron pot hanging above a small fire – the air thick with smoke and exotic spices – and the benches arranged in a circle. Hazibub was wearing a white robe and had a smear of red across his forehead. He picked up a smooth stick and stirred the contents of the pot.

'Now what nonsense am I being made to sit through?' Cupid said, his tiny face scrunched up into a frown. 'I haven't even had my breakfast yet.'

Katerina passed him a half-empty bottle of gin left on the table from the night before and waved an uninterested hand. 'Allow him his nonsense. It harms no one.'

Hazibub had collected a live rat from one of the traps that Harry used near the animal feed. Holding it by the scruff off the neck, he sacrificed it, letting the blood, still warm from the creature, drip into the simmering ingredients. He chanted words in a language that no one understood and then, using a thick cloth, lifted the pot from the hook and walked around the wooden benches, marking every single forehead, even little Esfir's, with a thumbprint of dark red.

To give them their due, a hushed reverence descended and the silly comments dried up, everyone entranced by the sincerity of his actions.

'What's this all about?' Samson finally asked, as Hazibub returned to the fire and sat cross-legged before it.

'You may be thinking this is unnecessary dramatics, but I am fearing for our safety, so I conduct this ritual to ensure that if any harm is coming to us after those threats, we might be given the opportunity to rise again.'

Mallory wondered if he'd seen any other deaths besides his own, but she was also confused by his words.

'Rise again? Do you mean be reborn after we die? Come back to live another life? Like the Buddhists?'

'No, my dear, a transmigration. Our souls, our very essence, will be taking an empty vessel to use as our own. Usually, the soul is leaving the body after death, but this spell will bind the two together, for I am seeing a most strange vision of falling bones and rising spirits. It is meaning this will be our chance to be living again.'

'Empty vessels? Like the body of a dead person?' Zella asked, shuddering. 'I don't want to come back in some wizened old lady who pees herself and is riddled with tuberculosis.'

'You will be finding that the arrival of your soul brings a renewed energy that heals much of what the body has suffered, although it cannot be turning back the clock.'

'I'd better come back as someone tall,' Cupid muttered.

'Don't get me wrong, Hazibub, old mate, but it sounds a right load of bollocks, if you ask me.' Harry scoffed and patted his knee for Po Po to come to him.

'You're the bloody reason they've taken against us,' Samson pointed out. 'Stealing the damn pig and getting into brawls. If I'm totally honest though, I'd rather Hazibub rustled up a little spell to stop us dying in the first place.'

'Don't worry, if anyone comes for us, I can have 'em in a fight.' Cupid jumped up, his fists balled, and hopped from foot to foot, ready for combat. His breakfast gin was kicking in nicely.

'Ve'll be gone soon enough. Just stay out of troubles for a few days. Now to vork,' barked Katerina. 'Hazibub has done what he needs to do.'

* * *

The following day was dry and gusty. Harry and the other lads set to work sanding and repainting the waggon that held the animal cages. The Caley sisters practised some new tricks with the monkeys, and Samson was lifting weights to keep up his strength.

Mallory was in a lot of pain that day. Her stomach hurt and even Katerina could see she was struggling and so ordered her to rest. She took herself off to the steps of the covered waggon, tipping her face to the weak sun, and looking across the common, feeling drowsy from the few drops of laudanum she'd discreetly taken. Hazibub, Katerina and herself were probably the only ones who appreciated the seriousness of her condition now. She knew that the waggon advertising The Living Wonders was not to be repainted until the new year. Samson's ever-prudent wife was leaving it until last in case the Toad Girl was no longer one of the attractions.

Zella appeared from the woods, skipping as she emerged from the trees but slowing to a wary amble when she noticed Mallory.

'Where have you been? Esfir was asking for you earlier.'

Samson had also noticed his daughter's absence but Mallory had covered for her.

'I'm not answerable to you.' The young woman stuck her chin in the air and tried to push past her friend to enter the waggon, but Mallory refused to budge.

'Were you with him again? The man from the big house? You mustn't.'

'You don't understand.' Zella sank to the steps and sat next to Mallory. 'He loves me.'

'You've barely known him a fortnight. How can you be so foolish! He's only after one thing, like your mother said.'

'You're wrong – he hasn't touched me like that, or suggested that we do anything improper. He's a good man. Such behaviour would go against his principles.'

Sarah had indicated as much to Mallory on the beach, insisting Master Felthorpe was not a man for dallying, as her grandmother had put it.

'But he's going to find out that you're not... that you have experience with—'

'I don't mean this unkindly but you don't know what it is to be in love. I can't explain it. When we first met that day on the common, there was this incredible pull between us – as though I'd always known him, like he was part of me – and he felt the same. Looking in his eyes makes my insides tumble over faster than any somersault I can perform.'

Mallory *tried* to understand. She'd been told that love at first sight was possible. When Samson was in his cups, he often told of how he'd fallen for Katerina within minutes of seeing her across a crowded quay. And that love had lasted for years. But, even if this thing with Master Felthorpe was genuine, Zella must know it was impossible.

'Your mother says we'll be moving on soon. Maybe even before the week is out. Do you seriously expect him to follow us around the country, when he's set to inherit a large estate? He's the son of a lord. He is not going to abandon that to join the circus.'

'Christian wants to marry me. His father returned from his London trip this morning and he's going to speak to him about letting us stay on the land for the winter. Try to soothe the rift between us and the villagers. It's got out of hand, but there's no reason we can't live companionably for the winter months. It'll give my parents a bit longer to get used to the idea—'

'*Marriage*?' Mallory was incredulous. 'You're as hot-headed as your father. How can you even think of being apart from Esfir?

And you'll abandon us, for what? To swan around a big house and have babies? The monotony of it will kill you. You were born to perform.'

'Marriage?' Katerina appeared from nowhere. It was something she did a lot – lurking in the shadows and overhearing things people didn't want her to know. It was another reason she ran the circus so efficiently: she knew everything that was going on. Although she was somewhat behind with regard to this gossip.

'Vot is it you're talking of?' she demanded.

Zella glared at Mallory, as though the eavesdropping was her fault, but her mother was standing in front of them now, her arms crossed and her face severe. No one dared lie to Katerina.

'You may as well know, seeing as the cat is out the bag, but I've met someone and he's asked me to be his wife.'

'And so your head has been turned again?' Her mother was furious. 'Did you learn nothing from before? Has vun of the fishermen been sniffing around you? I vill not tolerate this nonsense.' Katerina was firm in her assertion. 'I think he said this to seduce you, foolish girl, but even if the silly man thinks it is love, you are too precious to give yourself to some ignorant pudding-head.'

'He's not ignorant. He's a gentleman – Christian Felthorpe from the hall. Even you must see he's a good catch. He's promised to take care of me, and that means none of us need worry about money ever again.'

It was unusual for Katerina to be silent, but Mallory watched as all the colour drained from the older woman's face. Both girls had expected her to launch into another angry tirade but she stood frozen, her mouth agape and her eyes glassy.

'His father is back from London now and—'

'Mallory...' Katerina shook herself from the trance and spoke through her daughter, 'ask the hands to start packing up the contents of the big tent and get Harry to check the horses. Zella, tell your father ve leave tomorrow. I am putting the full stop to this foolishness this instant. I vill get the money ve need and then ve are on the road again.' She turned to go but spun back to face her daughter. 'You *do not* leave this camp until I return. Understood?'

And through her tears, Zella nodded.

Mallory did as she was bid and Harry muttered something about being glad to see the back of this sanctimonious backwater. But poor Zella could barely get the words out between sobs when she found Samson to explain her mother's instructions. Mallory caught the conversation as she helped Hazibub to pack circus equipment back into the large tea chests they used for storage.

'Why the hurry?' her father asked, as he nailed a new piece of wood to one of the waggons where rainwater had rotted the boards.

'Because she's determined to ruin my life. I've found someone who loves me and she can't bear it. She wants to tie me to this circus, but what if I want a different life? Not to spend my days travelling from place to place. I'm just a star turn to her. Something to perform, like the monkeys. Train, train, train. "Do it again, Zella! Do it better!" She doesn't treat me like a person with feelings, but she can't keep me an old maid forever.'

'Don't tell me one of those village lads has laid his dirty hands upon you?' Samson's quick temper reared its ugly head but Zella soothed him with her words.

'Nothing has happened, Daddy. No one's touched me. Quite the opposite. Master Felthorpe has behaved most gentlemanly towards me.'

'The entitled so-and-so who's been causing us all that trouble with his damn dog?'

Her expression answered for her and Samson laughed, so preposterous was the suggested love affair. He pulled his daughter close with his enormous bear-like arms.

'Your mother is quite correct; that is *not* a romance that will have a happy ending. It's them and us. Surely these last few days in Thistlewick Tye have proved that. She worries, that's all. And we don't want any more unexplained daughters popping up.' His attempt at humour fell flat as the young tightrope walker started sobbing again.

'Certainly explains why he's been a damn sight more pleasant to us but I can assure you, if your mother says we're leaving Thistlewick Tye tomorrow, my girl, then we *will* be leaving.'

* * *

The afternoon rolled on but Katerina didn't return from Felthorpe Hall. Mallory wrote a note for Sarah and persuaded Harry to run it into the village. The young girl would be terribly disappointed that the circus was moving on but she was determined to arrange a goodbye. She asked to meet up in the churchyard around dusk, as she understood it wasn't far from the Cleyfords' cottage and she hoped Sarah could slip out the house for a few minutes. Mallory hadn't been into the village as such, but if there was one thing that stood out in a landscape, it was the parish church.

'I can't stay long and I had to lie to Mother – which I hate –

but she's being so unreasonable about this whole thing,' Sarah said, as they sat together later that evening atop a generations-old burial vault. 'She's taken against you all and nothing I say will make her change her mind. When we were in the butcher's today, she told him that the vicious lies about the Reverend Marsham were the last straw. The vicar helped to set up the Benevolent Committee, after all, and she said that to speak ill of such a man only proves that the Devil has surely sent you all to test us.'

'Then your mother will be pleased to know that we're leaving,' Mallory said. 'But I couldn't go without giving you this.'

Mallory had spent the last couple of days embroidering a square of cotton, using threads and scraps of fabric from the workbox that she kept for the costumes. The young girl loved the sparkles and ribbons and so she had sewn the words, 'True friends are never apart, maybe in distance but never in heart', and surrounded them with a border of brightly coloured flowers. Tiny glass beads, gold thread and sequins were all incorporated into the design and she knew that it was some of her finest work. When the circus had moved on, which Katerina seemed to think would be imminently, Sarah would have this keepsake of their time together.

The young girl, whilst thrilled with the gift, was visibly upset. 'I can't believe the villagers are making you go. It's so unfair.'

'People always struggle with those who are different from them,' Mallory explained. 'It's as much us as it is the villagers. I'm not sure that, as travelling folk, we're always as respectful as we should be, even though I've found, time and time again, we're judged before we've done anything wrong.' She didn't explain that the budding romance between Zella and Lord Felthorpe's son had forced the issue. Katerina clearly wanted to nip it in the bud before her star act could get herself into trouble again. From what Mallory had witnessed, time was certainly of the essence.

'Will I ever see you again?'

'I honestly don't know.' It wasn't that she couldn't imagine Samson bringing the circus back up to this part of the world, but more that she wasn't sure she'd still be alive when he did. 'But thank you for your friendship. I'll never forget how kind you've been to me.'

They sat chatting for a while before their final tearful embrace, and then Mallory threaded her way through the gravestones and back out onto the common.

As she approached the camp, however, she was confused at the lack of noise. Usually by now, someone would be singing – often a drunken Cupid – and there'd be chatter from the big tent. The silence was unsettling in the extreme.

She came up behind the waggons where the horses were tethered. Beauty nickered softly to her as she passed. The two zebras were standing behind, their white striped bodies visible, even in the dim light. The monkeys were chattering away inside their cages but no human voices could be heard.

As she neared the big tent she stumbled over something on the ground. It was a pair of booted feet across the pathway – one of the hands drunk again, she assumed, and continued onwards. Much of the preparation had been done for their leaving, as the benches and trestles had been stacked on one of the waggons, but they'd need to sleep in the tent tonight, so dismantling would begin at first light.

She pulled back a corner of the canvas but there was no one inside. In the flickering lamplight, she could see that most of their possessions had been packed away, apart from the bedrolls and some of the cooking equipment. Of course, she realised, the troupe would be sitting around the fire. She unhooked a lantern and carried it out the other side of the tent, but it took her brain a few moments to catch up with the sight that met her eyes.

The fire was burning embers. No one had been tending it, but it gave off enough light for her to make out the slumped bodies of the troupe sprawled across the benches and lying on the ground. But this was not a drunken rabble, passed out from too much intoxicating liquor. As she held the swaying lantern aloft, she could see the tortured corpses and rictus grins of people who had seemingly been poisoned.

'No, no, no, no...' she repeated under her breath, as she ran from body to body in the vain hope someone was still alive. Cupid was face down on a bench, Harry and Po Po nearby, and the Caley sisters were the other side of the smouldering fire, curled together on a rug... but the most heartbreaking sight of all was Zella clutching a dead Esfir to her chest.

Two thoughts hit her with equal force. The first was that Hazibub had been right. He'd known something bad was on the horizon but, despite his circle of salt and strange ritual, the evil had come for them regardless. The second was whoever was responsible must surely still be out there. Would they now be looking for her?

Trying to suppress her sobs for fear of someone hearing, she stepped back into the twisting shadows and away from the devastating scene, trying to work out what could have possibly happened in the hour or so that she'd been gone. There was a clatter as her foot caught a couple of bottles standing on the ground and she used the lantern to illuminate a crate of wine bottles and a half-empty basket of foodstuffs that she didn't recognise. As someone responsible for the meals, she knew the current state of their larder, and it hadn't included these items. Was this what had killed them?

In the ensuing stillness, she heard approaching footsteps and low, mumbling male voices. Panic flooded her body and she gently placed the lantern on the ground and extinguished it, knowing that to carry it would give away her location immediately. This wasn't any of her troupe returning – she'd now accounted for everyone, save Katerina, whose body she hadn't yet come across.

She slipped back into the big tent, grabbed her small box of personal possessions and a blanket for warmth, and quietly headed for the woods. Too bewildered to make sense of the scene she'd stumbled across, and too emotional to think clearly, she knew she had to hide herself away and not do anything rash.

* * *

Mallory spent the night in the copse. She found a hollow to curl up in, but her sleep was fitful and she heard voices in the distance, weaving into her dreams. When she awoke, the air held the bitter pungency of smoke. What would daylight reveal when she returned to the camp?

But as she stepped from the trees, it was as if the horrors of the night before had never taken place. Hardly anything of the camp remained. The waggons and horses had gone, as had the boxes ready for loading, and the tent was a smouldering heap in a now almost empty patch of land.

We've been completely erased, she realised, staring at the flattened grass and muddy tracks – the only evidence that the circus had been camped there just a few hours before. *But why?*

38

Mallory stared at the barren patch of common. It made no sense but proved she'd been right to hide. Whoever was responsible for killing her friends had returned to destroy all the evidence that such a heinous crime had been committed.

Staying near the edge of the trees, she realised that the bodies of the troupe were also nowhere to be seen, although an ominous mound of soil was visible a few yards back from where the campfire had finally burned itself out. Someone had set the big tent alight, and she could see the charred remains of the large oak poles, the very skeleton of the structure, lying across the space at strange angles where they'd collapsed inwards. There were ruts in the earth where the waggons had been moved, and the deep impressions of horseshoes intermingled with foot-prints, where all this activity had taken place hurriedly during the night.

Mallory's whole world crumbled. There was nothing and no one left. The only person she trusted, the only person who'd shown her any kindness since arriving at Thistlewick Tye, was Sarah. She'd already decided on a plan of action as she'd lain curled up beneath the stars, but she couldn't execute it alone, and was still wrestling with whether it was fair to ask the help of someone so young. But, ultimately, what choice did she have?

After making her way back to the village, she tried to work out which was the Cleyfords' cottage from the shadows, eventually spotting the mother enter the house. She waited a while in nearby bushes, her cloak pulled down over her face in case someone should happen upon her loitering. It was nearly midday by the time she spotted the young girl, coming out the back door with a small basket looped over her arm, to collect eggs from the wooden coop in their garden.

Bouncing some stones off the tiny roof, she finally got Sarah's attention and the young girl was both horrified and delighted to see Mallory, as the pair tucked themselves out of sight.

'Why are you still here?' she asked, her eyes anxious and confused. 'The village is full of chatter about the circus leaving last night. How you've done more wicked things and were chased away. Your people have smashed windows on the high street and set fire to the Tutters' barn of grain. It's been blazing all night. And they're saying one of your men assaulted Mary Tutter. She's Dr Appleby's niece and he's unspeakably angry.'

'It's all lies. My people are dead. When I returned after we parted last night, I found they'd been murdered. Oh, Sarah...' The tears she'd been holding in came tumbling out, unstoppable and raw. 'It's only because I was with you that I wasn't part of the massacre.'

'Murdered? I don't understand. Who'd do such a thing?'

Mallory shrugged. 'More than one person but who and why, I don't know. Our silly feud with the villagers was becoming an issue, but to poison us...'

She explained what she'd found at the camp but kept the more unpalatable details to herself.

'Could it be an accident? I've heard Mother talk of cheap alcohol killing people before, or well water being contaminated?'

Mallory shook her head. 'This was a deliberate act, but I've not the strength nor the courage to investigate. I'm merely here to ask for help.'

She'd spent the night weighing up her options. Running away would mean starting again somewhere, and as a circus freak who was surely dying this was not an appealing option. Revealing herself to the people of Thistlewick would make her a target. She would either be taken advantage of or killed, like her friends. In reality, she didn't have a choice.

'Anything.'

Mallory swallowed hard. 'May I borrow a spade?'

'Of course. There's one in the shed. I'll leave it outside the door when I go back inside.'

'Also, I need you to be a brave girl and meet me on the common tonight. Go through the woods and come out by the fallen oak, just past where we camped and the horses were tethered. Wait until dark, and wear old clothes.'

Sarah nodded her understanding and, with her mother now calling for her, the two parted.

It wouldn't be easy, but Mallory knew what she had to do.

* * *

Perhaps if the pains hadn't been so bad, or she was a braver person, Mallory might have considered seeking justice for the crime that had been committed. But as she worked, she knew in her heart she was weary of it all. She was too tired to fight and it wasn't a fight she stood any chance of winning. Lies had been told about the circus from the beginning. And now to claim they'd set a barn alight and attacked a girl from the village...

Someone had taken against them and was spreading vicious falsehoods.

She stood over the hole that had taken two hours to dig. It wasn't deep enough, but the deeper she'd gone, the harder it was to get the soft sandy soil out. The sides kept collapsing and, in the end, she decided it'd do the job well enough.

'Is this a grave?' Sarah asked, her pale eyes wide in the shifting moonlight, but Mallory didn't give a direct answer.

'I'm terribly ill,' she said, reaching out for the young girl's hands and trying to stress her earnestness. 'And I can't go on without them. I belonged somewhere and now I don't belong anywhere. This is the first and only time I've had any real control in my life and it feels better than I'd expected.'

Sarah's bottom lip was wobbling, fearful of what her friend was about to say.

'Twenty-nine years isn't bad, and they've been largely happy. I was lucky to find people as understanding as Samson and Katerina. They weren't perfect, by any means, and I'm fully aware that I've spent my life being worked hard and exploited for profit, but people were always going to stare at me, so I figured I might as well be paid for their pitying looks.'

'You talk as though your life's over, but you can live with me. I can speak to Mother...'

Mallory didn't answer. She understood Sarah's concerns, but she couldn't live here, with these people, and they both knew it. And she simply wasn't brave enough to go out into the world alone. Bad things would happen. Besides, Mallory knew her health was declining rapidly now. It would be a drawn-out and painful end. This way, she trusted, would be painless.

'Taking your own life is a mortal sin,' Sarah whispered. 'Suicides aren't even allowed to be buried on consecrated ground.'

Mallory laughed at that. 'I was never going to be buried.

Didn't you hear what happened to Joice Heth? The hundred-and-sixty-one-year-old woman exhibited by P. T. Barnum as the nursemaid to George Washington? Her body was dissected in front of fifteen hundred people. She was a sideshow even in death. Or The Hottentot Venus, an African woman with an unusual body shape? Her skeleton, and parts of her anatomy preserved in jars, are on public display to this day. We're medical curiosities. I don't want to end up on an operating table, whilst three dozen students stare at my cadaver, then have my bones placed in some dusty museum for people to stare at. I've had enough of that in my lifetime.' She reached her hand out to her friend's shoulder. 'Trust me. This is the best way. No one will notice the disturbed soil between these trees. I want to be buried close to the people I loved.'

She thought back to the mound at the nearby camp and shivered, remembering the horrors of the previous night.

'All I ask now is you return in one hour. There'll be a blanket at the bottom of this hole. Push the soil back in with the spade and fill it up. Maybe scatter some branches over the top to hide the fact the earth's been disturbed but don't mark it in any way. If you want to remember me, do so when you walk along the beach; it was such a happy day.' She hoped that because she'd chosen a spot away from the main paths, no one would stumble across it for a while. 'My heart breaks that I'm asking you to do this, but I've absolutely no one else. You're so very grown-up and wise beyond your years, Sarah. Bright enough to understand my decision. Had I been blessed with a child, I'd have wanted her to be just like you. Hazibub gave me some special medicine that will take the pain away. I'll drift into a peaceful sleep and he assured me it's the most wonderful way to go...'

Sarah pulled back her shoulders and tipped her chin to the sky. 'I understand and I can do this.'

Mallory embraced the young girl, and they sobbed for a while, reluctant to let each other go, but the wind was whipping up, coming in from the sea, and the temperature was dropping fast.

Sarah eventually tore herself away. 'I won't let you down,' she promised. 'And will remember you always. "True friends are never apart; maybe in death but *never* in heart."' She echoed the words from the embroidered sentiment, her own eyes brimming with tears. And then she set off for home, without allowing herself to turn back.

When she was certain she was alone, Mallory climbed into the hole and out of the bitter wind. The moon was looking down at her – a white circle in the black – and for a moment, she thought the man in the moon was frowning. She slipped the small blue bottle from her skirts. The cork was stiff but she wriggled it free and brought it to her lips. It tasted sickly sweet and smelled of spring blossom.

A warm feeling spread from the centre of her body – a sleepy yet euphoric calm. She lay back in the dark and pulled the blanket over her shivering body, covering her head and closing her eyes, as her mind began to conjure up a thousand magical visions. There were leaping horses and tumbling acrobats, shooting arrows and flaming torches. A scattering of twinkling lights winked and whizzed above her head. Music drifted in the air surrounding her – not a tune she recognised, but an uplifting melody that filled her with joy. Her heart raced faster as the tempo increased and she imagined herself swirling about in a dreamlike carousel. And the colours! Mallory had never seen a sight quite so beautiful.

The spinning slowed and she realised that she was surrounded by people. All those she loved were there: Samson and Katerina, arm in arm; Little Cupid – rosy-cheeked and with a bottle of gin in his hand; Po Po casting her chicken bones and gazing at how they had fallen. She looked back up to Mallory, actually smiling, as though the fortune at her feet had predicted the very best of futures for them all. Zella called out from above, in her most glamourous bodice and stiff, sparkling tulle skirt, as she walked across the sky with so much poise and elegance. And little Esfir, twisting her tiny body into curious shapes and giggling as her arms wound around her legs.

Beauty and Star galloped towards her from somewhere in the distance, manes flying in the wind and muscles rippling. Beauty stopped barely two feet from where she was standing, whinnied and put his gentle face next to hers. She could smell the fresh hay, feel the soft velvet of his muzzle. Mallory grabbed a handful of mane and hoisted herself up onto his back and turned to the gathered crowd.

'Oh, my darling friends,' she said. 'You waited for me.'

'Of course,' Samson said. 'We wouldn't go anywhere without you, my beautiful little Toad Girl.' He smiled that familiar smile and put out his hand. 'You're family.'

39

EDWARD, 1895

Edward didn't interrupt her story. At first, he remained furious at the deceit. How could Maude, or rather Mallory, have kept this incredible truth from him? Especially when she knew he was investigating the disappearance of the circus. But he soon felt a thawing as she relayed her tale because, as a freak himself, there was much he could relate to.

He understood now why she'd been so frightened these past four years. Someone, or several someones, from the village had poisoned the entire troupe. She must have been petrified that her real identity would be revealed and they'd come for her, too.

Perhaps he should have spotted that she was not the real Maude Grimmer sooner, though. The clues were there from the beginning: her desire to give the bones a proper burial and keep them from washing out to sea; her sudden epiphany and decision to stop drinking; the tidy interior of the cottage and her kindness, so at odds with the stories he'd heard about the violent drunk. And then she'd harboured Noah, not because she'd known the youngest Garrod since childhood, but because he'd been inhabited by Samson Ballard, the owner of the circus and a father figure from her previous life.

As she told her tale, she stared into the fire, as though the story was playing out in the writhing flames before her, and kept her face shielded from his. It suddenly became imperative to Edward that they made eye contact so that he could seek out one further truth. How did she *really* feel about him? Because since their earliest encounters on the windswept beaches of this North Norfolk village, he'd been falling, slowly, almost imperceptibly, for this woman, whatever the truth of her identity.

He slid from the bench and joined her on the floor, but still she wouldn't look at him – her chin set defiantly forward. There was a beat, and then he reached over to touch her face and turned it towards his.

'I'm sorry we got angry with each other,' he said. What colour had Mallory's eyes been, he wondered, squinting at the mud-brown but endearingly earnest eyes that bored into his. 'You're right; I've lived a life claiming to have a gift that I do not. My entire livelihood is built on deception and trickery.'

She gave a small snort and raised an eyebrow.

'I may not have guessed your albinism but I knew you were a fraud long before you admitted it. I'd heard rumours that Mr Shaw had summoned a medium, and it was why I ran from you on the beach. I felt sure you'd know instantly that I wasn't Maude Grimmer but a spirit inhabiting her body, and yet you sensed nothing.'

A hundred questions were still circling his muddled brain, all fighting to be the first one out.

'So how long have you been in the body of Mrs Grimmer? You said the bones only started falling recently.'

'I wasn't buried with everyone else.' She shrugged and turned away, drawing her knees up to her chest and returning her gaze to the fire. 'I was much nearer the cliffs, and when there was a huge landslide four years ago, my body fell to the shore and I was somehow released.'

He was confused. 'But—'

'One minute I was Mallory Hornchurch, the Toad Girl – the young woman with her face and limbs covered in unsightly bumps – choosing to bow out from this world on my terms. The next, I woke up on the stone floor of this cottage in a pool of vomit, exactly as I described. Nothing made sense until I remembered Hazibub's bizarre ritual with the rat blood. He was right – slipping into Maude seemed to bring a renewed energy and a certain degree of healing to her ravaged body. I didn't have to endure days of sweating to wean myself from the gin, as I previously told you, but didn't want my recovery to sound suspicious.'

He risked shuffling slightly closer to her.

'Then, to be clear, you're not a married woman?'

She shook her head. 'But as I frantically pieced Maude's life together, there was certainly a time I worried that her husband would return. Apparently, he still has brothers living in Sheringham and I thought news of my recovery might reach him, so I carried on living her life to avoid being discovered. Whilst I feel nothing but pity for what he went through when Maude was at her most violent, I was anxious that his reappearance would lead to... expectations on his behalf that I wouldn't be happy to fulfil.'

He understood her meaning well enough and cast his eyes to the floor. He also didn't want Mr Grimmer back on the scene. Maude would certainly no longer be able to entertain him, as a friend or otherwise. He also acknowledged that the thought of another man touching her, kissing her, claiming her, was unbearable.

'I had to work out who I was, where I was, *when* I was and how to survive. I knew so little about Thistlewick Tye or the people in it back then because I'd hardly left the camp. But by scurrying around the edges of the village and listening to snatches of conversation, I worked out enough about her life to live it. Ironically, being shunned by the villagers was in my favour and I've managed well enough these last four years, even though I've carried a lot of worry with me – worry that someone might discover who I really was, that Maude's husband would return, or that I might die alone, never being loved by another person again. Because I've been so desperately lonely, Edward, and then you appeared, making me feel things I thought I'd never feel again...'

Finally.

She turned to face him, her bottom lip quivering in the flickering light. A lone tear dribbled down her cheek, but she said nothing further. The silence was excruciating and, in the end, he could bear it no longer and leaned closer, twisting his whole body towards hers, and grabbing her shoulders to pull her close. He gave her plenty of opportunity to move away, if that was what she wanted, but she didn't resist. His lips approached her face, tentatively at first, before he covered the salty droplet with his mouth, and kissed it away.

Her questioning eyes bored into his as he pulled back. 'Would you have done that if my skin was a grotesque mass of lumps?'

She was challenging him and he understood. When you were a freak, it was vital to establish that any kindness was not born of pity for the thing you couldn't change. A newfound desire to be completely honest with her from this moment on, until his last ever breath on this cruel and judgemental earth, swept over him.

'It's impossible to answer a "what-if",' he said. 'I wasn't even born when you were Mallory Hornchurch. But if I'd been wise enough to get to know you, then unequivocally yes. Your beauty is apparent in the way you live your life and your kindness towards me. I, more than anyone, know that it is not fair to judge a person solely by how they look, and am absolutely certain that you deserved that kiss, whatever skin you are in.'

Her mouth twitched and spread into a fleeting but genuine smile. 'That may just be the nicest thing anyone has ever said to me.' It appeared he'd given the right answer. 'So, no more lies? No more hiding? Between the two of us, if no one else?' she said.

It was as if the sparks of their earlier frustrations with each other, dancing around them like the angry embers from the fire, had now burned themselves out, cooled to grey, and drifted slowly to the floor, settling at their feet. All was calm; all was bright. And, as they sat before each other, any pretence that there was not an overwhelming attraction between them dissolved into the sour smoke of the room.

Rising to her knees, she bent over his snow-white head and planted a gentle kiss on his short-cropped hair, her lips playing with the velvety nature of it. To be loved for what he truly was – Edward felt a wave of rogue emotions wash over him. He swept his arms up to her hips and buried his face in the cushion of her bosom, losing himself in the soft folds of the fabric and inhaling the scent of her. Her arms wrapped themselves around his shoulders and he heard her contented exhalation. Had anyone ever touched this poor woman in a sexual way? He doubted it. Certainly not in the time since she'd become Maude, because after the husband had left, no one had dared approach her for fear of being attacked.

'No more lies,' he muttered. 'Because you, Mallory Hornchurch, are incredible and deserve nothing but love. You're strong, intelligent and kind. Your compassion humbles me.'

He deliberately used her real name and didn't mention her physical attributes, even though he'd be a liar to deny that there were things about Maude's body that attracted him. But, he acknowledged to himself, it was the *way* Mallory was touching him – her fingers tracing swirls and circles across the goose-bumps of his skin – that was truly sending electric pulses through his body. Not the way she looked.

She pulled back and smiled, dropping down in front of him once more, before lifting her hands up to the row of tiny cloth-covered buttons that ran from the neck to the waist of her worn wool dress. He was mesmerised as she began the tantalisingly slow process of pushing them through the snug buttonholes. The fabric parted, and more and more of her flesh was exposed.

Impatient, he got to his knees and placed his hand over hers, momentarily halting her disrobing, and leaning forward to claim her mouth with his own. Their kisses quickly established the hunger they both had for each other and she tugged at his cotton shirt with equal urgency, sliding it upwards, being mindful of the bandage as she pulled it over his head.

For only the second time in his life, he wasn't conscious of his body. Much like the day he'd fallen on the rocks, he had no desire to hide the snow-coloured hairs that clustered in the hollow of his chest, or the line that ran from his naval and down to another, intensely private, thick tangle of white.

There was no doubt where this was leading now and he felt the strain of anticipation in his trousers. He couldn't remove them fast enough, almost as if her acceptance of his albinism gave her the right to access every part of him. *This is who I truly am*, he was repeating in his head, the physical effect their shared kisses and caresses were having on his body now blindingly obvious. *And she still wants me!*

There were very few times in his thirty-six years he'd felt truly powerful, apart from possibly when he was commanding a roomful of desperate and hopeful grieving relatives, but in this small flint-built cottage, on the ravaged and windswept North Norfolk coast, with this innocent young woman, he felt like a god. Surely, even the huge Samson Ballard, as he stood in the centre of the ring, introducing his *Circus of Astonishing Spectacles*, had never felt this potent?

He bent forward to trace a line of kisses from the nape of her neck, across her collarbone, and then burrowed his lips between the dress and her skin.

'I miss my old body,' she admitted, from above. 'It was letting me down and caused me so much pain, but it was mine. I felt comfortable in it.' She stretched her arms out in front of her and he felt them brush past his ears. 'Who even am I?'

'You're still Mallory, just wrapped up in different paper,' he mumbled, between kisses. 'But let me help you learn to love this body, too.' He undid the remaining buttons and slid both the dress and cotton chemise from her shoulders, over her hips and down to the floor, before burying his face once more in her breasts. This time, however, he could taste the salt on her flesh and feel the warmth of her skin on his lips. Those arms that she was struggling to accept, instead accepted Edward, pulling him tightly to her nakedness.

They tumbled to the thick knotted rug, all intertwined limbs and frantic kisses, and he manoeuvred her body so that she was beneath him, steadying himself by placing his hands either side of her. And then, gently at first, he entered her. Their eyes locked together, and the world lost all focus as the sensation of being connected to this brave and beguiling woman, in the most intimate of ways, usurped everything else.

Maude was not his first, but the woman concerned had been paid handsomely for her services and her discretion. She'd never called him beautiful and certainly never compared him to an angel. She'd also kept her eyes closed every time, doubtless treating the whole experience as nothing more than a job. But he could never bring himself to visit those establishments where disease and desperation were rife. Nor would he spoil the purity of someone who had hopes that the physical act might lead to love. Because, he realised with astonishing clarity, that's exactly what he felt for the amazing woman beneath him, her eyes boring into his, as though she was afraid she might miss some important cue, as his hands explored the most intimate parts of her.

This was love.

And, even though he could not admit it to Mallory, maybe a small part of that *was* because she was a freak like him, and she understood him nearly as well as he understood himself.

She trembled at his touch, bucked as she reached her release, and let out an animal moan. Limp from the overwhelming wave of intense sensations, she lay spent, as he coupled with her once more, focused on everything and nothing, and found his own nirvana.

40

Mallory fell asleep in his arms and he carried her carefully up the tiny stairs, slid her into what had once been the marital bed of Mr and Mrs Grimmer, and then climbed in next to her, moulding his body around hers. He lay there in the dark, his heart aching for the young woman of all those years ago and everything she'd been through, until he, too drifted off.

* * *

A shaft of light falling across his face from the small window in the low-ceilinged room woke him up the following morning. He wriggled to his elbows and could see that the fog had lifted in the night, much as the fog had lifted from his eyes when Mallory had collected the skull from the blanket chest.

Her skull.

He turned back to the sleeping woman beside him and gently swept back a loose strand of her dark hair, flecked with silver. The revelations that had tumbled out the previous night were so incredible, he half believed he'd imagined them in those moments between his dreams and being awake. He'd been such a fool.

Mallory stirred and opened her eyes – confusion and, eventually, comprehension apparent across her face. 'You stayed?'

'There was nowhere else I wanted to be.'

Edward slid back under the rough blanket and she rolled over onto her side towards the window. His knees slotted behind hers, his chest pressed against her back, and one arm rested over her thigh. She reached for his hand and brought his fingers to her lips, kissing them softly, before returning them to her leg.

'Do you not feel uncomfortable that I am one person trapped inside the body of another?' she asked.

'Many of us are one person trapped inside another,' he replied. 'Don't you think, deep inside, the frail elderly lady is still the child eager to run across the meadow? Or the man stuck in a mundane job with a family to support still holds on to the dreams of travel and adventure he had as a child?'

'Perhaps.'

A tatty blackbird flew to the windowsill outside and looked in at the pair of them as it hopped back and forth along the sill. Being watched by the creature made him think of Mallory's experience.

'Did you have a consciousness at any point between your death and waking up as Maude?' he asked, curious to know if ghosts existed. Had she floated about, after her bones had fallen from the cliffs, looking through the windows of the people in Thistlewick Tye? Were there other spirits out there wanting to contact the living?

She was silent for a moment and then twisted her head back to look at him.

'It's difficult to explain but I remember a queer feeling, a tumbling, almost as though I was part of the mist rolling in from the sea. But the passing of time and any awareness of my surroundings were hazy. And then suddenly I found myself in this cottage, as though I was pulled to Maude's body the moment she died.'

'How does this thing even work?' he pondered. 'Does the whole skeleton need to be exposed before the soul is set free? And then it waits for an empty vessel – the body of someone who's passed away – to slide into?'

She shrugged. 'Hazibub said the soul would be tied to the body, and the only part of the body that endures is the bones. I found my skull two days after I became Maude, when I wandered down to the beach, trying to work out how to feed myself. From its position near the copse above, and because of the bony deposits on the surface, I knew instantly it was me. I'd died with my feet to the sea, so it would have been the last thing to fall – ironically not after a storm, but a stretch of hot, dry weather. The rest of me probably fell the previous winter because those bones had long been washed out to sea.'

'I presume, then, that no one rose up in Silas when he was pushed from the cliffs because another complete body hadn't fallen?' This had been his earlier hypothesis.

'Possibly. I'd only found four skulls by that point, and there were four possessions; Maude, the baby, Emma and Noah. I'm certainly not aware I had any choice in who I took over, and wouldn't have chosen this body... this life, if I had.'

'Oh, I don't know. Being Maude has served you well. She lived an isolated existence. You might have been discovered had you been thrust into different circumstances. Poor little Esfir was surrounded by people she didn't know and too young to make sense of what'd happened to her.'

'Oh, Edward.' She rolled her body towards his. 'I keep thinking how scared she must have been.' He noticed the wobble of her lip and concertinaed brow. 'She was just a child. Not even four. And suddenly she wakes up as Mrs Shaw. How frightened she must have been to look in the mirror and see the face of someone else – to be surrounded by strangers and not able to explain herself.

'It was a shock for Samson, too. He was drifting about in Noah's body for several days until he found his way to your cottage.'

'He stumbled across me by accident, but I already suspected the younger Garrod brother had been possessed because you talked to me about his strange behaviour just after Silas died. I asked him outright, because a drunk has nothing to lose by speaking nonsense, and he readily admitted his true identity. But, more shockingly, he told me that it was *Silas* who'd turned up to the camp with the contaminated gifts of food and wine.'

Silas Garrod had delivered the poison... Now things were beginning to make sense.

'The troupe assumed he'd either been sent by Master Felthorpe, because he'd stuck up for us, or that his speech in the tent had forced the villagers to examine their consciences and they were trying to make amends,' Mallory continued. 'We were preparing to move on the following day, so they were grateful for it, but within the hour it was obvious they'd been poisoned. He spared me the details, but I'd seen the bodies...'

'I agree that it's unlikely Silas was acting alone.' Edward was convinced Jacob Palmer was also part of this.

'Samson said he was the only visitor that night, but I know others were involved. More than one person returned to bury the dead and dispose of our belongings. But, of course, Samson knew nothing about this until I told him, much as I had no idea that Silas had delivered the food, because I was with Sarah.

Nobody liked us back then; to my mind, any of the villagers could have been part of it – even the vicar.'

Edward shook his head in disbelief. 'And there was me thinking Silas Garrod was an innocent man, murdered by an evil spirit. I certainly got that the wrong way round. Samson must have been incandescent to find himself on the common with the man responsible for killing everyone he cared about. One minute he was choking and coughing up blood, the next the perpetrator was standing right in front of him – albeit looking considerably older.'

'I know what he did was wrong but there is a part of me that understands completely,' she said. Edward understood Mr Ballard's actions, too.

'So why did he speak in a foreign language on the common?'

Mallory smiled. 'He picked up the odd word from Katerina – mainly curse words, using them so his girls didn't know he was swearing. I'll wager if he woke up in the body of a stranger and then found himself facing the man who'd killed his family, he'd *absolutely* curse.' She gave a small smile, clearly remembering the circus owner fondly. 'And when you saw him at my cottage, you'd just told him you were a spiritualist so he was panicking. He was convinced you'd expose him and he'd swing for his crime. How could he ever explain the truth to a judge? So, he planned to walk to Great Yarmouth and sail abroad; that part was true. I gave him what little money I'd saved, and the watch chain I'd snatched from you on the beach – it was his, anyway...'

Of course, Edward realised, she hadn't been selling the items found with the bones. They were the personal possessions of those she cared about. She'd have kept them safe. The gold chain would fetch Samson a bit of money and he was glad for it. It was unlikely that those burying the dead back then had time to thoroughly search the bodies. Plus, it was dark, and it wouldn't have occurred to them that the land would fall into the sea and reveal their shocking crime – not in their lifetimes, at least.

Now he understood why Samson hadn't attacked him on the common – his violence had only been aimed at the person who had done him wrong. But Edward also knew that this whole affair didn't end with Silas's death. He'd been wrong to suspect that the spirits were the force of evil when clearly someone from the village was behind all this wickedness.

'Silas surely didn't administer that fatal dose of morphine to Emma?' Edward frowned. 'To my knowledge he's never set foot in Barnabas's home, unless he climbed in through a window. And a three-year-old wasn't capable of assembling the syringe and injecting herself, or even being aware that the morphia would kill her, which probably means someone at Thistlewick House wanted her dead. We know that Esfir *was* the intended victim, not Mrs Shaw, because it's now obvious this all centres around the unjust murders of your friends. The mention of Zella and the waggons, even if the little girl's name itself meant nothing, would have been enough for someone to make a connection to the circus.'

Mrs Drayton was the only member of his cousin's staff who was old enough to have been alive in 1855. She'd been working for her family's grocery business back then, so had dealings with the travellers when they'd stayed on the common. Barnabas hadn't moved to the village until ten years ago, and the current Dr Appleby could only have been a small child.

'But Silas was dead by the time Carl was poisoned and I was shot at.' He thought back to his conversation with the landlord. 'Jacob became increasingly nervous when I questioned him about the missing troupe yesterday. He wasn't running the Sailmaker's back then. Like many of the men from the village, he worked for Lord Felthorpe, and was undoubtedly part of that gang who chased Harry into the camp.'

'Yes, I recognised both of them from my fleeting visits to the village as Maude. And yet even Samson didn't know why anyone would want them dead. Just a silly feud that got out of hand, I guess. All I know is that when I returned from saying goodbye to Miss Cleyford, everyone at the camp had been murdered.'

Edward took a moment to realise the significance of the name. 'Miss Cleyford is Sarah – the young girl you befriended?' She nodded. 'Ah, I had no cause to be told her Christian name, but it makes perfect sense. She kept the handbill you gave her. And she defended travellers to her mother when I visited. Does she know who you really are?'

Mallory shook her head. 'She was a child. And I made her do such a terrible thing. I've often wondered whether I was wrong to ask for her help and can't forgive myself.'

'You had no one else,' he pointed out, kindly, and then made another connection. 'You're the one who has been giving her the gifts all these years, aren't you?'

'It was the only way I could thank her. I got quite the shock when I realised that the fifty-year-old woman I'd occasionally seen about the village was the young girl who'd been so kind to me. It's sad that she never married and did, indeed, end up leading the dull life she was afraid lay ahead of her.'

'She's nursing old Dr Appleby at the moment – he's seriously ill with this wave of influenza that's sweeping through Thistlewick Tye. With all that terrible rain the night before last, I was worried more bones would fall.'

'They did,' she confirmed. 'I was out yesterday morning trying to recover them, but with the fog and a high tide washing much of the soil away, I doubt I got them all.'

This was concerning. How many more souls were floating about, imminently to wreak havoc?

'Barnabas told me yesterday the doctor didn't expect his father to last much longer. I was on my way there when the weather disorientated me and I was shot at. We need to go to the Appleby house as soon as possible, in case one of your friends has found themselves in his worn-out body.'

She snorted. 'No one's going to let the village drunk in to see a dying man.'

'Sarah will, because we'll tell her everything.'

Mallory shook her head. 'I can't face her. She won't remember me and, even if she does, she's not going to believe I'm who I say I am.'

'I think you're wrong,' he said, gently. 'The handbill from *Samson's Circus of Astonishing Spectacles* is one of her most treasured possessions, along with the embroidered sentiment that you gave her. It's been framed behind glass and hangs, pride of place, on the wall above the fireplace. You worry that you've caused her lifelong suffering by asking for her help all those years ago, but children are more resilient than you think. That friendship meant a great deal to her, however brief it was, and the joy that you'll bring when she learns you walk this earth once more will be immeasurable.'

Mallory shook her head but didn't argue further, and instead reached up to the bandage around his head. 'How's the wound?'

'Sore.'

She shuffled up the bed, grabbing a handful of blanket to preserve her modesty, and stared at him for a considerable amount of time.

'An inch or two to the left and you'd be dead,' she finally said. 'If someone's tried to kill you twice, they'll try again, and I can't bear for someone else I care about to be taken from me. So yes, I'll come with you to see Sarah, and let's root out the evil that lurks in this village.'

41

Edward again experienced the simple joy of watching Mallory's domestic routine as she prepared breakfast, before they headed over to the doctor's house.

As an adolescent, he'd believed love would be dramatic and colourful, and in some ways, his love for Emma had been like that. A week of theatre shows and fine dining, the buzzing city and the company of smartly dressed, well-educated individuals. But, here with Mallory, he knew that this cosy feeling of being loved, of existing alongside another human being with no expectations on either side, was what made a bowl of plain porridge taste so inexplicably heavenly, and that being with her in this tiny cottage, for all its smell of cheap tallow and damp walls, was the only place he wanted to be.

Then he smiled to himself as he recalled their activities of the night before and forced himself to be honest. Perhaps it was also the sex.

It was late morning before they stepped from her front door and he reached for her hand, wrapping his wide fingers around hers.

'Someone might see,' she said, looking nervously about.

Reluctantly, he let her hand drop.

They walked through the woods, all traces of the heavy fog now gone, and ventured up the lane to Dr Appleby's house. Miss Cleyford answered the door, wearing a long white apron, and nodded nervously at the woman she believed to be Maude Grimmer. She noticed Edward's bandage. Mallory had reapplied it that morning to incorporate his wig.

'Mr Blackmore, what on earth's happened to your head?'

'Someone wants me dead and I was shot at yesterday. Things are getting serious and we need your help.'

'The doctor isn't in.'

'It's his father we've come to see,' Edward said. 'How is he?'

'I'm surprised he's still here, to be honest. His breathing seems remarkably improved this morning but he's more muddled than before. He's talking of circles of salt and poisoned wine.' Mallory and Edward exchanged a glance. 'The influenza has really taken hold in the village now. Several of the children from the school have come down with it, and my own mother – who was not in the best of health before. I'm running backwards and forwards between my house and the doctor's. It's exhausting.'

'Can we see him, please?' Edward asked.

Miss Cleyford threw another anxious look at the woman by his side. 'You must know that influenza patients are isolated to stop the spread of the disease. I can't let either of you near him, I'm afraid.'

'Please?' Edward begged. 'We'll keep our distance. I have questions, and there are things I need to explain to him, and to you. Things you won't believe. But it's all connected to the circus that came to Thistlewick when you were a child, and the young woman you befriended.'

'Mallory?' Her voice was a whisper. Edward nodded, and felt Mallory stiffen beside him.

'Has your patient mentioned any names that sound as though they might be from the circus handbill you showed me?'

The older woman frowned and then gave a cautious nod, perhaps now realising the significance of his questions. She pulled back the door to let them in and directed the pair to a room at the back of the house, where the old doctor lay propped up in a small wooden bed.

He turned his face to the visitors, his eyes brighter than Edward remembered. This was not the confused and frail man of a few short days ago. Someone else had woken up to find themselves in this worn-out body, and he wondered if they were as scared as Esfir had been. He needed to break the news as gently as possible, acutely aware that Miss Cleyford was anxiously watching them both and had absolutely no idea what was going on.

'My name is Edward Blackmore. There's no need to be alarmed. I'm a friend and mean you no harm. The year is 1895 and we're in Thistlewick Tye, a small village on the cliffs of North Norfolk. If my guess is correct, it will seem only moments ago that you were camped up with the other members of Samson Ballard's circus, as you stopped here for a couple of weeks to make repairs to your equipment and rest your horses.'

The old man narrowed his eyes but nodded his head. Sarah couldn't have looked more astonished if a giraffe had loped into the room.

Mallory took a step forward and continued with the explanation.

'This happened to me, too. Try not to be frightened but you've come back in the body of another. The troupe was poisoned and later buried at the far edge of the common. Our bones have fallen into the sea and we've risen again, just as Hazibub promised. Do you remember his curious ritual? We all thought he was talking nonsense as he planted a thumbprint of some bizarre concoction on our foreheads. I certainly didn't believe there were any such things as spirits, but he was so worried that we were in danger. I know what I'm about to say sounds utterly unbelievable but I'm Mallory – the Toad Girl – and I, too, have come back from the dead.'

There was a thud as Sarah let out a squeal and collapsed into a chair by the wall. The old man nodded and a slow smile crept across his wrinkled face.

'Goodness me. It worked? Darling child, I am believing every word you say and am so glad to find a friend in this new time.' He smiled. 'I was always knowing that spirits could be revived, although it needed a very special kind of magic, for I was the one casting the spell.'

'Hazibub?' Mallory's voice was incredulous.

'At your service.' He dipped his head and then stretched his arms out before him and studied the twisted, liver-spotted hands. 'Although I was hoping for a more youthful vessel,' he admitted. 'I appear to have aged considerably overnight.'

Mallory started to walk towards him but Edward grabbed her arm, aware that even if Hazibub's possession of the old man's body had seen off the illness, there might still be a lingering miasma in the air.

'How I've missed you. If I could kiss you right now, I would,' she said. 'There's so much to catch up on but, for the moment, trust no one, except Edward and myself. Evil still walks through Thistlewick Tye.'

Hazibub nodded, as Mallory turned her attentions to Sarah, approaching her slowly, head bowed and biting at her lip.

'I hope we can trust you, also, not to talk about what you've heard in this room? Someone is trying to kill Mr Blackmore; they poisoned his manservant, and are responsible for the death of poor Emma Shaw. Because it really is me, Sarah; the woman you befriended when you were a child. The woman you never judged for her unsightly face, and who snuck you into the back of the big tent to watch the circus rehearse. You gave me a whelk shell, so I could always hear the sea, and I embroidered you a senti-ment about friendship, because your acceptance of me meant the world. I think of you often as I scour the shoreline and cook the bladderwrack or raid the seagull nests for their gamey eggs.' She let out a small snort. 'If only you knew how useful your lessons about scavenging along the foreshore that day have proved to be.'

'It can't be...' Poor Sarah Cleyford looked frightened and hopeful all at once, but Mallory's words could only be spoken by someone who'd shared those experiences with her.

'And then that awful night when I returned from the church-yard to find everyone dead. My people were murdered, remem-ber, Sarah? And now, as their bones fall into the sea, they're rising again. But, by choosing to bury myself so much nearer to the shore, my grave was exposed four years ago, and I've been living as Maude Grimmer ever since.'

The older woman was deathly white and mouth agape. Edward could see her hands were shaking as she clutched at the arms of the chair she was in. Her eyes started to fill with tears as she looked up at Mallory.

'Truly?'

'Truly.'

She got back to her feet and stared at Mallory for a long time, before stretching out her arms so the pair could embrace.

'Oh, my goodness, I can hardly believe you're here. My life has been haunted by that week. You opened my eyes to a world of wonder and then the circus was persecuted by people for reasons I couldn't understand. I grew up overnight and was never quite the same again.'

'I'm so sorry I asked you to do such a terrible thing. It torments me every waking moment, but I had no one else to ask.'

They pulled back and Edward could see how overjoyed both women were to have found each other again.

'Don't apologise. It wasn't your request that upset me, because I trusted that you'd passed happily and were free of pain. Instead, I was horrified when you told me that such a wicked crime had been committed – all those people killed – whatever your sins. And then the following day everyone around me was saying something completely different, and I was so confused. I went down to your camp, but the circus had gone – not a trace – and I began to wonder if you'd got it wrong. Perhaps you'd been accidentally left behind and imagined the deaths. Because, everyone in Thistlewick Tye was so definite, and when adults repeatedly tell you how a thing is, you doubt yourself. And then forty years later, I heard of the peculiar incident with Emma at Thistlewick House and the consequent arrival of Mr Blackmore, who was asking questions about the bones...'

'Oh, Sarah.'

'So, it *was* Esfir who came back in Mrs Shaw's body?' Miss Cleyford turned to Edward.

'*Esfir*? You must be telling me all that has happened,' Hazibub demanded, his brow wrinkled into a stern frown as he leaned forward.

Mallory and Edward shared what they knew. They suspected, but could not prove, that the first person to rise, after Mallory, had found themselves in the body of the blacksmith's baby, but the tragedy of the infant's death meant they'd never know who. Perhaps one of the hands, perhaps Cupid, or even Zella. Then they relayed the sad tale of Esfir, and finally how Samson had avenged them all by pushing Silas from the cliff.

'A reckless man, very quickly to use his fists, but someone who would always defend his own,' Hazibub agreed. 'I am pleased he is being out there somewhere with the chance to have a few more years of living. Let us be hoping he can curb his temper and come up with a scheme not too fanciful that will make him enough money to survive. But I'm still not understanding why those village men wanted us dead. To be giving us poisoned food and wine when we had committed no real crime.'

'Murder seems extreme,' Sarah admitted, 'but the village was full of talk about the terrible things you'd done, and what bad people you were, for weeks. It was hard to know what to believe. Mother told everyone you'd all but kidnapped me, and I knew that wasn't true. But your lack of faith, questionable morals and lies about the Reverend Marsham meant everyone was glad to see you gone.' Edward knew from Mallory that the vicar really was a voyeur, but didn't comment. 'Apparently, you set your snake on Lord Felthorpe's dog, stole the church silver and set the Tutters' barn alight. Then it came out that Mary had been assaulted by one of your men and was with child...'

Hazibub and Mallory exchanged puzzled glances.

'We weren't guilty of those things,' Mallory said. 'For a start, my people were dead before nightfall. By the following morning, all traces of the circus had gone. The Tutters' barn was either lit to hide the fact they'd set fire to our big tent, or purely as something else to blame on us and justify our persecution.'

'And the pig, too,' Sarah added. 'They accused you of stealing one from Lord Felthorpe.'

Three sets of eyes fell to the floor and no one commented on this particular accusation.

Sarah looked thoughtful. 'Several local farms suddenly

acquired new waggons and extra horses after you supposedly left. They were yours, I guess, although I don't know what happened to the monkeys or your zebras...'

Monkeys were easy enough to dispose of, but zebras? Edward thought of the old doctor's admission about eating zebra at Emma's funeral. He said nothing. The ladies didn't need to know.

'Whilst I don't believe the whole village was responsible for the deaths,' Edward said, 'I think they were so prejudiced that when it came to covering up the crime, they didn't ask too many questions. But it would have taken more than one person to bury the bodies and move all the equipment. Jacob Palmer must be involved. He has a shed full of circus paraphernalia. Maybe he simply couldn't bring himself to destroy the items, but they rather point to his guilt.'

'Jacob and Silas were good friends,' Sarah confirmed, and then pulled her face into a puzzled frown. 'Mary Tutter's child was born seven months after the troupe pitched up and, whilst I know babies can be born early, he was a healthy weight. No one says anything, but Charlie Tutter has the same smile as Jacob Palmer – you only have to look at his teeth. It makes me wonder if two young people, who were doing things they shouldn't, blamed such an accident on people who weren't there to defend themselves. Her uncle, the old Dr Appleby, would have been livid if he'd suspected she'd been dallying out of wedlock, and her best friend at the time, Freda Drayton – or Mrs Drayton as she's known now – would have been equally furious.'

Edward hadn't realised his cousin's housekeeper was friends with the Tutter woman, but the village was small and they were about the same age, so it made sense.

'It is seeming to me that we were blamed for a great many things,' Hazibub said. 'Considered evil because we were different. So, we must be using this second gift of life, however short it may be...' Hazibub again looked at his ancient hands, '...to expose the truth.'

'What do you need me to do?' Sarah asked.

'You've already been a great help by alerting me to the contents of Jacob's barn and letting us in to see Hazibub today,' Edward reassured her. He thought back again to the ramblings of old Dr Appleby at the funeral. 'Hazibub, I suspect the man whose body you now occupy was part of this. He certainly had something weighing on his conscience and, in his senility, may have shared it with his son. If you can keep up the pretence that you're his father, perhaps you can find out what?'

'This outbreak has the doctor rushed off his feet,' Sarah chipped in. 'He's left the care of the old man to me because he rightly believed there was little left that he could usefully do, so I can tell Hazibub everything he might need to know to carry out the deception.'

Edward nodded his appreciation. 'In the meantime, we must speak to a man about some hidden tea chests,' he said, and reached for Mallory's hand, so angry about the revelations that were coming to light that he no longer cared if they were judged for their perceived adulterous relationship, and set off to have words with Jacob Palmer.

42

Edward banged on the door to the Sailmaker's with his fist but there was no response. After a few minutes, the Reverend Fallow scurried past. His eyes flashed to Edward's other hand, still gripping tightly on to Mallory's, and he jolted his head back in surprise.

'I appreciate that neither of you profess to have any faith, but I must ask you refrain from displaying such inappropriate behaviour in public.'

'Mall... Maude and I are good friends...' Edward began, and then questioned why he was trying to appease the vicar's sensibilities when he cared nothing for the religion the man practised. 'More than friends,' he corrected.

'Really!' The vicar almost snorted the word in his shock. 'May I remind you, Mr Blackmore, that Mrs Grimmer is a married woman and, as such, should not be engaging in such intimate behaviour with another man.'

If he was shocked by hand-holding, he'd be absolutely scandalised by the other things they'd been up to. Besides, Edward decided that if there was a God, He would know that Mallory was a spinster, so they were breaking no commandment regarding adultery, even if He tutted at their sexual activities outside of wedlock.

'You can't have it both ways, Reverend. If you accept we do not follow your religion, then you cannot judge us by the tenets it upholds. I love Mrs Grimmer, with every part of my being, and if God exists, He can judge me for that when I pass to the other side. In the meantime, I have no intention of hiding the one thing that truly brings me joy.'

The vicar's face was now practically puce, but Mallory's, conversely, had drained of colour. Edward hadn't told her in words quite how powerful his feelings for her were, and should have done so before declaring himself to the Reverend Fallow.

'We will not condone this. We do not want immorality in this village. *Leviticus* would have you both put to death.'

'And who is "we", exactly?' Edward asked, wondering how strictly the man obeyed the Ten Commandments, and whether he'd ever mixed up a deadly hair tonic or if he owned a gun.

'All of the faithful and upstanding members of our community,' he blustered. 'And I shall certainly be speaking to the Benevolent Committee about your immoral behaviour later today.'

'But, as the good book says, Reverend, if we do not forgive those who trespass against us, our own trespasses will not be forgiven. Have you sins that need addressing? Because I know that I have many to forgive.'

'Indeed you do.' The vicar was almost shaking by this point. 'And telling scandalous falsehoods is amongst them. Claiming to be able to contact those who have passed on, only for Lady Temple to reveal that you have no such ability. I strongly suggest that when you inherit Thistlewick House, you might consider selling it and returning to London, where your heathen ways are more acceptable. This village does not want you, Mr Blackmore. You are not welcome here.'

'And yet there are many people who have told falsehoods in Thistlewick Tye over the years. Do you intend to persecute them all in such a manner? Ask them all to move out? Because you'll find the population of Thistlewick Tye sorely depleted, if you do. Jacob Palmer is a prime example, because I strongly suspect he's not been honest about his knowledge of the circus troupe that disappeared in this village forty years ago.'

Edward was done with maintaining the thin veneer of politeness and took a step closer to the vicar, using his height to intimidate the man, as he spat the words out.

'In fact, he was involved in the murder of over a dozen people – yes, you heard me correctly – and has some of their possessions tucked away in his back barn. And then look more closely at Charlie Tutter and ask why his mother might have cried rape back then, when he so startlingly resembles the landlord of this particular establishment. I've been told that the gap between his front teeth is quite distinctive. Because I intend to quiz Mr Palmer about all of this when he *finally* answers the door.'

He threw a look up to the tiny Tudor first-floor windows, hoping to see Jacob's round face peering down, but all was silent within. The vicar was subdued for a few moments, after the flurry of accusations, but finally spoke, perhaps thinking they would find out what he was about to say soon enough.

'Jacob started a fire in his back barn last night, just as the fog was clearing. The baker, who's always up and about in the early hours, saw him light it – but when the constable went to question Mr Palmer, he'd disappeared. Emptied the till and run.'

'Then I would say he was guilty of something – wouldn't you,

Reverend? And perhaps your perfect little village isn't quite as perfect as you thought, because I'm convinced that the bones falling into the sea by the common are from *Samson's Circus of Astonishing Spectacles*. And these unjustly persecuted dead travellers are now possessing people in the village and taking their revenge.'

'Absolutely preposterous! Spirit possessions are a heathen fabrication.'

'Really? Because we both believe, for different reasons, that death is not the end, so what is it you are struggling with, exactly? That spirits exist? Or that someone in your perfect village might be a killer?'

'And yet you've been publicly exposed as a fraud, so you've certainly not communicated with these alleged murdered souls. These wild claims have no basis in fact.' But the vicar looked less sure of himself now.

Edward locked eyes with the man, and kept his voice low and serious.

'I have recently spoken directly to a member of the troupe who wasn't at the camp that night and didn't ingest the poison. Someone who was not amongst the dead but who witnessed the crime, and who everyone forgot about. Forty years is really not so long ago...'

He didn't elaborate, feeling he'd said enough. Technically, two of the troupe were missing that night – Mallory and Katerina – but let him read into his words what he would.

The vicar started to look uncomfortable and tugged at his collar.

'I cannot listen to your nonsense any longer. I'm a busy man and have places to be. Do excuse me.' He gave a curt nod of the head, and strode off in the direction of Felthorpe Hall, but Edward knew that the man was rattled.

* * *

With no Jacob to question, Edward insisted Mallory came back with him to Thistlewick House, stressing he wouldn't countenance her being out of his sight. If his life was in danger, so was hers. She gripped his hand even tighter, perhaps for courage, and agreed.

They strode along Copperpenny Lane together, as the damp smell from the rotting leaves circled them in the breeze. Life was fleeting, he realised, and he intended to live every day as though it were his last. The conversation with the reverend had only strengthened his resolve. He *would* be with Mallory, whatever upset it caused.

'It was Jacob and Silas then,' she said, struggling to keep up with his long strides. 'Two angry young men who decided to wreak revenge on a group of people who'd disrupted the lives of all at Thistlewick. We did steal a pig, after all.'

But her conclusion didn't sit right with Edward.

'That doesn't make sense. The crimes the circus was accused of either didn't affect them personally, or were manufactured after your friends were killed. They both worked for the previous Lord Felthorpe. Perhaps he asked them to deal with the troublesome travellers? They were in his employ and would have done what he asked.'

'But he wasn't even in Thistlewick when we pitched up. Besides, he's long dead, so he can't be the one trying to kill you now.'

'How about his son, Christian, the current Lord Felthorpe?'

'He certainly gave us trouble when we arrived, eager for us to be gone and letting his stupid dog wander around our camp, but he fell in love with Zella,' Mallory said. 'I saw them together, Edward, and the pull between them was absolutely incredible. I find it impossible to believe he could've killed her, or have had any part in her death. They'd only known each other a matter of days before he proposed – that's a huge commitment, considering how different their worlds were. And when his father returned from London, he planned to speak to him about letting us stay on the common. We all witnessed him go from antagonistic to fully supportive within those few days, and I understand the poor man was so heartbroken that he never married anyone else after she disappeared.'

So, who else did that leave?

'Dr Appleby senior was rambling when I met him at Mrs Shaw's funeral. His son was quick to dismiss what his father was saying and blame his senility, but perhaps he was admitting to the crime? He told me he'd done bad things. Yet, he was too frail to have murdered Mrs Shaw or been out in the woods with a rifle. Mrs Drayton, however, could easily have removed the morphia from the doctor's bag when Emma was ill, and had ample opportunity to administer it, but I see no obvious motive. And you told me how the vicar back then was badly humiliated by Harry – a motive perhaps – but he's also long dead so certainly isn't around to take potshots at me in the fog. It seems to me that we've got people who had motive *or* opportunity... but no one who had both.' Edward sighed. 'We know multiple people are involved, but I can't see either Silas or Jacob orchestrating everything, either forty years ago or now, so who the devil's behind it all?'

They arrived at Thistlewick House and Barnabas dashed out into the hall, raising his eyebrows when he realised Edward was not alone.

'Barnabas. I'm sure you are acquainted with Mrs Grimmer?'

His cousin nodded briefly at Mallory but addressed Edward with a flurry of anxious words.

'Thank the Lord you're safe. Damn fool to go out in that fog yesterday – worst I've seen in years. What the hell were you thinking? I've been half expecting the constable to call and announce your body had been found at the bottom of the cliffs. And then Wright went down to the village first thing because we saw smoke. Turns out Jacob Palmer has been up to no good, and gunshots were heard in the woods yesterday afternoon. I've been so worried about you – especially after all that funny business with the hair tonic.'

Mrs Drayton appeared and helped Edward hang his coat on the hatstand and relieved Mallory of her cloak.

'And what the blazes has happened to your head?' Barnabas belatedly noticed the bandage.

'I'll explain everything. We need to talk. It's important,' Edward said.

'And Mrs Grimmer needs to be present, does she?'

'Absolutely, because she's pivotal to what I have to tell you.'

His cousin narrowed his eyes, but nodded, reluctantly leading them both into the drawing room and then addressing his housekeeper, who had followed them in.

'Some tea, please, Drayton. And tell Cook there will be three for luncheon.'

The housekeeper's thin lips pinched tight at the thought of entertaining such a disreputable woman, but she nodded. 'Very good, sir.'

The gentlemen waited for Mallory to take a seat, and Edward noticed how wide her eyes were as she looked about the tastefully furnished room. He doubted she'd ever been in such a well-to-do house in either of her tragic lives. She nervously patted her shabby skirts and picked at her fingernails.

'It won't be me ordering the staff about soon,' Barnabas observed, but without resentment. 'Fraud or not, it doesn't matter to me. The house will shortly be yours and I truly believe I will be happier in the little cottage by the church. All I want is to be near my Emma.'

Edward reached for his cousin's knee. 'That's what I'm here to talk about. I understand now why you so readily handed the house over to me after her death – because she meant everything to you and your life felt empty without her. I, too, have fallen in love and would equally sacrifice everything, all the wealth and comforts I thought I wanted in life, to be with the woman who's so completely claimed my heart.'

Mallory jerked her head in his direction at this dramatic declaration as Barnabas raised his head. Yet again, he'd announced his depth of feelings to someone other than the person he should be declaring them to. But he'd been certain of his love since she'd revealed who she truly was, and they'd engaged in that most intimate of acts on the knotted rug in front of her tiny fireplace.

'In love? With whom?'

'The woman you see before you today.' He allowed himself to smile as he looked across at Mallory's startled face. 'And I don't want your house, Barnabas, because she's taught me what is truly important in life, and it isn't money, or a big house, or fine foods. It's being accepted for who you are.'

'*Maude Grimmer*?' Barnabas's tone was incredulous, and then he remembered that the poor woman was sitting not five feet from him. His cheeks coloured as he turned to her. 'Apologies, but you are married and quite... erm... different to the sort of woman I imagined my cousin falling for.' He swung back to Edward. 'I always understood romance was not on your agenda.'

'She knows my secret and yet she's still here by my side. I acknowledge we're in an incredibly complicated situation and she's not free to marry, but I *will* find a way to be with her.'

He'd made a great many assumptions and turned to face Mallory, his eyes asking the questions he'd yet to voice. Did she feel the same? She was frantically blinking away building tears but she nodded, and Edward knew it was time to trust his cousin with the truth. Firmly closing the drawing room door behind Mrs Drayton after she'd presented the tea tray, he began to tell his cousin of a persecuted circus troupe and an astonishing spell cast by a mysterious snake charmer as a consequence.

At the end of his tale, he explained that it was Esfir, the young daughter of the circus owner, who'd found herself in Emma's body, and that Mallory, the Toad Girl, had been Maude for the last four years.

Barnabas looked shocked by his revelations. 'Is this more of your nonsense, Edward? Playing on my gullibility for your own ends again?'

'Not at all, cousin. You were correct about the spirits possessing people, but we were both wrong about their intent. We assumed they were maleficent, but it was the villagers who turned on the troupe. A couple of lads poisoned a gift of food and wine, and other members of the community were either actively involved in covering this up, or turned a blind eye to the distribution of their possessions and failed to scrutinise the lie that the circus had moved on.'

His cousin nodded and Edward was once again glad for his trusting nature, even though everything he'd told Barnabas this time was the truth.

'Then, my Emma died the night of the high fever?' Edward nodded, and shortly afterwards Barnabas nodded to himself. 'You never could have saved her. By the time I wrote to you, it was already too late.'

The room was silent for a moment. Poor Barnabas.

'The time has come to start asking direct questions and

demanding answers. Much like the detailed research I did before my séances, the information I now have at my disposal gives me an advantage. And by presenting an air of confidence, people will talk more freely because they will believe I already know the information they hold. So, if you would kindly ask Mrs Drayton to join us?'

Barnabas rang the bell and his housekeeper was summoned. She was obviously still rattled by the presence of Mrs Grimmer. Her eyes were wary and she was wringing her hands together as she entered.

'Dear woman.' Edward stood and gestured for her to take a seat. He began a slow pace, back and forth in front of the fireplace, his deep blue tailcoat flapping behind him as he walked. 'I understand you were a young woman when the circus came to Thistlewick Tye and I believe you know more about its disappearance than you're letting on...'

The older woman narrowed her eyes but didn't speak, so he continued.

'Mrs Shaw's earthly body was possessed by a little girl called Esfir – the youngest daughter of Samson Ballard, owner of the *Circus of Astonishing Spectacles*. Someone recognised her name and was worried that she'd reveal the dark truth of the troupe's demise. You were the only person with access to your mistress's room the night she died. You were also the only person to witness the delivery of the poisoned gift basket. So, I have to ask if you administered the morphia to your mistress to stop secrets from tumbling out? And whether you tried to kill me with tainted goods, too?'

'I loved Mrs Shaw!' The housekeeper looked horrified.

'I've no doubt. But someone wanted her silenced.' Mrs Drayton looked confused. 'You were best friends with Mary

Tutter back then and have understandably been angry if you thought she'd been attacked. Yet, even before that accusation, your family sold the troupe a sack of mouldy potatoes, and tensions were running high. For a woman who regularly attends church, your behaviour towards them wasn't very Christian.'

He was clutching at straws, trying to find a motive that would justify Mrs Drayton killing Emma, but the poor woman was now shaking.

'How do you know all this?'

Edward kept silent – another trick he'd learned over the years. It made people uncomfortable so they kept talking to relieve the tension, often saying more than they intended.

'I had nothing to do with Mrs Shaw's death, your hair tonic or the circus leaving. Ask who you like – even them spirits, if you really *do* have the ability to contact them.' She was indignant now. 'I'll be honest – I didn't like the circus folk one bit, and I didn't care where they went. I was just pleased to see them gone and didn't ask too many questions.'

'But they didn't go, did they? They were poisoned by food and wine delivered by Silas Garrod, and they died horrific deaths.'

Mrs Drayton gasped. 'The circus people were poisoned?'

Edward and Mallory exchanged a glance. The housekeeper's shock seemed real enough.

'Look, there were things that went on after the troupe disappeared that seemed odd, I'll grant you. The Tutters got a pair of carthorses and a new waggon, as did another farmer, out towards Cromer. Yet the Reverend Marsham *swore* that he'd seen them leaving in the night. That he'd had further words with Mr Ballard in the churchyard and that they'd stolen the silver plate.'

'You do know, don't you, that Mary wasn't attacked by one of the hands; Charlie Tutter is Jacob's?'

She bowed her head to avoid his eye and nodded. 'Not at the time, but it became obvious as he grew up. Truth is, the circus had done such wicked things, what did it matter if one more accusation was levelled at them? It saved Mary a thrashing.'

Mallory was furious and leapt to her feet. 'See! That's exactly the problem. Of all the crimes we... I mean, the circus, supposedly committed, only the theft of the pig was true. The hired lads didn't even start the fight outside the pub. That was young Jacob Palmer, sore because one of them was talking to the village girls, and probably where he got the idea to blame them for the pregnancy.'

'Mrs Grimmer has been helping me with my enquiries.' Edward noticed the housekeeper's confusion and hastily tried to explain away Maude's outburst. 'But she's quite correct. It's too easy to pin everything on those who have different morals to your own, especially if they've disappeared and aren't there to defend themselves.'

'Those people were mothers, daughters, fathers...' Mallory was close to crying. 'Many of them had extremely difficult lives, born with disfigurements, not wanted by their real families. The Giraffe Woman was stolen from her people, the Toad Girl was dying from the lumps that everyone laughed at, Harry had been beaten by his father as a boy, Samson grew up in a workhouse... All of them had unhappy pasts and were just trying to earn a crust. And yet there were people in this village who would see them dead.'

Mrs Drayton looked quite moved by Mallory's passionate speech. Perhaps she'd not thought of it from that point of view.

'I can promise you, sir—' she looked over to Edward '—I may have kept quiet about some of the things that went on back then, and perhaps my silence is a sin I need to atone for, but I had no part in any murder.'

The housekeeper's bottom lip wobbled as she spoke, but she held his eye. He was used to liars and knew the tell-tale body language that often gave them away.

'No,' Edward agreed, slumping back into his chair. He'd at least ruled out one suspect. 'I'm inclined to believe you.'

43

'I shouldn't be here. It's making everyone uncomfortable,' Mallory said, when they were left briefly alone in the dining room after luncheon. It had been a stilted affair, the formality of it clearly made her uncomfortable and she ate very little. She pushed back her chair, stood up and walked to the windows. Edward joined her.

'My cousin is still master here and the staff are paid to do as he instructs. It doesn't matter what they think. Besides, I'm simply not prepared to part with you now, or at any point in the future; partly because I fear for our lives, but also because I love you, Mallory Hornchurch: Living Wonder, *lusus naturae* and incredible Toad Girl – even though I seem to have declared this to everyone *but* you.'

'But we are very different people and we want different things, Edward. I have no desire for great wealth and am content with my simple life.'

'Amassing a fortune is no longer as important to me as it once was. I spent years striving to do just this as a compensation for the way I was born and the injustice I suffered at my father's hands. But last night, in your tumbledown cottage, there was no banquet to be had, no expensive port and no guest bed with feather mattress and silk coverlet. We didn't need money to have a hearty meal, a good laugh and an amazing evening.'

He bent down, closer to her face and she tipped her head up to his. Their lips met briefly, as his hands cupped her cheeks. He reached for her slim waist and pulled her close. She slid her arms up his body and rested them around his neck. They stood in silence for a few moments – the longing between them almost palpable. He let out a small groan, then released her. More than anything, he wanted to lead her upstairs to his room and demonstrate exactly how strong his feelings for her were. Being together in her isolated cottage, where they knew the truth of her identity, was one thing. But any such behaviour in his cousin's respectable household, was quite another.

Mallory, however, as much as he loved her, was currently a distraction and he needed to focus. They should return to the village and ensure the constable investigated Mr Palmer's involvement in the horrific events of forty years ago. His meandering thoughts wandered to the Benevolent Committee – the three men running the village back then, even though the old doctor had been the only one still alive until yesterday, and had at no point been capable of chasing him through the woods with a gun. They'd always been the moral backbone of Thistlewick Tye and yet, it was now apparent that the village had always been decidedly lacking in morals.

But even the committee's successors had no real motive for wanting Edward dead. The current Dr Appleby and Reverend Fallow were too young to have been involved with the circus, and Christian Felthorpe had been so desperately in love with Zella that Edward found it hard to believe he'd have been part of such a thing.

Mrs Drayton knocked and entered, still embarrassed by all that had passed that morning, but aware of her duties.

'Miss Cleyford is here to see you, sir. She seems rather agitated.'

A moment later, Sarah was shown into the room, looking quite flushed. 'It's my mother. She passed away a little while ago and I was with her when she took her dying breath—'

'I'm so sorry.' Mallory stepped forward and embraced her friend.

'I knew it was coming, regardless of the influenza, and we've had a difficult relationship over the years, but I will miss her.' Finally Sarah's voice cracked and she allowed herself a few moments of grief, her head resting on Mallory's shoulder, before she wiped her eyes and pulled herself together.

'It was her time, but it's not the reason I'm here. To my amazement, the very next moment she started rambling in a strong accent, anxious about the safety of her daughters. As unbelievable as the idea was, I could only assume the Russian fortune-telling lady had appeared in my poor, dead mother's body. So, when I saw the doctor leave for his rounds, I rushed across the road for Hazibub. We were able to explain everything to her and he's currently at my house, and disturbing truths are spilling out, thick and fast. He has news of his own and it's imperative that you and Mallory return with me.' She looked at Edward. 'Now.'

The pair didn't need telling twice and Edward led the ladies to the hall, grabbing their coats and his cane, and asking the housekeeper to let her master know they were heading to the village.

* * *

Ten minutes later, the three of them were standing in the Cleyfords' front parlour, with Hazibub and Sarah's extraordinarily sprightly looking mother sitting in the fireside chairs.

'This is the man I told you about,' Sarah said, pushing Edward forward. 'Mr Blackmore.'

'Ah, the man who spent a lifetime pretending to talk to spirits but had no such ability, and yet is the person I understand we must rely on to sort out this horrific mess?'

There was no trace of an accent, which surprised them both, after Sarah's claims.

'You don't sound like Katerina,' Mallory said.

Mrs Cleyford – or whoever was possessing her – sighed.

'The time for charades and lies has passed, don't you think, my little Toad Girl? The very reasons I pretended to be a foreigner all those years ago are the reasons I must own the truth now. Like many who join the circus, I was running from an uncomfortable past and created a new identity to make sure I was never discovered. I had befriended a young Russian artist, and was his muse for a couple of years, so I took on his nationality. It suited me to be dark and mysterious.'

'I knew it,' Mallory said, folding her arms across her chest.

'And I always knew you were brighter than most,' Katerina replied. 'The truth is this whole mess is my fault and I am responsible for all these deaths – both back then and now. I was hiding from my past and did not want to be recognised. I'd spoken with that accent for so many years, that by the end I was even dreaming in it.' She took a deep breath and shook her head. 'It became second nature, and even my beloved Samson didn't know the truth. I was Russian; I was exotic; I could be anything I wanted to be—'

'What is going on?' The door to the parlour burst open and young Dr Appleby entered the room, having clearly let himself into their house. 'My maid said she saw my father heading this way with Miss Cleyford earlier.'

Edward was cross at the interruption. Katerina had been about to explain why she felt the murders were her fault, although he couldn't imagine that she'd poisoned her family and friends... or had she? Mallory said the woman had disappeared the afternoon of the massacre and her body was not amongst those dead around the campfire.

'Ah, the man who was killing little Esfir,' Hazibub announced and the doctor looked as shocked as Edward felt by the pronouncement.

'Get the constable,' Edward whispered to Sarah. If accusations and secrets were to spill out, they must be witnessed. 'Go now.' She nodded and slipped out of the room unnoticed.

'Father, what *are* you doing here?' Appleby went to Hazibub's side and laid a concerned hand on his shoulder. 'You should be in bed. You're not well.'

'I am being greatly better than you think,' Hazibub replied. 'And I am also knowing now that you put the needle in Mrs Shaw's arm and watched her die. We discussed it not two hours ago, did we not?'

The doctor looked at the faces in the room and gave a half-chuckle. 'My poor father's infirm of both mind and body. Please pay no mind to his dramatic pronouncements.' He glared at the old man. 'Come now, Father, we must be going.' He put out his hand but Hazibub shook his head and remained in the armchair, as Edward worked through the logic of the shocking claim and the truth hit him.

'Of course! I'd suspected poor Mrs Drayton of the crime but this makes much more sense. It's been dancing around the edges of my brain – how Barnabas talked of rushing into the bedroom to embrace his wife's body, lifeless and pink. How he lifted up her soft, warm arm. But the significance of his words have only just occurred to me. She can't have died in the early hours, because the blood would have ceased to be pumped around her body and started to settle. Whilst it is true that the dead can remain warm for many hours, had she died when the doctor claimed, she would have appeared pale, and rigor mortis would surely have started to set in.'

Mallory gasped and Katerina threw the doctor a look that would have frozen over the hottest desert.

'You walked into her room,' Edward confidently surmised, 'arriving ridiculously early, quickly establishing that no one had been in to see her since the previous evening, and administered the overdose right there and then. She had been dead mere minutes when my cousin rushed to her side.'

'How dare you accuse me of such! You doubt the word *of a doctor*?'

Dr Appleby's eyes flitted between the faces of those assembled in the Cleyfords' front room and was horrified to realise that they did all believe him guilty of the crime. His challenging words had set off a chain of thought in Edward's brain: when someone was respectable, they tended to be believed. Figures of authority, like government ministers, vicars and teachers, would always be trusted over women or uneducated working men… or troublesome members of travelling communities. It didn't necessarily mean these upstanding citizens were always telling the truth though. Not one person had thought to challenge the doctor's pronouncement about the time of death and he'd rather relied on that.

Edward was suddenly furious with himself for not properly reading the man's reactions when they'd first met at Emma's funeral. Dr Appleby had been too quick to dismiss his father's claim to be guilty of bad things as senility, when the old man obviously had dark secrets in his past. His son had also engineered an invitation to the séance – flattering Edward with his interest in spiritualism. The interest was real, because if the spirit of a young girl linked to the circus was going to appear, he had to be there when it happened. His shock reaction at the news that Emma was left-handed was genuine, but he'd interpreted it incorrectly, believing the doctor was horrified that there had been foul play, when instead he'd just been annoyed that he'd overlooked this vital detail when he'd administered the morphine.

'Killing an innocent child is not a very nice thing to be doing,' Hazibub stressed. 'Even if you were doing it to protect your father. What did he do, I wonder, that you felt you had to be taking such measures?'

'What the hell is going on? What are you talking about, Father?' He looked at the old man and his expression changed as he contemplated the unthinkable. The man sitting before him was not who he thought. His hand flew to his forehead as he massaged his temples in his distress. 'Spirits aren't real.' He almost shouted his affirmation. He turned to Edward. 'You know this? Your livelihood has been based around this lie. You were good – very good – and almost had me believing you when you pulled that trick about my mother, but the newspapers have confirmed you to be a fraud.'

'And yet,' Edward said, 'you injected poor Mrs Shaw to stop the truth of your father's role in the murder of the circus troupe forty years ago from coming out. I suspect he supplied the poison used to kill them all. Likely strychnine, although I cannot be certain.' Now that he'd successfully established the man's guilt, he had nothing to lose by revealing his hand. 'But the souls of the people he so cruelly murdered have begun to rise again, in the bodies of those who are passing away in Thistlewick Tye. I saw

Noah die up on those cliffs yet seconds later he came back to life. The spirit of Samson Ballard had risen and realised that Silas Garrod – the man who had given them the poisoned wine – was standing before him. I believe the furious circus owner then pushed him from the cliff. Equally, this man—' he pointed to Hazibub '—is not your father, but I think you know that.'

As he had done so many times in the past, when he'd fished for information in his séances, he then stated a thing as fact in an attempt to draw the man before him out.

'Esfir knows that you injected the body of Mrs Shaw. Despite what the newspapers claim about my abilities, I've successfully contacted her spirit and she told us everything. It's no use pretending poor Barnabas's wife was responsible for her own demise any longer.'

Dr Appleby pulled at his collar and tiny beads of sweat started to form across his forehead. The man's predisposition towards the spiritual would be to their advantage.

'But... but Mrs Shaw was dreadfully unwell and not long for this world. All I did was try to ease her passing...'

'Mrs Shaw was long dead,' Katerina said, calmly from her chair. 'You killed my daughter. She was three years old, frightened and alone. You did an indescribably wicked thing.' Edward could quite imagine her as the strong, capable woman Mallory had described. Not hot-headed like Samson.

'You!' Dr Appleby yelled at Edward, spinning to face him. 'Everything has gone wrong since you arrived. You've got everyone riled up about these spirits. Charlatan or not, this was not your business to meddle in and you should have left well alone. I've just come from the weekly meeting of the Benevolent Committee and we have become increasingly concerned at your scandalous accusations. The Reverend Fallow is so worried about the lies you're peddling that he and Lord Felthorpe are currently heading to the cliffs to examine this so-called grave – which could, frankly, be hundreds of years old.'

'I have proof that those bodies are from Samson's circus. Possessions found with the bones date the grave and confirm their identity. Some of the villagers are old enough to remember them visiting that winter, and yet everyone claims they left after two weeks and sailed for foreign shores. So, I have to ask myself, why they would all lie?'

'What you don't understand, *Mr Blackmore*, is that the circus folk were bad people – freaks of nature, sexual deviants and thieves. My father told me about the wicked things they did. Details of which he only began to talk about in his senile years. Evil must be eradicated before it spreads like a creeping canker. This is an exemplary village and has a reputation that generations of us have striven to uphold. I will not allow the Devil to invade it again. My father may have supplied the poison, but he was doing God's work.'

The truth suddenly dawned on Edward. In this village, religion, which although not for him and something he generally understood to be a force for good, had been twisted to legitimise controlling behaviour. This man – like his father before him – was a hypocrite of the highest order, and an extremely dangerous one, to boot. Had he also shot at him in the woods, and poisoned Carl too?

But before Edward could challenge him, Dr Appleby lunged forward and grabbed his collar, twisting at it in a forceful and violent attempt to strangle him. The pair tussled for a few moments, before his attacker realised that Edward, although pale and quiet, was stronger than he looked. In his frustration, Dr Appleby pulled back his right arm and swung at his head. He caught Edward across the cheek, at the same moment as the door flew open and Sarah returned with the constable.

Mallory let out a little cry and rushed to his side. His face felt sore and he knew his eye would come up in a nasty bruise.

'What in the blazes is going on?' Constable Lovett exclaimed.

The doctor had sunk to his knees and was staring at his hand, as though he couldn't believe what he'd just done, so Edward supplied the explanation.

'As I'm sure you are aware, there have been dark things going on at Thistlewick Tye. I wasn't certain at the time, but I can tell you now that Silas Garrod was responsible for the deaths of a travelling circus troupe forty years ago; my manservant was deliberately poisoned, I was shot...' He pointed to his bandage. 'And the good doctor here administered the fatal dose of morphine to Mrs Shaw. Go back and check the coroner's report. She was a left-handed woman who wouldn't have injected herself in the left arm. Appleby admitted it to his own father this morning.'

'Sorry, my son, but this man is speaking truths and justice must be being served.' Hazibub looked at the doctor and nodded slowly, as everyone else in the room mumbled their agreement, and the constable scratched his head.

'There's definitely something peculiar in the air, 'cause I ain't seen nothing like it in all my twenty years in the job.' Edward stopped short of volunteering that the deceased souls of a whole circus troupe might be the peculiar thing in the air he was referring to. 'Always thought I'd landed on my feet, policing this village: there was barely an apple stolen from the market. And yet, if what you say is true, in the last couple of weeks, along with Jacob's strange behaviour last night, there've been murders and attempted murders left, right and centre. It beggars belief.'

'All lies!' Dr Appleby shouted. His eyes were wild and he was almost shaking, as he spat out the words and flailed his arms around. 'Who do you believe, Lovett? The respectable village doctor? Or two desperately ill, elderly people, a known drunkard and a man who has been exposed in the newspapers as a liar?'

'But, my son, you were admitting your crime to everyone in this room moments before the constable arrived.' Hazibub continued to play his part.

'This man is not even my father,' Dr Appleby shouted in his frustration. 'He's the spirit of a long-dead circus freak.'

'Right you are, sir.' The constable frowned at the doctor, now clearly convinced the man was either drunk or mad. 'However, in the meantime, you'll be paying a little visit to the cell to calm down whilst I sort through all this muddle because, whatever else you may or mayn't have done, you *have* just assaulted Mr Blackmore.'

'Never was I thinking a son of mine would be attacking another man, completely unprovoked, with his bare hands.'

Appleby looked defeated, or maybe he was just glad the whole sorry mess was out in the open. Constable Lovett produced a pair of iron handcuffs and led him from the room, turning as he stepped through the door. 'But I want to speak to you all down at the station before the day is out.'

'Of course, Constable,' Edward said. He wanted to feel that he'd secured justice for Emma, but the truth was she had never been murdered; she'd passed away in the night from influenza, and an innocent little girl had been killed by a desperate man.

'So, the doctor killed Esfir to protect his father?' Mallory said. 'I don't understand. Was old Dr Appleby behind it all? I realise the constable will get answers from him soon enough but why did his father want us dead? I don't even remember him having much to do with us back then. The allegation concerning his niece came out after the massacre.'

She looked over to Katerina who, Edward remembered, had been about to make a dramatic pronouncement just as the doctor had burst in on their gathering. In all the drama, he'd momentarily forgotten that Mrs Ballard, the common-law wife of the owner of *Samson's Circus of Astonishing Spectacles*, had claimed she was responsible for the deaths.

'It's all rather more complicated than that,' Katerina said, pulling herself up from the chair, all traces of her influenza gone. 'The doctor said the Reverend Fallow is with Lord Felthorpe examining the grave?' She looked at Sarah, who nodded. 'Then that's where we must go.'

44

Mallory looked anxiously at Edward, as the small group made their way along the lane and onto the common. The temperature hadn't risen much since they'd arrived at the Cleyfords' cottage, as there was no sun or patches of blue – just grey cloud hanging heavy across the sky.

Katerina and Hazibub walked at a slower pace. Their possession of the elderly bodies may have eliminated the influenza, but the flesh and bones of both had still been around for decades. Sarah held the old woman's arm, and Edward wondered if she still felt some connection to the woman who'd given birth to her, and whom she was undoubtedly grieving. He hoped there was no unpleasant miasma lingering near Mrs Cleyford but, having nursed both her and old Dr Appleby and not succumbed, her daughter was probably safe. Sarah remained, he reflected, a remarkable woman, living an unremarkable life. Look how she'd taken all their wild claims in her stride. Her mother said she was a dreamer, her head full of bookish nonsense, which had made her open to such outlandish phenomenon. But she was also kind, she was trusting and she was loyal.

In the distance, the figures of Reverend Fallow and Lord Felthorpe were peering over the cliffs and gesticulating at the ground beneath their feet. The vicar was wearing his vestments, and carrying a large crucifix in one hand and a small, stoppered glass bottle in the other. Edward could only assume the latter contained holy water, as it appeared the pair had just conducted a ritual of some description... or were preparing to.

'I'm not sure why Katerina's so keen to speak to the vicar. He wasn't even around back then,' Mallory whispered.

The reverend saw them approach and strode over to meet them, concern etched across his face, but Lord Felthorpe had his back to them, scrabbling about in the soil.

'Dear Mrs Cleyford, what on earth are you doing out of bed? Especially on such a chilly day as this?' He looked quite alarmed. 'I find it somewhat irresponsible of your daughter to expose you to the elements so.' He gave Sarah a chastising look as a swirl of wind tugged at the edges of his white surplice.

'Reverend Fallow, what are *you* doing on the cliffs in such inclement weather?' Edward turned his question around and the vicar narrowed his eyes. He could sense the man was wary of him after their last encounter. Mallory's love had given him the courage to step from the shadows and stop worrying about what others thought, and the vicar hadn't liked his honesty about their relationship one bit. He could hardly put Edward across his knee and give him six of the best, like he did with the schoolchildren.

'Mr Blackmore.' He nodded his head and begrudgingly acknowledged Edward but didn't answer the question.

'I see you're here in an official capacity. Could it be that you and Lord Felthorpe have finally accepted my cousin's wife *was* possessed of a long-dead spirit and are attempting to protect yourselves from future transmigrations?'

'Not that it is any of your business, but I am indeed exorcising this area of ground at Lord Felthorpe's behest. It's a precautionary measure because, whilst I find the idea of such a phenomenon unlikely, I accept that there are things in heaven and earth that I cannot hope to fully understand. The bodies beneath our feet belonged to wicked heathens. A circus came to this village forty years ago and attempted to corrupt the good people of Thistlewick Tye and, if spirits do indeed exist, then I cannot have them rising to commit such unholy acts again.'

Interesting, Edward thought, that he was now accepting these bodies were the missing troupe, when everyone had so strenuously denied this when he'd first enquired about the falling bones.

'And has the unjust nature of their passing been explained to you, Reverend? Because they certainly didn't die of natural causes, burying themselves in the process.'

The vicar frowned and then his eyes briefly expanded in horror, this aspect of the situation apparently not having occurred to him.

Katerina slipped her arm from Sarah's, and walked towards Lord Felthorpe, who'd remained closer to the cliff edge, only belatedly realising they had company.

'The true wickedness,' she muttered as she strode forward, 'was not found in the people beneath our feet, but instead in the man that, I've been told this morning, the entire village of Thistlewick Tye looks up to. The man who professes to be a Christian. Ha!' She snorted. 'Never was an individual more inappropriately named.'

'Mrs Cleyford. Miss Cleyford.' Lord Felthorpe greeted them as they approached. 'Did I hear my name mentioned?' He gave his usual pleasant smile and bowed his head.

'What did you do, Christian?' She stopped in front of him and tipped her small, grey head upwards to meet his eyes.

'Killing me, I understood. But a whole group of innocent people?'

Hazibub, Mallory, Edward and the vicar drifted over to witness this extraordinary confrontation. Was Katerina claiming that Lord Felthorpe had murdered her all those years ago? Edward exchanged a startled glance with Mallory. He knew the fortune teller had disappeared to the hall that afternoon to confront the Felthorpes about the romance. Had Christian taken the news badly and refused to give Zella up?

'My dear woman, what are you talking about?' He turned to Sarah. 'Your mother really shouldn't be out here in this dreadful weather. I understand she recently contracted influenza and it seems to be affecting her mind.'

Katerina ignored his patronising comments and waved a bony finger at him.

'Forty years ago, a crime of indescribable magnitude was committed right here, on this common land. A whole troupe of circus folk were murdered. It took me a while to work out what happened that night, but having talked to Miss Cleyford at length, I'm now utterly convinced you were behind the mysterious gift of poisoned food and wine.'

Mallory and Edward exchanged another surprised glance. But he'd been a friend to the troupe back then because he was desperately in love with Zella, and keen for the villagers and the travellers to heal their rift.

Katerina continued. 'Everyone in this village does as you say for the fear that God will punish them if they don't – as it was with your father, before you. The great triumvirate of lord of the manor, vicar and doctor was as strong back then as I understand it is now. The three men most respected in Thistlewick, with your holier-than-thou demeanours but righteous indignation.

Even as heir to the estate, you commanded enough authority to have men do your bidding.'

Lord Felthorpe couldn't even be bothered to reply to an old woman he clearly suspected was off her rocker, and instead addressed her daughter.

'Miss Cleyford, please return your mother to bed. The doctor tells me she's dangerously ill and has clearly now entered a state of delirium. The reverend and I are dealing with a potentially serious matter, and she is talking nonsense about things that don't concern her.'

Katerina stepped forward and narrowed her eyes. 'But it does concern me, Christian. I *was* there. You murdered my people. You killed the man I loved. And before that, you took a gun from your father's cabinet and shot me.'

Even Edward was confused, and he'd thought himself fairly well apprised of the events from Mallory's past life. Christian snorted and looked about him with a broad smile on his face, clearly finding the whole drama highly amusing – or wanting those about him to think that he did.

'Poppycock,' he said, dismissively.

'But you wouldn't be out here with the reverend exorcising this land if you didn't suspect there was some truth to the rumour of spirit possessions,' Edward pointed out. 'Because these are the bodies of *Samson's Circus of Astonishing Spectacles*. So, why would everyone lie about the troupe moving on? Why would Jacob Palmer set fire to a barn containing their equipment? Why would Samson himself, risen in the body of Noah Garrod, push Silas from the cliff? And why would Dr Appleby confess that he injected poor Mrs Shaw, when she claimed to be the spirit of a long-dead little girl called Esfir from that very company? Because Constable Lovett currently has the third member of your tight and oh-so-dubious Benevolent Committee locked up in the Thistlewick Tye police cell for admitting exactly that.'

'That's the biggest load of tosh I've ever heard anyone spout. You, Mr Blackmore, have quite the reputation for spinning fanciful and utterly ridiculous lies.'

'Christian.' Katerina barked his name in a surprisingly aggressive manner. 'Please pay attention to what we're saying. In the same way Esfir jumped into Mrs Shaw, and Samson into poor Noah Garrod, you should know that Hazibub, the snake charmer, is currently in the body of old Dr Appleby.' She gestured behind her. 'And standing before you now, in the body of old Mrs Cleyford, is Katerina Ballard, born Elisabeth Sutton, who married your unhinged father, Lord Felthorpe, in the April of 1829 and lived to rue the day. I abandoned you when you were a young child, but had to escape the rigid control imposed upon everyone in this village, *and* the madness of my husband. A man who believed he was chosen by God to make Thistlewick Tye an earthly utopia – a paragon of the perfect English parish. And woe betide anyone who didn't conform...' Her voice softened slightly and she looked up to him with tears in her eyes. 'I'm your mother, Christian.'

Everyone turned their faces to Katerina in shock. The current Lord Felthorpe froze. All colour drained from his face and his cheeks paled to grey. His smug self-assured manner was dissolving before their eyes. Even his confident stance evaporated, and Edward noticed his shoulders drop.

'Did you know he used to beat me?' she continued. 'That he only lay with me to conceive you, and then our intimacy ended? And, yes, he rewarded the faithful, bestowing charity and kindness on the righteous, but the sinners, his wife included, were made to pay for their perceived sins. One day, I'd simply had enough of the violence and ran off with a Russian artist who decided I was worthy of attention – even if it was only because he wanted to paint me. I stayed with him until he tired of me, and then met a man on Liverpool docks, with wild plans but a big heart, and truly fell in love.'

Even Edward was moved by Katerina's condensed life story.

'No. You can't be.' Christian Felthorpe shook his head.

'Why not?' She remained calm and her voice gentle. 'Because you shot me dead at the hall? I must at least thank you for burying me with my true family. Did you carry the dead body of your mother to the common yourself?' she asked. 'Or did you order one of your men to do it?'

'I say, Christian? Is any of this true?' the reverend tentatively enquired.

'No,' Lord Felthorpe said again, but Edward could tell he was less sure of himself now.

'And yet everyone here knows that as those bones have been falling, the dead have been rising,' Edward said. 'When Mrs Cleyford passed away from the influenza this morning, Katerina Ballard slipped swiftly and silently into her body, finally able to speak the truth.'

Lord Felthorpe's gloved fists were now in tight balls and he began a slow pacing, back and forth, in front of them all. 'Stay out of it, Blackmore. We all know you to be a fraud. The newspapers were full of your shameful exploits. You've been the thorn in my side since your arrival – asking questions and sticking your pasty face into business that has nothing to do with you.'

'So much so that you tried to poison me, and when that failed, you took potshots at me in the woods.' Edward wasn't certain if his accusation was accurate, but Felthorpe's belligerent response suggested it was.

'Prove it.' He was angry now and not a man used to being challenged.

'Would someone *please* tell me what's going on?' the reverend asked.

'Oh, do shut up,' his friend snapped. 'This pathetic little band of sinners and liars are talking rubbish. We know Blackmore sneaks about uncovering half-truths to convince gullible people that he's speaking to the deceased – his tricks were exposed by his former manservant – and this is doubtless what's occurred here.'

Katerina took another step closer to her son. 'I *am* the woman who gave birth to you on a snowy February night in 1830, who nursed you for a year, watched you take your first shaky steps and read fairy tales to you in the evenings until you were four years old. And yet you shot me with a rifle from your father's gun cabinet in the drawing room at Felthorpe Hall on a cold November afternoon…'

The swirling winds, dancing across the cliffs and whipping about their feet, were the only sound as everyone considered the implications of her words. Edward understood now the reason she'd insisted the circus travel to Norfolk all those years ago. Mallory told him how the Ballards had argued. Katerina had promised Thistlewick Tye would provide the answer to their financial worries, so he could only assume that she'd returned to extort money from her husband. Perhaps to blackmail him into handing over a large sum or she'd reveal her true identity – something that would destroy his reputation and bring chaos into his ordered life and perfect village. But he'd been unexpectedly absent, away in London, and they'd had to await his return. And then something else about this whole twisted mess occurred to Edward. Something really quite unpalatable…

He heard Mallory gasp and knew that they were six steps ahead of Sarah, Hazibub and the reverend.

'You brought it all upon yourself.' Christian exploded with a sudden burst of temper, finally accepting she spoke the truth. 'Twice you ruined my life, Mother. Firstly, by disappearing and leaving me to be brought up by the man you so despised. And then by returning unexpectedly twenty years later to destroy our lives. As if running off with freaks and whores wasn't enough, you brought them back to our lovely village.'

'And now I'm here to ruin everything for you a third and final time.' They could all see she took no pleasure from this statement, as she gave a resigned shrug of her thin shoulders. 'You ordered one of your father's men to deliver poisoned food and wine to the camp. Hazibub told me that Silas Garrod arrived bearing gifts and offering to build bridges. My husband, in his death throes, realised they'd been tricked and swore to kill you all – probably the last thing poor little Esfir heard, and the threat she repeated in her confusion at waking up in Mrs Shaw. You killed *almost* everybody I loved, Christian, because, despite everything, I do still love you. A mother's love endures, because her offspring remains a part of her very being, regardless of whether that child is good or bad.'

'But I am still not understanding. Why would he be wanting us all dead?' Hazibub was confused. 'Because we were stealing a pig? Because we were breaking their commandments? Because we were speaking with foreign accents, looking different to them, and were not believing in their god?'

Lord Felthorpe locked eyes with the elderly woman he now understood was his mother. Edward saw the pity etched across Katerina's face, but Christian was trembling, his hands still scrunched into tight fists, as he shook his head vehemently from side to side.

'Don't say any more. If you truly love me, Mother, then don't say it out loud.'

Katerina's crinkled cheeks were now damp from the flow of

tears. She briefly closed her eyes, as if she was trying to transport herself away from this moment.

On the edge of the horrifying scene, Sarah, like Mallory only moments before, gasped.

'Oh my God. *Zella was his sister!*' She hastily silenced herself by clasping both hands to her mouth.

The six of them had now surrounded Lord Felthorpe – a horseshoe of people confronting him for his past sins, as he backed away, towards the cliffs. This final revelation made everything clear to Edward. A sin so bad that, even if it had been committed in ignorance, he couldn't allow it to ever be exposed – even if it meant committing further sins to cover it up. All of which was indicative of his unstable mind, religious fanaticism and mercurial emotions. He'd fallen passionately in love in a heartbeat, and then chose to erase all those who might have knowledge of it, in another.

The reverend remained confused. 'I don't understand, Christian. Did you order the performers to be killed? That's a mortal sin. There are no circumstances that justify such wickedness.' He turned to the others, panic across his face. 'I had no part in this.'

The Reverend Fallow hadn't yet been born in 1855, but had been chosen as a replacement for the Reverend Marsham, Edward suspected, because of his equally extreme religious fervour. His appointment allowed the great triumvirate of vicar, local landowner and doctor that Katerina had talked of to continue under the guise of the Benevolent Committee, orchestrating the rules, punishments and rewards of Thistlewick Tye. But the village was no more real than Edward's own elaborate illusions. The parishioners would not drink to excess; they would attend church every Sunday, remain faithful in their marriages, work hard and educate themselves, keep the village looking beautiful and willingly look after their own. Those who broke the rules, or outsiders who set no store by them, were another matter, however. They'd be evicted, sent to the vicar for punishment, perhaps fall suspiciously unwell after a visit from the doctor... Edward considered all the tales of supposed divine retribution that had likely come straight from his medicine cabinet. Yes, Thistlewick Tye had the appearance of a godly and caring community, but those who directed it were guilty of the most heinous crimes.

'Is it true?' Edward asked. 'Did you order Silas and Jacob to kill the whole troupe because you fell in love with a girl you didn't know you were related to?' He wanted to hear Felthorpe admit it aloud. 'Mallory was right – you really did love her – and it was such a shameful secret that you couldn't afford for it ever to come out.'

Desperate and panicked, Felthorpe let out the most guttural roar, his face scarlet and strings of spittle hanging from his mouth. He rushed at his tormentor and pushed him violently to the ground. As Edward's head smacked into the dirt, his hat, bandage and wig tumbled from his head. There was a shocked silence as everyone took in his brilliant white hair and the implications of this.

The older man's vitriol twisted into disgust as he stood over the fraudulent spiritualist. 'Now it all makes sense. You're a freak like the rest of them. It's bad enough that I had to put up with that imbecile Noah for fifty years – at least he attended church and tried his best. But you were created by the Devil Himself, and flout every law and moral we strive to live by.'

Edward felt the slow rise and fall of his own chest as his whole body began to seethe, finding himself on his backside and at a distinct disadvantage. How dare Felthorpe mock his albinism? Mallory had shown him it wasn't a thing to be ashamed of, and he felt guilty for continuing to conceal it. She was a much braver person than him and spent ten years allowing her differences to be laughed at. Whilst it had obviously been difficult at times, she'd found more love and acceptance, surrounded by people who also didn't fit in, than she ever had with her own father. If Mallory loved Edward regardless, what did the opinions of others matter?

'And yet, your largesse only extends to people who fit into your perfect world, because Thistlewick Tye is an illusion, a sham – a village overseen by murderers, liars and zealots, who have no compassion for anyone who's different. You may think badly of me but, unlike you, Felthorpe, I have never killed a man... until now. Because you don't deserve to take one more lungful of this glorious sea air.'

He scrabbled to his feet, grabbed his fallen cane and twisted the skull. He was not a violent man by nature – far from it. His gentle soul was another of his father's favourite criticisms – unable to countenance a son who criticised hunting, wouldn't properly whip a dog for bad behaviour and refused to learn to box. But the fox, the hound and the opponent in the ring had done nothing to deserve his wrath. The man standing before him now, however...

He drew out the long silver blade, and leapt forward, brandishing it in Christian's face. His speed, and the fact the cane concealed a weapon, both took Felthorpe by surprise. Edward raised his right arm and held the tip of his blade inches from the man's throat, absolutely determined to use it.

'Esfir was an innocent child, for God's sake. You're the real Devil here.'

He pushed the sharp point further and further, until it pierced the skin and a tiny scarlet blob appeared. He wanted more than anything to thrust the whole sword forward and finish the man off.

'Don't do this, Edward,' Mallory pleaded. 'You'll be hanged for murder. I love you and I need you. Don't make me spend the remainder of my life alone.'

'Put the blade down, Mr Blackmore,' Katerina echoed. Her voice was firm and brooked no dissent. Edward could only imagine how intimidating she'd been, barking orders in her fake Russian accent.

He allowed his hand to drop slightly.

'You'll pay for your crimes twice over,' he said to the man before him. 'Once on this earth and then for an eternity in the next.'

Lord Felthorpe rallied, now that his life was no longer in immediate danger. 'But who will believe you? There's absolutely no evidence to back up your spurious accusations.'

It was true – they couldn't prove any of it. It would be Lord Felthorpe's word against theirs, and Edward suspected this would play out as it had since time immemorial; the respectable citizens would be believed, and the disreputable freaks would not.

'Zella must never know about any of this,' Katerina said, turning to Edward and Mallory, with a strange look in her eyes. 'Promise me? If she comes back, tell her how much she was loved. I was only severe because I wanted the best for her.' She turned back to Christian. 'I must take the blame for all of this. It was wrong of me to leave you with your father, and I should've told you who I was as soon as we pitched up on the common. I'm so very sorry.'

'Surely, you can tell her your—' Mallory began, but Edward suddenly knew what Katerina was planning.

The thin body of the determined octogenarian lifted her head to the heavens and rushed towards her son with an energy that surprised everyone. There was a moment, Edward caught it in Christian's eyes, when he also realised what his mother was doing, but he didn't have time to react, as she launched her tiny body at his. The element of surprise and his proximity to the edge made everything that followed inevitable, as they both tumbled from the cliffs and fell to the ground below with a sickening thud. The wind whipped up from the beach to the clifftop and carried the echoes of their harrowing cries.

Edward stepped forward, as far as he dared, and peered over the edge. He heard nothing for those few moments apart from the crashing of the waves below. Even with his poor eyesight, he could see that mother and son lay dead together on the sand: Katerina with her arm across his body, where she had pushed him backwards, looking, for all the world, as though she was holding him in a final embrace.

Perhaps she was.

45

Christian Felthorpe had spent the last half an hour trying to convince his returning father that the arrival of an itinerant circus troupe in Thistlewick Tye was not the calamity he supposed. Yes, they were heathens and there'd been run-ins with the locals, but perhaps if the village had been more welcoming, these deluded people could be made to see the light. No one had taken the time to teach them right from wrong. The young tightrope walker, for example – whom he loved more than he'd ever loved anything in his life before – was a bright and lively young woman, open to his teachings, and they'd spent much of their precious snatched time together simply talking. Her atheist parents had never taken her to church. It wasn't her fault. She listened to the things he told her, asked intelligent questions about his religion and was intrigued by a life where you could put down roots, have the security of four walls, and nurture and tend to a garden.

But Lord Felthorpe was not a man to be argued with, and certainly not the sort happy to entertain the idea of a lousy bunch of travellers polluting his beloved village. He had no time for freaks and liars. If only Dr Appleby had done his job properly when the Garrod woman had fallen pregnant from a dalliance outside her marriage, then Thistlewick Tye wouldn't be lumbered with a motherless halfwit. Whatever potion he'd given her to make her pay for her sin had affected the development of the child no one knew she was carrying. The idiot boy even survived being dragged out to sea several years later. But, he told his son, God had come to him in a dream and told him the sins of the mother should not be visited upon the child, so he'd done his best to tolerate little Noah.

'Silas Garrod tells me they've been thieving. They stole one of my pigs, have been lying about being sold mouldy produce by the Draytons and all but kidnapped the Cleyfords' daughter.' He was angry. 'And the vicar's full of the debauchery they practise. Are you aware the owners of this abomination of a travelling show aren't even married?' He spat the words out. 'Dr Appleby said they drink to excess because old Jessop has been happily serving them at the Sailmaker's – that damn man needs to retire; he doesn't keep a proper watch on his customers as I've repeatedly demanded,' he said, as an aside. 'I want them gone from Thistlewick Tye, Christian, as soon as possible.'

His son began to plead for leniency when their butler entered the room and informed them that a Katerina Ballard was at the door, insisting she spoke with Lord Felthorpe on a matter of the utmost urgency.

'Talk of the devil,' his father said. 'And I use that term advisedly.'

The exotic, raven-headed woman entered the room, her eyes lined in thick kohl and a long scarf draped over her head. She fixed her gaze on his father.

'Henry,' she said, and it took Lord Felthorpe a moment.

'*Oh, sweet Lord in heaven.* Elisabeth?' His father began to shake.

She swung her attention to Christian. 'Did you touch Zella?' she asked, her face fierce and her tone sharp, and then decided to explain a few things to the returning Lord Felthorpe. '*Your* son seems to have formed a most undesirable romantic attachment to *my* daughter. They've been meeting in secret and she's under the impression they'll marry.'

Christian was confused. Where had this woman's thick Russian accent gone?

'I hope for your sake you didn't, son,' his father said, his eyes frantic. 'For even God would find it hard to forgive such a sin.'

'And we all know how highly you value God,' Katerina said. 'You always were a sanctimonious bastard. Trying to create the perfect village and punishing those who trespassed against Him, as though you were his chosen one.'

'I don't understand. How do you know my father?' Christian felt that he was missing something fundamental, but wasn't sure what.

Lord Felthorpe staggered backwards and slid into the high-backed leather chair behind him, clutching at his temples, and his forehead creased into the deepest frown.

'You don't remember, do you? How could you? You were so young when she abandoned us both.'

Christian's eyes flitted between his father and this relative stranger, as he tried to come to terms with the suggestion that this woman was the mother who'd run off when he was barely four years old.

'It's imperative that you tell me you didn't touch the circus girl, son.' His father was now gripping at the chair arms and so furious that he could barely force the words through his clenched teeth. It was at that moment that the sickening truth hit Christian.

Zella was his half-sister. That sparkling, raven-haired marvel, with her dark hypnotic eyes and beguiling smile. The connection they'd both felt the very instant they met – that inexplicable pull, as though he somehow knew the young woman from somewhere, even before the moment he'd first seen her on the common. Now he understood and it made him sick to his stomach.

Panic, fear and disgust rammed into him like a speeding train.

He said nothing and walked calmly from the drawing room and along the corridor, down the steps to the lower floor, and took the second door on the right into the gun room. He unlocked the glazed cabinet and took out a hunting rifle, loaded two bullets into the magazine and, using the bolt action, chambered the first round. He retraced his steps and re-entered the room, where his father was now on his feet again and talking to... to... his mother. He lifted the gun to his right shoulder and took aim. His father's shocked expression alerted the woman to his presence. She spun around and started to speak but he didn't want to hear one more word from her vile, lying mouth, so he gently squeezed the trigger and shot her in the centre of her chest.

Katerina Ballard slumped to the floor and her thick, red blood began to pool on her dark dress and then spill out over the Turkish rug.

'This can't get out,' Lord Felthorpe said, strangely calm and unemotional, considering his wife was lying dead at their feet. 'My reputation... yours... everything I've striven to create here in Thistlewick Tye.'

Christian nodded and dropped the gun to his side.

'Leave it with me, Father.'

And he swept from the room to speak to the two young men he knew would do his bidding without question. All loose ends must be silenced – even Zella. The Devil had sent her to tempt him and he'd failed to spot His deviousness. His father frequently called upon Dr Appleby to administer justice, and the man would have something in his medicine cabinet that should do the trick. These obliging villagers would all be rewarded on earth by him tenfold, and in heaven by God for eternity.

His mind was racing as he made his way to the stables. The people of Thistlewick had already taken against the circus and he would encourage this by adding to their crimes. He'd tell everyone they'd sailed to St Petersburg from King's Lynn. If that bitch wanted to be Russian so badly, he'd send her there in his fictional ending to her wicked story. His father had told him the truth of their marriage and it wasn't the version she'd spouted in front of the fire only minutes before – instead, he'd spoken of her disobedience and constant questioning of the one true faith. And for her to allow that snake of a temptress, in the form of Zella, into their Garden of Eden... He'd thought it was love and had never felt anything so pure in his life, but it was a heinous trick that his mother had somehow been a part of.

She deserved to die... They all did.

* * *

Eleven hours later, in the light of a pale moon, as it began to shy away from the creeping dawn, Christian Felthorpe brushed the loose dirt from his hands and stared at the low mound in the patch of common land that held all his secrets. Jacob and Silas began to harness the carthorses to the waggons and take them back to the hall. They would be repainted and, along with the horses, given to good, honest, hard-working folk to make their lives a little easier – a reward for their faithfulness. He looked out at the black sky, as it met with the raging sea below, confident that this dark chapter of his life was dead and buried.

But as he turned away, and walked back to the village across the common, he didn't sense the cliffs, creeping up behind him.

46

EDWARD, 1895

Edward stepped back from the edge to a row of expectant faces. He shook his head in reply to the unasked question. No one spoke for a few moments.

'It's up to you, Reverend,' Sarah said, displaying a surprising confidence. 'But I strongly suggest you resign your living immediately and leave Thistlewick Tye. Dr Appleby has admitted to the murder of Mrs Shaw, and Lord Felthorpe is dead at the bottom of the cliffs. Because if you choose to ignore me, I hope you can come up with a satisfactory explanation as to why the elderly Mrs Cleyford would want to push such an upstanding member of the community to his death. I, for one, shall be demanding that the Bishop of Norwich investigate the missing circus from all those years ago and turn his eye to scrutinising the work of the Benevolent Committee, from its inception until the present day. If you don't contact him by the end of the week, I may even suggest he pays particular attention to how harshly you deal with the children that are sent to you.'

Edward gave her a silent cheer in his head.

'But I had no idea—'

'Then I shall write to the bishop this very afternoon. I've precious little else to fill my time now that my poor mother has passed.'

'May I request,' Edward said, 'that whilst you mull over Miss Cleyford's ultimatum, you kindly fetch Constable Lovett and tell him there's been a terrible accident. We'll watch over the bodies until he arrives.' He wanted to discuss the implications of what they'd just witnessed, but not with the vicar present.

The Reverend Fallow nodded and mumbled words of agreement, still clutching the crucifix and holy water, and looking quite terrified as he scurried off.

The remaining four people stared at each other in disbelief – a reverential silence to acknowledge the horrors of what had just unfolded.

'Are they both about to be possessed by members of the circus troupe?' Sarah nodded to the cliffs, as soon as the vicar was out of earshot.

'No bodies have fallen recently so I don't believe there are any ousted spirits waiting to slip into Christian Felthorpe or your mother. She can be at peace now,' Edward said, and then turned to Hazibub. 'But, if there are another handful of bodies waiting to fall, then we could be in for some troubled times. So far, the spirits have jumped into people of their own sex, but will this always be the case? It could prove quite distressing for your friends if it isn't.'

The snake charmer shook his head and let out a deep sigh.

'I am now knowing that I did not think this through. It is much likely to be the very old who die next in Thistlewick and I am wondering what sort of second life that will be for strong men such as Harry and our most athletic Caley girls.' He looked again at his liver-spotted hands. 'It is not being much of a life for me.'

'Undo the spell, Hazibub,' Mallory begged. 'Stop the rest of them rising – Harry, Cupid, Po Po, Zella and the others. It's done now and, as much as it breaks my heart to think I won't see them again, they should be allowed to rest in peace. We have our revenge and the truth is out. Edward is right. Put an end to this madness.'

'Of course,' he replied, and placed his hands together, as if in prayer, and bowed his head to hers. 'I will be setting about it this very evening, when I have gathered what I need.'

Edward shook his head slowly in disbelief.

'That real magic should exist and can be performed by man. As if it wasn't enough to discover that spirits really do exist. Everything I thought I knew has been turned on its head.'

Hazibub stepped towards him and placed a hand on Edward's chest, leaving it there for several moments.

'I am seeing that you are a good man, and one with an extraordinary future laying ahead of you. But that is not being for me to share. Time is short for me, but there are things I can show you, my son, that will be bedazzling you.' He smiled and stepped away.

Edward felt his breath catch in his throat. No one had ever called him 'son' before, not even his own father.

'Your ear's bleeding again.' Mallory tore a strip of cotton from her petticoats and approached him to dress his wound. He looked at the three people standing with him on the gusty clifftop and thought of their kindness, finally understanding that real family need not be related to you. The only benevolence he'd ever received had been from a place of duty, or because those concerned expected something in return – usually for him to contact the deceased. He smiled inwardly at the irony as he bent down to plant a small kiss on the head of a woman who'd been dead for forty years.

'I was not knowing that Katerina was from here,' Hazibub said, staring out across the sea. 'That it was the reason she brought us to this place.'

'None of us did – not even Samson,' Mallory said, tucking in the loose end of the makeshift bandage. Edward slipped his arms about her. She was starting to shiver. 'He laughed when Zella told him Christian wanted to marry her. Had he known the truth, his reaction would have been thunderous – not amused. Katerina had reinvented herself as this Russian fortune teller, with her draped scarves and kohl-lined eyes. I guess the villagers who'd known her as a young bride, were not looking for a middle-aged foreigner. Perhaps only her husband would have recognised her when she turned up – and he wasn't here when we first arrived.'

'I am blaming myself. I saw that something bad was coming but could not see clearly what.' Hazibub shook his head.

'You're not responsible for the depraved actions of an obsessive zealot,' Edward said, still simmering that the troupe, although not exactly snow-white, had been treated so badly. 'Even Katerina felt guilty. It makes me angry that those who were committing the terrible crimes were doing so with a clear conscience, truly believing it was all for the greater good. Christian's father had schooled him to continue his legacy, as two generations of Felthorpe men tried to create their own little utopia. But without you and your transmigration spell, the five men at the heart of this would never have been uncovered.'

'Looking back, it explains Christian Felthorpe's behaviour in the months following the disappearance of the circus,' Sarah said. 'I didn't know about his love for the high-wire girl, but he shut himself away for the remainder of the winter, and there was never any further romance in his life. How could he live with the knowledge that he'd shot his own mother and then ordered the annihilation of a whole group of people? It also explains why the exceptionally young Jacob Palmer was made landlord of the Sailmaker's, and Silas was given a small house in the village and his brother a job. They were being paid for delivering the poisoned goods and for covering up the crime afterwards. Who knows which other young men were involved in the burial of the bodies and distribution of the circus equipment?' She shook her head from side to side. 'How can I have lived amongst such evil people all these years and not known? Perhaps I should have asked more questions and trusted my instincts.' She looked quite forlorn.

'You were a child,' Edward said, gently. 'And I've learned that we're very much shaped by the adults who surround us when we're young. It was natural you believed the things you were told by them.'

Hadn't he always felt responsible for being born an albino? Logic told him it was not his fault, but a whole childhood of being blamed, and consequently rejected, had taken its toll. Perhaps it was time to celebrate his differences and recognise that the problem was entirely his father's...

The sound of agitated voices drifted across the common. The vicar was returning with Constable Lovett and it was likely some difficult questions were about to be asked.

'I must be leaving this village in the morning, as soon as I have performed the spell, and before the sins of old Dr Appleby are laid at my feet,' Hazibub said, looking anxiously at the approaching men.

'So soon? But what will I do without you?' Mallory whispered, her bottom lip quivering. 'There'll be no one left from the circus. You're my family.'

'Ah,' he said, taking her hand and gently kissing it. 'But I was always seeing your happiness as clear as the brightest of days, even though I knew you would have to wait, and—' he looked up at Edward and then briefly turned to Sarah '—I am very much thinking that you have found a new family now.'

As Edward contemplated Hazibub's words, he wondered if the solitary life he'd craved for so long was really what he wanted. He'd never been part of a loving family, or even a caring community, but perhaps he'd been looking in the wrong places.

47

CHRISTMAS EVE, 1895

The day was bitter, but the interior of Maude Grimmer's cottage was just as cosy as Edward remembered. It was Christmas Eve and his arms were wrapped around the woman he loved, as she sat in front of him, on the floor, before the fire in her tiny cottage. He'd not worn his wig nor dyed his eyebrows since the moment Christian Felthorpe had exposed him at the top of Thistlewick cliffs. He was learning to suffer the pitying looks and thoughtless comments, because the one person whose opinion really mattered still looked at him in wonder, as though he were the most beautiful thing she'd ever seen. Besides, the villagers had so much to contend with, that the albino currently cohabiting with the adulterous drunk on the other side of the woods was only of passing interest.

The Felthorpe family solicitors had successfully chased down a distant cousin of Lord Felthorpe and informed him that he was to inherit the hall. Rumour had it, the fellow was married to the daughter of a renowned liberal theologist. Their progressive view of Christianity would certainly shake things up in Thistlewick Tye, and not before time, thought Edward.

The bishop was waiting for the new Lord Felthorpe to take up residence before securing someone to fill the vacancy left by the sudden and unexpected resignation of the Reverend Fallow. The villagers deserved a vicar who would bring them light and joy, because they had been foolish sheep, easily led and needed a good shepherd to guide them. Their local landowner was dead, and lovely young Dr Appleby, with the kind eyes, was to stand trial for the murder of Mrs Emma Shaw in the new year. Not to mention the upset caused by the dramatic deaths of Silas Garrod and Old Mrs Cleyford, and the news that Jacob Palmer was a wanted man.

Meanwhile, a neighbouring priest was overseeing the church services, which had recently included the funeral of another elderly influenza victim. At least the dead were staying dead, much to everyone's relief and thanks to a clandestine midnight ceremony performed on the cliffs by Hazibub. Luckily, the constable was far too overwhelmed by everything to consider that Silas's death was anything other than the accident he had always supposed it to be. Edward was certainly not about to demand Noah be traced and made accountable.

Several officials from Norwich had arrived the week of Lord Felthorpe's death to investigate reports of human bones falling into the sea. Edward advised his friends to play down the spirit possessions, as only Barnabas and Dr Appleby, outside the four of them, knew the truth with certainty. Both these men, for different reasons, chose to say nothing, and Mrs Drayton, the only other person they'd told, had never been fully convinced.

Instead, Sarah claimed that as a young child, she'd seen the massacre of the circus troupe on that very spot, but had been too scared to speak the truth whilst Christian Felthorpe was alive. The constable, who was instructed to investigate these historic murders, almost wept when he realised the monumental task that lay ahead of him. From being the most underworked policeman in Norfolk, he was shortly to be one of the busiest.

Maude Grimmer played no part in the allegations and kept to the shadows. The drunkard who lived outside the village boundary was, after all, nothing to do with any of this...

Edward gently kissed the top of Mallory's head and then leaned back on the bench, inhaling the incredible smells drifting about the small space – no longer vying with the odour of cheap tallow candles. Barnabas had insisted on donating several items to Mallory to make her life easier – including two smart oil lamps and a box of the finest beeswax candles... and, that afternoon, a brace of partridge.

'I've never eaten partridge,' Mallory said, twisting her head to look up at him. 'I hope I've done the birds justice. Your cousin's being overwhelmingly generous.'

'He's atoning for his past transgressions,' Edward pointed out. 'It makes him happy, and anything that keeps him away from the drink, and stops him wallowing, is a good thing in my book. He's also been incredibly generous to Sarah. They're both giving up their spare time to volunteer at the church and keep things ticking over until the new vicar is appointed. He'll never get over Emma, but I can't help but hope that in time this friendship will develop into something more.'

'Sarah is a woman in her mid-fifties! There must be nearly fifteen years between them.' Mallory looked slightly scandalised.

'There's over thirty years between us, and you don't find that an issue,' he teased.

Barnabas had finally accepted that his cousin would not take Thistlewick House but insisted that he kept the five hundred pounds – he had, after all, solved Emma's murder. Edward had issued instructions for what remained of his London possessions to be auctioned, and the proceeds, along with the money in the Cattisham Orphanage Fund, were donated to a real orphanage. He had no desire to return to the city.

'Open it then,' he urged, pointing to the small envelope tied in ribbon that was resting on Mallory's lap. They were exchanging gifts, as was the Christmas Eve tradition. She undid the bow and slid out three tickets for a steamship liner sailing to America in the following February.

'But—'

'After we've tied up everything here, we'll leave with only what we can carry and when we arrive in New York, we shall present as man and wife.'

'And the third ticket?' she asked, frowning.

'Your elderly father is coming with us.'

Edward had used some of the money from his cousin to spirit Hazibub to Liverpool, where he was to wait patiently in rented accommodation until his friends could join him. Coincidentally, old Dr Appleby had allegedly been seen by Mrs Grimmer, walking into the sea, the day after his son had been arrested. A pile of his clothes was left on the beach and no one was surprised that in his senility, he'd committed such a tragic act. But his body would never wash up on the shore.

'Katerina wasn't free to marry when she met Samson, but they made their life together nonetheless,' Edward continued. 'I want to make mine with you and Hazibub – in a place we're not known and can start again.'

'And where will we live? What will we do for money?'

'About that...' he said, grinning. 'I've a mind to set up a travelling show. *Alberto the Albino – Magician and Living Curiosity.*' He waved his hands through the air, imagining his name across a huge banner in the sky. 'It suits me to perform under canvas, away from the sun, and I have an eye for fancy clothes and a talent for the dramatic. We can start small and pick up acts as we move around the country, making sure everyone is treated well and paid fairly. There's something that appeals to me about gathering up our chosen family along the way. Samson and Katerina had the right idea – surround yourself with people you like, and stand by their side always, so they never feel alone. Our circus, however, will have far less debauchery.'

'And far less alcohol,' she declared. Edward smiled; she was warming to the idea.

'Whoever we scoop up, we will not ask them about their past, nor judge them for their differences. I'll embrace what I am and wear all white. My impossible illusions will be talked about far and wide, and you'll be my sensible head and stop me buying zebras.'

Hazibub had offered to pass on all his secrets and spells to the man who had made his Toad Girl so happy, knowing that his time on this earth was limited and wishing to leave a lasting legacy. The pull of such a promise had been too strong for Edward to resist. After all those years of cheap tricks and illusions, he'd shortly have access to real magic. Now wasn't that something?

'So, despite telling me that the happiest you've ever been was at my tiny cottage, eating stew, and living a simple life, you now wish to travel to America, set up a circus and perform in front of admiring crowds?'

'Yes,' he confirmed, dropping his head to the back of her neck and leaving a trail of tiny kisses. 'As long as you're by my side.'

She placed both her hands over his and smiled.

'Although the truth is, if we never make a bean, I'll still be happy, because you, Mallory Hornchurch, Toad Girl and Living Wonder, are all the riches I need.'

* * *

MORE FROM JENNI KEER

The next book from Jenni Keer is available to order now here:
https://mybook.to/JenniKeer6

ACKNOWLEDGEMENTS

Huge thanks to the usual suspects – my editor Iso Akenhead, copy editor Helena Newton, proofreader Anna Paterson, and cover designer Alexandra Allden. The whole team at Boldwood make every book an utter joy to work on. Also, to my wonderful agent, Hannah Schofield, always by my side.

A grateful nod to my son Evan, who was brainstorming with me when I initially wondered who I could bury on a clifftop. (These really are the sort of questions that I come out with over dinner. Our house is anything but dull.) I'd started to look into pirates when he suggested the circus, so this book really wouldn't be what it is now without his input. He may also be partially responsible for some of the darker elements that are creeping into my work, as he keeps forcing me to watch horror films, even though he's the gentlest soul I know.

A special thanks to Rosie Hendry for showing me around West Runton, which is nestled between Cromer and Shering-ham, and was very much the inspiration for Thistlewick Tye. We walked along the beach and I saw, first hand, the dramatic erosion of the coastline. Incidentally, a mammoth was found there in 1990 but, thankfully, no buried circus troupe. Thank you, dear Rosie, for your time and patience that day, and for answering my many subsequent questions.

I'd also like to thank Nicola Knight and the Redwings Horse Sanctuary at Caldecott. I spent a lovely afternoon being educated about 'all things horse'. As a woman who was initially unsure which end you feed, I feel my equine knowledge has come on leaps and bounds. If you love horses, please consider supporting this marvellous charity: www.redwings.org.uk

For anyone interested in Mallory's condition, it was loosely based on Gardner syndrome, which was only properly recognised in 1951. In Mallory's day, it wouldn't have been understood at all. Heartbreakingly, life expectancy is between thirty-five and forty-five years and there is still no cure.

Just to repeat what I said at the start of this novel, writing historical fiction is a challenge when the terms used in a particular period are no longer acceptable. I hope readers appreciate that it's sometimes difficult to keep the vocabulary historically accurate and not be offensive. Dwarf, freak and simple, in particular, sat uncomfortably with me, but to describe Cupid as a man of short stature would be anachronistic. Thankfully, we've moved on from such language and I sincerely hope no one is offended.

To my many writing friends, especially the Famous Five, fellow members of the RNA and all those who support authors by helping to produce, distribute, sell, read and review our books. To my family for keeping my glass topped up, to Anne Stuart (my high school PE teacher) for Copperpenny Lane, and to Louise Foulger for providing me with THE BEST writing chair. Thank you, darling.

Lastly, huge congratulations to Carol Willison who won the competition in my author newsletter to name a dog in this novel. She suggested the name Banjo and he now exists, running around the pages of this book, and barking at a man he knows for certain is not Noah Garrod.

As ever, dear friends, you keep reading and I'll keep writing.

Jenni x

ABOUT THE AUTHOR

Jenni Keer is the well-reviewed author of historical romances, often with a mystery at their heart. Most recently published by Headline and shortlisted for the 2023 RNA Historical Romantic Novel of the Year.

Download your exclusive bonus content from Jenni Keer here.

Visit Jenni's website: www.jennikeer.co.uk

Follow Jenni on social media here:

facebook.com/jennikeerwriter
x.com/JenniKeer
instagram.com/jennikeer
bookbub.com/authors/jenni-keer

ALSO BY JENNI KEER

No. 23 Burlington Square

At the Stroke of Midnight

The Ravenswood Witch

The House of Lost Whispers

The Peculiar Incident at Thistlewick House

Letters from
the past

Discover page-turning
historical novels from
your favourite authors
and be transported
back in time

Join our book club
Facebook group

https://bit.ly/SixpenceGroup

Sign up to our
newsletter

https://bit.ly/LettersFrom
PastNews

Boldwood

Boldwood Books is an award-winning fiction publishing company seeking out the best stories from around the world.

Find out more at www.boldwoodbooks.com

Join our reader community for brilliant books, competitions and offers!

Follow us

@BoldwoodBooks

@TheBoldBookClub

Sign up to our weekly deals newsletter

https://bit.ly/BoldwoodBNewsletter

Printed in Dunstable, United Kingdom